The Bone Thief

The Bone Thief

BREEANA SHIELDS

PAGE STREET
PUBLISHING CO.

PAGE STREET
PUBLISHING CO.

Copyright © 2020 Breeana Shields

First published in 2020 by
Page Street Publishing Co.
27 Congress Street, Suite 105
Salem, MA 01970
www.pagestreetpublishing.com

Distributed by Macmillan, sales in Canada by The Canadian Manda Group.

24   23   22   21   20   1   2   3   4   5

ISBN-13: 978-1-62414-930-6
ISBN-10: 1-62414-930-8

Library of Congress Control Number: 2019948962

Cover and book design by Kylie Alexander for Page Street Publishing Co.
Cover illustration by Mina Price

Printed and bound in the United States

To Ben,

who first made me a mother

———◆———◆———◆———

Chapter One

I have blood on my hands.

I stand in the Forest of the Dead, next to our family tree, a knife dangling from my fingers. My palms are raw and seeping. I've been digging into the bark for nearly an hour, and I've only managed to carve a shallow furrow. I didn't think it would be so difficult, but Gran once told me these trees were special—strengthened by the magic of the bones that have hung here for generations. And these branches have seen more power than most.

A bead of sweat slips from the nape of my neck down my spine. I slide to the ground and rest my back against the tree trunk.

Summer has given way to fall, and the trees are aflame with hues of red and orange, as if the whole forest is on fire. It makes me feel as if I'm inside a bone reading, seeing all of my possible futures, dozens of paths stretching before me.

But my mother isn't on a single one of them.

It's not just that she's dead; it's so much worse than that. She's also missing.

Latham stole her body, and if I don't find her bones, she's lost to me forever. I think of how Gran's bones were used for my kenning, of how her gran's bones were used for hers. Our entire family is sealed together this way—the bones of one generation guiding the fate of another. If I can't get my mother back, whose bones will be used for my own daughter's kenning? Will they belong to a stranger? Someone who never stroked her hair when she was ill? Who never looked into her eyes after a nightmare to tell her she was safe? Who never loved her?

With a start I realize that even if I do manage to find my mother's bones, she will never comfort my daughter like Gran comforted me. Never hear the sound of her laugh or clean her sticky fingers. Death is one cruel revelation after another, unfolding like a map of heartache with ever-expanding borders. And now this: My mother will never know my daughter.

Then again, maybe I won't survive to have a daughter at all.

Grief and rage combine and swell in my throat. My fist clenches tightly around the knife in my hand. I tilt my head toward the sky, and a single crimson leaf drifts onto my shoulder.

Autumn used to be my favorite time of year. I found it

poetic—the fierce, bold colors of leaves just before they tremble from their branches and die. As if the last moments of life were the most powerful of all.

But now I prefer the tender, gentle colors of spring.

I shift my body so the leaf floats to the forest floor. The air is heavy with the scent of rot. A few rows away, a burlap sack hangs from a sturdy branch. Inside is the body of Eli Higgins, who took his last breath two weeks ago. And in another tree nearby is Hester Ollif, whose heart stopped beating just yesterday. Both trees are draped in colorful blossoms, the names of the deceased freshly carved into the trunks below other family members who have gone before. At least a dozen trees across the forest are burdened with the bones of the dead.

But our tree is empty. There's no place to hold my sorrow.

I stand and brush the dust from my skirt. A sudden awareness prickles at the base of my skull and I freeze. Gooseflesh races up my arms. It's a sensation I've experienced multiple times in the last few weeks. It feels like a pair of eyes are focused on my back. Like a breath at my collar. Like someone is watching me.

I spin around, but no one is there. It's just my imagination. Just the fear of Latham's last threat: *I'll see you soon, Saskia. You can count on it.*

Each night since my mother's death I've had the same nightmare. Just as I drift off, my mind replays each detail of her murder. Latham thrusting a knife through her back. Her eyes going wide with shock before she falls into my arms. Her blood thick on my fingers.

Then the dream shifts to a place I've never seen before:

a room full of spell books and bones, incense and strange weapons. Latham strides toward me—a Mason-crafted sword in his hand—a look of such dark delight in his eyes that it makes my blood run cold. Each time, I know I'm about to die, but I wake just before the blade falls.

Latham is coming for me. Even when I try to forget, my mind reminds me in my sleep.

And now I'm imagining things that aren't there while I'm awake, too.

My heart pounds, jackrabbit fast, but I pull in slow, deep breaths until I'm steadier. Then I lift the knife in my fist and begin to scrape at the trunk again, deepening the groove I created earlier. Usually Oskar, the master of the bone house, carves the names of the deceased into the bark when he hangs the burlap bag from one of the branches. But there is no bag to hang, no bones to prepare. I set off for Ivory Hall tomorrow, and I can't bear to leave an empty space where my mother's name should be; I may not have her body, but I won't rob her of the honor of being remembered.

I scrape into the wood until the joints in my fingers scream in pain. Oskar must have better tools for carving than my father's old knife.

A throat clears behind me. "Saskia?"

I turn to find Bram, his brown eyes soft with concern. A bright spark of surprise goes through me. "You're back," I say. Bram came to Midwood after my mother died, but only stayed a short time before returning to Ivory Hall to finish his first-term exams. I'll be joining the apprentices for the second term, so I

4

didn't expect to see him until then. "What are you doing here?"

"Norah sent me back to travel with you." He gives me a wry smile. "I think she'd feel better if every Breaker in Kastelia were by your side."

Norah is Steward of Ivory Hall. She offered me a placement to train as a Bone Charmer, and wanted me to go to the capital immediately after the funeral, but I needed time to grieve. And time to figure out how I'm going to hide the fact that I'm both more and less qualified than Norah thinks; I already have a Bone Charmer mastery tattoo because my mother was training me in secret, but I lied about being matched as a Charmer. I wasn't. Not in this reality, at least.

"I think Norah just feels guilty that one of her instructors murdered my family," I say, dragging the toe of my boot through the pile of leaves at my feet.

A shadow falls over Bram's expression. "Maybe that's part of it, but she also cares. You'll see once you get to know her better." He rakes his fingers through his hair—a gesture I feel like I've seen a hundred times. I've known him for years, so it shouldn't shock me that he's so familiar. But it's *how* familiar that both thrills and unsettles me. Because it's not our childhood that taught me the planes of his cheekbones, the angle of his jaw, the way he strums his fingers when he's nervous. It's the vision of my other path I saw in Gran's healed bone. A different possibility, one Bram has never seen. To him, I'm just a girl who once judged him unfairly. But to me . . .

"Anything I can do to help?" he asks, his gaze skipping between the blade in my hand and the tree behind me.

Suddenly an image of his lips on mine rises in my memory. Heat floods my face. I bite the inside of my cheek and hope he doesn't notice.

He cocks his head to the side and gives me a quizzical look. "Unless you want to be alone? I don't mean to intrude."

He's misread my discomfort. Good.

"You're not intruding." I hold out the knife to him. As he takes it, his thumb feathers along the love tattoo on my wrist and I inhale sharply.

Bram's eyes go wide, as if he's just as shocked by the touch as I am. He snatches his hand away. "Do you . . ." He pulls on the back of his neck. "Do you miss him?"

At first, I'm confused by the question. And then I realize he's talking about Declan. Of course Bram would think that's where I got the love tattoo; Declan and I were matched at the kenning. But still, the thought makes my stomach clench.

"No," I say, "not even a little." Declan's betrayal feels like a fresh burn that can't withstand even the lightest contact without stinging. "I just miss my mother." What I don't say: *I also miss the future you and I never had.* A thousand images of Bram jostle in my mind—they're almost, but not quite, memories; almost, but not quite, mine. Some are blurry and indistinct, and others are vivid and alive with color. But together they're a storm of confusion that rages in my chest.

I can't afford to fall for him. The love tattoo is a remnant from my other path, so given time, it should fade. Things that aren't nurtured eventually wither. Latham is far less likely to kill me if it disappears.

Bram gives me another odd look, as if I'm a puzzle he can't quite figure out. He turns the knife over in his hand, examining the blade.

"This isn't bone-made," he says. "And it's also too dull. You'll be here all night."

I shrug. "It's all I had."

He slides the leather satchel from around his neck and digs through it, producing a small bone-handled folding knife. He opens the blade and inclines his head toward the tree. "May I?"

I nod and step aside. Bram holds the knife perpendicular to the ground and carves my mother's name in deft, confident strokes. My gaze wanders to the muscles in his arm, flexing as he works.

When he finishes, he turns toward me. "How is that?"

He's engraved my mother's name—DELLA HOLTE—in neat block letters, along with her death date.

Warmth spreads through my chest. "Perfect," I say, my voice catching a little. "Thank you."

My fingers twitch—longing to reach for him—but I shove them into my pockets. We're about to spend weeks together on a ship to Ivory Hall. And after seeing a glimpse of what we could have been together, it will be so hard not to rely on Bram for comfort. Not to feel his hand fold around mine like a promise to double my joy and divide my pain. But I have to try.

My life depends on it.

Ami and I wander arm in arm through the streets of Midwood. The sun sits low on the horizon and the sky is awash in shades of pink and gold. We've been trying to say goodbye for hours, but neither of us can seem to find the words. So we keep walking, keep chatting about mundane things, as if we'll be together forever. As if I won't sail away tomorrow and Ami will stay here and for the first time in our lives we won't see each other every day.

As much as I want to pretend things are normal, I can't.

Everywhere I turn, I see the ghosts of my family—my mother coming out of the Marrow, a stone basin tucked beneath her arm like it weighs no more than a feather; Gran heading into the Sweet Tooth to buy the lemon-flavored candies she favored; my father fishing on the banks of the Shard, a contented smile on his face. The memories fill me with bittersweet longing.

But other images crowd in too—Declan threading his fingers through mine, making promises he had no intention of keeping; standing beside my mother in the bone house, gazing into the empty box where Papa's remains should have been; walking into my own home, what had always been a cocoon of safety and love, to see Latham with a blade at my mother's throat.

Midwood won't ever be the same. I can't imagine staying. And yet I can't bear the thought of leaving, either.

We end up on the riverbank, as if our feet carried us there by habit. But it's too cold to peel off our boots and sink our feet into the water. So we sit in the grass, bundled in our warm cloaks.

Ami nudges my shoulder gently with her own. "What are you thinking?"

Finally an honest question. She must sense the time slipping away too, like water held in cupped hands, seeping through our fingers no matter how desperately we try to hold on.

So I give her an honest answer. "I'm just wishing I weren't such a coward."

She turns to me, her eyes wide with surprise. "Why would you say that?"

I run my hands over the grass, letting the blades slide between my fingers. "I'm scared all the time, Ami."

She's quiet for a moment. "Of what?"

I sigh. There are so many answers to that question. "What if the Grand Council finds out my mother illegally trained me? Her reputation will be ruined." I bite my lip. "Or they could punish me."

"Everything will be fine," Ami says. "They have no way of knowing unless you tell them."

I give her a pointed look. "Yes, they do."

"Saskia!" Ami looks stricken. "I would never betray your trust like that."

I roll my eyes and tug her dark, glossy braid playfully. "Not you. My mastery tattoo."

But an uncomfortable realization uncoils in my chest. Ami isn't the only one who knows I've used unbound magic. My fingers clench around a fistful of grass.

"No one is going to examine you for unexpected tattoos," Ami says, interrupting my thoughts. She's right. Tattoos are considered deeply personal, and it's rude to ask about them.

A relieved breath sags out of me. "I worried my trainer

might, as a way to gauge my progress."

A shadow falls over Ami's face. "Oh."

"Has Oskar asked about your mastery tattoo?"

Her hand closes around mine. "Not right at first. But yes, eventually." She squeezes my fingers. "Don't worry, though. By the time anyone asks, you will have been bound to bone charming long enough that no one will be suspicious. Just make sure to keep it hidden until then."

I'm suddenly grateful the weather has shifted. It won't be unusual for me to wear long sleeves until spring, and by then my mastery tattoo will no longer be incriminating.

"Bram knows too," I say softly.

Her mouth falls open. "About the tattoo?"

"No, but he knows I used unbound magic. I did a bone reading in front of him last spring after my mother died. I wasn't thinking clearly."

For the first time, Ami's expression mirrors the tumult raging in my chest.

"Will he say anything?" she asks.

"I don't know. I'd like to think he won't, but he's not the same person in this reality. Latham was mentoring him."

She bites her thumbnail. "That's not good. But he didn't know what Latham was capable of, right?"

"I don't know what he knew," I say. "I don't know who I can trust anymore."

"Trust yourself," she says. "Trust your gut."

"That's what I did with Declan and look how that turned out."

Her eyes go soft. "Not everyone is Declan."

"No one else is you, either."

Her lower lip trembles and she wraps me in an embrace. I hold her extra tightly, until she finally pulls away and gives me an evaluating look.

"Maybe all this worry is just a proxy for what's really bothering you," she says.

I give a harsh laugh. "You're right. I'm worrying about nothing—unbound magic isn't *that* illegal, my mother's bones aren't *that* lost, the Charmer determined to kill me isn't *that* evil."

She purses her lips and glares at me. "Are you done?"

"Yes," I say. "So what do you think is really bothering me?"

"I think you're trying to avoid how much leaving Midwood will make you feel even further away from your mother when you're missing her so much already."

Tears prickle at the backs of my eyes. This is so like Ami. To take my worries from me, package them in her unique brand of love, and hand them back to me in a way that makes me feel truly seen.

"What if this is a huge mistake?"

She shakes her head. "It's not. You're doing the right thing, Sas. Talk to Bram. Ask him to keep your confidences. And then find your mother's bones and bring her home."

The twilight melts into darkness, and finally we walk back to my house, where we talk until we drift off to sleep.

I wake at dawn and gather my things, moving as silently as I can. Then I pause and let my eyes scan across this room with so many memories. My parents cozied in front of the hearth, giggling and whispering like a pair of intendeds even though they'd been married for years. Sitting near the window with Gran while she brushed my hair in long, careful strokes. My mother hunched over her spell book, her lips pursed in concentration.

And now Ami, lying with her hands pillowed beneath her cheek, her face smooth and unworried in sleep. I rest my palm gently on the crown of her head, careful not to disturb her. If she wakes and I have to say goodbye again, I won't be able to force myself to leave.

My whole life, I've wanted nothing more than to stay in Midwood forever. But now, if I want to find my mother's and Gran's bones, I have no choice but to leave. I'm standing at the intersection of twin miseries—no matter which way I turn, sadness will follow.

Right now, Ami is the only person in the world I trust.

And I have to leave her behind.

Chapter Two

$\mathcal{I}$ was worried about time alone with Bram on the journey to the capital, but it turns out I have the opposite problem. I barely see him at all. Norah sends a wing-fleet vessel full of Breakers from the Ivory Guard to escort us to Kastelia City. I'm constantly under watch, and Bram spends most of his time playing games of dice with the crew and the off-duty Breakers.

It's both a relief and a disappointment. Even though I know I should keep my distance, the pull toward him is almost irresistible. But I keep reminding myself that my feelings aren't real. They're just a remnant from a life I never lived. If my other path actually had any influence on this one, Bram would feel the same way, and it's obvious he doesn't. When we see each other in passing, he waves and sometimes even smiles, but his eyes only flick to mine for a moment before continuing his conversation. He's friendly without being affectionate.

But his indifference toward me poses an even bigger problem than my wounded pride. I'd planned to talk to Bram about keeping my secret, but so far, the two of us haven't been alone for even a moment.

I spend much of my time on the deck—icy wind in my face—gazing toward home. When I took the journey to Ivory Hall on my other path, did I feel this alone? As if there's not a shoulder in the world where I can rest my head?

As we get closer to the capital, my anxiety grows until I feel as if I've swallowed an entire hive of bees. I'm not going to get an opportunity to talk to Bram unless I make one. We're never going to be alone. I wasn't looking forward to this conversation when I thought we'd have privacy, but imagining broaching the subject with spectators around makes me want to launch myself overboard and sink to the bottom of the Shard.

I find him the next evening, as he's finishing a meal with one of the other Breakers. The two of them lean back in their chairs, hands clasped loosely behind their heads. As I approach, their laughter dies off in a way that makes me feel like an interloper.

I rub my palms on my pants to dry them. "Can I talk to you for a minute?" I ask Bram. My gaze slides to the other Breaker. "Alone?"

"Sure," Bram says, standing.

His dining partner raises his eyebrows and gives us both a knowing look that makes my cheeks go hot.

I grab Bram's elbow and pull him far enough away so the Breaker won't be able to hear us.

"Saskia, what's going on? Is everything all right?"

I shove my hand into the pocket of my cloak and curl my fingers around Gran's healed bone. I couldn't bear the thought of leaving it behind, and now I cling to it like a lifeline. "We were matched on my other path." The words fly out of my mouth before I can stop them. It wasn't what I intended to say—not exactly. My already-flushed skin now feels on fire, and I wish I could melt into the deck and disappear.

Bram's eyes go wide and then he starts laughing. The sound stings like a slap.

"Why is that funny?"

"It's just—you and I—that seems . . . an unlikely pairing."

My fingers unconsciously circle the love tattoo around my wrist, which is as bright as it was the day it appeared. "Yes, well . . ." I stammer.

"Well, what?" His voice is still full of humor. "Why are you telling me this?"

Now that I've seen his reaction, I'm asking myself the same question. I guess some part of me was hoping his feelings were similar—an unexplained closeness that he can't account for. A longing to be together that makes no sense. But I'm being ridiculous. My feelings aren't real. Not in this life.

I stare out at the water, shimmering in the gentle light of the setting sun, while I gather my thoughts. Then I turn back to Bram. "I just wanted you to know that in some version of reality, you cared about me. That you wouldn't want to see me harmed."

"I don't want to see you harmed in *this* reality," he says. "We've had our issues in the past, but I'm not a monster."

"I know, but you've seen things that could get me in trouble. That could sully my mother's legacy." I can still picture the shock in his expression as he watched me do a reading on Gran's healed bone after my mother had died.

But you aren't trained, he said when I prepared to prick my own finger. *Are you?*

I'm trained enough.

My cloak suddenly feels too tight and I tug at the collar. "I just want to make sure you won't betray me."

The amusement vanishes from Bram's face, and something dark flashes across his expression so quickly, I think I might have imagined it.

"Of course I won't." His voice is gruff.

I don't know if I can believe him. Ami advised me to trust my gut. But what if my gut doesn't know the difference between this reality and any other?

My fingers twine together so tightly that my knuckles turn white. "No one can know about my other path," I tell him, my voice low and urgent. "No one can know that my mother taught me bone charming."

He touches my shoulder lightly. "I won't say anything. You can trust me."

An image of Declan rises in my mind. His bright green eyes dancing with laughter. Color flooding his pale cheeks the first time we kissed.

"The last time I trusted someone, he got my mother killed."

I turn away to find a cluster of Breakers looking back and forth between me and Bram with curious expressions.

Behind me, Bram starts to say something more, but then one of the crew members comes past us carrying a bundle of tangled fishing net. "Could I get a hand with this?"

"Of course." Bram hurries forward and whatever he was going to say is forgotten. Our ship arrives in the middle of the night. The harbor is lit by a full moon and puddles of pale yellow light from the oil lamps lining the pier. It's quiet, except for the occasional screech of the Watcher-controlled birds that circle overhead.

Ivory Hall gleams in the distance like a diamond against a velvet sky.

Norah meets us onshore. "Saskia," she says, catching my hands in hers, "I'm so relieved to see you." Her silver hair glimmers in the moonlight, and is twisted into a knot at the back of her head.

"It really wasn't necessary to send so many people to travel with me."

She gives me a tight smile. "I assure you, it was."

A chill goes through me, and I pull my gray cloak more tightly around my shoulders. The Grand Council's search for Latham must not be going well.

Norah's gaze sweeps over the group of Breakers and lands on Bram, who is standing a few steps closer than the others. She turns to him. "I'd like to speak with Saskia alone. Why don't you go on ahead? I'm sure you're exhausted."

Bram's eyes meet mine just for a moment. He lifts one hand

in a silent farewell before jogging toward the broad lane that leads to Ivory Hall. All but one of the Breakers follow him, and I'm left alone on the pier with Norah and a huge man with chiseled features and dark hair cropped close to his scalp. He wears a black cloak with a thick white stripe on the sleeve.

"This is Rasmus," Norah says. "He'll be assigned to you for the duration of your training. You'll be safe enough within the walls of Ivory Hall, but if you need to leave for any reason, Rasmus will accompany you."

I swallow. "A bodyguard?" Being constantly watched on the trip here was bad enough, but the thought of someone following me for months makes me feel like boarding another ship and sailing straight back to Midwood. "Am I in that much danger?"

"It's out of an abundance of caution," she says. But her worried expression tells a different story. She touches me lightly on the shoulder. "I assure you, Rasmus will be discreet. You'll barely know he's there."

The Breaker is the size of a small mountain. I'm certain I'll know he's there.

"There's something I wanted to discuss with you," Norah says. She threads her arm through mine and we begin walking. "I'm sure you're still devastated about what happened with your mother."

Beside her, I stiffen. "Latham killing her, you mean?" I have no patience for my mother's death being dipped in sugar to make it more palatable.

She doesn't respond for so long, I think she's reconsidering her intentions for this conversation, but then she sighs. "I don't mean to downplay it. But I do need to know I can trust you."

My breath lodges in my throat. Does she know I lied about being matched as a Bone Charmer?

"What makes you think you can't trust me?" I try to keep my voice steady and hope Norah can't hear my heart thrashing against my rib cage.

"When grief mixes with anger, it can work on us like a poison. Make us do things we otherwise would never consider."

She knows. She must.

I glance over my shoulder at Rasmus, who looks alert and ready to spring into action. Maybe he's here to detain me instead of protect me.

"I never intended to—"

Norah pats my arm. "I'm not accusing you of anything," she says. "The Grand Council just needs to know that you're going to let them take care of searching for Latham and meting out justice. I'm sure vengeance is tempting—it would be for anyone—but this is something the council is far better equipped to handle. Promise me you'll let them?"

I'm so grateful we've moved away from the lamplight, so that the darkness hides the relief I can feel melting over my expression. She's not confronting me about something I did in the past. She's worried about what I'll do in the future.

And she should be.

But I can't let her know the truth—that something ugly has been festering inside me for weeks now: a hatred that burns so brightly, I feel as if I'm on fire. And along with it an aching desire for revenge.

"If I knew how to find him, I would have tried already." It's as honest an answer as I can muster. Because I'm determined to recover my mother's bones no matter what assurances the council wants. But staying in the capital—in Norah and the council's good graces—will give me the best chance of success. Latham lived and worked here. He must have left clues behind.

Silence stretches between us, an empty space that Norah is waiting for me to fill with a vow.

"I don't have a plan for revenge," I say finally. "I just want my mother's bones back." Strictly speaking, it's true. Latham will pay for what he's done—I intend to make him wish he'd never drawn breath—but I don't have a strategy at the moment. My skills are no match for his. Not yet.

"We have our best people working on returning them to you," she says, squeezing my arm. "I promise."

Norah and I continue toward the wide lane that climbs to Ivory Hall, and my erratic pulse slowly returns to normal. Rasmus follows behind, moving as silently as if he were weightless. It occurs to me that Norah intends for him to be my jailer as well as my guardian. I can't search for Latham very effectively if I'm being followed every time I leave Ivory Hall.

At least she accepted my response without forcing me to make a commitment. Norah didn't get a promise from me tonight.

But I'm glad I got one from her.

"Brace yourself," Norah says when we reach the enormous entrance to Ivory Hall. Bright moonlight illuminates arched double doors inlaid with a design of branches that mimic the Shard River. We've been climbing the hill for the better part of half an hour and my legs are tired and twitching.

"Brace myself for what?"

"You'll see."

Rasmus goes in first, and Norah and I follow closely behind.

I press a hand to my chest. It's as if we've stepped directly from the crisp autumn air into a winter palace made of snow and ice. The floors, walls, and ceilings are made from the same white stone as the exterior of the building. Huge chandeliers hang from above, casting soft light around the grand foyer. Dual staircases—with white steps and white banisters—curve elegantly toward the upper floors.

A gentle hum comes from somewhere in the distance.

Norah touches my elbow. "Are you feeling all right?"

"Yes," I say, turning toward her. "I just didn't expect it to be so beautiful." A furrow appears between her brows, and a thread of unease goes through me. I feel as if I've failed some important test. "What is it? Did I say something wrong?"

"Ivory Hall is made entirely of bone," she says. "Most Charmers become quite ill upon arrival."

Inwardly, I wince at the misstep. I search my memory from reading Gran's bone. How did I react in my alternate past? An image rises in my mind: the room spinning, a buzz in my ears, overwhelming nausea. Why don't I feel any of that now? I shouldn't have come here. I have too many secrets to keep, and eventually one of them will land me on Fang Island.

Suspicion sparks in Norah's eyes as she studies me. I press the backs of my fingers to my mouth, and her expression relaxes just a fraction. Maybe she's mistaken my panic for illness. It might be the only thing that saves me.

"Could I sit down a moment?" I ask.

"Ah, it's caught up to you," she says, not unkindly. "Of course you may."

Norah guides me to a chair and a strong feeling of having sat in this exact spot before overtakes me. I think of my mother's words as she cradled Gran's broken bone at my kenning. *We've done this before.* I wonder if she felt then as I do now—like she was hearing the melody of a long-forgotten lullaby, but the words were just out of reach.

A pang of longing for her hits me so hard that it snatches my breath away. The grief comes in waves, crashing over me when I least expect it, before receding again. But I don't think it will ever disappear. It will be lapping at the shores of my mind forever.

The hum in the room grows louder. I look around, but I can't tell where it's coming from.

"What is that noise?" I ask.

"It's just the walls whispering," Norah says nonchalantly. "It will fade." She holds out a hand and pulls me to my feet. "Let's get you some rest. Tomorrow will be a long day."

Norah leads me down a corridor off the main foyer. We pass a large dining hall with tables that stretch the length of the room, and beyond that a kitchen that looks big enough to feed the entire town of Midwood. Finally she opens the door to a small room just big enough for a narrow bed and a small bureau.

"We'll find you more permanent sleeping arrangements tomorrow," Norah says, "but I don't want to traipse through the girls' dormitory at this hour and wake all the apprentices."

She must see something unexpected in my expression, because she pauses for just a moment, her fingers curling around the door frame, and gives me a sympathetic frown. "I know this is a lot of change all at once. I'll do my best to make sure you have friends here. That you feel welcomed."

I want to tell her I don't need her help making friends. I'd rather have her focus on making sure Latham pays for what he's done. On getting my mother's and Gran's bones back before Latham uses them. But the words stick in my throat, and I just nod.

Norah pats my arm again. "Get some rest, and if you need anything, just call out. Rasmus will be close by."

I think of all the times over the last few weeks I've felt the weight of a gaze at my back, and wonder if Norah had people watching me in Midwood, too.

After she leaves, I change into my sleeping clothes and crawl under the covers. I pull the blanket all the way to my chin. The sounds in Ivory Hall are unfamiliar, and I feel unsettled in such a strange place. But home wasn't the same without my mother anyway. And it won't be the same until I have her bones back, and Gran's, too. It takes me a long time to drift off, but eventually the promise of revenge lulls me to sleep.

◆———————◆———————◆

The nightmares follow me to Ivory Hall.

I dream of my mother's death in vivid, horrid detail. Followed by Latham coming toward me with a weapon in his hand.

I jolt awake, sweating and gasping for breath. I stuff my knuckles into my mouth to keep from screaming.

Only a bad dream, I tell myself. Only my mind using my fear as fuel to re-create traumatic memories and invent new worries.

I reach for the wall to steady myself so I can sit up. But the moment my skin makes contact, I'm yanked back into the nightmare. I stand in a large space of some kind. The walls are lined with shelves overflowing with spell books, boxes of bones, unusual weapons, candles in various stages of use.

Music floats on the air.

I turn and see Latham, eyes eager and bright. And then the sword begins to fall.

I pull away from the wall and wrap my arms around my knees. Slow, cold horror settles over me. Norah's voice echoes in my head: *Ivory Hall is made entirely of bone.*

What if my dreams aren't nightmares? What if they're premonitions? Just now, when I touched the wall . . . I don't know how it would be possible without blood or flame, but it felt just like a bone reading. Of the future.

Of my death.

Chapter
Three

he next morning, I wake to gentle rapping. I scrub
at my eyes, disoriented. It takes me a moment to figure out
where I am, but when I do, the night before rushes back, and
my stomach lurches. Another knock sounds, and a girl around
my own age pokes her head through the door.

"Saskia?"

I pull myself into a sitting position. "Yes?"

The girl enters and gives me a bright smile. She's holding
a tray laden with fruit and bread. Her wide brown eyes are
framed by thick lashes, and dark curly hair tumbles down her
back all the way to her waist. She reminds me of someone, but
I can't figure out who.

"Are you hungry?" I open my mouth to answer, but she slides the tray across my lap and keeps talking. "I guess that's a silly question, since it's nearly time for the midday meal and you haven't had anything to eat since yesterday. Unless Norah offered you a light meal last night? It doesn't seem like she would have, but she surprises all of us sometimes."

She pauses and tilts her head to one side as if she's waiting for a reply.

"No, Norah didn't offer me a meal." I pick up a deep purple berry from the tray. "And yes, I'm hungry."

"I thought you would be." She sits on the end of the bed. A smattering of white star-shaped tattoos curve around the back of her ear, and her right arm is covered in indigo swirls. "I'm Tessa, by the way, your new roommate."

Suddenly the pieces fall into place. I saw her in the bone reading; she was my roommate on my other path as well. Chills race up my arms. What are the chances I'd end up sharing a room with the exact same person? Unless we were fated to meet no matter which path survived?

She must notice a change in my expression, because her eyes go soft. "Are you feeling ill? Norah said that sometimes Bone Charmers have a harder time adjusting than the rest of us. It sounds miserable, but I could probably help if you aren't feeling well. I could do a spell for nausea if you need it."

"Thank you, but I'm fine," I say, though it's a lie. The nightmare—or was it a bone reading?—flits at the edges of my thoughts and it's all I can do to keep the panic at bay. I pop the berry into my mouth and chew slowly. "You don't have a roommate already?"

"No," she says, drawing out the word so it sounds both humorous and annoyed. "There were uneven numbers, so I was assigned a solo room. But it's been so dull all by myself—not to mention lonely—and I can't tell you how happy I am that you're here." Her hand folds around my ankle.

Normally, I would find her chattiness grating, but a wave of affection washes over me that I can't explain. She feels like an old friend, lost and then found again.

I keep eating while Tessa talks. She tells me all about how her first term went, how she's finally feeling more confident in her abilities, how she can't wait until she can introduce me to her friends.

"I want to know all about you, too," she says after several minutes, "but it will have to wait until later. Norah wants to see you in the great hall"—she motions toward the food—"as soon as you're finished eating, of course."

The great hall. That can only mean one thing: a binding ceremony. My appetite vanishes and I push the tray away.

"I'm done," I tell her. "Let's get this over with."

Norah hasn't asked me about the details of my kenning. Including which of the three Sights my reading showed.

I can tell her anything I want.

Tessa and I walk down the corridor toward the great hall. As she fills me in on what to expect during the ceremony, I think of my father's lessons in strategy. Should I say I have

Third Sight? Assuming Norah has hired another instructor to replace Latham, they would presumably be using his old office. Latham might have left behind clues there that could help locate him.

Then again, I could say I have First Sight. Maybe focusing more heavily in reading the past would help me determine his plan in more detail.

And not choosing Second Sight might be protective—if I'm bound to the same Sight as either my mother or Gran, will Latham really acquire the bones of all three Sights by killing me?

The large doors of the great hall come into view, and an image rises in my mind. A huge rectangular room bathed in sunlight. Soaring ceilings supported by massive bone columns. Hundreds of folded cloaks resting beside stone basins. A shiver tingles down my spine. It's as if a ghost has sidled up beside me to whisper secrets into my ear. Memories of things that never happened to me but would have if I'd been on a different path. If Gran's bone had never broken.

But when Tessa opens the door, the scene before me looks nothing like the one in my memory.

The day is overcast, and so the stained-glass windows aren't flooded with light and color. No rows of long tables. No stacks of colorful cloaks. No grandeur at all.

And the room is empty.

"Oh no," Tessa says, "you had more time to eat and I rushed you. I'm sorry."

I laugh at the sincere look of regret in her eyes and take her fingers in mine. "You're a good friend, Tessa."

Her eyebrows disappear into her hairline, and it takes me a moment to realize my mistake. We've only just met, and my response was far too familiar. I let go of her hand and my cheeks flame.

She studies me with a perplexed expression, and I scramble for some way to explain. "I'm sorry, I—"

The door at the far side of the great hall swings open. But it's not Norah who enters the room. It's Bram. My heart leaps at the sight of him, and a wave of confusion slams into me. My hands twitch at my sides as he approaches, and I resist the urge to reach up and sweep aside the lock of chestnut hair that has fallen across his forehead. It's as if my body is a stranger, responding to things I don't remember. What my heart *should* be feeling is panic. Bram knows enough to ruin my life. He knows my mother had Gran's bones illegally prepared for my kenning. He's seen me use unbound magic. And now he's here at my binding ceremony, where I will make promises that turn me into a hypocrite. The realization is like soap drizzling into my eyes during a bath. A moment ago, I was fine, but now Bram's presence is uncomfortable. Irritating.

He vowed to keep my secret, but will he?

"Hello," I say. "I wasn't expecting to see you here."

"The binding ceremony requires witnesses," Bram says. The wine-red shirt he wears brings out a hint of ruddiness in his complexion. "Norah asked me to attend." She could have chosen anyone for a witness. Why Bram? "She thought you might appreciate a familiar face," he says, as if I've spoken my concerns aloud.

I'm startled by a sudden, upsetting impulse to embrace him. I think of the tattoo around my wrist that I'm hoping will fade. About the way he laughed when I confessed we were matched on my other path.

"Oh." I infuse my voice with indifference, as if his presence is no more significant than one of the Poulsen twins showing up to my binding. We're from the same town, that's all. "Well, then, thank you for coming." Bram starts to say something more, but he's interrupted by the door opening again. Norah enters carrying a stone basin loaded with supplies. On top is a neatly folded wool cloak. She's accompanied by a Bone Charmer—just one—dressed in red silk robes.

"Sorry to keep you waiting," Norah says. She dips her head toward the woman beside her. "This is Kyra. She's our Second Sight Charming Master. Kyra, this is Saskia."

"A pleasure to meet you," I say. Kyra's skin is warm brown, and her black hair is braided and twisted into a bun at the back of her head. Her face is unlined and has an ageless quality.

She takes my outstretched hand in hers. "The pleasure is mine. It will be refreshing to have an apprentice for the upcoming term. I look forward to working with you."

I turn back toward Norah. "But I don't understand. I never told you I was matched with Second Sight."

A look of alarm flits across Norah's expression. "Was I wrong? Were you matched with another Sight?"

I swallow. There's no good way to handle this. I wasn't matched as a Bone Charmer, so Norah couldn't have access to the results of a reading that gave me Second Sight when one doesn't exist. But on my other path, my mother *did* match me with Second Sight. So what if Norah somehow knows that's my fate?

"You weren't wrong," I say, finally. "I just wondered how you knew."

She and Kyra share a look. "We have reason to believe Latham might have been targeting your family based on you having Second Sight." She clears her throat. "It's rather unusual to have three generations of Bone Charmers, and even more rare that they each have a different Sight."

This time it's me and Bram who share a significant glance. Back in Midwood, he promised to help me stop Latham, and his eyes spark with interest at Norah's declaration.

But it's reassuring that Norah knows some of what Latham was after. Maybe the Grand Council will be successful in finding and stopping him.

"Shall we get started?"

Norah goes to the small wooden table in the center of the room and places the basin on top. Inside is a collection of bones.

My palms begin to sweat as I think of what my mother told me about the binding ceremony. That it involves apprentices agreeing to confine their magic to one specific area. *It's like pruning a garden. The magic is directed and confined. And eventually the potential in other areas withers and dies. And the nurtured magic grows stronger.*

But I don't want to lose my ability to see into the past or the future.

My mastery tattoo isn't the one I'm trying to lose.

Kyra takes out a piece of flint and a small sharp needle. She reaches for my hand and cradles it in hers.

"Saskia Holte, you have been chosen as a Bone Charmer with the Second Sight." *And the First and the Third, too,* I say in my own mind. "Today you will bind yourself to this magic as it has bound itself to you."

She reaches for my hand and pricks my index finger with the needle. "In front of you are the bones of Charmers who have come before. Do you witness with your blood that you will honor their legacy?"

"Yes," I say, tipping my finger to allow a single drop to fall into the basin.

"Do you vow to use your gifts for the benefit of others and not for personal gain?"

I hesitate. Will using bone magic to plot revenge against Latham be breaking this promise? But seeking justice isn't selfish. I won't be doing it just for myself. I'm doing it for my mother. For Gran. For everyone else Latham has hurt, and will hurt in the future if he isn't stopped.

"Yes, I do." I let another drop fall on the bones.

"Do you vow to help your fellow citizens find happiness, while matching their talents to the needs of the country?"

"Yes." A third drop of blood spills into the basin.

"Do you promise to follow every tenet of your training, to uphold the values that you learn within these walls, and to use your magic for good?"

"Yes." I squeeze my finger to force another drop to fall, while saying my own words silently: *I vow to use all three Sights to seek justice.*

Master Kyra sets the bones on fire. She pulls a pouch from her pocket and sprinkles its contents over the basin. The flames turn a vibrant blue and shoot high into the air.

"Saskia Holte," Kyra says, "you have been bound to this magic and you are now authorized to don the training cloak."

As I wrap the red fabric around my shoulders, I can only hope my silent additions to the binding ceremony keep all three Sights intact.

I need every advantage I can get if I have any hope of finding my mother's bones before Latham uses them to control the future.

"You must be hungry. You hardly ate earlier," Tessa says as we walk away from the great hall. "We should probably get you something to eat."

I can't help the laugh that bubbles up my throat. Tessa hasn't stopped trying to feed me since we met.

"What's so funny?" The register of her voice elevates just a fraction, and I realize I've hurt her feelings.

"Nothing," I say. "I was just thinking that it's so obvious you're an oldest child."

Tessa's eyes go wide with astonishment. She stops walking and spins to face me. "How did you know that?"

My stomach squirms uncomfortably. The truth is, I'm not sure *how* I know. But I do. It's the same way I know my father loved the scent of woodsmoke—a thing I never remember actually learning, but the knowledge is written on my heart just the same.

33

"Well, you've done nothing but try to take care of me since I got here." I gently bump her hip with mine. "It's clear you've had practice."

A series of images flash through my mind: Tessa's cool knuckles resting against my forehead; Tessa kneeling in the grass beside Bram as she performs a healing spell to take away his pain; Tessa sliding a tray of food onto my lap, her brow furrowed in concern.

The tips of her ears turn pink. "Am I that transparent?"

My chest suddenly feels tight with emotion. I touch her wrist lightly. "Yes, but in the best way possible. You must be an incredible Healer. And for the record, you're right. I'm starving."

We round the corner into the dining hall, which is a cacophony of noise and color. Servers circulate with platters of fragrant meat and fluffy bread. "I want you to meet everyone," Tessa says, taking my elbow and guiding me to a table at the far side of the room, where a group of half a dozen apprentices are already deep in lively conversation.

"This is Jacey," Tessa says, pointing to a girl dressed in a purple robe. Her skin is golden brown, and her heart-shaped face is framed by a tumble of dark curls. "She's a Mixer."

Jacey gives me a small wave, and Tessa turns toward the rest of the table, making a series of rapid introductions that fly by so quickly, I'm sure I'll never remember them all. I search my memory of my reading of Gran's bone, but none of these names or faces are familiar.

The more time I spend here, the more my mind is flooded

with images from another life. I remember a boy with auburn hair, pale skin, and a sprinkle of cinnamon freckles. A Breaker girl with raven locks and a penchant for snark. But neither of them are here.

This morning, when I realized that Tessa and I were roommates on my other path, I assumed her other friends would be the same as well. But they're all different. How is it possible that Gran's bone breaking changed Tessa's entire group of friends? The thought gnaws at me all through the meal. Were none of us fated to be close? Was the vision I saw wrong? Are the others even *here*?

A wave of homesickness washes over me. I wish I could talk to Ami and get her advice.

"Saskia." Tessa's voice pulls me back to the present. Her tone makes it clear this wasn't the first time she's said my name.

"I'm sorry," I say, "what was that?"

"Jacey asked how your binding ceremony went."

I shift my focus to Jacey, who is studying me with an eager expression. "I'm just trying to imagine all that pageantry for one person. Was it awkward?"

I shake my head. "My ceremony was nothing like yours. No tables full of cloaks. No learning about the meaning of the stained-glass windows or the history of the Grand Council. We pretty much just skipped right to the binding."

"Wow, Tessa really filled you in on every detail." She smiles and nudges Tessa's ribs with her elbow. "That sounds nothing like her. She's usually so *quiet*." Jacey's tone is full of gentle sarcasm. No one who has spent more than a moment with Tessa would ever sincerely describe her as quiet.

Tessa gives Jacey a playful glare. "For your information, I didn't have time to tell her anything about our binding. So I must not be the only talkative one around here."

I flinch at my mistake. I keep losing track of what I *should* know and what I only know from my other path. I fiddle with the napkin in my lap, flicking the corner between my thumb and forefinger. "My mother attended Ivory Hall, so I had some idea of what to expect."

Tessa shakes a basket of bread in front of me. "Do you want more?" I grin and raise my eyebrows. Crimson floods her cheeks. "I really do keep trying to feed you, don't I?"

"Yes." I snatch a chunk of bread from the top of the heap. "But it's endearing."

Jacey offers me a plate with tiny roses carved of butter. "Was your mother a Charmer too?"

A lump forms in my throat. "She was." I look away to discourage further questions.

The conversation shifts to the upcoming bone games. By now I've figured out they're a series of challenges during second term, but most of the information about them is rooted in speculation and rumor. I'm just grateful we're not talking about my mother anymore. It's a wound too raw to bear prodding.

Chapter
Four

The rest of the day is a whirlwind. Norah takes me on a tour of Ivory Hall—from the grounds of rolling hills and colorful autumn trees, down to the brightly lit workshop in the basement, and finally to the training wing, where she announces that my first session with Master Kyra will be tonight. I had hoped for more time to settle in—one day, at least—but Norah remains insistent.

"You're months behind the others," she says. "I'm afraid you'll need many extra hours of practice to catch up before the bone games."

I start to ask what she means by bone games, but she's already walking away.

Now I stifle a yawn as I sit at a circular table opposite Master Kyra. Several small animal bones are scattered on a cloth in front of me.

"I'm holding a small object in my left palm," Kyra says. "I'd like you to attempt to divine what it is."

She lights a bundle of incense, and the smoke curls around us in lazy circles. When the sharp scent of sage hits my nose, memories of my mother rise in my mind—her sitting in front of a stone basin performing readings for the townsfolk, the soothing certainty in the cadence of her voice, the delicate beauty of her hands wielding small needles and pieces of flint. My throat aches. I squeeze my eyes closed.

"Saskia?" Master Kyra's voice is tinged with worry. "Is something wrong?"

I shake my head. My grief feels too raw to share. Too personal. "I'm fine."

She frowns. "Are you sure?"

I touch a single finger to one of the bones, anxious to end the conversation. "You're holding a coin," I tell her. "A silver one."

Her sharp intake of breath closes a fist of fear around my throat. Too late, I realize that she expected the task to be far more difficult. My heart hammers beneath my rib cage. The mastery tattoo hidden under my sleeve suddenly feels as if it's on fire.

Master Kyra opens her palm to reveal a small silver coin. "Are you sure you've never attempted a reading before?" Her tone is light, but there's an undercurrent of suspicion beneath her words that makes me feel as if I'm on trial. I try to remember how long it took on my other path to gain a level of skill for these kinds of simple tasks, but the reading of Gran's healed bone wasn't clear enough to give me every detail.

"Maybe it's beginner's luck?" My voice comes out strained.

Kyra frowns. "Unlikely. In my experience, luck and magic don't usually join hands."

I feel like a rabbit caught in the sudden bright beam of a hunter's lantern. Trapped. Exposed. I need to say something to erase the wariness from her expression.

"My gran always said she thought I would have an aptitude for charming," I say. And then after a pause: "Before she died."

Kyra's eyes fill with sympathy. Her fingertip trails along the edge of the velvet cloth as if she might find an explanation in the bones themselves.

Finally her gaze meets mine and she smiles. "It seems your gran was right. You must be exceptionally gifted. Perhaps it won't take you as long to catch up as we feared."

Despite all my worry, the statement gives me a little stab of satisfaction. The more talent and training I have, the better my chances of finding Latham and getting my mother's bones back. And then I'll make him pay for what he's done.

"Shall we try something more challenging?"

"Sure."

She taps her bottom lip with her index finger and stares off into the distance. "Can you divine the weather . . ." My heart does a little leap because weather is easy. But then Kyra continues: "In Midwood?"

Until Master Kyra lit the incense, I had actually managed not to think about my mother for a few hours. But the moment she entered my mind again, it was like ripping open a barely healed wound. Focusing on home right now would be unbearable.

I swallow. "Does it have to be Midwood?"

Kyra's head tilts to one side. "Anywhere else would be impossible for you to see." My expression must reveal my confusion, because she explains further. "Our homes leave an indelible imprint in our memories. Your connection to Midwood will make it far less challenging than trying to read something in a town or village you're unfamiliar with. Even so, with such limited training, you're unlikely to be able to reach that far." She smiles gently. "Despite being gifted."

It's as if she's presented me with two poisoned goblets and asked me to choose. If I pretend to fail, Kyra will go back to easier tasks and I'll lose an opportunity to stretch my abilities. But if I succeed, she'll suspect that I've trained before. Starting an apprenticeship in the middle of the year is already unusual, and the last thing I need is to draw even more attention to myself. Under the table, I curl my fingers into my palms. Either choice is a risk, but only one of them will get me closer to my goal.

And I'm still shaken by the worry that my recurring nightmare was actually a bone reading. But even if it wasn't, I still know the truth: One way or another, Latham is going to kill me. If I have any chance of changing my fate—of besting him and making him suffer—I need to learn as much as I can as quickly as possible.

I cover the bones with my palms and close my eyes. A tug low in my stomach pulls me into a vision and I'm suddenly in my house in Midwood. I had intended only to see the town square. To get a quick look at the sky. Instead I'm standing next to my mother's favorite rocking chair, staring out the window. Rain patters softly against the glass. It's the kind of day when we would have a fire burning in the hearth. A pot of stew bubbling on the stove. But the house is cold. Empty. A body without a soul.

I will never be able to escape this sorrow. It will follow me everywhere. Haunt my nightmares and darken my days.

I yank my hands away from the bones. "It's raining," I tell Kyra without meeting her eyes, "and chilly."

"Well done," Master Kyra says softly. Her voice has a quality that draws my gaze upward. She looks unsettled, and her hands tremble as she gathers the bones and deposits them into a small bag. "I can see why Latham—" She suddenly stops talking and presses the back of her hand to her mouth as if the words escaped without her permission.

"Why he wants me dead?"

She sighs, her eyes full of regret. "Why he thinks your bones would be especially powerful." She touches my shoulder gently. "But please don't worry. We're close to finding him, and he can't hurt you. Not here."

I think of Rasmus ready to accompany me if I leave the grounds. Of Norah's promise to keep me safe. Of the earnest expression on Master Kyra's face. And for the first time since Latham killed my mother, a tiny seed of hope sprouts in my heart.

Maybe I don't have to do this alone.

Maybe I really will be safe here.

Both Bram and Tessa are waiting for me when I leave the training wing.

"Our new room is ready," Tessa says brightly, threading her arm through mine. "And Bram wants to see if it's better than his. Right, Bram?"

Bram gives a half smile that suggests he said no such thing.

The path to the girls' dormitory—just as everything else in Ivory Hall—looks vaguely familiar. Like something out of a dream. Candelabras made from deer antlers are spaced at regular intervals and bathe the white walls in a gentle light. The flames flicker as we pass, but bone magic keeps them from snuffing out. Beneath our feet is a plush rug with swirling patterns of green and gold, and I know the exact spot where it's grown threadbare—a detail plucked from my memory, even though I can't locate the source.

Tessa stops halfway down the corridor, at a door in the center of the block of rooms.

"Let me," Bram says, reaching for the knob. But it won't open. He wiggles it and tries again. "It's locked."

"That's strange." Tessa reaches for the knob, and at her touch, it turns easily and the door swings open wide.

"Whoa, where'd you get a Mason-crafted lock?" All three of us startle at the voice. We turn to find an apprentice in an orange cloak studying the knob with an expression of naked admiration. He takes in our confused faces and dips his head toward the door. "It will only open for the room's occupants."

Tessa's eyes go wide. "That's amazing"—she leans toward me and lowers her voice—"and a little terrifying that it's necessary."

I couldn't agree more.

The room is much larger than where I slept last night. Two beds are situated on either side of a big window, with a bureau and desk for each of us pressed against the opposite wall. A neatly folded stack of linens sits at the foot of each bed. And on one of the pillows is a gift, wrapped in brown paper with delicate designs stamped across the surface in red ink. Tessa fingers the tag. "Saskia, it's for you."

I take a step forward and see my name written in delicate script.

"No one gave *me* a gift when I started training," Bram teases. "It hardly seems fair."

Tessa hands me the package. "Open it," she says, flopping on one of the beds. "Let's see what it is."

I sit on the floor and work a finger under one seam until the paper rips. Inside is a leather-bound book.

Tessa props herself up on one elbow. "Wow. Kyra must have a lot of faith in you. I didn't get a spell book until I'd been here for months."

I can't help but feel a swell of pride and anticipation. Maybe I actually managed to impress Master Kyra instead of arousing her suspicion. The thought wraps around me like a warm blanket.

And then I turn the book over and my blood runs cold. I drop it as if it were on fire.

"What's wrong?" Bram says, kneeling beside me. "Saskia, what is it?" Blood pounds so loudly in my ears that it sounds like his voice is coming from the bottom of a pit.

"This isn't from Kyra." I press a hand over my mouth.

For just a moment before the binding ceremony, I'd foolishly hoped the Grand Council had things under control. That maybe they really could find Latham. Punish him. Return my mother's bones to me.

But they can't. If I want to survive, I'll have to save myself.

Because the spell book is covered in markings I would know anywhere. My mother's mastery tattoo—a vertical oval inside a larger horizontal one, both framed by thick, arching lines on the top and the bottom. The small butterfly tattoo that appeared above her heart on the day I was born. The jagged scar on her collarbone that my father's death left behind.

Acid-laced terror pushes up my throat. Latham was in this room. It didn't matter that the door was protected by bone magic. Or that Norah has hired a bodyguard. Latham wants me to know he can get to me anytime. Anywhere.

This is a spell book made of my mother's skin.

Chapter
Five

ram and Tessa stare at me in openmouthed horror as
I explain what the book is, what it means.

It's as if the temperature in the room has plummeted.

"How?" Bram says. "Why?"

They're the same panic-tinged questions that dart through
my own mind. But I already have the answers. "Latham wants
me to know I'm not safe. That I'll never be safe." I swallow.
"And he wants to torture me before he kills me so that my
bones will be more powerful."

Tessa inhales sharply. "Isn't Latham the instructor who
went missing at the end of last term? Why would he want you
dead? How does he even know you?"

I fill Tessa in on the details of how Latham killed my gran and my mother. As I talk, the color leeches from her cheeks. When I finish, she jumps to her feet. "I'll get help."

I put a hand out to stop her. "No. Wait."

She pauses, and then as the silence stretches between us, her brow furrows in confusion. "We have to tell Norah. She'll know what to do."

But something inside me has gone very still. I feel as if I've been both hollowed out and made of stone. "It won't do any good. Norah can't protect me. No one can."

Tessa's eyes go wide. "You can't just *not* tell her." She throws a panicked look at Bram, as if pleading for support, but his gaze is fixed on the book.

He lays a palm on my arm. "Do you want me to get rid of it?"

"Yes," I say, and then I shake my head. "No."

The book is an abomination. An evil I can't quite force my mind to accept.

And yet.

It's the only thing I have left of my mother. I can't bear to keep it and I can't bear to let it go.

Bram studies my face, then gingerly picks up the book and wraps it in the brown paper. "I'll put it in a safe place," he says, "until you decide what you want to do."

Relief sags from me as Bram slips out the door with the book. Tessa stands and paces back and forth along the length of the room. Her shoulders are curved and she chews her thumbnail as she walks. Several times she pauses, opens her mouth, and then seems to change her mind.

"Just say it," I tell her finally.

She spins to face me. "Say what?"

"Whatever it is you've almost said a dozen times."

"I . . ." She hesitates. "I don't want our relationship to start out on the wrong foot."

I nearly laugh. For me, meeting Tessa feels like thumbing through a book only to realize that I've already read the first few chapters. It doesn't seem like starting so much as remembering. But her pained expression pulls me up short. It's something more than worry about the book Latham left.

Tessa's fingers wander to her hair, wrapping tightly around one of her curls and tugging as she stares off into the distance. She grimaces, as if unaware she's causing her own pain. And suddenly I recognize her expression: guilt. Does Tessa know more than she's letting on?

I sit up straighter. "What are you hiding, Tessa?"

Her eyes narrow and her expression grows fierce. "I'm not *hiding* anything. I'm trying to keep you from doing something stupid."

The way she's looking at me—like I'm a stranger who just insulted her—makes my insides go cold. I'm nobody to Tessa. I'm just a girl she met yesterday who is already asking her to keep a secret. I'm not sure which is worse—to know for certain you're all alone or to see a glimpse of what *could* have been, of people who *might* have loved you, but to be on your own just the same.

"I'm not doing something stupid," I tell her, my voice flat. Something in her expression changes. She sinks to the floor and rests her back against her mattress.

"But what's the harm in getting Norah's advice? Not telling her is reckless. Don't you trust her?"

"I *do* trust her," I say. "But involving her will just give Latham more power."

Tessa purses her lips. "Saskia, I don't think—"

"If we tell Norah, she'll just wrap me in a thousand layers of protection, and the only effect will be to hold me down so Latham can kill me more easily." Tessa opens her mouth to argue, but I keep talking. "He's a spider. I'm a fly. And Norah's attempts to help will be the web that pins me in place to be devoured. But she won't realize until it's too late."

I can see Tessa weighing this image against everything she knows about Norah. Everything she doesn't yet know about me. Still, I can tell she wants to believe me. She just needs a little push.

I sit next to her, press my shoulder against hers. "We were friends once," I say. "In another life."

She looks at me as if I've spoken in a foreign tongue. "What are you talking about?"

It's a risk to tell her the truth, one I may come to regret. But if I'm going to have any chance of stopping Latham, I need allies. And everything I know about Tessa makes trusting her feel like the right answer. Ami's words drift through my mind: *Trust your gut.*

I tell Tessa about Gran's broken bone. About the path that didn't survive. About the friendship we almost had, but didn't.

"It's how I knew you were an oldest child," I tell her. "It's how I know a lot of things about you that I shouldn't."

Her expression is unreadable, and my chest constricts. What if this was a terrible mistake?

"Did I ever tell you that my father is imprisoned on Fang Island?"

The statement hits my ears like shattering glass, startling me so much that every other thought flies out of my head. I half expect to look over and see that Tessa is reading from a letter or a book.

But she's not.

Her fingers curl around her knees. Her eyes are distant, as if she's deep in a painful memory.

"No," I say carefully, "you didn't."

Is she testing how much I know about her? About how close we were on my other path? Worry snakes through my stomach.

Tessa exhales—a ragged sound filled with emotion. "He loved to gamble. Cards, horses, kenning results." She worries the edge of her thumbnail with her teeth. "But his ambition outmatched his supply of coin."

"You can get sent to Fang Island for gambling?" I ask. The prison is remote, heavily guarded, and reserved for the worst criminals in Kastelia.

Tessa gives a harsh laugh. "No. But you can get sent there when you try to numb your stress with too much ale, and then hurt your family because you're drunk."

"Oh, Tessa . . ." I cover her hand with mine. "I'm sorry." We sit like that for a few moments, as questions bubble inside me. Why would she suddenly share something so personal? Is she trying to tell me that I'm gambling away my life? That she doesn't tolerate people who break the rules?

"May I ask . . . ?" I pause, unsure how to put my thoughts into words without offending her. Finally I give up and just finish the question. "Why are you telling me this now?"

Her eyes meet mine. "Because someone hurt my mother once too, and for years I'd counted myself lucky that he didn't do worse. I can't imagine the pain if I'd actually lost her." She flips her hand over and threads her fingers through mine. "I'm telling you so that you know I'm on your side."

The door opens, and Bram slips back into the room. The spell book is gone. His gaze roams over my face, searching, and then falls to my hand, intertwined with Tessa's. His expression darkens with something I can't quite read. Worry? Fear?

"I took care of . . ." His voice fades away, as if he's not sure what to call such a thing. He pulls at the nape of his neck. "If you ever want it back, just let me know."

"Thank you."

His eyes soften. "You're welcome."

A spark lights in my chest. And then I remember he's here out of obligation to Norah. She asked him to come back to Midwood to travel with me, invited him to my binding ceremony. And the idea of us together made him laugh out loud. The memory slides under my skin like a sliver. A painful reminder of all I've lost.

Inwardly, I wince. I haven't lost Bram—we were never together. If I can manage to ignore the feelings from my other path, they'll eventually disappear. And I need to be focused on Latham.

Revenge is a jealous master, Gran used to say. She meant it as a warning—a plea to always seek forgiveness instead of vengeance. But that was before Latham killed her. Before he killed my mother.

Now I've given my entire body—heart and soul—to my plan for revenge. I'm the handmaiden of vengeance.

There's no time for love.

The spell book changes everything.

I had planned to be cautious in my training with Master Kyra. To hold back at least a little and find a delicate balance, making steady progress without improving so quickly that it becomes obvious I've trained before.

But Latham is coming at me with everything he has. I can't afford to move slowly.

During our next session, Master Kyra presents me with a set of bones from the vertebral column of a jackal. "I'd like to test your range today."

"My range?" I can't quite keep the disappointment from seeping into my voice. I reached all the way to Midwood during our last session. Does she really think I need to work on my range?

"Not distance," she clarifies, as if hearing my thoughts. "Time. I'd like to know how far into the past and the future you can reach." A little thrill of anticipation goes through me, followed almost immediately by panic. I have all three Sights. How can I possibly allow her to test my range without giving myself away?

My mind scrambles for a way to avoid the task. So far, I've never been able to tell which Sight I was using—I've thought I was seeing the present when I was actually reading the past, or the future when I was attempting to see the present. What if I try to see later today and end up reading next week instead? Is that too far in the future to be believable?

If I get expelled from Ivory Hall, I'll never hone my skills enough to stop Latham. I'll never find my mother's and Gran's missing bones. Blood roars in my ears. The room feels far too warm, and I shrug the heavy training cloak from my shoulders.

"How far can new apprentices typically reach?" I ask.

Master Kyra studies me, her mouth pressed into a thin line, and I have the sensation of being turned inside out and inspected. She always seems to see more than I'd like her to.

"Everyone is different."

"How far can *you* reach?"

The question is impertinent, and for a moment I think she'll refuse to answer, but then she gives me a measuring look. "A few hours. A day at most."

The pressure in my chest lightens just a fraction. At least it gives me a reference point.

Master Kyra lights the incense—lavender—and sits across from me. "I'd like you to attempt to see what will be served for the evening meal tonight."

It's an impossible task—every meal looks the same except for the menu. I'll know what I'm seeing, but not *when*. I swallow. But maybe that's the point. Maybe Kyra suspects me, and she's carefully designed this exercise to force me to reveal my abilities.

"Are you cold?" Master Kyra asks, her head tilted to one side like a quizzical bird.

I'm confused until I realize my hand has gone—unbidden—to my upper arm. My palm covers the mastery tattoo hidden beneath my sleeve. It's an intricate knot design with three corners. One for each Sight.

Heat creeps into my cheeks. "A little," I say, pulling the cloak back around my shoulders, grateful for yet another layer between Master Kyra and the tattoo beneath my sleeve.

"You may start whenever you're ready," she says.

I take a deep breath and place my fingers over the bones. The room tilts slightly, and I squeeze my eyes closed. The familiar pull low in my stomach greets me like an old friend. I direct my focus to the dining hall, and a vision forms behind my lids. Servers carry large dishes filled with meatballs in a rich cream sauce, and platters of boiled potatoes and roasted vegetables. Small bowls of sugared berries sit at even intervals down the length of the table, along with pitchers filled with cider. I look around for some indication of the day, or time, but find nothing to suggest either.

I nearly pull myself from the vision and tell Master Kyra that I couldn't see a thing—it's a much safer course of action than describing the meal only to realize I've reached too far forward or backward. But maybe there's another option. Maybe with a little more focus, I can find out what day this is. I think back to the tour Norah gave me the morning after I arrived. To the enormous kitchen adjacent to the dining hall.

With my shift in focus, the scene changes and I'm plunged into the middle of chaos. Undercooks stand on both sides of a long wooden table, chopping bundles of herbs and slicing vegetables. A small, round woman—probably the head cook, judging by the way everyone moves a little faster whenever she looks in their direction—shouts orders. On the back wall, inside the huge hearth, are three giant cauldrons bubbling with fragrant fish stew. Loaves of dark bread—dozens of them—cool on another table.

Panic swims up my throat. This is an entirely different meal. Somehow by changing my focus, I've slipped backward or forward in time. The vision dims, fractures, spins. I feel as if I'm rolling down a steep hill, utterly out of control. I think of my mother's lessons. Of her telling me to focus my thoughts as tightly as possible. To a single pinprick—one person or one moment in time. But I don't know which moment I'm looking for. I have no sense of where I'm starting. This could be years in the past or years in the future.

So I do the only thing I can think of. I focus on the cook—on her stout, round frame. Her gray eyes. The soft wrinkles of her cheeks. The vision stabilizes, though now the kitchen is empty and clean. The cook stands with her hands on her hips, her gaze sweeping over the room like a queen surveying her kingdom. I follow her into an anteroom adjacent to the kitchen.

She stands near a small desk, her fingers drumming gently on the wooden surface.

I failed. If the cook isn't bustling around surrounded by help, then I'm likely far from *any* mealtime, evening or otherwise.

What am I going to tell Master Kyra?

The cook drops into the chair in front of the desk, and I wish I could join her. Sink into a soft seat and rest my head in my hands. She slides open a small drawer and pulls out a stack of papers. On the top is a small bit of parchment with a list of supplies written in delicate script: dill weed, flour, juniper berries. She glances at the document briefly and then shifts it to the bottom of the stack. Beneath is a crudely sketched table—columns and rows of squares, each with a menu written carefully in the center. My breath catches. It's a *calendar*. The cook's finger trails along the page, while I frantically search for anything familiar. And then, finally, near the bottom of the page, I spot a meal I recognize: smoked salmon, buttered greens, and crisp bread topped with cheese. I look at the neighboring square, and commit it to memory before I yank myself from the vision.

When I open my eyes, Master Kyra is watching me, her chin resting in her palm. She raises her eyebrows. "So?"

"Meat pie," I say.

"Is that all?"

My pulse races. I shake my head. "I couldn't see anything else."

She studies me, her expression inscrutable. What if I got the menu wrong entirely? The cook must repeat meals often. Maybe I should have claimed I couldn't reach as far as this evening. But then Master Kyra gives me a small, tired smile. "Well done, Saskia. You missed the spiced apples, but I'm impressed you were able to reach as far as the first part of the meal. You're making excellent progress."

I suddenly feel weightless. Buoyant.

I'm coming for you, Latham. And there isn't anything you can do to stop me.

Chapter
Six

ife at Ivory Hall falls into a comfortable rhythm. I continue to train with Master Kyra—holding back just enough to avoid suspicion while trying to perfect my craft, attend seminars in the workshop with the other apprentices, and eat meals in the dining hall with Tessa and her friends—they haven't quite started to feel like *my* friends yet.

Tessa keeps her word and doesn't tell Norah about the spell book. Bram hasn't either, but I'm still cautious. Declan's betrayal is never far from my mind.

But not having anyone to confide in is a slow acid that eats away at me and leaves an aching hole in the middle of my chest. Each night as I fall asleep, I imagine I'm talking to Ami.

That we're sitting on the banks of the Shard, dragging our toes through the water, as I discuss my problems. In my mind, I tell her about my options one by one, and she picks them up, examines them, and offers her opinion before setting them down again.

I could break into Master Latham's old office and search for clues there, I tell her. *As far as I know, he hasn't been replaced yet, and his belongings should still be there.* Maybe I'll find some clue about Avalina, the girl he fell in love with in his youth.

My imagined Ami scoffs at the idea. *If he managed to sneak into your bedroom to leave the spell book, I doubt he would be so careless as to leave anything incriminating behind.*

I could try to find a set of bones powerful enough to attempt a reading on him and discover his location.

Ami shakes her head at this, too. And she's right. With the protective magic he has at his disposal, seeing him in a reading is likely impossible.

"Are you still awake?" Tessa asks softly. We turned off the lights hours ago, and my imagination has been so full of Ami that for a moment I think Tessa's voice belongs to her. A wave of joy swells in my chest before crashing into disappointment.

"I'm awake," I say, turning on my side to face her, though she's nothing more than a shape in the dark. "What's keeping you up?"

Tessa sighs. "I keep thinking about Latham. How you told me he wants you to know you're not safe."

"Yes?"

"What if you're wrong? How do you know for sure that's what he's doing?"

"It's hard to explain," I tell her. "I just know."

But her question unlocks something in my mind. I understand Latham. As much as I despise him, I understand how losing someone you love—being prevented from living the life you imagined for yourself—might drive a person to unspeakable actions. In his mind, he's trying to right a wrong.

That's how I know deep down that the key to stopping him isn't searching his old office or finding him through a reading. I've known since he showed up in Midwood and killed my mother that the key to finding him is Avalina.

What I don't know is how to find her.

I think of the first time my mother told me about Latham. I've thought about it every day since she died. My mother said Latham was friendly when they first met. Likeable. *He was bone-matched with a girl named Avalina. From all appearances they were deeply in love. But halfway through the year, she abruptly left Ivory Hall, and no one ever saw her again. After that, Latham was different. He kept to himself and seemed to resent everyone around him.* My mother hinted that there were swirling rumors. A scandal that changed Latham forever.

I might have thought nothing of the story—young love gone wrong is unlikely to turn a man into a monster—but, before he killed my mother, Latham mentioned Avalina. He said they would be together if not for the Grand Council. Which makes me think that my mother was on to something. She clearly had a gut feeling about his motivations. If this woman was the branch point for Latham turning down a dark path, maybe finding her will give me the answers I need.

Tessa makes a sleepy, disoriented noise at the back of her throat. I doubt she'll remember much of this conversation in the morning. So, for just a moment, I pretend that Tessa is Ami. That I can trust her with my secrets.

"Latham was in love once," I say out loud. "With a woman named Avalina. I need to find her."

"Did she train here?" The words slur blearily together, and I can tell Tessa is drifting off.

Still, the question makes my mind spark with possibilities. If she was an apprentice at Ivory Hall, there should be records.

"Tessa, that's brilliant," I say. But she doesn't answer. Her breathing is deep and even. Suddenly I'm homesick, not only for Ami, but for the Tessa on my other path. The one I knew, and who knew me.

Is this my fate? To only feel close to versions of friends who don't exist in this reality, while my one friend who does is far away?

Knowing that I might be able find more information about Avalina without ever leaving Ivory Hall should make me feel better, but it doesn't. Because maybe searching for a plan gave me something to occupy my thoughts as I lay awake. I'm always exhausted, but terrified of falling asleep.

Of dreaming.

Of encountering a vision of a bleak future each time I close my eyes.

Just when I think I have my training schedule figured out, fate—in the form of Norah—throws me for a loop.

"Apprentices," she says, from atop a small stage in the center of the workshop's amphitheater, "the moment you've been anticipating since second term started is finally here. Everything is about to change."

The room fills with animated chatter, and I feel like I missed a step. I turn toward the girl sitting beside me—a girl with sandy-brown hair named Ingrid. She's the only other Bone Charmer training at Ivory Hall.

"What's going on? What is Norah talking about?"

"Bone games," Ingrid whispers.

Of course. They've been mentioned a few times, but I've been so focused on finding Latham and ignoring Bram, I haven't given them much thought.

But now a memory tickles at the back of my mind: tables spread along the length of the workshop, a pile of bones placed in front of me, a contest to assemble and identify them as quickly as possible. Bram's face floats behind my eyes and my cheeks go hot. He was there. I can nearly feel the ghost of his fingers brushing against mine. Weren't those games? It's like a key in a lock that doesn't quite fit but feels like it might if I just wiggle it a little.

"Haven't we already played bone games?" I ask. And then I catch my mistake. "Haven't *you* already played them, I mean? Before I got here."

Ingrid shakes her head. "No, it's a second-term thing. They started including them a few years ago. It was my brother's favorite part of training." She tilts her head to one side. "Are you thinking of bone races?"

Bone races. That's right. The words click into place in my mind, along with the rest of the memory from my other path. The hard set of Bram's mouth as he worked. The triumphant expression on his face as we slid the last *Bradypus* bone into place and won the contest. But then something slips inside me. It's not a memory. It was only a possibility and it never happened. Not for him.

"Yes," I say, "that's right—bone races."

Norah brings a bone amplifier up to her lips and clears her throat. "If you'll quiet down, I can continue."

Ingrid turns away from me and leans forward. She's not alone. Every apprentice is perched on the edge of their bench, waiting to hear the details.

Norah smiles as if pleased by the effect her words have produced. "Until now, you have primarily worked and trained within these walls. But this term, you'll need to push yourselves further than you ever have before."

She paces along the length of the stage, her palms pressed together in front of her. It's so quiet, I can hear each swing of the pendulum housed in the clock mounted on the back wall—a massive contraption made from the bones of a red-necked ostrich.

"When you leave Ivory Hall, you will be assigned to various villages across Kastelia. Many of you will serve on town councils. You will be required to work with other bone magic specialties to solve complex problems. In the past, we found our apprentices were well trained in their own magic but ill prepared for leadership and problem solving. So, several years ago, we devised a solution." She stops pacing and turns to face us. "Those of you with siblings who attended Ivory Hall have no doubt heard all about it. But for the rest of you, I'm excited to introduce you to the bone games."

Another chorus of whispers ripples over the assembled apprentices. My gaze wanders around the room, over the benches painted in various colors to match our cloaks until I land on a sea of black. Bram sits with his back to me, talking to the other Breakers. He leans forward, seemingly absorbed in the conversation. I watch him for several moments, still confused by the pull I feel toward him. He turns and meets my gaze and my heart lurches. I can't let myself be taken in by emotions from my other path. I harden my expression and let my eyes slide right past Bram, as if I never saw him at all. From the corner of my gaze, I see his brows knit in confusion. A pang of longing hits me square in the chest, but I don't look back.

"These challenges," Norah says with a tone that silences all the chatter, "will require you to work in small groups of five or six—roughly the size of a town council—and will take you all over Kastelia. The games will be graded on a pass-or-fail basis, with the same score given to the entire group, so choose your teammates wisely. You'll want a good blend of specialties and a variety of talents. If you fail the games, you fail your apprenticeship. Now go. Make good decisions."

The room erupts into chaos, and Ingrid is immediately overwhelmed with requests to join a team. There are only two

Bone Charmers available, and no one wants the girl who just started training. A pit opens in my stomach as I think of childhood games of Dead Man's Prisoner. I remember the nagging worry of being chosen last and bearing the shame, not only of being declared the least worthy but having an audience for the humiliation.

A tap on my shoulder makes me spin around, and relief floods through me at the sight of Tessa. Her arm is looped through Jacey's.

"Can we join your team?"

My gaze skips between them. "I think the more appropriate question is, can I join *yours*?"

Jacey laughs, her dark eyes bright. "You're going to be in high demand," she says. "Trust me, no one is clamoring for extra Healers and Mixers."

"Well, in that case," I say, sweeping my arm over the empty space beside me, "yes, join my illustrious team."

Tessa grins. "Excellent. Now, if we can find a Mason, a Watcher, and a Breaker, we'll be one of only two teams with all six specialties."

At the mention of a Breaker, my traitorous eyes go searching for Bram. And like a homing pigeon, I locate him immediately. He's standing near a group, but I can't tell if he's part of a team yet. And then I see Norah approach him. Touch his elbow. Whisper something in his ear. Bram nods. He lifts his head to search the room.

And then aims straight for me.

Hot shame races up my neck as I think of Norah's words

when I first arrived. *I'll do my best to make sure you have friends here.*
Did she tell him to join my group? Does she think I won't have a team otherwise? I don't want Bram's pity. His obligation. His false friendship borne from duty.

"Hey," he says as he approaches us, "do you have room for a Breaker?"

Tessa grabs his sleeve. "Yes, that's perfect!"

Bram's gaze flicks to me, but I look away.

All I want—all I've *ever* wanted when it comes to romance—is a choice. To choose who to love. For someone to choose me. It's why I begged my mother not to give me a reading for a bone-matched partner.

Latham has stolen everything from me, and only one good thing came out of all that loss—my bone-match to Declan died with him, so I recaptured the ability to love who I choose. And even though I vowed to keep my distance from Bram so I could protect us both from Latham, each time he looks in my direction, my resolve slips like a shawl over bare shoulders.

I can't help the foolish hope that keeps blossoming inside me. It's a desperate kind of wanting that feels as essential as breathing. But is it my choice? Am I drawn to him because of what I saw on my other path, or because it's really how I feel here and now? The worries have been twisting together inside me since Bram showed up in Midwood, making me feel as hopelessly tangled as the box of silver chains Gran used to keep on her nightstand table. I would sit for hours trying to separate them, but only managed to knot them more tightly together.

But now, seeing him join our group only after Norah

nudged him in my direction, casts a heavy shadow over me, and all my hope shrivels. Dies. The idea of us together is laughable to Bram. He's here, not of his own free will, but as a favor to Norah. And *my* free will is all tangled up in emotions that don't belong to me.

Fate is mocking me. It will be an exquisite kind of torture to be around Bram, but not *with* him.

Hatred for Latham pulses through me. It's fire in my veins. A bitter poison that coats my tongue. He's snatched the happiness from my past, present, and future.

Bram touches my arm, opens his mouth to say something, but then we're interrupted by a loud voice behind us.

"Did I hear you guys say you need a Watcher?"

I spin around and my heart jumps into my throat. A tall apprentice in a green cloak stands in front of me. He has a messy mop of ginger hair and his nose and cheeks are dusted with cinnamon freckles. He was on my other path. I've been looking for him since I got here.

I grasp for his name, but before I can find it, he sticks out his hand.

"Talon," he says, and I feel the name click into place in my mind. The rightness of it. The familiarity.

When Tessa introduced me to her friends, I assumed Talon would be among them. But maybe he was fated to be on *my* path, not hers. But how can that be when I remember her introducing me to him before and not the other way around?

My mind is spinning so fast, I can't find the words to respond.

Tessa leans across me to take Talon's hand. "I'm Tessa," she says. "And this is Jacey and Bram. The frozen one beside you is Saskia."

Talon puffs out his chest and tugs on the collar of his cloak. "No worries. I'm used to rendering people speechless."

A sudden warmth floods my chest; it's the same instant affection I felt upon meeting Tessa. I squeeze his elbow gently. "I'm so glad you're here."

He grins. "Well, good. And I must say, this is a much more welcoming group than the one I nearly joined." He motions toward a clump of apprentices all dressed in green. They're clearly his friends, judging from the goofy faces he's pulling at them. "They thought a group with only one specialty was a bad idea."

"I'd say they had a very good point," Jacey says, her voice full of amusement. "Six Watchers on a team seems like you'd be begging to lose."

"So is that a yes?" Talon asks. "Can I join you?"

Jacey quickly looks around the group for confirmation. We all nod. "That's a yes," she says.

Talon bounces lightly on his toes. "So what next?"

"Ideally, we need a Mason," Tessa says. "But if we have to double up . . . maybe another Mixer?" She chews her lip as she glances around the room. "Most of the teams look full."

"I have an idea," Talon says. "Wait here." He jogs over to an apprentice with straight jet-black hair and tawny skin. The two boys chat for a moment, and then return to the group together.

"This is Niklas," Talon says. "He's agreed to join our team."

Niklas acknowledges all of us with a small nod. He has a slim silver ring on his left hand that he keeps unconsciously spinning as Tessa peppers him with questions.

Jacey and Talon strike up a conversation about what format the bone games might take, and how lucky we are to get all six specialties. Which leaves me and Bram standing awkwardly beside each other.

"Saskia," he says, his fingertips brushing against my scapula. Even through my cloak, the touch is unbearable. A reminder of everything I want. Everything I can't have. Everything I don't know if I can trust. I turn slightly so that his hand falls away. His brow furrows. "Is something wrong?"

How to answer such a question? With the truth? That I'm mourning memories of the two of us that aren't real? That my feelings for him are as strong as they are mysterious, and I'm not even sure if either of us are the same people in this reality? But I can't say any of that.

"Everything is fine," I tell him. "I'm just tired."

"I wanted to talk to you about something," he says. His voice is low, meant just for me, and his breath dances across my earlobe, sending shivers down my spine.

My closed-up heart cracks open just enough to let in a small, shimmering sliver of hope. "What is it?"

"In Midwood—after your mother died—I promised I would help you." He glances around to make sure no one is listening. "And after seeing that spell book . . . we need a plan."

Oh. The fissure in my heart clots over, seals tight. More duty and responsibility and keeping promises.

"You don't have to . . ." I falter, distracted by the intensity of his expression. The way he is focused solely on me, as if we haven't just received news that our training is about to become much more complicated and difficult.

"Yes, I do," Bram says. "Don't forget that Latham wronged me, too. He befriended me, and then sent me back to Midwood to help you grieve the loss of your mother without telling me that he was the one who killed her." He shakes his head. "He did that for a reason, and I need to find out what it was."

My fingers trace the red tattoo around my wrist. It's supposed to be growing fainter, but if anything, it's brighter than before.

"I don't want you to help me because you feel obligated."

"But I *am* obligated," he says. "I loved your mother."

A lump forms in my throat. "I know you did."

But I don't say the rest of what I'm thinking. That I'm heartbroken she's the only reason he wants to help me.

Chapter
Seven

Instructions for the first challenge of the bone games begin arriving later that evening.

Tessa and I sit on a plush, oversized bench in the library—a space so breathtaking that I find it hard to focus on my studies. It's a soaring atrium six tiers high, supported by graceful, carved bone columns that stretch from floor to ceiling. Each level has a low-walled balcony made from slender bones interwoven in a lattice pattern, giving the illusion that they're fashioned from lace. Light pours in from large windows, casting the entire room in an otherworldly glow.

A sudden flurry of activity causes both me and Tessa to look up from our spell books. Two instructors—a blue-cloaked

Healer and a purple-cloaked Mixer—enter holding large wooden boxes. They glance around the room briefly, then split in opposite directions—one heading for the staircase that curves toward the upper levels, the other stopping at a table nearby and presenting the box to a stunned-looking Watcher.

"What's going on?" Tessa asks at the same moment the phrase *bone games* darts through the room like a whisper on wings.

"Were we supposed to get a box?" I ask.

"I don't know." Without even thinking, I stand, as does every other apprentice in the library. We are—all of us—drawn to the nearby apprentice who received a box.

A crowd gathers around the Watcher, who shuffles from one foot to the other as his peers pummel him with questions: *What's in the box? Where's the rest of your team? Are you nervous?*

"Back up and give him some space," the Mixing Master says, making a gentle flicking motion with her hand. "This group's challenge has nothing to do with yours. You'll each get your own instructions in due time."

"But when?" a voice at the back of the crowd shouts.

"The challenges are unique to each team—specifically designed to test your strengths and expose your weaknesses. You'll receive them as soon as they're ready."

"Maybe all of our maneuvering to get each bone magic won't matter," Tessa whispers.

"I had the same thought," I say. If the challenges are individually designed, we may have earned ourselves a more difficult set of tasks.

Tessa's fingers twine together. "Let's find the others. It's possible someone else on our team has our box."

My gaze flicks to the desk at the front of the library. "Go ahead. I need to take care of something first and then I'll catch up with you."

"Are you sure?" she asks, but her eyes are already on the grand double doors and I can tell she won't feel settled until she finds out if we've gotten our instructions yet.

"Yes, go ahead. I won't be long."

"See you soon." Tessa squeezes my elbow and scurries away.

The information desk is small and curved, with a spiral pattern carved on the front that encircles the librarian like the shell of a gastropod. She even looks a little like a snail, with a pair of spectacles perched on top of her head like small antennae.

She leans forward as I approach. "What can I do for you?"

"I wondered . . . is there any way to access the records of past students?"

The librarian frowns. She retrieves the spectacles from the top of her head and settles them across the bridge of her nose. The frames are made of bone—magic, then—and I wonder if they help her see clearly in more ways than one.

My hands begin to sweat.

"That's an odd request." She folds her hands together in front of her and studies me, clearly waiting for me to explain myself.

"My mother was a student here, and she recently died." I tug on my earlobe, my restless fingers longing for something to occupy them. The words are still hard to say. "I was hoping to contact her former classmates so I could record their memories of her. For a keepsake."

The librarian's face softens. "I'm so sorry for your loss. But that would be highly unusual. I can't just give out contact information of old students. Perhaps you could talk to some of her old friends. See if they can help you?"

"There's no one to ask," I tell her, "or I would have tried that first."

She shakes her head. "I'm sorry, dear, but it's just not possible. It would violate their privacy. Even if I'm sure many of them would be sympathetic to your cause."

My fingernails dig into my palms. I have to convince her to help me, but I don't know what else to do. She seems resolved.

"It's important," I say. "Please?"

She turns away and begins tidying the papers on her desk. Her movements are brusque. Efficient. "Will there be anything else?" she asks without looking up.

"Could you . . . could you at least find me the surname of one of the apprentices who trained with her? Someone she mentioned once? Maybe that will give me enough to go on."

The librarian pauses. Cocks her head to one side as she considers my request. Then she sighs. "I don't see how a name would hurt anything."

"Thank you," I say, taking my first deep breath since the conversation started. "That would be so helpful."

She stands and motions toward a junior librarian to take her place behind the desk. "What is the apprentice's first name?"

"Avalina," I say. "She started the same year as my mother, Della Holte."

"Old student records are on the sixth floor, so it's going to take me some time. Wait here."

And I do.

I wait and wait and wait some more.

The light in the library grows dim. Shadows fall across the shelves. I pace the length of the library, as if keeping my feet moving might speed the process. The junior librarian—a young man only a few years older than me—keeps casting anxious glances toward the staircase, as if he, too, thinks his superior has been away overly long.

Finally I hear the click of boots on the bone steps, and my pulse quickens.

The librarian rounds the corner, her arms empty. "I'm sorry. There's no apprentice by that name in the records."

"But that makes no sense. She trained here. How could there be nothing?"

"Sorry," she repeats, lifting one shoulder, nonchalant. "I can't produce something that doesn't exist." But there's something in the set of her jaw, in the careful way her eyes avoid meeting mine. She knows more than she's saying. She saw something in those records that she isn't willing to share.

Anger flares in my chest, but losing my temper is unlikely to sway her. "What am I supposed to do now?" I ask under my breath. It's a question directed more to myself than to the librarian, but she answers anyway.

"Maybe it's time to let this project go. Your memories of

your mother are the ones that matter most anyway."

Her words make my throat ache, and I wish I could tell her that there's so much more at stake than memories. Avalina is my best chance at finding Latham. And finding Latham is the only way I'll find my mother's bones.

But I'll need a different plan. It seems I'm searching for a ghost.

That night, I wait until Tessa falls asleep, and then I pull out Gran's healed bone. If I can't find clues in the library, I'll need to search for them the only way I know how—on my alternate path.

The last time I attempted to read the bone was shortly after my mother died. I was grieving then. Shaken. And though I've thought about exploring it further, I haven't had the courage. I don't want to see myself interacting with Latham unaware that he was Gran's murderer and had plans to kill me and my mother as well. To watch myself fall in love with Bram. To witness my own death.

But now I have no choice. I need to search for clues in my interactions with Latham that might give me some idea of where to find him. And how to stop him once I do. I set the bone on my lap, and stare at it. My throat goes dry. I can't bring myself to do another reading. I'm not sure I have the stomach to encounter Latham, but that's not what's holding me back.

It's Bram.

If watching our story unfold once tangled my feelings so hopelessly, I can't imagine the damage repeated readings would cause. If I want my love tattoo to fade, I need to forget my other path, not torture myself with it. How can I find clues to stop Latham without encountering a version of Bram that makes me want to disappear into another reality? I wrestle with the decision until I can't keep my eyes open anymore. I don't have to explore the path today. I can wait until I'm stronger. Until the tattoo has started to fade. So I fold my fingers around the bone and give into the temptation to close my eyes and drift off to sleep.

Tessa's anxiety about the bone games has reached a fever pitch. Over the past few days, most groups have received their instructions, and Ivory Hall has slowly emptied of apprentices as the teams have dispersed all over Kastelia to work on their tasks.

The six of us sit together at an otherwise unoccupied table in the dining hall. Tessa has been talking nonstop since we got here—a frenzied stream-of-consciousness rant that makes me feel as if we're all perched on a slender branch in a windstorm.

"Do you think the bone games are timed somehow? Are we going to be at a disadvantage because we're starting so late? What does it mean that we're one of the last groups to get instructions?" Tessa doesn't breathe between questions to leave time for an answer. But finally she falls silent.

"Someone has to be last," Talon says cheerfully. "Why not us?"

Tessa wrings her hands. "I'd rather be in the middle. There's safety in the middle."

"But no excitement," he says around a mouthful of bread. "Safety is boring." He licks the crumbs from his fingers, oblivious to the way she's glowering at him.

I lay a hand on Tessa's forearm. Even though I don't share her apprehension—I have much more pressing matters to occupy my worry—I understand it. Her role as a Healer is to alleviate pain, to end suffering. When she sees discomfort, she longs to magic it away. But this is a problem that can't be fixed with anything but patience, and it puts her on edge.

"Everything will be fine," I tell her. "I promise."

"Saskia's right," Jacey says. "All we can do is wait."

Tessa takes a deep breath. "I know. I'm trying."

Niklas and Bram, who have been quietly talking to each other, suddenly fall silent. Bram nudges Tessa's shoulder with his own. "Look, maybe you don't have to wait much longer."

Master Kyra walks toward us with a large wooden box. She plunks it down unceremoniously in front of Tessa, as if she knows exactly who needs to see it most. "Good luck," she says.

I practically feel Tessa exhale.

Jacey reaches for the latch, but Tessa places her palm flat against the wood to prevent her from lifting the lid. "Let's take it upstairs where we have more privacy."

We all glance around the room. Two other groups sit clustered together, both a sizable distance from each other, and so far from us that we can't hear a word they're saying. Can't even make out their facial features.

"I really don't think—" Jacey starts, but the pleading expression on Tessa's face seems to change her mind. "All right. I suppose an extra layer of privacy couldn't hurt. Let's open the box somewhere else."

The room I share with Tessa isn't small, but with six people crammed in a circle on the floor between the two beds, it feels tiny. Bram ended up next to me, his legs folded in front of him, feet crossed at the ankles. His shoulder presses against mine, and it makes it hard to think. Hard to breathe. I try to shake off the feeling, annoyed that my body still can't seem to tell the difference between my two paths.

"Is everyone ready?" Tessa asks. The wooden box sits in the center of the circle.

Jacey gives a playful, dramatic sigh. "Just open it already. The anticipation is killing me."

Tessa lifts the lid. Inside the wooden box is a thick cube of silky-smooth bone. It's about the size of two loaves of bread resting side by side. At first glance, I might call it a box, except for the fact that it has no hinges, no visible seams of any kind. Tessa turns it over, examines it from every angle.

"Um . . . thoughts?"

"That looks Mason-made," Talon says. "Give it to Niklas."

Niklas takes the contraption from Tessa and runs his palm along the surface. "My best guess is that it's a puzzle box."

"So how do we open it?" Bram asks.

Niklas shakes his head, his fingers still roaming over the surface. "They're all different. Some open to a distinct series of movements on the surface, some open only in a designated location, others work with a specific fingerprint."

"Like the lock on our room," Tessa says.

"Yes," Niklas says, "the magic is a little different, but the principle is the same."

I think of the box that my mother had commissioned to hold my father's bones. It was made by Midwood's town Mason, beautifully crafted from the crushed fragments of a whale's rib cage and inlaid with diagonal stripes of lapis lazuli. It had a lock that would only open—was *supposed* to only open—for me or my mother.

And yet Latham managed to steal my father's remains anyway.

The memory rekindles my anger. Which, I suppose, is better than the frozen awareness of Bram next to me—the pressure of his humerus against my own, the way our patellas brush together, separated only by cloth and skin. Anger focuses my mind. Fashions it into something blade-sharp and ready for action.

"What are we going to try first?" I ask.

Niklas sets the box down and stares at it uncertainly for several long moments. "I think the series of movements is the most likely."

"So give it a go," Talon says.

Niklas swallows. Cracks his knuckles. And then with his finger begins to trace a pattern on the surface of the bone—a quick swipe downward, a half circle back up, and then another. We all watch him, transfixed. It takes me a moment to figure out what he's doing, but when I do, it makes sense. His fingers are tracing letters, moving slowly, deliberately. B-O-N-E G-A-M-E-S. As he reaches the final curve, we all lean forward, our breath held against our ribs with wild hope.

79

But nothing happens.

Niklas's shoulders slump. He deflates a little.

"No worries," Talon says, slapping him on the back. "We'll try something else."

And we do. We pass the box around the circle, each of us examining it from every angle. Testing out our fingerprints, looking for seams that might indicate a mechanism for opening, trying out different number and letter combinations: each of our names one by one, the sum of our ages, IVORY HALL, and even—courtesy of Talon—HELP!

Jacey tips her face toward the ceiling and exhales loudly. "This seems like a silly challenge. How does a guessing game serve any purpose?"

The statement makes me sit up a little straighter. "Wait. Maybe you're onto something."

She lifts her head, lips pursed. "What do you mean?"

"Norah said the purpose of the bone games is for us to learn to work together."

"That's what we've been doing," Tessa says. "For *hours*."

"But we've been taking turns trying to solve it. Maybe we all need to touch it at the same time."

A ripple of optimism pulses through the circle as we each lay a palm against the silky surface of the box. For a moment, everything is still.

And then, beneath our fingers, the bone begins to move.

The box opens like a flower blossoming.

The top separates into individual segments, slender pieces that alternate between moving forward and moving back.

At the same time, the sides divide and fall away. The slices at the top of the box rotate downward and weave between the others. It happens slowly, and we all gape, mesmerized. When the bone finally stops moving, it resembles a basket more than a box. Resting at the bottom is a velvet pouch containing a small set of bones and a single parchment folded in thirds and tied with a slender leather cord.

Tessa is the first to thaw enough to move. She lifts the document and places it on her lap.

"What does it say?" Jacey asks, her voice full of the same reverence I feel.

Tessa doesn't answer right away. Her eyes roam over the page, her expression changing from excitement to dismay.

"What?" I ask. "What is it?"

"Our first task is here."

"Yes," Talon says carefully, his brow wrinkling in confusion. "We knew it would be, right?"

"I mean that we aren't going to another town. We're staying *here* in the capital."

Disappointment seeps into me like cold. I hadn't realized until this moment how much I was looking forward to exploring Kastelia. And judging from their heavy sighs and downturned expressions, the others feel the same.

My thoughts go to Rasmus—the bodyguard Norah said I'd need if I left the premises—and guilt worms through my stomach. I can only think of one reason why we'd have to remain at Ivory Hall while all the other teams get to travel to other parts of Kastelia.

"It's probably my fault," I say softly.

Beside me, I feel Bram tense. "Why would you say that?"

I tell him what Norah said about me leaving the grounds.

"No," he says, "if she hadn't made provisions for you to participate fully, she just would have excused you from the games."

"But if I weren't in your group—"

Tessa's hand shoots out and grabs my forearm, making the rest of the sentence die on my lips. "Look at this." She hands me the parchment. My eyes roam over the page—it's filled with basic information about the task. Each of our names is listed in neat block print at the top, along with the location of the challenge (Ivory Hall) and the time frame we have to complete it (one week). Nothing that makes me feel the slightest bit better. My need for a bodyguard has probably ruined the games for everyone.

But Tessa motions for me to continue, so I keep reading. When I get to the bottom of the document—the actual instructions for our first bone game—my breath catches.

I was wrong. This isn't a task that could be completed during regular training. This task makes me wish for the safety of working in the training room with Master Kyra.

"What's going on?" Niklas asks finally.

"Yeah," Talon says, "tell us about our first bone game."

Game. The word hits my ear and I cringe. The title of this challenge couldn't be less appropriate.

"It's not a game," I say. "There's an actual trial being presented to the Grand Council next week." I swallow the lump in my throat and look up from the page. "And the six of us have been assigned as the jury."

Chapter
Eight

trial.

The words thrum through my mind and make it impossible to sleep. For a moment tonight, I hoped—we all had—that perhaps this was simply a mock trial. A test to see if we will choose the correct sentence for the accused. Kastelia doesn't typically need outside juries. Town councils decide small local matters and the Grand Council decides more serious cases. Juries are only called if needed to break a tie. Maybe we'd hear the evidence, tell the Grand Council our decision, and afterward, they would be the ones to actually render a final verdict. Or maybe this case happened long ago, and the defendant is either living free or has been punished; our task is simply to see how well our judgment tracks with the Grand Council's.

But then we checked with Norah and she confirmed our worst fears: The trial is current, and we are the only jury. A stand-in for the Grand Council, who has agreed not only to assess the competence of our opinion, but to stand by it whether they agree or not.

"People tend to be at their best when there's something at stake," Norah said, not unkindly. "Now why don't you all get some sleep and revisit this tomorrow? I'm sure you'll do fine."

I think of all the times I thought it was unfair that my mother wielded power over my future—over the future of the rest of Midwood. When she performed readings, I used to imagine her as a puppeteer maneuvering the strings of a person's future until they danced in a way that pleased her.

But I was wrong.

I was no marionette. I could reject what she chose for me, refuse to move in the direction she preferred.

But this decision . . . the defendant can't simply discard our verdict. He can't walk away or refuse to dance.

We have to get this right. We hold a man's fate in our hands.

"This initial statement is marked 'preliminary,'" Bram says.

We sit around a table on the fourth tier of the library—the only level that was vacant—the document resting on the table in front of us. I'm bleary with lack of sleep, and a headache pulses behind my eyelids.

Talon traces his finger along the edge of the page. "Which means what? That the facts might change?"

Bram clears his throat. "Not necessarily. But it's definitely incomplete. When the Ivory Guard is tasked with conducting an investigation, they do just enough work to decide if a trial should be held. The real work comes later."

"*We* have to do the real work," Jacey says, her voice bleak, "even though none of us are properly trained for this."

An uncomfortable silence follows, as the words hang in the air between us like a chill. She's right. None of us feel prepared for this. After poring over the document, we all agree that the facts of the case—what few we were given—are muddy at best. A man was accused of using unbound magic, and though there were several witness statements, it seems no one actually saw him do it.

Niklas pulls his ring from his finger and spins it on top of the table. "He was probably a leftover."

Jacey's mouth twists into a knot. "That's a terrible thing to say. Just because someone can't afford a kenning, doesn't make them a criminal."

Niklas snatches the ring and slides it back onto his finger. "I didn't mean it like that. But he must have been someone with magical tendencies who didn't get a kenning. Otherwise, how would he be able to use unbound magic?"

I shift uncomfortably in my seat.

"That makes sense." Talon picks up the parchment and squints at it, as if he's expecting new words to appear to con-gratulate us on guessing correctly.

"I don't think we'll know anything for sure until we investigate more," Bram says.

Tessa reaches into the box and scoops up the pouch of bones and offers them to me. "A bone reading seems like a logical place to start."

I raise my eyebrows in a question. "What makes you think doing a Second Sight reading is the way to go? What could I possibly see that would help us?"

Tessa shrugs. "The bones must have been included for some reason, and none of them need to be healed or broken, so they're useless to both me and Bram. Niklas already helped us open the box, so I doubt they're meant for him." Her gaze flicks to Jacey then Talon. "And we don't seem to have need of a Mixer or Watcher at the moment either. That leaves you. We can question the prisoner, and you can do a reading to see if he's telling the truth."

"You want to go to the prison now?" I say. "All of us?"

Tessa tilts her head to one side. "We're supposed to work together."

My secrets burn inside me, and my tattoo throbs like a pulse. I think of my training session with Kyra the other day. The slick, choking panic of not knowing if I was seeing the past, present, or future. But this isn't a menu. It's a man's life.

The rest of the team watches me expectantly. I have no choice. I can't avoid doing readings in front of them forever. Although— an idea starts to form—maybe I can give myself better tools.

"I don't have any of my supplies," I say. "I'll need to stop by the training wing first."

"Let's go then," Jacey says, already standing and gathering the documents into a pile. The others follow her lead. Talon stretches as he stands, and Niklas nestles the bone box back into the wooden one.

I shake my head. "No need for us all to go. I'll get my things and meet you downstairs."

I walk away before any of them can argue. I'm outside the library when I realize that Bram has followed me, and I startle.

"I thought you might need some help," he says.

A pang of gratitude goes through me, followed immediately by a flutter of unease. Does he suspect that I'm about to bend the rules just a bit, if not outright break them? Not telling Norah what he saw months ago is one thing, but will he keep my secrets if he sees me break the rules again?

I push the thought away. Bram already knows enough to sink me if he wanted to. "That would be nice," I say. "Thank you."

My heart beats faster as we reach the training wing, and I ease open the door for one of the bone charming rooms. But Master Kyra is nowhere to be seen. Relief sags out of me. I move quickly, gathering a burner and a bundle of incense, a piece of flint, a velvet cloth.

Then I turn to Bram, dipping my head toward the back of the room, where a few stone basins sit on a narrow wooden table. "Would you mind grabbing one of those?" I hope he misses the tremble in my voice, the way my eyes slide away from his.

Master Kyra and I haven't worked on using flame in readings—it's an advanced technique that she hasn't introduced yet.

But I already know how to do it. My mother taught me not so long ago.

I think of the desperation in her voice when she offered to train me. *Teaching you would violate my code of ethics.* Yet she had done it anyway. She risked everything to protect me.

Bram doesn't hesitate before hefting the heavy basin into his arms. I chew the inside of my cheek as I watch him. I can only hope that none of my friends are aware that I'm not supposed to be doing flame readings yet. Since I know very little about the details of their training, I doubt they know the intricacies of mine. But when I think about how much trust I'm putting in Bram, a wave of apprehension goes through me. Why would he follow me without being asked?

"Why are you helping me?" The question comes out more harshly than I intended, and a flash of irritation darts across his expression.

"Um . . . you're welcome?"

I sigh. I wish I could find a way to break down the barriers separating us. To bridge the gap between what I know and what he does. At least then I could test my feelings to see if they're real or just a relic from a life I never lived.

"You just don't seem the type to help for no reason."

He flinches—it's a tiny movement, barely perceptible, but his mannerisms are so familiar that I know I've wounded him.

"I'm sorry," I say. "I didn't mean it that way."

"It's fine," he says. "You don't even really know me."

And now it's my turn to flinch.

It was like this on my other path too—a tension between us

until we finally saw each other clearly. I search my memory for what finally made the difference. Maybe I can use what I know about my other path to connect with Bram here?

"Do you remember that time the prison boat docked in Midwood when we were children?" The question seems to catch him off guard and he shifts the basin from one arm to the other.

"Yes," he says, his tone guarded. "What about it?"

I swallow. This is going to be harder than I thought. "I was unfair to you back then. The prisoner frightened me, and"—I stumble over the exact words I said in my other path—"I was scared, and I made assumptions. I'm sorry."

He gives me an odd look. "Don't worry about it. All is forgiven."

A sharp stab of disappointment goes through me. "That's it?"

"What do you want me to say? That I hate you?" He gives a dark laugh. "It was a long time ago, Saskia. People make mistakes."

A stone drops into my stomach. I was stupid to think that the same apology that brought us together in my other reality would work in this one. But at least now I know for sure—my other path doesn't matter. Bram and I are different people here.

I massage my temples. "Forget I said anything."

He pulls on the back of his neck, and lets out a long sigh. "I'm helping you because we're on the same team. And because your mother helped me when I needed it most. I feel terrible about what happened to her."

"It wasn't your fault."

His eyes slide away from me, and his expression shutters. "Anything else you need?" He's not wearing his cloak and the fabric of his sleeve strains over the muscles in his upper arm, which are flexed to support the basin.

Heat prickles my cheeks, and I quickly look away.

"No," I say, my voice catching. "I think I have everything I need."

The prison is adjacent to Ivory Hall, in a nondescript structure that lacks all the majesty of the main building. Both are made of bone, but the prison is fashioned from rough-hewn bricks, unlike the smooth, gleaming surface of Ivory Hall, which must have taken hundreds of Masons and many years to craft.

A female Breaker meets us at the entrance. Her black cloak has thick white stripes on the sleeves that designate her as a member of the Ivory Guard.

She frowns. "It takes six of you to question a prisoner?"

"We're supposed to be working as a team," Talon says.

Her expression sours even further. "You won't have long. Use your time wisely."

We all nod our assent, and she leads us through a small side door into a decidedly mundane room. A cluster of prison guards stands in one corner, engaged in a quiet discussion. Other members of the support staff rush around shelving boxes of bones, poring over thick stacks of parchment, assembling trays of food. Only a few of them glance up long enough to notice as we file past.

"Watch your heads," the Breaker says as she directs us to a narrow stone stairwell.

As we descend, the air chills. Turns dank and musty. It takes my eyes a moment to adjust to the dimmer light, but slowly the space comes into focus. A passageway stretches out in front of us with a row of cells on either side. A pair of Breakers stands at each end, and another paces up and down the corridor.

"Your man is the last one on the left," the Breaker tells us. "Make it quick."

I push ahead of the others and hurry toward the cell at the end of the passage. A man sits in the corner, shackled to the wall. His clothes are filthy, his beard unkempt, as if he's been incarcerated for many weeks. His feet are bare, and his head is bent at an odd angle. My stomach drops to my feet. Is he hurt? But then he lets out a deep, shuttering breath and I realize he's sleeping.

"Excuse me," I call out. "Sir? Can you wake up?"

The prisoner stirs. Flinches. Groans as he rolls his neck in a slow circle.

"Excuse me?"

Finally he looks our direction and surprise flits across his expression. "Who are you?" he asks, and then, without waiting for a reply: "What's going on?"

"We were hoping to ask you a few questions," Tessa says. "We're in charge of deciding your case."

His jaw drops. "They're leaving my fate to a bunch of children?"

"I'm afraid so," Talon says.

The prisoner throws his head back and laughs. It's not an amused sound, or even a surprised one. It's unhinged. Like a man who knows he's going to lose everything he cares about.

"We'd like to help you," I say gently. At the edge of my vision, I see Jacey's warning glance. We're not supposed to help him; we're supposed to judge him. But I don't correct myself. "Would you like to tell us about what happened that landed you here?"

"No," he says, his voice gruff and weary, "I don't believe I would."

The six of us exchange worried glances. What are we supposed to do if he refuses to cooperate?

"I need to get a little of your blood for a bone reading," I tell him.

He fixes me with a hard stare. He lifts his shackled ankle a few inches off the floor and gives his foot a little shake. "I'd love to oblige, but I'm a little tied up at the moment."

"I'll come to you." I turn and nod at Tessa, who hurries to the end of the corridor and returns with a guard.

The Breaker unlocks the door and lets me into the cell. I crouch next to the prisoner, and pull out a needle and a small vial.

"May I?" I ask, nodding toward his hand.

"Do I have a choice?" The question is sarcastic, and I can tell he doesn't actually expect me to answer, but I stop what I'm doing and sit back on my heels.

"Of course you have a choice," I say. "But it will make it hard to decide your case if I can't see what happened."

A flicker of hope lights up his expression. "So you're a First Sight Charmer?"

My gaze slides away from his. My hands tremble. "No," I say quickly, "Second Sight. But if you're thinking about the day in question while I do the reading, I might be able to see it."

His eyes narrow. I can tell he doesn't believe me, but he doesn't challenge my statement. He simply offers me his hand. I prick his index finger and gather several drops of blood into the vial.

When I'm finished, I stand. "Thank you."

"Good luck." Something in his tone sends a shiver down my spine, and I get the sense he's talking about more than just the reading.

I exit the cell and the guard locks the door behind me.

"Is there somewhere here that we could work for a bit?" Tessa asks the guard. "We might have follow-up questions for the prisoner after Saskia finishes the reading."

He sighs as if this taxes his patience. "There's an empty cell over here. Follow me."

Talon's jaw drops as he turns to me. "He expects you to do this *behind bars*?" His voice is low, but apparently not low enough.

The guard spins around. "You got a better idea, kid?"

Talon clamps his lips tightly together and shakes his head. "Nope. It sounds great. Perfect."

The Breaker lets out a low grunt. "That's what I thought." And then he opens the cell and ushers us inside.

Chapter
Nine

'*ve never performed a bone reading with this big of an audience before. I'm not sure I can. The small space is hazy with incense, overheated with too many bodies. I can't draw a proper breath.

I sit on the hard floor in front of the stone basin. The rest of the team has moved to give me space. Talon and Niklas sit together against one wall, the others settled on the opposite side. But the cell is still too cramped.

My magic feels private. More like bathing or dressing than performing, so it's a vulnerable thing to be watched, studied.

I place the bone in the bottom of the basin and sprinkle it with a few drops of blood from the vial.

"What am I looking for?" I ask, letting my gaze fall on each of my teammates. I've been trying to formulate a point of focus that won't make it obvious I'm using anything other than Second Sight, but I'm not sure how to direct my thoughts. "What are we supposed to find?"

"Evidence, I suppose," says Talon with a small shrug that suggests he knows it's not the most helpful answer.

I bite my lip. I guess the only way forward is through.

I pick up the flint in one hand, the small smooth stone in the other, and spark them together. Then I set the bone on fire. I wait a few moments until the bone is sufficiently blackened, until the putrid smell snakes through the incense and assaults my nostrils before extinguishing the flame with a heavy iron lid. Then I tip the bone onto the ground.

The pull of the magic is immediate and intense. It sings to me—beckoning me to dance—and the blood in my veins leaps in response, tugging me into a vision.

The prisoner sits just as we found him—on the dirt floor of his cell, one ankle shackled to the stone wall. His knees are bent toward his chest, his head thrown back. Jensen. The man's name slides into my mind as easily as dark slipping into daybreak. One moment it isn't there, and the next it is—bright, clear, and unmistakable.

Emotions roll through Jensen like a storm—thunderclaps of anger, drizzles of self-pity, but hanging over it all is a thick fog of worry. In his mind, I see his family. His partner, Fredrik, a man both bigger and gentler than Jensen. And their young son, Boe, with his curious brown eyes and golden-bronze hair.

What will become of them if he's convicted of a crime? Boe's mother died when he was a baby. If Jensen never goes home, will Boe's grandparents allow Fredrik to raise him? He can't bear the thought of Fredrik losing both his partner and his child in a single cruel moment. Or of Boe losing the only two parents he's ever known.

Outside the vision, I tense. This hardly seems like evidence. I need to know what Jensen actually *did* to end up here. As if responding to my thought, the scene shifts: the gentle rhythm of horse hooves on a pebble-strewn trail, Boe's laughter floating on the breeze like a melody.

Jensen sits astride a brown mare. Boe rides in front of him, his expression full of delight as he points out trees, rocks, and plants.

"Did you see that bird back there, Papa? It had a purple chest and a blue head."

"You have sharp eyes," Jensen says. "I missed that one."

"It would be funny if you had a purple chest and a blue head."

Jensen chuckles. "Indeed it would. Do you think Da would still love me if I were purple and blue?"

"Probably?"

Time stretches and Jensen gets lost in his thoughts. He's on the way to see a patient in a neighboring village—a woman who developed an infection after she cut herself while cooking. Jensen treated the infection when he first saw her, but now it's time to follow up and make sure she healed properly. Normally, he would leave Boe at home with Fredrik, but it's harvest season, and Fredrik will be busy in the fields until sunset. Easier for Jensen to take Boe along on an adventure for the day. And who knows? Maybe Boe will be matched as a Healer at his kenning and the experience will prove useful.

Boe yawns. "How much farther, Papa?"

"Not too much longer now," Jensen says. "We should be there before dark."

Boe looks up at the bright blue sky. "That seems like *a lot* farther."

Jensen chuckles. "We'll stop in a bit so we can stretch and eat a little something. How does that sound?"

Boe makes a noise of agreement and scrubs at his eyes. Soon he's slumped against Jensen, fast asleep.

Jensen doesn't see the rabbit—a streak of white, racing across the open field next to the trail, a fox in pursuit. The rabbit races across the path in front of the horse, and the horse spooks. Jensen tries to calm her, pats her neck, speaks softly.

And it might have worked if Boe hadn't startled from sleep, if he hadn't cried out.

But the sudden sound makes the horse rear back. Boe slides to one side, and Jensen scrambles to steady him. He had to loosen his grip on the boy—just a bit—to soothe the horse, but it was too much.

It all happens in a flash. Boe slipping sideways, falling, shouting. And then the horse coming down hard on Boe's leg. Jensen hears the crack of his son's femur, and his blood runs cold.

He scrabbles from the horse, cradles his son in his arms. "You're all right," he says. "I've got you."

Boe is screaming, a desperate, piercing wail. Blood soaks his pants. Jensen lays him gently on the ground, rips the fabric away, and assesses the wound. An open fracture. A fragment of Boe's femur has punctured the skin. It's the most dangerous kind of break.

"Help me, Papa," Boe cries. "Please."

"Shhh," Jensen says, "I will, son. I will."

Jensen presses his fingers to the wound, lets magic flow through him until he can see clearly inside Boe's leg—to the tendons, ligaments, and muscles beneath the skin. And then he curses under his breath. The sharp bone has sliced through a blood vessel. The bleeding is uncontrolled. He'll never make it to a Mending Healer in time.

The bone needs to be set here—on this rocky path at dusk; there isn't time for anything else.

But Jensen is bound to Disease. Not Mending. And yet . . . as a boy, when his magic first started to blossom, he thought he might be matched to Mending. He could heal broken bones, could stitch torn skin, could control pain. Maybe . . .

"Papa!" Boe's small hands are curled into fists. His back arched in agony.

Jensen doesn't even think. He grabs a set of bones from his satchel and uses them to send relief into his son's small body. Boe's expression relaxes. His hands unclench, fingers falling open.

"That's better, Papa."

Jensen empties his Healing satchel, spreading his supplies on a cloth next to him. He reaches for another set of bones and begins to heal the break. His fingers stay in contact with the boy's flesh as he closes his eyes. I can see inside his mind—how he directs his magic to put pressure on the damaged vessel, clamping down hard until the bleeding is controlled, before directing it to suture itself back together. Then he tackles the bone—repositioning the fragments into their original location—and then beginning the process of fusing them back together. He's working so intently that he fails to hear the hoofbeats behind him.

"Do you need help?"

Jensen startles at the voice. He turns his head to find a couple—a man and a woman, each on horseback. Both wear identical expressions of concern.

"My boy is ill," Jensen says. "I'm a Healer, but we could use some help getting to the nearest town." His gaze sweeps across the landscape. "Our horse seems to have bolted."

Jensen turns back toward Boe and continues working on the boy's leg. He misses the suspicious look that passes between the couple. The way they study Jensen and Boe with furrowed brows. His supplies—vials of bone dust to calm fevers, creams to sooth chronic skin problems, tools to examine eyes and peer down throats—are clearly those of a Disease Healer, but Jensen appears to be mending. The boy's leg is soaked in blood, and it was the sound of screaming that made the couple sit forward in their saddles and urge their horses into a run. This was clearly an accident—a bad one from the looks of it—that resulted in a broken bone. But now the boy is alert and calm. Breathing easily. In no pain.

Either this man is a Disease Healer practicing mending or a

Mending Healer in possession of items that he shouldn't have access to.

"We'll ride ahead to the next town," the man says. "Secure a wagon and a place for your boy to rest."

Jensen wipes his forehead with his sleeve. He doesn't turn around. "Thank you."

Outside the vision, my heart begins to pound. I want to warn Jensen. To tell him to find his missing horse, take Boe, and ride toward home. But I'm powerless to do anything except watch. What will Jensen find when he shows up in the neighboring town? The magic responds to my question. Yanks me forward in time to the exact moment occupying my thoughts.

And I have my answer.

Jensen lifts Boe from the back of the wagon. The color has returned to his small, soft cheeks and he even manages a faint smile. Jensen cradles Boe in his arms as the couple leads the way toward a small cottage.

"You'll be safe here," the woman says.

But she's lying.

Because when Jensen steps over the threshold, he's greeted by a delegation from the Ivory Guard.

I wrench myself from the vision, breathless.

"He's not guilty," I say, though it's not precisely what I mean. According to the laws of Kastelia, he probably *is* guilty. But he shouldn't be. It's not right.

For a moment the only sound is the rushing in my ears. Then everyone starts talking at once.

"What did you see?"

"How do you know?"

"Did you find out exactly what he did, so we can try to interview him again?"

The questions trip over one another, coming so fast that I can't pair them with their speakers. And then cold dread seeps into me.

I can't tell them the truth. If I explain what I saw, they'll know I did a reading of the past, and I'm guilty of the very crime that Jensen is accused of committing.

"How do you know he's innocent?" Bram's voice cuts through the noise. I look up and our eyes meet. He studies me for a long, silent moment, as if he can see my thoughts. "You're splotchy." The observation only makes me flush more. I have that uneasy sense of familiarity again, as if we're acting out a play that was written long ago. Has he said that to me before? I press my palms to my cheeks to cool them.

"I get a bit spotty sometimes when I'm ill," Talon says. "It's the fair skin, I think."

Bram opens his mouth to say something more, but then seems to think better of it. *Saskia gets splotchy when she's nervous.* The words float into my mind like a memory. Suddenly I'm certain that's what he was about to say.

I scramble for a way to explain what I saw without incriminating myself. The rest of the team stares at me expectantly.

I press my lips together while I gather my thoughts. "His

name is Jensen. He wasn't someone without magical tendencies, like we thought. He's a Healer, and he was accused of
using a different healing magic than he was bound to."

"Is that even possible?" Niklas asks, leaning forward. "I
thought the binding ceremony stifled all other magic."

"I thought so too," Tessa echoes.

A bead of sweat slips from the nape of my neck and inches slowly down my spine. The air in the cell is damp and so
thick that it's suffocating. "No, it's abiding by the promises in
the binding ceremony—ceasing to practice magic in all but one
small area—that causes any other abilities to slowly ebb away."

Jacey dabs her forehead with her sleeve. "Tell us what else
you saw."

So I do. But I'm careful not to reveal that I saw the past.
Instead I tell them the story came from Jensen's memory as he
sat in the cell. I give them as much detail as I can from beginning to end, hoping they'll feel as I do—that Jensen had no
choice. That any father would do the same. They listen carefully to the end.

"But I thought you said he didn't do it," Niklas says. "Now
you're saying he did?"

"I said he wasn't guilty. What else was he supposed to do?
Let his son suffer? Considering the circumstances, how could
we possibly convict him?"

"Maybe we should go talk to him again," Jacey suggests.

"Yes," I say, unable to keep the tremble from my voice. "We
should." I stand up and hurry out of the cell without waiting
for the others.

"Jensen," I say when we reach him, ashamed that I didn't ask his name before. "Tell me what happened with Boe."

He looks up sharply. And then his eyes go soft, like his child's very name is a ray of sunlight that can soften his edges and melt away his severity. Now his expression looks more like the father I saw in the vision than the callous man we encountered when we first arrived.

"He got hurt," Jensen says, his voice barely above a whisper. "And I healed him."

"With what magic?" Tessa asks, not unkindly.

Jensen's gaze finds hers and holds it. "With the magic he *needed.*"

"But, what I mean is, did you—"

He holds up a hand to stop her. "Is there anything I could say that would make a difference?"

Tessa frowns. "You could say you didn't do it."

He sighs. "The law is the law. And I'd do it again to spare my boy. Just tell me this: When is the trial?"

This time it's Bram who answers. "It's in three days."

We leave the prison in an even more somber mood than when we arrived.

"We can't convict him," I say as we walk back to Ivory Hall. "He did what any parent would have done in the same situation."

But the others are quiet, and it makes the discomfort inside me squirm like a restless serpent. "Doesn't anyone agree with me?"

"How old do you think he is?" Tessa asks softly.

I turn to face her. "Jensen or Boe?"

"Jensen."

I shrug. "Thirty-five? Maybe forty?" I turn to the others. "What do you guys think?"

"I agree," Niklas says. "I'd guess late thirties."

"So his binding ceremony was at least eighteen years ago."

"Yes," I say, not sure what his age has to do with anything.

She sighs. "So if he still has access to Mending Magic, that means he must have been using it regularly. This whole time."

All the breath leaves my lungs as the implications slam into me. Jensen won't be judged by his humanity in this one moment. He'll be tried based on the fact that the moment was possible at all.

"We don't know that," I say, my voice small. "Not for sure."

Tessa leans over and rests her hand lightly on my elbow. "Maybe there's something we're missing. Let's use the next few days to study the law. There must be some exceptions in extreme cases."

"I agree," Jacey says. "We shouldn't jump to conclusions before we have all the information."

But certainty spills over me like a pot of spilled ink, blotting out my optimism. In the eyes of the Grand Council, Jensen and I are the same.

And eventually, we'll both face the same fate.

Chapter
Ten

he next morning we sit in the library, poring over every book we can find on the laws governing unbound magic in preparation for the upcoming trial. But no matter how many times I read the text of the law, I can't find a loophole that will save Jensen.

I dig my fingers through my hair. I wish I'd paid attention to all the conversations between my mother and Gran about council business. Often, over the evening meal, my mother would ask Gran's advice on some case she was deciding. Gran would always offer a nugget of wisdom—usually in the form of a story from her own days on the town council.

As a child, I found these discussions unbearably dull, but

oh, how I could use their combined wisdom now. A stab of longing goes through me. I miss them both so much. And my father, too. I'm an orphan with nowhere to turn for advice.

I wish I could rely on my team for support, but I feel separate from everyone else—like I'm observing them from a distance. As we've worked together over the last few days, I've started to learn each of their rhythms. How both Tessa and Niklas are worriers, but they have completely opposite ways of coping: Tessa chatters when she's nervous, but Niklas gets even more quiet than normal. I've noticed Bram's silent leadership, Jacey's take-no-prisoners approach to life, and the way Talon jokes around to ease the tension.

But I have no idea how they see me.

Maybe it's because I don't fit in with everyone else. Or maybe I just can't see myself clearly. Maybe none of us can.

Gran used to make a dessert she called caramel-core cake. The first time I ate it, I thought it was a misnomer. The cake was white and fluffy, and there was no caramel in sight. *Keep going*, Gran said when I told her I thought she'd given me the wrong dessert. *One taste doesn't make a meal.* And then my fork hit a pocket of caramel, and sweet gooey sauce spilled over my plate, soaking the cake and transforming it from ordinary to divine. It made me wonder if people are like that too—if we have to dig a little to find whatever is at their core.

But my core is full of secrets, and I can't let anyone get close enough to see who I really am.

My thoughts are interrupted by the librarian, who makes a small sound at the back of her throat. Once she has our attention, she gives us a thin smile. "I need to step out for a bit, and my assistant stayed home ill today, so it's just me. Is there anything you need before I go?"

My pulse spikes, but I force my expression into a calm mask and avoid meeting her gaze.

Luckily, Tessa is quick with both an answer and appropriate eye contact. "I think we're fine for now, thank you."

"Excellent," the librarian says. "I'll return shortly."

Her boots click on the bone floors as she walks away, and I feel the sound in my chest, like a beating heart. I wait for her footsteps to recede down the corridor and out of earshot before I stand.

"Is something wrong?" Bram asks.

"No. I'll be right back."

I rush up the steps as fast as my legs will carry me. I've been waiting for a chance like this for weeks. The librarian's words echo in my head: *Old student records are on the sixth floor.* My legs burn as I climb. This was probably a terrible idea. Who knows how much time I have? She could return at any moment.

When I reach the top of the staircase, my stomach sinks like a stone. This level is massive, with shelves fanning out in every direction. I'll never find Avalina's records in time. But I have to try. I hurry along the shelves, skimming labels and book titles for anything that might give me a hint where to start. I pass stacks of kenning results going back decades, financial records, books of maps, histories of prominent Kastelian families.

And then I see something that stops me in my tracks. A section of shelves marked APPRENTICES. It's filled with dozens of leather-bound volumes. I pick up one at random and thumb through the pages. The book is filled with information about former apprentices—their names, bone magic specialties, towns of record. And there are multiple entries for each student, written in different penmanship, with updates added year after year as circumstances changed.

I glance over handwritten notes that document major life events—moves to a new town, joining ceremonies, the birth of children, illnesses, but I don't recognize a single name. And most of the records include a death date. Too long ago then. I pick up volume after volume until finally I find something that makes my lungs constrict. My mother's name and vital details written in neat, delicate script: *Della Holte, Third Sight Bone Charmer, Midwood.* Other facts are here as well. Her appointment to the town council, her bone match to my father (and the date of their joining ceremony), my birth.

At the bottom, in block print, is the word "deceased." The ink is a smidge darker than all the other entries, as if this could have been written yesterday, and I can't help but imagine the librarian pulling this book from the shelf and unceremoniously scribbling the date my mother died, her mind occupied with other things. My eyes sting.

I force myself to breathe, to blink. And then I reach for a different emotion instead. I let fury blaze through me and evaporate my unshed tears.

Now that I've found the correct book, I don't need to worry about Avalina. I'll find Latham's record instead. Discover where he lives, who he knows. How to hurt him.

Frantically, I turn the pages, but find nothing. I flip back to the beginning and start again, going more slowly this time, careful to read every name before moving to the next. Halfway through, my eye catches an irregularity. A jagged edge of paper juts up from deep in the seam. I stop and move the book closer to my face. Tiny scraps poke out from the middle of the book. Someone has torn out a series of pages. Certainty falls over me like a cloak. Latham's entries. They must be.

I search the rest of the book for Avalina's name, but she's not here either.

I have the sudden urge to slam a fist into the entire row of books and send them soaring. I pace up and down the aisle, taking deep breaths and trying to rein in the rage that bubbles up my throat like poison. How is it that Latham manages to rip the heart from everything that matters?

I drag the toe of my boot along the smooth bone floors, wishing I were outdoors, where there are rocks to kick.

On the bottom shelf, another label jumps out at me. INCOMPLETE. Above the word is only a single, slender volume. I pick it up and leaf through the pages. It's identical to the apprentice records, except these entries are shorter.

And they include a date of expulsion.

These must be from students who didn't finish their training. My breath quickens as I think of my mother explaining that Avalina left Ivory Hall abruptly. I search through the book, hardly daring to hope. And then, like a sudden burst of sunlight through clouds, her name appears. Avalina Berg. A rush of energy vibrates through me.

Footsteps thunder up the staircase and I go rigid. Panic

closes a fist around my vertebrae. I glance around for somewhere to stash the book, but I left my satchel and my cloak on the first level. I don't have any choice, except to slide the book back on the shelf where I found it and allow it keep its secrets. But I won't get another chance like this again.

The footsteps grow louder. Closer.

I can't let Latham win. Carefully, I rip the page from the book, fold it, and shove it into my pocket. Then I race down the aisle, onto the wide landing, start down the staircase.

And run headlong into the librarian.

"What are you doing up here?" Her face is red, and a vein bulges near her temple.

"Looking for a book," I say, trying to infuse my voice with a weightless quality.

Her eyes narrow. "What book?"

I twist a lock of hair around my finger and widen my eyes slightly—an expression cultivated during my childhood whenever I needed to convince my father of my innocence. *What are you doing, bluebird?* he would ask after catching me tiptoeing from the kitchen in the middle of the night with chocolate-smeared lips. *Didn't I tell you only one dessert?*

I forgot, Papa.

"I wanted to find a better explanation of Kastelia's laws regarding unbound magic." I purse my lips. Lift one shoulder. "But I'm not having any luck."

Her expression relaxes just a fraction. "That's because you're looking in the wrong place. You should have asked me for help. Apprentices aren't allowed on this level."

"I'm sorry," I say. "I would have, but you stepped out."

She sighs—a sound that is equal parts frustration and disbelief. She studies me for a moment, and I resist the urge to touch my pocket to reassure myself the paper is still there. After a beat, she presses her lips together and motions for me to follow her down the stairs.

We arrive back on the main level to find my team arguing about how to approach the trial. "We need some kind of strategy," Bram says. "Otherwise, we're going to look like bumbling fools in front of the Grand Council."

"Our strategy should be figuring out what's fair," Jacey says. She's pacing back and forth in front of the table, her dark curls bouncing with each step. "If he did it, he's guilty. It's as simple as that."

"I don't agree," Bram says. His gaze finds mine as I approach the group. He's the only one who knows I'm guilty of using unbound magic too. Although he isn't aware that I can use all three Sights, he does know that my mother trained me, that I used charming magic before my binding ceremony. A wave of gratitude goes through me. "I think there's a lot of gray area."

"What kind of gray area?" Talon asks. He taps his fingers on the tabletop. I notice his knuckles are sprinkled with freckles as I slide into one of the chairs beside him. The parchment in my pocket feels as if it's on fire.

Bram rakes a hand through his hair. "Maybe Jensen wasn't aware the magic was illegal? Or maybe he thought he was justified in using it?"

Jacey blows a puff of air through pursed lips. "That's what were supposed to decide. Was he justified or not?"

Tessa gets quiet. "Even if he was, it still doesn't explain how he was able to use the magic so many years later."

"Maybe he's an anomaly," I say. "Maybe his ability never faded, and he was able to access Mending Magic in an emergency."

"Even if that's true," Jacey says, "he still used unbound magic."

"But it goes to intent," Bram counters.

We go back and forth until nightfall. Finally Niklas groans. "We're getting nowhere. I think we're just going to have to wait until we've questioned the witnesses at trial to form an opinion." He's hardly said a word all evening, which somehow makes his opinion more forceful.

"You're right," Tessa says. "I'm willing to listen to what the witnesses say before I make up my mind."

And so, we all agree. We'll wait until the trial to decide.

Tessa is particularly chatty that night as we prepare for bed. She gives a long commentary on everything from the bone games to her Healing training—Master Dina has been particularly demanding lately—to wondering if Niklas is so quiet because he's homesick or if he simply has a more reserved personality.

"Or maybe he's just slow to warm up," she says, pulling the tie from her hair and using her fingers to untangle her curls.

"Do you think he might talk more once he knows us better?"

"Probably?"

"You seem faraway tonight. Is something on your mind?"

The question catches me off guard. My mind keeps jumping back and forth between worrying about Jensen and obsessing over the folded parchment in my pocket. All I can think about is Tessa falling asleep so I can read it.

"I'm sorry," I say. "I'm being a terrible listener and a worse friend."

Tessa flops down on her bed. "You didn't answer the question."

"You noticed that, did you?" I keep my voice light, teasing, but inside, my nerves clatter together like a pair of cymbals. Should I tell her? Can I trust her with the truth?

Her face goes serious. "Is it about Bram?"

"No!" Heat rushes to my cheeks. "Why would you say that?"

"It just seems like there's something unfinished between the two of you."

"I stole something from the library," I say, as much to change the subject as anything. But when Tessa's eyes go wide with alarm, it makes me wish I could snatch the words back. "I'm planning on putting it back," I amend, though I really can't return a ripped page.

Tessa's expression softens, and she reaches for my fingers. "Tell me what happened."

My mouth goes dry as I sit beside her and retrieve the page from my pocket. Some irrational part of me is worried that it will disintegrate the moment I try to open it. Or burst into flame. A nagging fear that Latham will have found a way to keep me in the dark again. But the parchment stays solid as I unfold it across my lap.

"Oh," Tessa says when she sees Avalina's name. "*This* is why you risked the wrath of the librarian by going to the sixth floor. Not for a law book."

I nod absently as I study the entries. "She was a Mixer," I say aloud. "From Leiden."

"The City of Glass? My childhood tutor moved to Leiden a few years ago," Tessa says. "I could write a letter to him and ask if he knows anything about her."

I lay a palm on her forearm. "Yes, that would be helpful."

"How strange," Tessa says. "It doesn't say why she was expelled."

But my gaze has drifted to the bottom of the page, and a spasm of relief goes through me. The most important information in the entry is what *isn't* here. A death date.

Avalina is alive.

Chapter
Eleven

The Grand Council Chamber takes up the entire top floor of Ivory Hall.

It's a section of the building usually off-limits to apprentices, so Norah meets us at the guest entrance on the main level and guides us up the curving staircase. The only sound is the click of our boots against the bone floors as we climb. We pass the tension around the group like a musical ensemble sharing a melody—Bram tugs at the back of his neck, leaving a bright red handprint against his skin; Niklas incessantly spins the silver ring around his finger; Tessa chews her lip; Jacey's hands curl into fists; and Talon's pale fingers tap against his leg as if his thoughts are searching for a rhythm. My secrets have burned a hole in my center, and I feel hollowed out and empty.

When we reach the top floor, Norah turns and gives us a gentle smile. "Try to relax. You'll do fine."

But I'm not convinced any of this will turn out fine. I lay awake deep into the night, haunted by the resigned despair of Jensen's expression when we left him, as if he'd already glimpsed the future and knew nothing good awaited him there.

But when Norah pulls open the doors to the council chamber, every thought flies out of my head. I've never seen anything more beautiful. Sunlight spills through the banks of floor-to-ceiling stained-glass windows on both our left and our right. Beneath our feet, a giant map of the Shard is inlaid into the bone floor with brilliant blue sapphire, the branches of the river spilling out richly in all directions. Straight ahead is a tall dais with ten thrones intricately carved from bone. Each features a mosaic design fashioned from gems—a different color for each of the bone magics. The Charmer's throne features a blooming rose of rubies, the Watcher's has an emerald eagle, the Mason's a set of tools in vivid spessartite. Beside me, Bram gives a low whistle, and I follow his gaze to the Breaker's throne, which has two crossed swords made from silver-lined obsidian. And next to it, the Healer's seat features two open hands fashioned from sapphire, while the Mixer's chair has a mortar and pestle made from amethyst. The four chairs for the non-magical members of the council are resplendent as well, each of them inlaid with intricate designs in mahogany.

"Well, that's not intimidating at all," Talon says. "My gramps decorated his dining room in this same style."

We all laugh, and I feel the knot in my chest loosen just a little.

"I'll tell them you're ready," Norah says. She makes her way to the front of the room and raps her knuckles on the plain wooden door behind the dais.

A moment later the door swings open, and the members of the Grand Council file into the chamber dressed in silken robes that match their thrones. Embroidered on each of their sleeves is a golden knot designating them a member of the council. I'm expecting them to take their respective seats, but instead they descend the small staircase and sit on the bench in the front row.

I turn toward Norah, looking for some clue of what we do next.

"Take your seats, apprentices," she says softly.

"Here?" Jacey asks, indicating the bench directly behind the council.

"No," Norah says with a shake of her head. "Up there." She nods toward the dais, and my stomach plunges. We have to sit on their *thrones* while they evaluate if we can do their jobs as well as they can?

My mouth couldn't be any drier than if I'd swallowed a handful of dirt.

"It feels like *we're* the ones on trial," Talon whispers behind me.

"We are," I say softly.

As soon as I sit down, a jolt goes through me. Startled, I clutch the arms of the chair, and the room tilts sharply to one side. I squeeze my eyes closed. A series of images flashes behind my lids—a woman sitting on a stone ledge studying a pile of bones as the wind whips her black hair around her face; a man dropping a handful of carpal bones into a silver goblet filled with blood; a pair of twins—a boy and girl no older than six or seven—arguing about whether the mandible on the table between them belongs to a black bear or a grizzly.

My eyes snap open and nausea threatens at the back of my throat. Low in my stomach is the familiar pulling sensation that suggests I'm about to be swept away into a full-fledged vision.

I think of touching the walls in my room when I first arrived at Ivory Hall, of my nightmare coming to life even though I was wide-awake. This throne must be made from the bones of dead Charmers. Their combined history calls to me—I long to grip the arms of the chair and fall headfirst into their stories. It takes effort to keep my eyes open.

Sweat prickles on my brow. I can't lose control in front of the Grand Council. I focus all my attention on staying in the present, fixing my gaze on a spot in the back of the room where bright rectangles of light fall on the floor. I yank my hands from the arms of the chair and rest them in my lap. Slowly, the sensation subsides, and I feel more anchored to the present. I pull in a deep breath and dry my hands on my cloak. When I look up, the entire Grand Council is watching me. The Bone Charmer—a bald man with a heavily lined brown face—studies me particularly intently.

"Are you unwell?" he asks.

I press my lips together and shake my head. "I'm fine."

His gaze doesn't move from me. Seconds tick by.

My hands go cold. I interlace my fingers and press my palms together, but I don't look away. I have the distinct feeling that I'm being tested, and to break eye contact would be to fail. From the corner of my eye, I see the other members of our team shifting uncomfortably in their seats.

Finally the Charmer gives a small nod of concession. He turns to the other members of the council.

"Shall we begin?"

The Mixer—a woman who looks far too young for such a prestigious role on the council—stands and produces a large wooden box. She places it in front of Jacey on the narrow table that runs from one end of the dais to the other.

"Begin whenever you're ready."

Jacey looks like she might be sick. She hesitates a moment, probably hoping for more instruction. But it doesn't appear that any additional information is forthcoming. Her fingers tremble as she lifts the lid and takes out a set of bones, a mortar and pestle, a half dozen tubes of different liquids in a variety of colors, and a clear flask.

"Are these the ingredients for truth serum?" Jacey asks.

"We're only here to observe," the Mixer replies. "No questions, please."

Jacey swallows and pulls her shoulders back. She places the bones into the mortar, and then, with practiced hands, begins to crush them with the pestle. The tools look like they're made of marble, but they must be infused with bone fragments to be able to pulverize the contents so efficiently. Soon the small bowl is filled with white powder.

Jacey unstops a vial of pale green liquid and dribbles a stream into the mortar. Then she uses the pestle to stir the mixture into a thick paste. She continues adding ingredients—a drop of yellow liquid, ten drops of orange—until finally she seems satisfied. She deposits the paste into the flask and fills it with crystal-blue water, stirring it vigorously until the paste dissolves. When she looks up, her eyes widen, as if she's forgotten she was being watched.

"It's ready." Jacey's voice is even, but her knees shake beneath the table.

"Call in the witnesses," the Mixer says.

Even though there's no one at the back of the room, the double doors swing open and a dozen people are led forward by black-cloaked members of the Ivory Guard. First among them is Jensen, who looks more like himself than the man we met in prison a few days ago—he's been bathed and shaved, though he's a little thinner than he was in my vision. An image of him cradling Boe in his arms flashes through my mind, and I bite the inside of my cheek almost hard enough to draw blood.

Most of the witnesses file into the bench behind the Grand Council, but Jensen sits on the opposite side of the room, in the front row. The wide aisle between the two groups seems like an impassable gulf.

"How would you like to proceed?" the Bone Charmer asks.

Our team exchanges glances.

"One moment, please," Tessa says, motioning the rest of us

toward her. The six of us huddle together around her chair to discuss. "Let's save Jensen for last," I whisper. "He deserves to hear what the others have to say so he can defend himself."

Bram nods. "I agree."

"Who should go first?" Tessa asks.

Niklas sighs. "I'm not sure it matters."

And he's right. I've turned the case over in my mind again and again, pored over the wording of the Kastelian law, and there isn't a solution that ends well.

Unless Jensen claims he didn't do it. But based on our conversation with him, he seems disinclined to lie. And the truth serum will make it impossible anyway.

Once we've finished talking, we settle back into our seats, and Tessa addresses the council. "We'll interview the witnesses one at a time, and end with the accused."

The morning tips into afternoon, and stuffy heat infuses the chamber. We've been at this for hours and haven't learned anything new. Each witness points to the same basic facts: Jensen alleviated his child's pain with magic he wasn't authorized to use. The couple who approached Jensen and Boe on the trail testified that they heard the desperate screams of a child, but by the time they reached Boe, he was sitting calmly—seemingly pain-free—while his father healed his leg. I tried to push back in my questioning: *Could it have been a different child screaming? Could Boe have been in shock? How can they really know*

for sure what Jensen did when they didn't see it for themselves?

But it hardly makes a dent in the avalanche of testimony that follows.

Members of the Ivory Guard testify that the moment they began questioning Jensen, Boe proudly announced that his papa had fixed his leg and made the pain go away.

A Mending Magic Healer testified that he examined Boe shortly after the accident and found evidence of a newly healed femur fracture. In his opinion, there is no question that the boy broke his leg and received a healing spell.

Finally it's time to question Jensen himself. I feel as if my nerves have been wrung out like a wet cloth.

Tessa invites Jensen forward and he climbs into the witness seat slowly, like a man twice his age. Jacey pours a bit of the truth serum into a small drinking horn and offers it to him.

Jensen grimaces as he brings the *keras* to his lips, and I'm forcefully reminded of my encounter with the foul-tasting liquid after my father's bones were stolen. I remember the horrible, lurching feeling of not having control over my answers. Of the words practically leaping from my mouth the moment a question was asked. The memory makes bile rise in my throat.

Jensen downs the truth serum in one swallow.

Bram has the first question, and he leans forward slightly in his seat. "Can you tell us your name?"

"Jensen Niles." The answer comes almost instantaneously.

"Do you have bone magic?" Talon asks.

"Yes, I'm a Healer."

"Which kind?" Talon presses.

"Disease."

When it's my turn, I shift in my chair so I can meet Jensen's gaze. "Can you tell me what happened the day Boe broke his leg?"

Jensen relates the story more or less the way I saw it in the vision. He took Boe with him on a house call. The horse got spooked. Boe fell and broke his leg. As Jensen talks about his son, the lines around his mouth soften. His eyes shimmer.

"What was it like to watch him in pain?" I ask.

From the corner of my eye, I see a few of the council members react to this question with raised eyebrows or frowns. But I don't care. They need to hear it.

"It was torture," he says.

"What would have happened if you hadn't healed Boe's fracture?"

"He would have died." Jensen's gaze is steady.

I nod at Jacey to indicate I'm finished. I wish I could handle the entire interrogation myself, but we agreed to limit ourselves to just a few questions at a time before ceding to the next team member.

"Did you use forbidden magic to heal your son?" Jacey asks.

I press my lips together and stare at my lap. It's a good question for getting to the truth, but a terrible one for helping Jensen.

"I didn't have a choice," Jensen says, his voice even. "Any parent would have done the same."

"Did you perform a healing spell by accident?" she asks.

"No."

"So you did have a choice." Her tone indicates it's a statement, not a question, and Jensen must interpret it the same way, because he doesn't reply. "Go ahead, Niklas."

Niklas leans forward in his chair. "Do you have a mastery tattoo?"

"Of course," Jensen says.

"May we see it?"

One of the Grand Council members—a woman without bone magic—clears her throat. "That's an unusual request. Why are you asking?"

"While preparing for this case, I did some research on the time before the binding ceremony was introduced. And it led me to believe that mastery tattoos are different when more than one specialty is conquered."

She gives him an appraising look. "Different how?"

"Their design indicates the number of different magic elements that have been mastered. For example, a double-edged sword for someone who learned two different types of magic, a block-shaped design for someone who controlled four."

The Grand Council members whisper to one another, clearly impressed. They hadn't expected any of us to know such a fact, let alone think to ask about it.

But my mother knew.

A drumbeat of panic builds in my chest. Blood rushes in my ears.

I hear my mother's voice in my head. *Your mastery tattoo has three corners.* I didn't fully understand what she meant at the time.

Suddenly I feel as if *I* am in the witness seat. As if the Grand Council will demand I pull up my sleeve to reveal what lies beneath. And all the evidence they need to convict me will be rendered in graceful, curving lines in hues of violet and cobalt. With a jolt, I realize I'll have to hide my tattoo forever, not just until I'm further along in my training. It will testify against me for my entire life.

"Very insightful," the council member tells Niklas. Then she turns to Jensen. "Typically, we would never ask to see a tattoo without the consent of the witness, but I believe a good case has been made for revealing yours. Pull up your sleeve, please."

Jensen complies. His mastery tattoo is a pair of wings.

"We have to convict him," Jacey says.

The Grand Council removed the witnesses and left the six of us alone to discuss our decision. We moved from the dais to the benches in the front row of the chamber.

"We don't *have* to do anything," I say. "Our instructions said that the Grand Council would abide by our decision, so let's do the right thing and find him not guilty."

Tessa lays a palm on my forearm. "But, Saskia, this is a test. The challenge is to see if we will make the same ruling they would. And they'd convict him."

"What did Jensen do that was so terrible?" I can hear the edge in my voice, but I can't seem to soften it. "He saved a child's life. We're really going to send him to rot on Fang Island for that?"

Talon paces back and forth in front of the dais. "But it's not as if it was only that one time, Saskia. He had a dual mastery tattoo."

"Maybe that's just the way the tattoo manifested. It could mean *nothing*," I say.

"In context, it means something," Niklas says. "I'm bound to Instruments and Tools, but if I were accused of constructing a building, and my mastery tattoo supported that—"

I spin to face him. "You've said practically nothing for more than a week, but now that a man's life is on the line, you're suddenly feeling chatty?"

Niklas puts both hands in the air, palms facing me, and takes a step back. "I'm just trying to help."

"Saskia." Tessa's voice is reproachful, but her fingers close gently around mine. I take a deep breath and try to rein in my anger. She turns toward Bram. "You haven't said much. What's your opinion?"

Bram rakes his fingers through his hair. "Breakers don't subspecialize—we're simply assigned to Bone Breaking—so I'm not sure I'm the most qualified to give an opinion. It's complicated. I agree with Saskia that it's not fair, but I also agree with the rest of you that Jensen broke the law."

"He had a good reason," I say, letting my gaze sweep over each them. "Doesn't that matter to any of you?"

"We weren't asked to decide if he had a good reason," Jacey says softly. "We were asked to decide if he's guilty."

I feel like a loose thread inside me has snagged on something sharp, and now I'm slowly unraveling. If my team thinks Jensen deserves to be punished, they would surely think the same of me. If they saw my mastery tattoo, would they even listen before they condemned me? Would they care that my mother only taught me bone charming to save my life? Would it matter to them that my magic was able to grow wild and free because I didn't have a binding ceremony until I arrived at Ivory Hall? Or would they simply see three corners and call me a criminal?

For the past few weeks, I've let myself indulge in a fantasy that I might be able to have friends here. Allies. That, when the time was right, I'd be able to tell them everything and they would have my back. But I was wrong.

A deep well of sorrow opens in the pit of my stomach. I have nothing. No one.

"Fine," I say, "if everyone else agrees, then I won't interfere."

"Saskia—" Bram says, but I hold up a hand to stop him. I turn toward Jacey.

"Tell the Grand Council that we've made a decision."

Chapter
Twelve

he next few days pass in a blur.

Ivory Hall is bustling with apprentices again. Round one of the bone games is over and all the groups are back in the capital.

And no one had a challenge as brutal as ours.

Chatter about the games floats through the corridors between training sessions and across the dining hall at meal-time—stories of one group tackling an obstacle course, another working as a team to cross a chasm, yet another who had to find their way through a giant maze made of bone. As far as I can tell, none of the other teams faced something with last-ing consequences. Most of the apprentices seem to be in good spirits, as if the challenges have given them more confidence in their abilities. But a thick fog of foreboding hangs over me that I can't quite shake. The Grand Council sentenced Jensen to fifteen years on Fang Island. He will miss Boe's entire childhood. It makes me feel ill every time I think about it.

And I know my future isn't any brighter. I feel like I'm in a bone reading, looking down two equally dismal paths—either my life ends at Latham's hand, as it has so many times in my nightmares, or it ends as a prisoner on Fang Island once my secrets are exposed.

I long for the comfort of my mother's good advice or Gran's warm hands around mine or my father's gift for telling me just the right story that puts everything into perspective.

But I can't have any of that.

I'm homesick, but it wouldn't matter if I were in Midwood. After Gramps died, I visited the Forest of the Dead often, finding comfort at the base of our family tree. But now, with my mother's and Gran's bones still missing, it would only be a painful reminder that I have no way to connect with them. Except . . .

I do have one of Gran's bones—the healed one that I've been avoiding since I got here. Looking down my other path won't allow me to visit memories of my father or Gran—they were both already gone before the bone broke. But I could see my mother again. I could finally look for clues about Latham. And now that I'm better about feeling my way forward and backward through time, maybe I can avoid seeing too much of Bram. The extra practice navigating through the reading might be good for me. It could help me in later visions to know if I'm seeing the past, present, or future.

My loneliness gives me the courage that my fear never could. I sit on my bed and fold my legs in front of me.

I close my eyes and touch the bone with a single finger. I feel the familiar tug in my belly and then I'm swept into a vision that feels as real as it does familiar. Like pulling a well-loved sweater over my head and finding it exactly as I remembered.

I linger on my mother's face as I entered the Marrow for my kenning—the way the candlelight danced in her eyes. I watch as she placed her red training cloak around my shoulders before I left for Ivory Hall, as she took my hand in hers, her fingers brushing against the petal-shaped tattoo on my thumb. But then I speed past my terse responses, grateful I lived in a reality where she knew how much I loved her.

At Ivory Hall, I pay special attention to my training sessions with Latham. I examine every visible inch of his office, hoping for any small clue to indicate where he might be hiding. I stay in the reading for as long as my focus allows.

And then the next day, I read the bone again.

At first, I told myself I was reading my other path to look for clues about Latham.

But now, days later, the readings have become more than practice. More than searching for ways to stop Latham. More than trying to find Gran's and my mother's missing bones.

The readings have opened a gateway to another life. One where I don't feel so disconnected from everyone around me. I sink into the feeling of friendship there as I study my other path over and over again.

And each time it becomes less about Latham and more about Bram.

I watch the hard set of his mouth when we were first matched. Hear the rich, low sound of his laugh as he reacts to some joke I told. See his hand dart out to circle my wrist and spin me around.

I watch us argue. I watch us stumble through the forest, running from Latham. I watch his defenses slowly melt away, and see his eyes go liquid each time he looks at me.

Day after day, I linger on the feel of his mouth against mine, our tears mingling together before my eyes close for the final time.

I fall in love with him over and over only to come back to a world where he feels nothing for me but friendship. Where I don't know if my feelings for him belong only to another path or if they're real on this one too.

It makes me hate myself, but I can't stop.

Between studying Gran's bone and lying awake at night worrying about Jensen, I get so little sleep that it's impossible to focus on my training.

"You seem distracted today," Master Kyra tells me at our next session. A handful of tiny ossicles lie on the cloth in front of me—malleus, incus, and stapes—and I've been using them to try to determine the location of the nearest pack of wolves in the hills surrounding Ivory Hall. The small bones of the inner ear are particularly useful for readings that involve hearing, but each time I get close, I lose my focus.

"I'm sorry," I say. "I'm not my best at the moment."

Master Kyra sinks down into the chair across from me. "Something you want to talk about?"

She rarely asks me anything personal, so the question catches me off guard. "I . . . No, I guess not."

Kyra laughs. "Well, that's a yes masquerading as a no if I ever heard one. What's on your mind?"

I swallow, unsure how truthful to be. "I'm just a little shaken by our first challenge."

"What happened?"

I tell her about the trial, and she listens intently, her expression thoughtful. When I'm finished, she makes a throaty sound of disbelief. "Whoever designed that challenge wasn't pulling any punches, were they?"

My heart leaps into my throat. "Who designs them?"

"It varies. Usually a member of the Grand Council. Occasionally instructors or prominent members of the community."

I think of the Bone Charmer who watched me so carefully during the trial, and gooseflesh races across my arms. Did he suspect my mother of practicing illegal magic? Was he testing me to see if I'd give anything away?

"What specifically is troubling you?" Master Kyra asks.

"I don't feel like we did the right thing."

"The right thing for the challenge or the right thing for the accused?"

"For the accused." I give her the details of Jensen's story, and she listens carefully, her lips pressed together in a thin line.

"I don't blame you," she says. "That's a difficult case. What specifically is troubling you?"

"It just seems so unfair. Jensen was trying to help his son. He did something good—something merciful—and we punished him for it."

"Ah, but 'fair' means different things to different people." I raise my eyebrows in a question, and she continues. "Let me ask you this: Did Jensen know the law?"

"Yes."

"So he knew when he mended Boe's leg that the magic was forbidden?"

I let out a frustrated sigh. This is the same circular argument I had with my team over and over again. "Yes, but—" Master Kyra holds out a hand to silence me.

"Jensen understood the risk he was taking, and he decided Boe was worth it." Her eyes are soft. "He was an adult. He was willing to face the consequences for his child. But imagine how unfair it would be to let him go just because you understand his choices, when others have been punished for the same crime. And their motives might have been equally understandable if we knew the full story. Jensen was a good father, Saskia. His fate was in his own hands, not yours. All you can do is honor his sacrifice."

Her words pierce me to the core. I think of my mother offering to train me as a Bone Charmer to protect me from Declan. *Teaching you would violate my code of ethics—I could get in a lot of trouble if anyone finds out—but you still should be able to learn.*

All this time, I've been thinking Jensen and I are the same, when really, he has more in common with my mother. She was willing to die to keep me safe. Jensen's words float through my mind. *The law is the law. And I'd do it again to spare my boy.*

I have no doubt that my mother would die again to protect me. She'd choose that path over and over again if she had to. And I will accept whatever consequences come from making sure Latham pays for her death.

Master Kyra's hand closes gently around my forearm. "I wish I could tell you it gets easier, but it doesn't. Leadership is full of difficult choices."

Somehow her honesty, her acknowledgment that this is hard—and will always be hard—is what I needed to hear. She's the first person who hasn't tried to talk me out of my sadness. I blink back tears. "Thank you."

"You're welcome. Now, shall we try again?"

This time, when I close my eyes and touch the bones, I hear it. The distant, plaintive howl of a single wolf separated from his pack.

He sounds as lonely as I feel.

◆───◆───◆

I arrive early to our seminar in the workshop the next afternoon. Norah is scheduled to give a lecture called *Comparative Vertebrate Anatomy and Magical Applications,* so I'm poring over my spell book while I wait. Unlike the sea of Healers and Watchers at Ivory Hall, if Norah has a question related to charming, her choices are limited to either me or Ingrid. I need to be prepared.

"Saskia!"

I turn to see Tessa rushing toward me. Her cheeks are flushed, and I can't tell if it's from panic or excitement.

I stand up and close the distance between us. "What is it?"

"We got our second challenge for the bone games." She's waving a folded piece of parchment as if it's an invitation to a grand ball. But I don't share her enthusiasm. I'm not interested in more difficult choices.

"What do we have to do?"

Tessa bounces on her toes. "Not what. Where."

"Oh," I say flatly. "Then where?"

She sighs and thrusts the parchment into my hands. But before I can unfold it, she says, "It's in Leiden, Saskia." She leans toward me and lowers her voice, even though no one else is within earshot. "We can find Avalina."

A ping of alarm goes through me. "Our challenge is in Leiden?"

Tessa's face falls. "I thought you'd be excited."

"Don't you think it seems odd? We were just talking about finding Avalina, and our next bone game is in the exact town she's from?"

"You think someone is sending us there intentionally? But who? Why?"

It doesn't make any sense. Norah warned me against taking action against Latham on my own, and I can't imagine who would want me to find Avalina. Even if the Bone Charmer on the Grand Council suspects my mother trained me, what connection would that have to Leiden? Still, the coincidence makes me uneasy.

Tessa puts a hand on my arm. "I think you're worrying over nothing. The bone games must take months to prepare. I'm sure this was planned long before you expressed an interest in finding Avalina."

I sigh. Maybe my paranoia is getting the best of me. I take a deep breath, and a small bubble of hope inflates in my chest. I could finally get the answers I need to start searching for Latham.

But then a hand falls on my shoulder and I turn to find Norah standing next to the bodyguard I met my first night here, his arms folded across his massive chest.

"Hello, girls," Norah says. Then she indicates the man beside her. "Saskia, you remember Rasmus."

The sight of him is a sharp pin that collapses my optimism in one swift motion.

I'd nearly forgotten about Norah's stipulation that a bodyguard accompany me if I leave Ivory Hall. Suddenly I feel as transparent as a windowpane. Like my scheming is on full display for Norah to see.

I try to school my expression into something calmer than I feel. "Of course." I turn to Rasmus. "Hello again."

He doesn't move. He barely makes eye contact. The only sign he heard me is a subtle dip of his chin.

"Rasmus will accompany you on your next challenge," she says. "I understand you're headed to Leiden."

"Yes," Tessa says brightly, "we are."

My jaw tightens. "May I ask you something?"

Norah smiles. "Of course. What is it?"

"Who designs our bone games?"

Her expression falters. "Why do you ask?"

"Just curious."

Her eyes skip to Tessa, and the two share a glance—as if neither of them knows what to make of me and they're each looking to the other for an answer. Something hot and angry sparks in my chest.

"I don't know off the top of my head, but even if I did, I couldn't tell you. It's against policy to share that information with apprentices. At least until the bone games are over. Now, if there's nothing else, I better get going on this lecture before everyone leaves." She pats my arm. "Rasmus will meet you at the pier tomorrow."

"What was that about?" Tessa asks as soon as the two of them are out of earshot.

I'm not sure if she means me questioning Norah or Norah assigning me a bodyguard, but I'm not really in the mood to talk about either one.

"Saskia?"

"I forgot about Rasmus," I say softly. "We'll never be able to slip away now."

"Of course we will. There's only one of him and six of us."

"And he's trained in magic that we're not."

She smiles. "Yes, but we're also trained in magic that he's not."

"Where was this rebellious streak a few days ago when it could have saved Jensen?"

Tessa's expression falls. She takes a step back as if I've slapped her and she needs a bit of distance for safety. "Saskia, you know that was different."

I lift one shoulder and let my gaze slide away.

"So will you never forgive me?" Tessa's voice is small. Vulnerable. And it melts the last of my anger.

"There's nothing to forgive," I tell her. "I just wish for a different world sometimes, that's all."

"I know," she says. "I do too. But someday we'll be the ones with power—for real, and not just for one trial—and we can change it."

I don't tell her the truth—that I won't ever have power in Kastelia. Soon I'll either be dead or in prison. I'm relieved that Tessa wants to change the world, but she'll have to change it without me.

The next morning, we stand on the deck of a small boat and watch Ivory Hall fade into the distance. Leiden is north of the capital, and not far from the coast. The journey would normally take a few weeks, but Norah has commissioned a small wing-fleet vessel that can get us there in less than one.

We've been given no information about what kind of challenge might be waiting for us when we arrive.

Tessa sidles up beside me and rests her hand on the railing. "I think we need to let Bram in on our plan," she says softly.

"We don't *have* a plan," I say.

She nudges my shoulder with hers. "Good point. Let's make Bram do that part."

Despite myself, I laugh. Tessa's easy optimism feels like a

patch of sunshine, tempting me to curl up and let all my worries drift away.

For a moment, I wish it were possible—to let go of my hatred for Latham and move on with the rest of my life. That my need for revenge didn't burn so brightly inside me that sometimes I worry it will consume me long before it hurts him. But I can't. I need to find my mother's bones, and Gran's, too. And Latham has to pay for what he's done. Besides, even if I *could* let go, Latham never will. He won't rest until I'm dead.

So I won't rest until he is.

But the last thing I need is for Bram to get tangled up in my plan. Better for Latham to think I've fallen for someone else in this reality, and that Bram has nothing to do with the slender red tattoo etched around my wrist. If I can't save myself, I can at least save him.

"I think the fewer people who know what we're up to the better," I tell Tessa. "It's going to be hard enough for two of us to get around Rasmus."

"That's where Bram can help."

"Help with what?"

Both Tessa and I spin around to find Bram standing behind us. I shake my head. "Nothing."

At the same moment, Tessa says, "A little side trip in Leiden."

Bram's gaze skips between us. Then he leans so close, I can smell the soap he used to bathe this morning. "Is this about Latham?"

Tessa watches me closely, inclining her head slightly and widening her eyes for emphasis. *Tell him.*

"Yes," I say, finally. There's no point denying it. Bram was there when I found the spell book Latham left. And he did promise to help me before we left Midwood.

Tessa quietly fills him in on the details, and his total focus on her gives me license to study him without fear of being noticed. His hair is wind-tousled, and he has a bit of scruff along his jawline. Both only add to his appeal. He taps his thumb absently on the callous at the edge of his forefinger—a callous no doubt acquired from quickly snapping small bones in training. A crease appears between his brows as Tessa tells him we plan to find Avalina.

"Rasmus is going to be a problem," Bram says quietly.

"Yes," I say, glad he agrees with me. "That's what I keep telling her."

"It's not like I haven't thought this through," Tessa says. "I have an idea."

Bram gives her a skeptical look. "To trick a member of the Ivory Guard away from his post?"

"Just hear me out." Tessa turns to me. "Rasmus is duty-bound to protect you from Latham and to keep you from going off in search of him. Correct?"

"Yes."

"But Norah promised you would hardly notice he was there. So I assume he has orders not to interfere with your training. Or your fun. Or your"—her eyes slide away—"relationships."

"Tessa," I say, my voice low and full of warning.

"I'm just saying, it would be easier to cover for you if Rasmus thought you and Bram snuck off to be alone."

Bram clears his throat. "She's not wrong."

I go hot from my scalp to my toes, open my mouth to speak, and then snap it closed again.

Bram pulls on the back of his neck. Shifts his weight from one foot to the other. He's obviously as uncomfortable as I am, but still, his eyes grow distant and bright, as if Tessa's words lit a spark that has caught fire. He paces in front of the railing. "It won't be easy, but it could work. If Rasmus thinks he knows what you're up to, he's less likely to be as vigilant. Especially if you aren't sneaking off alone, but with another Breaker."

Tessa doesn't know what she's unleashed.

I've spent so long studying Gran's healed bone. Immersed in my other path. Longing for a reality that doesn't exist. I'm not sure my bruised heart can handle Bram pretending interest where there is none. It might break me.

"Bram, no. You don't have to . . ."

His fingers close around my elbow. "I told you I'd help find Latham. And I'll do whatever it takes to keep that promise. Even this."

Even this. The words ricochet in my mind like a bone-crafted arrow, cutting wherever they touch, but never slowing, never losing the power to wound.

Even this. Even this. Even this.

Chapter
Thirteen

atham couldn't have designed a better way to torture me if he'd planned this himself.

The moment I grudgingly agreed to Tessa's plan, she waggled her fingers between me and Bram. "You two should start acting cozy right away. Give Rasmus some time to warm up to the idea of you as a couple before we get to Leiden."

And now Bram and I sit on the deck away from the others, our heads bent together in a conversation that we hope looks intimate but is really anything but.

"This will never work," I say softly. Rasmus hovers over my shoulder, so I don't bother trying to mask my worry, but Bram's face is toward him. He can't afford to show anything but affection. He gives me an earnest, gentle smile.

"Not with that attitude it won't." His voice doesn't match his tender expression.

"Bram—"

"Your mother is the reason I moved to Midwood," Bram says. "Did she ever tell you that?"

Grief pushes up my throat. Because even though I knew, it wasn't my mother who told me. She rarely confessed her good deeds, and it was only after her death that I realized how many lives she'd changed for the better.

"No," I say, my voice tight, "she didn't."

"She rescued me at a dark time in my life. The least I can do is help you return her bones to Midwood, where they belong. I owe her that. And Latham"—a muscle jumps in his jaw—"I'd love nothing more than to see him suffer for what he did."

"But is this really the best way to go about it?"

"Do you want my help or not? Because I don't see another option."

"Of course I do. I just—"

Bram reaches up and tucks a stray hair behind my ear, and I freeze mid-sentence. My thoughts go hazy and spiral away. The gesture is so real, so *familiar*, it fills up that empty, aching part of me that reading my other path always leaves behind.

"For the benefit of our audience," he says in a low voice. The backs of his fingers still linger on the side of my face.

My heart ices over and fractures into two distinct halves— fantasy and reality. The Bram who loves me, and the Bram who is only playacting. The Saskia who had a chance for happiness and the Saskia who does not.

I can't mix them up. I have to remember what is real and what isn't.

"I'm trying to act natural," I tell him, through clenched teeth. I'm answering both his spoken concerns and my unspoken ones. How can I convince Bram I'm acting while simultaneously convincing Rasmus that I'm not?

"Try harder."

It's good advice for both sets of worries.

By the time the ship docks in Leiden, Rasmus has begun rolling his eyes every time he sees me with Bram.

Tessa says it's a good sign.

The town is on the coast, and from the small river port, we can see the black stone of the craggy shoreline in the distance. A small lighthouse perches on a hill nearby. Waves slam into the rocks, sending up sprays of foamy water. It's desolate, but beautiful.

"Welcome back to land," the ship's captain says as we prepare to disembark. He's holding a large, flat leather pouch that he waves in the air. "I was told to give you this upon your arrival. Who wants it?"

Jacey jumps up and snatches it from his hands, and the captain chuckles. "Good luck. I'll see you in two days for your journey back to the capital."

I hurry off the ship after Jacey, but when I set foot on the pier, my breath catches.

Leiden. The City of Glass.

I haven't been here since I was a small child. My father

brought me one summer to pick out an anniversary gift for my mother—a special window he had commissioned for their bedroom. Leiden's main industry is glass, and the town is most well known for supplying stunning stained-glass windows for buildings all over Kastelia and beyond. "I want your mother to wake up every morning bathed in light," he told me after he met with the artist. I rolled my eyes at the time—my parents' affection for each other was beyond embarrassing. But still, my memories from that trip are filled with a sense of wonder.

I remembered it being beautiful, but I wasn't expecting this. The pier is brimming with hundreds of glass sculptures—giant turquoise seashells gape open just enough for us to catch a glimpse of the pearly pink orbs inside. Delicate purple seaweed sprouts from the ground and seems to undulate in the breeze. An enormous yellow fish with black stripes and orange eyes bobs in the water alongside an emerald octopus. Trees made entirely of glass line the boardwalk. They're rendered in a multitude of hues and in such intricate detail that the veining on each individual leaf is visible. Everywhere the pier is bursting with color.

It's a feast for the eyes, and for several minutes we all gawk in stunned silence, turning in slow circles to absorb it all. But it would take hours to see every detail.

A flock of geese flies overhead, honking to one another as they pass, as if they, too, are entranced by Leiden's beauty.

"Should we get started?" Jacey asks. We all gather around her as she pulls a single sheet of parchment from the leather pocket, her gaze roaming over the words.

Talon makes an impatient sound. "So? What does it say?"

Her brows pull together. "We're supposed to stay at the Swallowtail Inn tonight, and the challenge will take place tomorrow at the Fortress."

Beside me, Bram goes still. Rasmus is standing a distance away, but I could swear I see him flinch.

"What's the Fortress?" Niklas asks.

"The Fortress is a training facility for select members of the Ivory Guard," Bram says. But his tone suggests something more than that. Something darker.

"What kind of training facility?" Tessa asks.

Bram's mouth is set in a grim line. "Let's just say I've never heard anyone speak of the place fondly."

"But surely they aren't going to expect us to fight," Talon says. "We wouldn't need that kind of training to serve on town councils."

"The Fortress doesn't train soldiers to fight," Bram says. "It trains them to survive torture." A shiver goes through me that has nothing to do with the cold. I pull my cloak more tightly around myself. Bram's hand goes to my upper back, his fingers resting lightly on my scapula. A comforting token of affection for Rasmus's benefit, I'm sure. I resist the urge to shake him off. I resist the urge to move closer.

A chilled silence settles over the group as we consider the implications of a challenge in this particular location. I kick a loose pebble with the toe of my boot and send it tumbling toward the river.

"Don't worry," Bram says, finally. "I doubt they actually plan to hurt us."

But the words come out forced and empty. We don't really know what Norah and the Grand Council might be planning.

"So what are we supposed to do until tomorrow?" Jacey asks.

"Let's explore the town," Tessa says, her voice false and overly bright. I shoot a quick, panicked glance at Rasmus, but his expression is the same as always.

Tessa strides off toward the center of town without waiting for a reply. Jacey shrugs and follows her. Then Talon and Niklas do too. Bram and I stay at the back of the group. He now rests his palm at the small of my back. The gesture makes my heart stop briefly, then gallop ahead at twice the speed.

A memory tickles at the back of my mind and I feel the ghost of Bram's fingers in the precise spot they rest now. Strong. Protective. But that was on another path, in another time. And it meant something different then.

I quicken my steps just enough so that his hand falls away.

The town square in Leiden is even more spectacular than its pier. Every building—humble or grand—is graced by colorful stained-glass windows, and sculptures like the ones we saw on the pier. We pass a bakery with a window depicting a scene of a woman removing a steaming round loaf of bread from a red-hot oven with a long wooden paddle. In front of the building, a giant glass basket overflows with shimmering pastries.

The calligrapher's shop has a series of windows showing scenes of apprentices learning the craft, heads bent over scrolls of parchments, inky black drops spilling from feathered pens. Across the road, the cobbler boasts a display of glass shoes—slippers, boots, sandals—sculpted in hues of crimson, green, and blue.

The breeze carries the briny scent of the sea.

As we walk, Tessa threads her arm through mine. "I'm going to stop in one of the shops and ask after my childhood tutor," she says softly. "He should be able to tell me where we can find Avalina. Why don't you go with everyone else to the inn to drop off bags and I'll meet you there?" She hands me her satchel and squeezes my arm before darting into a butcher shop.

Rasmus doesn't even turn to watch her go. It's a stark, unwelcome reminder that he's only here to guard me. Nothing else matters. Maybe I'm torturing myself with Bram for nothing.

I should know better than to get my hopes up, and yet the possibility of failure dances along every nerve ending, making me anxious and jittery. Avalina might not live in Leiden anymore. She might be unwilling to talk to me at all. I try to imagine the kind of woman Latham would fall for. Ambitious. Heartless. All angles and sharp edges.

The kind of woman who might take one look at me and kill me herself to save him the trouble.

We turn a corner, and the inn comes into view—a large L-shaped structure made from dark stone that highlights the stained-glass windows that stretch three stories high.

A group of children chase one another around the cobblestone courtyard in front, while weary-looking travelers unload trunks from wagons. It's busier than I expected based on the emptiness of the pier. As we get closer, I hear snatches of conversations in foreign tongues. Cistonian, with its long, melodious vowels, and the rough, clipped consonants of Novenium. Suddenly the bustling inn makes more sense. Most of these travelers probably arrived by sea instead of sailing down the Shard.

Several heads turn to watch us as we cross the courtyard, and suddenly I realize how strange we must seem in our colorful cloaks. A handful of bone magic apprentices so far from the capital and trailed by a hulking bodyguard.

The innkeeper is a small man with a slender frame and round wire-rimmed spectacles. He looks up briefly when we enter. "Ivory Hall?"

"Yes," Niklas and Talon say at the same moment.

The innkeeper takes two sets of keys from a pegboard behind him and hands one set to Niklas, and one set to me. "Turn right at the top of the stairs and take the last two rooms at the end of the hall."

After the grandeur of the rest of the town, I had high hopes for our accommodations, but our room turns out to be disappointing—small, with two questionably clean mattresses shoved against each wall, and a bedroll resting on the floor in between them. My neck aches just looking at it. I can't believe Norah sent us all this way but couldn't spare enough coin for an extra room or two so no one would be forced to sleep on the floor.

I toss Tessa's satchel on one of the mattresses and drop my own on the bedroll.

Jacey gives me a grateful look. "Thank you."

"Don't mention it."

I feel as if I owe them both—Tessa because she's helping me find Avalina, and Jacey because I've been misleading her about my relationship with Bram. She'd be hurt if she found out I'd trusted Tessa with my secrets but left her in the dark. Giving her the mattress assuages some of my guilt, if only a little.

"Hey there," Talon says, poking his head into the room at the same time he knocks on the door frame. He hooks his thumb toward Bram, who stands beside him. "We thought we'd grab a bite downstairs. Do you want to come?" Then he looks around. "Where's Tessa?"

Jacey rolls her eyes. "You just now noticed she's missing?"

"There are a lot of us," Talon says defensively. "And I've been rather focused on my growling stomach for the past few hours."

"She was hoping to visit her childhood tutor who moved here a few years ago," I say, grateful I can be honest, at least about this. "She stopped to make some inquiries about where he lives."

"Well, she must have been sneaky about it," Talon says. "I didn't even see her slip away."

Bram and I share a significant look. If Talon—who is one of the less observant members of our team—finds Tessa's disappearance suspicious, what must Rasmus think?

Bram claps Talon on the shoulder. "I'm hungry too. Let's eat."

I only manage to pick at my food. I break off a bit of bread from the loaf, only to realize a few minutes later that I've rolled it into a ball between my thumb and forefinger without ever bringing it to my mouth.

Tessa has been gone too long. I shouldn't have agreed to this plan. If something happens to her, I'll never forgive myself.

My eyes keep darting to the door, hoping to catch sight of her. Rasmus stands at the back of the room, silent, watchful. He could help me track her down. It would mean giving up all hope of meeting Avalina, but it would be worth it to know Tessa is safe. Eventually the pressure building in my chest becomes unbearable. I start to rise, but Bram puts a hand on my arm. His gaze flicks toward the door.

Tessa.

Her cheeks and nose are pink from the cold. When she spots us, her face breaks out in a wide smile. Good news, then.

My breath sags out of me.

Talon hops up and grabs an extra chair from a nearby table, presenting it to Tessa with exaggerated chivalry. "Ah, there you are. We missed you."

Jacey gives a derisive snort. "He just feels bad because he didn't notice you were gone for an embarrassingly long time."

Talon shoots her a glare. "You didn't have to *announce* it."

Tessa laughs and flops down into the chair. "Who wants to go see how glass is made?"

It's so completely different from anything I thought she

might say that I just stare at her, slack-jawed.

She takes a chunk of meat from my plate and pops it into her mouth.

"Really?" Niklas says. "How would we manage that?"

Tessa finishes chewing and swallows. "My tutor's son was recently apprenticed as a glassblower and he's invited us to his shop to watch him work." She shrugs. "But only if everyone is interested."

"I am," Talon says.

"Me too," Niklas adds.

Jacey pushes her empty plate to the center of the table. "I'm in. When?"

"Tonight," Tessa says, licking a crumb from her finger. "Now."

I can't figure out how this fits into Tessa's plan, but by the way she has schooled her expression into nonchalance, I know it does.

We leave the inn and stroll through the candy-colored town square to a more remote part of Leiden, where the buildings are farther apart and the windows are made of plain, unadorned glass.

I casually make my way to the front of the group and walk beside Tessa. She doesn't turn her face to acknowledge me, but after a few minutes she starts speaking in a voice low enough that I have to strain to hear. I fight the impulse to dip my head toward hers. "Avalina lives two streets south of the inn. Her house is built of rose-colored brick with white shutters. It has a big oak tree in front. Leave with Bram, but not until I give you the signal."

"Got it," I say just as Bram slides his hand into mine. I take a deep breath. I can do this. I have to.

The glass workshop is on the outskirts of town in a building that would be nondescript if not for the large cone-shaped protrusion on the roof.

As we approach, Rasmus puts his arm out to block me. "Wait here."

He disappears inside the building and doesn't return for several minutes.

Finally he emerges and waves us forward.

We step through the door into a dimly lit room so warm that it smothers the air from my lungs. I shrug off my cloak, and several others do the same. Even Rasmus tugs at his collar, as if he's considering shedding his Breaker attire.

Glassblowers work at various stations. One girl stands in front of a huge oven holding a long metal pole with a purple blob of molten glass on the end. She shoves the pole into the flame as if she's feeding a dragon.

On the other side of the room, another man blows into a metal pipe, and the liquid glass on the end expands into a delicate bubble. I'm transfixed by the sight, so much so that for a moment, I forget why we're here. And then, with a start, I realize that's the point. Tessa has planned the perfect distraction.

Rasmus stands at the edge of the room as mesmerized as anyone else. Carefully, I drape my cloak over the back of a chair in his peripheral vision. He's already swept the building for potential threats, so his guard might be down. Perhaps if he sees a flash of red from the corner of his eye, he won't be tempted to look away from the demonstration. Slowly, I back away. Without needing an explanation, Bram appears at my side, again threading his fingers through mine. The glassblower in front of the oven pulls the metal pole from the fire and then starts to spin it. Rasmus leans forward and watches as the glass ripples into a new shape. Tessa gives me a sharp look. *Go.*

Bram and I back out of the workshop, ease open the door, slip outside.

And then we run.

The crisp air is a shock against my bare arms. The cold bites at my nose and ears. I risk a glance over my shoulder, relieved that no one is following. At least not yet. We run until my legs ache. Until my lungs feel both on fire and coated in ice, like the burn that comes with frostbite.

We weave through alleys and between buildings. Rasmus can't stop us if he can't find us.

Finally we slow and then come to a stop. I put my hands on my knees and suck in a lungful of frigid air.

"You all right?" Bram asks.

It takes me a moment to get enough air to answer. "Yes. You?"

"I'm fine."

"After all this, she *better* be home."

The pressure in the air changes just a fraction—the breathless space between when I know Bram will laugh and when he actually does. Finally a full-bellied sound escapes him, rich and full as melting chocolate. "I hope so."

I'm filled with bittersweet longing.

"Ready?" Bram asks.

"Not really. But it's too late to back out now."

Chapter
Fourteen

valina's cottage is just where Tessa said we'd find it. The giant oak in front conceals the house from the road, but once we get closer, its cozy facade comes into view— rose-colored brick, white shutters, a small flower bed whose blooms have wilted. For a moment, I'm tempted to turn away. To march back to the glass workshop and tell Tessa that Avalina wasn't home. As if reading my thoughts, Bram once again slides his hand into mine and squeezes it reassuringly.

It gives me just enough courage to lift my fist and knock.

I'm torn between yearning for her to answer and hoping she won't. But we don't have to wait long.

The door swings open, and a woman stands in front of us.

She wears a thin, loose-fitting blue dress, and her raven hair reaches nearly to her waist. Her eyes are startlingly blue, and her mouth curves into a kind smile.

"Hello there. What can I do for you?"

"We're looking for someone named Avalina," I say, certain this can't be her. Latham couldn't love someone who looks so . . . ordinary.

"Lucky girl," the woman says, "you've found her."

I'm not sure what I was expecting. Obviously, she wasn't going to open the door dressed in armor or with a weapon in hand, but something about her friendly, unguarded expression throws me off. She's so different from who I imagined.

"We're apprentices at Ivory Hall," Bram says. "We were hoping we could ask you a few questions."

At that, her brows pull together. "You're a long way from the capital."

A shiver goes through me, and I rub my arms for warmth.

"Oh my," Avalina says, "the two of you are freezing. Come in, come in."

We step inside, and she pushes the door closed behind us. My gaze sweeps over the room. Off to one side is a small kitchen with a rough-hewn wooden table in the center. A bowl of fruit sits on top, and bundles of dried herbs hang from the ceiling.

Avalina leads us to the other side of the cottage, where several mismatched chairs are positioned around a hearth that glows with a crackling fire. "Have a seat," she says. Bram and I comply, both of us leaning toward the flames and rubbing heat back into our frigid limbs. "Now, you were saying?"

My gaze slides to Bram, but he's clearly leaving space for me to take the lead. "We have some questions about Latham," I say.

Avalina sucks in a sharp gasp as if I'd struck her. She stands, her chair scraping loudly against the wood floor. "Who are you? Why would you come here?"

I knew her friendly demeanor was too good to be true.

"I'm Della Holte's daughter," I say softly. "Latham killed my mother. And my gran."

Her eyes go wide. She drops her head into her hands, her long hair falling across her face like a curtain. Then, just as suddenly, she straightens and rushes from the room. Bram and I share a dark look. Was that a dismissal? Do we stay? Do we go?

She comes back a moment later with two bone amulets, each suspended on a leather cord. Without a word, she puts one over my neck, and then does the same to Bram.

"It will keep him from watching you," she says.

An icy finger trails down my spine. "Defensive magic," I say, remembering the necklace my mother left for me on my other path.

She nods and then bites her lip. "Please," she says, "tell me what you're doing here."

My thoughts are muddy and it takes me a few moments to clear them enough to speak. "After Latham killed my gran and then my mother, he stole their bones. He wants me dead too. I have to find him before he finds me." I tell her the story—how Latham is determined to collect the bones from three generations of Charmers. How he used Declan to spy on me and to try to win my affections so I'd have all three essential tattoos. How he wants to kill me slowly so that my bones will be as powerful as possible. Bram's brow furrows as he listens. His gaze falls to the tattoo on my wrist, and I feel my cheeks heat.

Avalina's fingers worry the bone charm that rests in the hollow of her throat. Her expression is bleak. "I haven't seen Latham in years. I wouldn't have the first idea how to find him."

"And yet you're still protecting yourself from him."

She drops the necklace, and her hand falls into her lap.

"You must know he's still obsessed with you." I dip my head toward her amulet. "You wouldn't need to wear that otherwise."

"I can't help you." Her voice is small, uncertain.

"Maybe you could just tell us a bit about him," Bram tries. "What he was like when you knew him. It might help."

She shakes her head. "You need to leave. Please."

My mind snags on the *please*. The courtesy of it. The civility, even as she's trying to kick us out. She wants to help, but she's afraid.

"I'm going to die soon." My voice is soft, but steady. "I've seen it in a vision—over and over again. There's probably nothing I can do about it. Probably nothing you can. But when you hear the news, I wonder if you will torture yourself with what could have been? What you might have said that could have made a difference."

Her expression is stricken. So is Bram's. "You're trying to manipulate me," she says. She sounds horrified. Indignant.

"Yes," I say, because that's exactly what I'm doing. "But I'm also telling the truth. I know what it is to stare down an alternate path and wonder at the different choices you might have made. It's not a fate I would wish on anyone."

A hundred emotions flicker over her face, and worry puddles in my chest as I wait for which one will prevail. But finally, her expression settles into resignation. "It's a very long story. I'll make us a kettle of tea."

As soon as she's out of earshot, Bram whips toward me. "You were lying, right? About having a vision of yourself dying?"

His concerned expression makes me hesitate. I want to say something reassuring, protect him from the truth, but the words stick in my throat. "No. I wasn't."

"Saskia!" My name explodes from his mouth in an urgent hiss. I feel it rush across my cheek like an angry gust of wind. "How am I supposed to help you if you don't tell me everything?" His gaze falls to the love tattoo around my wrist. "You never told me that Declan betrayed you."

I bite my lip. Say nothing.

"Did you fall in love with him?" The question makes me want to retreat. To curl up inside myself and avoid what's coming.

I shake my head. "No."

In the kitchen, the tea kettle whistles.

Bram narrows his eyes. "Then who?"

"We'll talk about it later," I say, watching Avalina arrange the kettle and a selection of teacups on a tray.

"If you weren't in love with Declan, then how did you get that tattoo?"

Avalina picks up the tray and starts to turn.

"Bram," I say sharply. *"Later."*

Avalina comes back into the room and slides the tray onto a low table. She pours a cup and offers it to me. Fragrant steam curls around my face as I take a sip.

Both Bram and I watch Avalina expectantly. Finally she sits in the chair closest to the hearth. She curls her feet beneath her and takes a deep breath.

"My parents had an unhappy pairing." Her index finger traces the rim of her teacup. "They fought constantly. My gramps once said that he'd never seen two people more suited to make each other miserable than my mother and father. They seemed to know exactly how to bring out the worst in each other. They rarely agreed on anything, but the one exception was their hopes for my future. They both desperately wanted me to be bone-matched. It was more important to them than anything, even than saving for my kenning. I think they wanted to spare me the misery of a pairing like theirs."

I lean forward in my chair, fascinated. My own parents had an unusually happy relationship, even for a bone-matched pairing. It's hard to imagine growing up any other way.

Avalina stands and adds a log to the hearth, prodding it with a fire iron until it settles. Then she sits back into her chair and continues with her story. "My parents spent a modest amount to have bones prepared for my kenning, but they spent a small fortune on the ones designated for the matchmaking portion of the ceremony. And they made their intentions clear to the Bone Charmer: He should use the less powerful bones for the kenning, and the stronger ones for the bone-matched partnership. So that's exactly what he did. He matched me with a boy I had never met, never even heard of. Latham Thorn."

With a start, I realize I've never heard Latham's surname before. It hits my ear strangely. As does listening to Avalina describe him as a boy.

"My parents were thrilled," she says, "relieved that they'd set me up for the life they'd never had. We made arrangements to visit the Thorn family immediately. His town held their kenning later than mine because their apprentices didn't need to travel far to reach Ivory Hall. So Latham hadn't yet had his reading when we arrived."

She stops then, her eyes becoming unfocused and faraway, as if overtaken by memories.

"Was it horrible?" I ask. "Meeting him for the first time."

Avalina smiles. "Quite the opposite. He was handsome and kind. I'd never experienced such an instant connection to another person, and I could tell Latham felt the same way. But his father was"—a shadow falls over her expression— "displeased. To say the least."

"Why?" Bram asks. "I would think he'd be happy your parents had saved him the expense of a matchmaking reading."

She sighs. "Latham's father was on the Grand Council. He had big plans for his son and thought the match was beneath him. I wasn't from a prominent family. I hadn't been matched to a bone magic specialty."

A jolt of surprise goes through me. "But wait, I thought you were matched as a Mixer?"

She frowns. "No. I was assigned to Ivory Hall as a chef's apprentice." My gaze goes to the dried herbs hanging from the ceiling, and the little pots of spices that line the windowsill in the kitchen. "It suited me perfectly. It still does."

"But your record at Ivory Hall said you were a Mixer. And my mother talked of you as if she'd known you, as if you'd trained in bone magic."

Avalina refills her teacup. "Ah yes. Well, as I said, Latham's father was unhappy with the match, and he decided that Leiden's Bone Charmer must have been in error. That perhaps he mixed up the bones from my kenning with the ones from my matchmaking reading. He convinced his colleagues on the Grand Council to demand a second reading from a different Bone Charmer. And once they heard that the more powerful bones were used for my matchmaking instead of my kenning, they agreed. My second reading matched me as a Bone Mixer." Her eyes fall to her cup. "And it also declared I had no suitable partner as a bone match in the entire country."

I pull in a sharp breath. The unfairness of it is staggering. "But I still don't understand what happened with Latham," I say. "If you weren't bone matched anymore, then why was he so angry?"

"Latham believed the results of the first kenning, not the second. We both did. It was so clear that we were meant to be together. We could talk about anything. He used to laugh at my jokes before I even got to the punch line. Latham's father tried to keep us apart, but we met in secret. And once I started training in bone magic, it was easy to be together. We fell in love despite everything—Latham's father, the Grand Council, the second kenning—we didn't need an official bone match to know we were fated for each other."

My heart constricts. Her tone is full of tenderness. How can she be talking about the same man who killed my mother? Who killed Gran? She leans forward and lays a palm on my forearm, as if she can guess my thoughts. "He was different then."

I shake my head. "No. People don't change that much. He tricked you."

"I know it must seem like that," she says, "especially after all that has happened since. But I think I'm a pretty good judge of character. I let *you* through my door, didn't I?"

Normally, her gentle humor would soften me, but I can't make sense of what she's saying. I expected her to tell me Latham was always a monster, that she ran from him—as fast and as far as she could—at the first opportunity.

"So what changed?" Bram asks.

Avalina sighs. "Latham's father was enraged when he found out we were still seeing each other. He demanded Latham call off our pairing. Latham refused. So his father went to the Grand Council again. And this time, he accused my parents of bribing our Bone Charmer for a false reading. Latham thought it would never work, assured me everything would be fine. But he underestimated how much power his father had over his colleagues on the council."

"The rest of the council *believed* him?" I ask.

She massages her forehead. "Either they believed him or they were willing to be complicit in his lie. It's hard to know which. But in either case, my parents were convicted and sent to Fang

Island. Leiden's Bone Charmer was too. And I was expelled from Ivory Hall and stripped of any right to practice bone magic."

Horror pushes up my throat. "But they're not still there, right? You must have been able to reverse such a terrible decision."

Her eyes shimmer with unshed tears. "Fang Island is a cruel place. All three of them died before they could be vindicated."

I think of Jensen and my stomach seizes. What will become of him? What will become of Boe in his absence?

"So is that why everything changed between you and Latham?" I ask. "Because of what his father did?"

"Of course not," she says, like one person's family betraying another's in such a heinous way wouldn't be enough to tear most couples apart. Her hands tremble as she smooths invisible wrinkles in her dress. "I didn't hold him responsible for what happened. We don't choose our parents. But yes, it changed things. Or I should say, it changed *Latham*. He became bitter. Obsessed with revenge."

I squirm uncomfortably in my seat as I think of my own fantasies of exacting vengeance on Latham. I don't want to fathom that the two of us could ever have anything in common.

"At first, we stayed together. But increasingly, I realized he had become a different person. His father's actions—and the Grand Council's—had unlocked a darkness in his heart that no amount of love could overcome. He started dabbling in dark magic, seeking out those who used it, learning to practice it himself. It frightened me."

"What kind of dark magic?" I ask. Did he know about the spell that required the bones of three Charmers even then?

Had he been planning to kill my mother since he was my age?

"Terrible things. Using healing magic to cause pain instead of relieve it, Mason-made weapons that should never exist, bone potions that induce panic if swallowed . . ." She stops talking, pressing her lips together as if she's ashamed the words have escaped. "I thought maybe in time he'd learn to forgive, to let go of all his hatred, but it only got worse. So I left him. I moved away from Kastelia City and came home."

"Did he try to win you back?" Bram asks.

"For many years," she says. "He seemed to show up at odd times, to know precisely where I'd be on a given day. Finally he admitted that he'd been reading my future. We fought." She touches the pendant at her throat again, as if to reassure herself that it's still there. "I told him I never wanted to see him again. But . . ."

"But what?" I ask.

"He respected my wishes . . . at least he seemed to. He stopped contacting me. He started tutoring at Ivory Hall. His life seemed to settle. But over the years, I got the sense that it was just an interlude. That he was planning something else. Something bigger." She frowns sadly. "It seems I was right."

"Do you know where he might be?" I ask. "The Grand Council hasn't been able to find him."

"Like I said, I haven't seen him in years."

"Yes, but you know him. Better than anyone. Where would he hide?"

Her gaze gets faraway again. She bites the inside of her cheek as she thinks.

A swarm builds inside me—hundreds of small, fluttering worries. What if she knows something but won't help us? What if she's still protecting him? What if we risked so much for nothing? The questions cleave together, coalesce, become a cord that winds tighter and tighter inside me until it nearly strangles my breath. What if Latham gets away with this?

I see the moment an idea occurs to her—a sudden light behind her eyes. A strike of a match in a dark room.

"What is it?" I ask.

She shakes her head. "Probably nothing. But when we were courting . . ." Her voice wobbles, as if thinking of Latham, the way he was then, is painful. "His mother inherited a small shop in Kastelia City. It had been in her family for generations. It changed over the years—it started out as an apothecary, then became a bookstore, and once it had even been a menagerie of sorts—selling colorful songbirds and small furry pets. When Latham and I met, it was a shop that sold a variety of musical instruments—all bone-carved—that would play in tune regardless of the skill of musician."

"You think he'd hide in a music shop?" I ask, confused.

"It had a secret room." Her cheeks flush. "We'd meet there sometimes to be alone."

It seems unlikely, but at least it's something. And maybe whoever works there can tell us something about Latham or his family that will help.

Avalina scrawls the address on a bit of parchment and gives it to me.

"Thank you." Darkness has crept over the room. Rasmus

must be livid by now. I rise to my feet. "We better get going. If you think of anything else . . ."

"Yes," she says as she walks us to the door, "I'll let you know." And then, after a pause: "Be careful. I don't know what he's capable of."

I turn to face her. "Oh, but I do."

She pales. Her shoulders sag. "I'm sorry. Of course, you know. I didn't mean . . ." She trails off. I think about how bright and happy she was when we first arrived, and now she looks wilted, as if we've snatched the sun from her sky. "He was a good man once," she says softly. "He could have been a good man still if only . . ."

I stiffen. "If only what?"

She sighs. "If only his family had accepted his fate. If only the Grand Council hadn't interfered."

"If only he'd made different choices?"

Avalina bites her lip. Nods.

"But isn't that true of everyone?" Bram asks. "Aren't we all just a collection of the choices we've made?"

"Yes," she says, "I guess we are."

Bram hesitates, his hand on the doorknob. "When did you finally lose hope that Latham would change?"

Avalina's expression grows thoughtful. "I suppose when I realized he'd mastered the darkest magic of all—the ability to pretend to be someone he wasn't."

Chapter Fifteen

e step out of Avalina's cottage to frigid air.

Shivers race up and down my body, and I wish I hadn't abandoned my cloak at the glass workshop. I fold my arms across my chest and run my palms along my skin.

Bram shrugs off his Breaker cloak and wraps it around my shoulders. "Here," he says, "this should help." It smells faintly of freshly cut straw from the floor of the Breaker training room.

"But now you'll be cold. I don't want—"

Suddenly his hand closes around my elbow, and he spins me toward him, pressing my back against the tree in front of Avalina's house.

"Saskia," he says, his voice ragged. His eyes search my face.

"May I kiss you?"

The question is low and urgent. My eyes go wide, and I'm flooded with feelings I can't name. They swirl inside me, hot and bright. I think of Bram's gaze falling to my wrist. *If you weren't in love with Declan, then how did you get that tattoo?* I should tell him no. I should try to protect him from Latham. But the tattoo isn't fading, and I'm not sure it ever will. He moves closer, still waiting for my answer. My heart lodges in my throat. I nod.

"Good," Bram says, his breath close to my ear. "Rasmus is coming."

And then Bram's mouth is on mine. Warm. Familiar. His hands slide under my hair and curve around the back of my neck. His thumbs trace the contour of my jaw.

I am drowning in him.

But then understanding slams into me like a blow to the stomach. For a moment I had forgotten our ruse. And yet I gave him permission to kiss me. I *wanted* him to. I long to curl up inside myself and disappear. To love someone who doesn't love you back is an aching thing.

I should pull away, but I don't.

Reality and fantasy melt together, and before I know it, I'm kissing him back. My fingers tunnel through his hair. I let myself imagine I'm the Saskia on my other path, and I pour all of my heartache and longing into the space between us.

And then Bram is yanked away from me. Cold rushes through my body, and I open my eyes to find Rasmus, his face twisted with rage.

"What do you think you're doing?" he shouts. I could ask myself the same question. I try to formulate an answer, but I'm distracted by the vein bulging at his temple. And the stunned expression on Bram's face, two fingers pressed to his lips as if he's not sure what just happened.

"I'm sorry," I say.

"Not as sorry as you're going to be." He shoves my training cloak into my arms. "Put that on, and get back to the inn. *Now.*"

I take off Bram's cloak and give it back to him. Rasmus glowers at me as I wrap my own around my shoulders. It's ice cold, as if he's been wandering through the streets with it for hours.

"I really am sorry—"

He clenches his jaw and gives me a look so severe that I snap my mouth closed.

Bram and I walk in silence, the shadow of Rasmus looming behind us like a threat. Usually, his steps are muffled, but tonight each footfall lands with a thud. I've never seen him so angry.

My feelings are a tangle inside me. I'm not sure what I expected—I knew Rasmus would be angry, but I wasn't counting on him to look so betrayed. Guilt stabs through me like invisible blades.

And I certainly wasn't counting on Avalina to force me to see Latham from a different angle. I thought if we found her, she'd either be his match or his opposite—someone as evil as him, or an innocent victim of his schemes who would be as eager for revenge as I am. I didn't think it was possible that she could make me understand him better. Or at least understand the boy he used to be.

And then there's the dizzying memory of that kiss.

We reach the courtyard of the inn. The cobblestones are bathed in soft pools of yellow lamplight. In the distance I hear the gentle sound of waves lapping against the shore.

I stop at the entrance and turn to face Rasmus. "What now?"

"Now you go to your room and *stay there* until morning."

It's not what I'm asking, and he knows it. I tilt my head and fold my arms across my chest while I wait for a better answer.

"What I should do is escort you directly back to Ivory Hall, where you can explain yourself to Norah." He turns to Bram. "And you too. As a Breaker, you should know better than to disappear with a bodyguard's principal."

Bram drops his chin, looking thoroughly chastened.

"Please don't send us back," I say. "I promise it won't happen again." Rasmus lets out a long sigh, and I see some of the frustration leach out of his expression. I touch his forearm. "I'm sorry I frightened you."

He looks affronted. "I'm a Bone Breaker and a member of the Ivory Guard. I don't *get* frightened."

I let out a soft laugh and then clap my hand over my lips. Mocking him right now is probably not my smartest move. "Well, I *do* get frightened, and you scared me nearly to death back there. One minute I'm kissing Bram and the next I'm staring at your grumpy face." I keep my voice light, teasing.

The corner of Rasmus's mouth twitches. "You'll be seeing

a lot more of my grumpy face if you ever pull a stunt like that again."

I put my hand over my heart. "I swear never to kiss anyone outside your presence ever again."

He snorts. "Let's not go to extremes."

"So you won't tattle on us?"

"I've tried hard not to interfere in your training or your friendships since we left Kastelia City. But this crossed a line."

"I know, I—"

He holds up a hand to stop me and I press my lips together. "You get one free pass. *One.* If anything like this happens ever again, I won't have any choice but to report you to the Grand Council." His expression softens just a fraction. "I'm here to keep you safe, not to restrict your freedom."

I strain to keep my face from showing that, at the moment, those feel like the same thing. I must succeed, because Rasmus gives a sharp dip of his head and then pulls open the inn door. Bram and I share a look behind his back. Bram's expression is part relief, and part something else that I can't name. There's a question in his eyes I don't want to answer.

We climb the stairs and at my door, Bram hesitates. "Saskia—"

"Don't even *think* about it," Rasmus says, giving Bram a little shove toward the boys' room. "I'll see both of you in the morning."

The Fortress is perched on a peak overlooking Leiden. Its gray stone and rounded towers stand in sharp contrast to the movement and color of the glass in the town below. My legs ache as we climb the rough, uneven staircase set into the hillside. The morning is bracingly cold, and my breath precedes me, billowing from my mouth with each labored breath.

Bram hikes wordlessly at my side. A pressure builds between us that feels thick enough to touch. Talon and Tessa are in the front of the pack, talking animatedly about what kind of challenge might be waiting for us today. Tessa keeps throwing glances over her shoulder. We haven't had a private moment to talk since Bram and I snuck out of the glassblowers' workshop, and I know she's anxious to hear about what happened with Avalina. Jacey and Niklas walk several paces behind, and though I can hear the low rumble of voices, their conversation is too quiet to make out. Rasmus follows closer than usual, as if making a point to remind me of his presence.

Finally we reach the top of the hill. The Fortress is protected by an elaborate gate with rails that look like delicate thorn-studded vines, each stretching upward until it curls into a spiral at the top. I would assume the gate was made from wrought iron if not for its pale color. Such elegant beauty seems completely out of place in front of this severe structure.

I reach out to stroke one of the vines, when a throat clears behind me. I yank my hand back and turn to see a Watcher, who seemingly appeared from nowhere. Her hair is completely gray and hangs in a long braid behind her back.

"I wouldn't touch that if I were you," she says. "The thorns are filled with poison."

I take a step back and shove my hands into the pockets of my cloak.

"Whoa," Talon says beneath his breath. "That's one way to ruin a day."

"Welcome to the Fortress," the Watcher says, spreading her arms wide, as if we've arrived for a garden party. "I hope you came prepared." The words are tinged with a warning—maybe even a hint of menace—and our team exchanges nervous glances. How can we prepare when we have no idea what to expect?

The Watcher makes a circle in the air with her hand, and the gate swings open. We follow her toward the front of the Fortress, but before we reach the entrance, she makes a sharp turn to the right and leads us to a steep, narrow stairwell that plunges so low, it could only lead to the dungeon level.

At the top of the steps, she turns to Rasmus. "Stay here. You won't be accompanying the apprentices below."

Normally, I would welcome the break from Rasmus's watchful gaze, but the look of alarm that crosses his expression sends a chill through me.

"You've cleared this with Norah?" Rasmus asks.

The Watcher gives a harsh laugh. "My post, my decision. But yes, she knows." Rasmus's hands curl into fists at his sides, but he takes a step back.

She gives him a curt nod, then turns to the six of us. "Follow me."

We descend the staircase in a single-file line. At the bottom, the Watcher opens the door and moves aside to let us enter. Once we've all stepped over the threshold, she starts to close the door.

"Wait," Tessa says. "What are we supposed to do?"

The Watcher gives a wolfish grin. "Simple," she says. "You're supposed to escape."

With that she slams the door closed.

And locks us in.

Chapter
Sixteen

t takes several moments for my eyes to adjust to the dark room, but slowly shapes emerge, and I'm able to take stock of my surroundings. The room is tiny and overly warm. The walls appear to be made of metal. In the center of the room on top of a small table are three baskets filled with bones.

Jacey smacks the door with the palm of her hand. "Open up! Let us out!" For the first time, I notice that the door is completely smooth. It's missing a handle on this side. "We have to get out of here." Her voice verges on panic. She pounds on the door with both of her fists, and then tries to wedge her fingers into the seam to pry it open.

Tessa lays a hand on Jacey's back. "We'll get out," she says, her voice low and soothing. "We just need to stay calm and figure out what the challenge is."

Jacey's breath is coming in short gasps. She's usually so unruffled.

"I don't do well in enclosed spaces," Jacey says, answering our unspoken questions.

"Let's sit down for a bit," Tessa says, guiding Jacey to a spot against the wall. "Just close your eyes and breathe with me."

I think of my father holding my face between his palms when I was scared. *Deep breaths, bluebird.* A wave of affection washes over me—for both my father and for Tessa. She's a natural Healer.

"If this is anything like the last challenge, we're probably going to need to work together." I touch Tessa's shoulder lightly. "But for now, you take care of Jacey, and the rest of us will start working on how to get out of here."

I join Bram, Niklas, and Talon in the center of the room.

"Where should we start?" I ask.

"Let's find out what kind of bones we have to work with," Bram says, pulling one of the baskets close.

We rifle through the contents, but they're just ordinary human bones—not prepared for magic.

"Are we supposed to assemble a skeleton?" Niklas asks. "Like we do in bone races?"

I rub my forehead. "That would make sense if there were more variety, but without long bones or skulls, there's nothing to assemble."

Talon mops his brow with his sleeve. "If the goal is to get

out of here, maybe we should look for another door."

Niklas leans his forearms against the table. "I doubt it's going to be that simple."

"Or maybe it will be," Talon counters. "Maybe it's like a riddle where the most obvious answer is the correct one."

"Let's just start with a general exploration of the room," Bram says. "Each of us can take a quadrant and look for clues."

"Or doors," Talon says.

Bram laughs. "Or doors."

The four of us peel apart. I head for the far side of the room, but Bram spins in the same direction. Our shoulders collide in the small space.

"Oof." He reaches an arm out to steady me. "Sorry. I thought you were going over there."

"Don't worry about it." I don't quite meet his eyes.

Talon looks back and forth between us. "What's with you two?"

"Nothing," Bram and I answer at the same time.

But Talon doesn't let it go. "Lover's quarrel? You better patch things up quickly; we don't have time for fighting."

The tips of Bram's ears turn scarlet, and he mumbles something before turning and heading in the opposite direction.

The room seems even warmer than when we entered, and I'm not sure if it's my discomfort or if the temperature has actually increased.

I run my palms along the smooth metal of the wall farthest from the entrance, searching for anything that might indicate an escape route. No luck.

I crouch down and my eye catches something—a series of indentations on the floor that look much like the thumbprint locks I've seen on some of the doors at Ivory Hall.

"I think I found something."

Bram, Talon, and Niklas rush to my side. Their upper lips are both beaded with sweat. The room is getting warmer. And smaller, too. Are the walls closing in?

"Is it a door?" Talon asks.

I move to one side and point to the row of depressions. "No, but it could be a lock to one."

Bram runs his fingers along the wall. "There's a seam here. I think Saskia is right. The lock must open this wall."

Niklas crouches down too. "Maybe it works like the puzzle box. Should we all try it together?"

"But there are seven spots and only six of us," Bram says.

My heart sinks. He's right. "Do you think Rasmus was meant to be here after all?"

"I hope not."

Tessa comes up from behind. "What did you find?" She has one arm around Jacey's waist. Jacey's breath is shallow and she looks green around the mouth.

"We're not sure yet," Talon says, then turns to Jacey. "Feeling any better?"

Jacey nods. "A little. I'll be fine once we're out of here."

"Then let's get out of here." He leans down and presses his thumb into one of the indentations and we each do the same. Nothing happens.

"Maybe one of us needs both hands?" Niklas says.

Bram lifts the hem of his shirt and wipes the sweat from his face. "But that doesn't make sense. It seems like they'd give us seven spaces for something that can be solved precisely with an answer of seven."

"No harm in trying," Talon says. So we do.

We each press our thumbs to one of the depressions in the lock. Nothing happens. We try every permutation we can think of—each of us taking turns providing the seventh thumb, different finger combinations, touching the lock one at a time in order of ascending, then descending age. Soon the metal is slick with our sweat. The room seems smaller than ever, and the air is so thick, it's difficult to draw a proper breath.

Finally Bram groans. "I really don't think this is the answer."

"Neither do I," Tessa says. "What else do we have?"

I glance toward the table. "Maybe the bones are the key."

Tessa's expression lights up. "Do any bones come in sets of seven?"

"The cervical vertebrae," Bram and I answer at the same moment. Our eyes meet and something sparks between us.

"Yes!" Tessa jumps up and starts passing around the baskets "Everyone, start looking."

Bram sits next to me on the floor and we dig through the basket together. It's filled with small bones—phalanges, metatarsals, nasal bones. We avoid touching each other as our fingers dart around the basket, but I fight the urge to catch his hand in mine, to force him to look into my eyes, to ask him all the questions that bubble at the back of my mind. *Are you just helping me out of duty? What do you see when you look at me? How could you kiss me like that if you were only pretending?*

But if Latham wins, none of it matters. I'll die whether or not Bram cares about me.

Finally I find a ring-shaped bone—the atlas—and a jolt of triumph goes through me. "Got one."

Jacey waves her hand in the air. "Me too."

"Good," Tessa says, "keep looking."

We help the others search and find precisely seven cervical vertebrae. A weight lifts off my chest. This is the answer. It has to be.

"That was actually kind of satisfying," Talon says as we gather the bones and take them to the far wall. I know what he means. I don't have the sick pit in my stomach I did at Jensen's trial. Solving a riddle is a relief compared to the last challenge. I place the atlas in the first space. Niklas drops the axis in the second, and then we arrange the bones in descending order just as they would sit in the spine.

But the door stays closed. We're pressed shoulder to shoulder. Closer than we were a few moments ago. A wave a dizziness washes over me.

We try putting the bones in reverse order. Still nothing.

The color drains from Jacey's face.

Niklas curses and slams the side of the wall with his fist. "I was sure that was it."

"We all were," Tessa says. She sinks to the floor. "What now?"

The room is sweltering. Sticky. The thought no sooner goes through my mind, when Jacey takes off her purple cloak.

"It's hot in here," she says.

Talon tugs at his collar. "I was just thinking the same thing."

Tessa and I exchange a look. The increased temperature isn't an accident. We need to solve this, and soon.

"I still think the bones are the answer," I say. "They wouldn't be here otherwise."

"Or they're trying to lead us astray," Niklas says.

"They don't *want* us to fail," Tessa says, and I wish I shared her optimism. "Is there another way we could use them? There's nothing here to heal or mix or break. Saskia, maybe you're supposed to do a reading?"

I shake my head. "The bones aren't prepared for magic, and besides, they didn't leave us the appropriate supplies to use them for our specialties." I don't have a basin or flint or a cloth. Jacey doesn't have a mortar and pestle. "There must be another set of bones that make sense in the lock."

"Maybe seven sets of the same bone?" Bram asks.

We scatter and start searching through baskets. We try seven scaphoids, seven lunates, seven capitates. But nothing works.

My hair is wet and plastered to my forehead. A bead of sweat drips down my spine. The air has only gotten warmer and more stifling.

"We're going to die in here," Niklas says dryly.

Tessa shoots him a sharp look and then jerks her head toward Jacey, who sits against the wall, her head between her knees. "Not helpful."

My shoulders ache. I roll my head slowly from side to side.

Then I stretch out my legs and draw an invisible circle in the air with my toes. My ankles crack and I freeze.

"What's wrong?" Bram asks.

"The cervical vertebrae aren't the only set of bones that come in seven."

Bram follows my gaze and a slow smile spreads over his face. "The tarsal bones."

The energy in the room shifts suddenly. Tessa and Niklas both sit up straighter. Jacey lifts her head from her knees.

Talon grabs my foot and plants a kiss on my ankle. "Saskia, you're brilliant and your ankles are lovely."

I laugh and kick him playfully. "You might want to wait to sing my praises until we find out whether or not I'm right. But either way, my ankles appreciate the compliment."

"My darling," Talon says, putting one hand over his heart, "I've always said you had top-notch tarsal bones."

Bram shifts and scratches the back of his neck. There's something in his expression I can't read. He clears his throat. "Let's start looking and see what we can find."

Searching through the baskets is more challenging this time. My palms are so hot and clammy, the bones slide though my fingers like they're covered in butter. I wipe my forehead with the back of my hand.

It takes a while, but finally we gather the seven bones we're looking for: calcaneus, talus, cuboid, navicular, and the medial, middle, and lateral cuneiforms.

We place them in the indentations one at a time. The air is so thick now, I can scarcely breathe. My throat is dry. Bram holds the last tarsal bone between his thumb and index finger. "Everyone ready?"

"Do it," Talon says.

Bram places the bone in the small depression, and suddenly the wall begins to move. Cold air rushes toward us and bathes me in relief. We did it. We escaped.

But when I look up, my stomach plummets. The door doesn't open to the outside.

It leads to another room.

Chapter Seventeen

cy air snatches the breath from my lungs.

The room stretched before us is the polar opposite of the one we're standing in. Bright instead of dim. Frigid instead of sweltering. Vast instead of cramped. I don't dare step over the threshold. But Jacey shoves me aside and practically leaps into the new room, pulling in great gulps of air on the other side.

And then she starts to shiver.

"This doesn't look good," Tessa says.

Bram's jaw tightens. "No, it doesn't."

A loud clang splits through the air, and the doors start to slide closed. We have no choice but to step into the next room, or risk getting trapped on the other side.

Frantically, we gather our things. I scoop up Jacey's discarded cloak along with my own and hurry through the doorway. "Do we have everyone?" I ask.

Niklas is the last to squeeze through before the door slams shut. "Yes," he says, out of breath. "I'm here."

I toss Jacey her cloak and pull my own around my shoulders. My teeth are already chattering. The ceiling soars above us, lit by tiny pinpricks of light that somehow manage to make the room look as if we're standing in full daylight on a cold, cloudless day. I can't tell what the walls are made from, because they're covered in a thick layer of ice.

We move a few steps farther into the room and find a long wooden table with a handful of bones, a mortar and pestle, and tubes full of colorful liquids.

And six *kerata*.

I run a finger over one of the drinking horns, and a knot of anxiety wedges beneath my sternum. These ingredients look completely different from the ones Jacey used to mix the truth serum. So what are they expecting us to drink?

Everyone else must be thinking along the same lines, because we all start talking at once—and every question is directed at Jacey: *What's going on? What kind of potion do you make with these bones? Is this going to hurt?*

"Stop!" Jacey throws her hands in the air. "I don't know. Let me think for a moment."

She examines the ingredients, her lips pressed together. And then she shakes her head. "I've never seen this combination before. I have no idea what it's for."

Talon's eyes go wide. "We can't just drink some mystery potion. What if that's part of the challenge? To see if we're stupid enough to poison ourselves?"

"It wouldn't be here if it weren't necessary," Jacey says. "At least I don't think so."

"Maybe we should hold off on the potion and explore the rest of the room first," Bram says. "It might give us some hint about what Jacey will be mixing."

It's a good idea, and we quickly separate and scour our surroundings. But there's very little to see. The room is stark white, well lit, and utterly empty but for the table. Small prickling sensations dance across my fingertips. Bram's lips are tinged blue. We can't stay in this room long without freezing to death.

"I don't think we have a choice," I say. "We're not going to be able to move forward until we drink."

Tessa tugs at her curls, spinning a lock of hair around her index finger. "You're probably right, but I hate the idea."

Jacey grinds the bones and adds the ingredients one by one. The mixture becomes a paste and then thins to a liquid as she works. Finally she finishes and fills each *keras* one by one.

"Maybe it's a warming potion," Jacey says as she passes them around.

The speculation gives me enough courage to tip the liquid into my mouth. I would do almost anything for a bit of warmth. The potion is sweeter than I was expecting. It tastes good as it slides down my throat. I wait for something to happen, but I feel just as I did before. Cold and all.

"What is that?" Niklas says, his voice filled with revulsion. I follow his gaze and suck in a sharp breath. A hole has opened in the back wall like a giant gaping mouth. Bones dangle from the top and jut up from the bottom.

"Are we supposed to . . . ?" Tessa lifts one hand toward the opening, her sentence trailing off, as if she can't force herself to finish.

"Go in there?" Talon says. "I think so."

Bram scrubs a hand over his face. "I'll go first." He moves forward without waiting for a reply. Just before he reaches the cavity, a wall of fire erupts in front of him. He lets out a startled yelp and jumps back.

And then I hear a noise.

A high-pitched keening. A plea for help in a voice so faint, I could believe I'd imagined it, if not for my own horror reflected in the others' expressions.

"Someone is trapped in there," Bram says. "We have to help them." But he doesn't move. His eyes are tight, his body is rigid. A sudden flash of realization goes through me. Bram's parents died in a fire. This is his worst nightmare.

"Someone else go first," I say, taking Bram's hand in mine and gently turning him away from the flames.

The crying grows more desperate.

Talon runs forward and plunges into the fire. But the moment he makes contact, the blaze transforms into water, rushing over his head, engulfing him. His eyes bulge. Instead of swimming to the surface, he flails in the water, his face a mask of panic.

Bram springs into action, diving into the water and yanking on Talon's arm. But Talon is thrashing so violently that Bram can't get purchase. The two struggle until finally Bram wraps an arm around Talon's neck and pulls him to safety.

The moment Talon is free, the water morphs into fire again, and Bram backs away.

Talon sinks to the ground and begins to cry. Great gulping sobs that make him seem years younger than seventeen years. Tessa crouches beside him and takes his hand in hers. She doesn't say a word; she just sits with him until he calms.

The voice in the fire begins to wail, and my heart pinches tight. How can we help someone we can't find? I'm so cold, I can't think clearly. My mind slows. Turns. Catches the thought before it spins away.

"The flames aren't hot," I say.

The others look at me with blank expressions.

"We're not getting any warmer despite the fire. And look, Talon isn't wet. It's an illusion."

Slow realization dawns over Bram's expression. "Based on our fears."

A band tightens around my throat. I think of Avalina's comment about Latham dabbling in dark magic . . . *bone potions that induce panic if swallowed.*

Tessa squeezes Talon's hand. "Is that true? Are you afraid of water?"

"I almost drowned as a child," he says. His eyes are haunted.

"I'm sorry," Jacey says, her voice small. "If I had any idea what the potion would do, I never would have . . ."

"Don't." I lay a palm on her forearm. "It's not your fault. There was no other way."

Niklas groans. "So what do we do now? How are we supposed to get through that tunnel if we can't even make it inside?"

"I'm guessing it's like the other challenges and we have to find a way to work together," I say, eyeing the flames.

"But how?" he asks.

"The only way out is through," Tessa says, though her voice sounds uncertain.

"Then let's go through," I say.

The six of us join hands in one long chain and march toward the flames. Suddenly I'm worried I was wrong—that the fire isn't just an illusion, that it will scald us the moment we make contact. I hope I'm not leading my teammates to our death. But as we get closer, it doesn't get warmer. Bram's hand trembles in mine.

We step through the blaze into a nightmare. I fight through a wall of smoke so thick, I can scarcely breathe. Panic claws inside me. My parents are somewhere close by. I can feel them. I try to call out, but smoke fills my lungs and I erupt in a coughing fit instead. My eyes sting. And then strong arms close around me. Someone pulling me toward safety. But I don't want to leave without my parents. The fresh air that rushes at me brings relief, but also shame. Flames lick up the side of a cottage. I left them there. A drumbeat grows inside me. *My fault. My fault. My fault.*

A hand tightens around mine, but when I look, there's no one there.

And then I remember. Bram. This is *his* nightmare, and he

needs my help to survive it. I try to open my mouth, but the illusion is too strong. Too real. I force myself to try again—he needs my help.

I squeeze his hand. "You're safe. It's not real, Bram. You're safe."

Abruptly, the vision dissipates. The six of us stand hand in hand at the edge of the cavern. Despite the cold temperature, Bram's face is covered in sweat. He's shaking. The rest of us are too.

"What *was* that?" Talon asks.

"Bram's parents died in a fire," I say quietly. "He was very young."

Bram's expression changes. His eyes are soft, alive with some new realization. His fingers tighten briefly around mine before he lets go.

"Whoa," Talon says. "That must have been . . ." He shifts his weight from one foot to the other, his face full of emotion. He was obviously as immersed in Bram's memory as I was, and he looks shaken. Talon claps him on the shoulder. "I'm so sorry."

Bram nods in acknowledgment.

Niklas clears his throat. "Should we keep going? If we wait, I'll lose my nerve."

We move into the mouth of the opening. Bones dangle from the roof like icicles and push up from the floor like spikes. It's too narrow a space to join hands, so we move single file, staying as close as possible to one another.

Jacey takes the lead, placing each foot carefully. We all seem to have the same instinct to avoid contact with the bones. I try to step precisely where she steps, moving as cautiously as possible through the space. It seems to be working.

And then Jacey trips.

I reach out to steady her, but I'm not fast enough. Jacey's hand juts out and grabs one of the bones near her knee. She yelps as it stabs her palm.

We all freeze. Jacey presses on the wound with her opposite hand. A fat drop of blood falls to the floor.

And the world goes dark.

I'm swept off my feet and stuffed into a tight space. My knees are wedged beneath my chin, and my back aches as if I've been in the same position for hours. Rough fabric covers my face, scratching at my cheeks and pulling toward my mouth with every breath. My entire body sways slightly as if—cold horror seeps into me—as if I'm stuffed in a bag dangling from a tree. I try to claw my way out, kick my feet, raise my arms above my head, but the space is too tight, and the only thing I succeed in doing is making the bag swing more violently.

My nose is filled with the scent of rot and death.

Nausea pushes up my throat. How did I get here? My thoughts spin wildly, grasping for something just out of reach. I'm too constricted to think clearly.

I don't do well in enclosed spaces.

Jacey. As soon as her face floats into my mind, I hear a piercing scream next to me. It's as if my mind has punched through the illusion and allowed a pinprick of reality to seep in.

This isn't real, I tell myself. *My feet are on solid ground. There's nothing blocking my nose or mouth. It's not real.*

Slowly, the room comes back into focus. Jacey is crouched at my feet, rocking back and forth, her fist shoved into her mouth. Tessa are Niklas are both curled in a fetal position. Bram and Talon stand near each other, wide-eyed and frozen. I wonder if we're all experiencing precisely the same thing, or if the potion works with each of our minds to create something unique—a custom-tailored agony.

I kneel next to Jacey and wrap my arm around her shoulders. "Jacey, can you hear me? It's Saskia."

Her head tilts in my direction, but she doesn't stop moving. "It's not real, Jacey. You're safe."

I keep talking softly to her, and gradually her eyes focus. "Saskia?"

I squeeze her arm. "Welcome back. Now help me with the others."

As we remind the others of where they are, of what is real and what isn't, Bram's words float through my mind: *The Fortress doesn't train soldiers to fight. It trains them to survive torture.*

And I realize I lied to Jacey earlier. She's not safe.

None of us are.

We wouldn't have the courage to move forward if not for the cold. But my skin prickles with needling sensations. What if the cold is causing irreparable damage? We have to keep going.

The cavern has so many twists and turns, it's impossible to know how far we have left to go. Each time we turn a corner, I'm hopeful we might see the exit, but so far, it's been nothing but an endless maze of fear.

Avoiding the bones is the only strategy that makes sense, but it's nearly impossible to execute. Niklas brushes against the tip of one bone while trying to dodge another, and suddenly a sea of enormous spiders emerges from the floor and races across our toes. Tessa screams and tries to kick them away. But her foot makes contact with another bone, and we're subjected to an image of her father—drunk and raging—that makes us all feel as if we're five years old, helpless and scared.

"I can't do this," Tessa says, once we've finally managed to pull ourselves from the illusion.

"You can," I tell her. "You are."

But I'm not sure I can do it either. My nerves are stretched so thin, I feel like I'm fraying at the edges.

As horrible as the hallucinations have been, none of them have belonged to me yet, and waiting—worrying about what might manifest—is its own kind of torture. Will I see the prison boat? Gran's death? My mother's?

Does it count as a fear if it's already happened?

Maybe if I'm very careful, I can avoid getting sucked into an illusion.

The terror would be bad enough, but giving my teammates a glimpse into the dark recesses of my mind—to have all my protective layers peeled away until I'm laid bare—is even more frightening. What would they think of me if they knew I was using unbound magic? Would they see me differently if they knew how often I fantasize about making Latham suffer?

I move slowly, keeping my arms tucked at my sides, watching every step. A variety of smaller illusions jump out at us as we brush past the bones—a group of peers mock us from the sidelines, calling us cowards and laughing at our failures. The floor in front of us seems to vanish, leaving us perched on the edge of precipice. We fail apprenticeships and get sent back home without our cloaks.

Finally we round another bend and an exit comes into view. Hope leaps in my chest, and I quicken my pace, mindful to place my feet carefully.

"Saskia!" Bram's hand shoots out to grab my wrist. "Watch your head."

But he's too late. A razor-sharp bone grazes my scalp. I let out a startled cry of pain and press a palm to my head. My hand comes away bloody. No.

If I can just get to the exit . . .

I start to run, heedless of the other bones. I keep my gaze glued to the spill of light ahead that gleams like a ray of hope.

And then Latham steps into the cavern. His hands are shoved casually into the pockets of his cloak, and he gives me a smile that manages to look carefree and menacing at the same time.

"Hello, Saskia," he says. "Going somewhere?"

My muscles go rigid.

"You're not real," I tell him. "You're just a figment of my imagination."

He laughs—a genuine laugh, as if I've actually amused him. "Am I? I had no idea. Then what a marvelous imagination you must have."

A chill inches down my spine. "You aren't here."

"Of course I am." He takes a step toward me. Not real. Not

real. But no matter how I try to convince myself, the illusion won't dissipate. He takes another step. I shrink away, and back into Bram. He puts a reassuring hand on my shoulder.

"Don't listen to him. You're all right."

But wait. Remembering that Bram is here should be enough to pull me back to reality. That's how it worked with all the other fears.

My pulse is erratic. Does this mean it's not an illusion? Is Latham really here?

"Go," I tell him. "My friends won't let you kill me. Not here. Not now."

"Oh, I disagree—I think now is the perfect time. You've spent the last several hours terrified." His eyes flick to Bram. "And you've never been more in love. Your bones would be particularly powerful if I killed you now."

He takes another step in my direction, and I make a small noise at the back of my throat. Bram's hand tightens around my shoulder. "Saskia, look at me. He can't reach you."

I start to turn toward Bram, when Latham pulls a knife from a sheath at his waist. It looks exactly like the weapon he used to stab my mother. My ears fill with a roaring sound. He spins the knife in the air, catches the handle deftly in his palm. Throws it again.

"How would you like to do this, my dear?" Latham asks. "Any thoughts?"

My mouth goes dry. "How would I like to do what?"

He rolls his eyes, as if I've taxed his patience by asking a silly question. "How would you like to die? I could kill each of your friends one by one in front of you. Or I could kill you first so they have the horror of watching you die slowly. Which would be worse for you, I wonder?"

"Bram," I say softly, "take the others and run."

I hear movement behind me, but I can't make myself look away from Latham, who is nearly close enough to touch. I hope they listened to me. I hope they're getting as far from here as possible.

Latham strides forward and lifts my chin with the tip of the knife. "I heard you visited Avalina," he says. "A clever idea, but ultimately useless. You can't run, Saskia. And you'll never be able to hide well enough that I can't find you."

He presses the blade against my throat. I feel a trickle of blood drip toward my collarbone, and tears gather in my eyes. I wanted so badly to get Gran's and my mother's bones back. To stop Latham. To make him pay for everything he's done.

But I failed.

It's the last thought I have before Latham's knife slices into my neck and the world goes dark.

Chapter
Eighteen

"askia, can you hear me?"

The voice sounds faraway. My mind is slow and heavy, as if it's wrapped in a thick layer of gauze.

A warm palm rests on my cheek. I turn my head and lean closer.

"Saskia?"

My eyes flutter open. Bram's face hovers above mine, his brows drawn together.

"I'm not dead," I say.

He gives a tense laugh. "No, you're not dead."

"But Latham . . . he was here. He was about to kill me."

Bram shakes his head. "It was only an illusion."

I pull myself into a sitting position. "No, this was different. I didn't get sucked into a vision. I knew where I was. Latham was here. I'm sure of it." My voice trembles.

"It only felt real," Bram says. "Think about it. If he was here, where did he go? He couldn't have just disappeared."

"But he knew things," I say, and then I lower my voice to a whisper. "Like how we visited Avalina."

"No, *you* knew those things, and your mind used them to conjure up your worst fears. You're safe, Saskia, I promise."

But I'm not convinced. I press my fingers to my throat and they come away with a faint smear of blood.

A shiver goes through me.

"Just a scratch from one of the bones," Bram says. I can still feel the press of Latham's blade against my windpipe. What are the chances that a bone grazed my skin in that exact location? Master Kyra's words dart through my mind. *Whoever designed that challenge wasn't pulling any punches, were they?* What if Latham is designing our games? But he couldn't be . . . unless someone at Ivory Hall gave him access to me. A lump forms in my throat. I hate not knowing who I can trust.

Bram studies my face, and his eyes go soft. "You're safe now, I promise."

He's wrong, but there's no point arguing with him, so I swallow my worry and take in my surroundings. We're in a different room—a warmer one. I have feeling in my hands again. I stretch my fingers wide and curl them into fists. "How did I get here?"

"We couldn't shake you out of the vision, so I carried you," he says. "I thought it might help to be away from the bones."

I feel my cheeks pinken, and I drop my gaze. "Did we finish the challenge, then?"

Bram pulls on the back of his neck. "I'm afraid not. But we're hoping this is the final area." He points to a window high above our heads that deposits a disk of sunlight on the floor. We must be close to the outside. Bram offers me his hand and pulls me to my feet.

The room is in the shape of a pentagon, with all five walls made of thick stone, and a round table in the center where the others are gathered, examining our available supplies. When Bram and I join them, Tessa reaches for my hand and laces her fingers through mine.

"That was intense," she says. "How are you doing?"

"I've been better." I glance around the table. "But I suspect that's true for all of us."

"Wasn't that one of the instructors at Ivory Hall in your hallucination?" Talon asks.

I swallow. "He was. Not anymore."

"Does he really want you dead?"

The question cracks something open inside me. Something about hearing the words said aloud gives them even more power.

"Yes." I fold my arms across my chest, as if it might help me feel less exposed.

"Why?" Jacey asks.

"It doesn't matter. Let's just figure out how to get out of here."

Jacey's face goes tight. "Saskia—"

"Please," I say, and my voice comes out strained, "let's just finish the challenge." My teammates stare at me, wordless. For a moment, I worry they might push me to reveal more than I want to. And if they push me right now, I might shatter. My soul feels as tender as a fresh burn.

A slow, silent beat passes. And then finally Bram stands and scrubs at his eyes with the heels of his hands. "I agree with Saskia. Let's finish this and go home."

His words hit me at an odd angle. Home. He must mean Ivory Hall, but a pulse of longing for Midwood goes through me that snatches the breath from my lungs. I want to go home. I want my mother so much that it hurts.

I have to focus.

We examine the items on the table.

They seem straightforward—the femur of a raven, carving tools, a handful of smaller bones. And at least the temperature is normal.

Niklas picks up the femur. "This one is obviously prepared for me," he says, and then inclines his head toward Talon. "I'm guessing I'm supposed to carve a flute for you."

"There must be a raven outside that I need to control," Talon says.

"Do you think it's hurt?" Tessa asks.

Talon cocks his head to one side. "Why would it be hurt?"

Tessa scoops up the small bones in her palm. "These are prepared for healing. I'm trying to figure out why we'd need them."

"I guess it's possible," Talon says.

"Maybe we should start with what we know for sure," Bram says. "Niklas, how long will it take you to carve a bone flute?"

"It's a small one, so I should be able to do it in a few hours."

Jacey groans. "Hours? I was really hoping you could have it done faster."

I bite my lip and pace back and forth. "It doesn't have to be fancy. It just needs to work."

A muscle jumps in his jaw. "Have you ever met a Mason? I can't just snap my fingers and magic the thing into existence. Carving takes time."

Niklas sits at the table and begins to work. The knife moves deftly in his hands, bone dust drifting on the tabletop like snow as he whittles. The rest of us explore the room, hoping for some other clue of how to escape, but it seems we can't do anything else until the bone flute is finished.

Eventually Jacey curls up in a corner and falls asleep. I wish I could do the same, but I doubt I could rest right now if my life depended on it. My mind is still reeling, tripping over my worries. The vision of Latham felt real in a way that the other illusions didn't. Maybe it was the same for all the apprentices— that their own fears were more alive than the fears of someone else. But still, my stomach feels like a writhing nest of snakes.

Finally Niklas holds up the femur bone and blows on it gently to remove the last of the dust. "Finished."

The flute is delicate. Beautifully carved. And suddenly I'm impressed that Niklas could create such a thing in so little time instead of frustrated he couldn't make it faster. Niklas gives the instrument to Talon.

"Moment of truth," Talon says. He brings the flute to his mouth and plays a sorrowful melody. A few moments later, a dark shape darts in front of the window. A flap of black wings. A gentle tap of a beak against the glass.

Jacey presses her palms together. "Thank the bones it's working."

"What do you see?" Tessa asks. But Talon ignores her and keeps playing. The bird disappears from sight. The tune goes on and on, and it feels like a raven—like sadness and bad omens and death. But it's also beautiful.

The melody drifts away and Talon lowers the flute. "There's a lever on the outside of the building that opens the door," he says. "The raven wasn't strong enough to lower it."

"Then how do we get out?" Jacey asks.

Talon goes to the far wall and runs his palms along the stones. "There must be a way to access the lever from this room. If I could just find a loose section—" One of the stones wiggles a bit, and Talon's eyes light up. He yanks harder and the stone comes away in his hand.

"And that's how it's done." He places one arm over his waist and gives a deep bow, as if he's onstage.

We give him a smattering of applause and his face breaks out in a wide grin.

Tessa peers through the opening. "So where is the lever?"

"It should be below," Talon says.

Tessa sticks her arm through the hole in the wall. "I can't find it."

My heart sinks. I should have known it wouldn't be

straightforward. Every time we think we have a solution, the ground seems to shift beneath our feet. Talon picks up the bone flute. "Let me see if I can guide you to it." He plays a short melody then lowers the instrument. "I don't think your arm is long enough. It's directly below you, but I'm not sure you can reach it."

"Who has the longest arms?" Tessa asks.

"Bram," Jacey and I say at the same moment.

But when Bram tries, he isn't any more successful than Tessa was.

"There must be something we're missing," Niklas says. "Maybe it's about who is more flexible?"

"Let me try," I say. I reach through the opening, my fingers trailing along the cool stone of the Fortress. I push my arm as far as it can go, until my shoulder is shoved against the inside wall at a painful angle. And my fingers brush against metal.

"Yes, Saskia, you've almost got it," Talon says, taking the flute from his mouth for moment. But no matter how much I strain, I can't quite reach far enough to push the lever all the way down.

"It's just right there," I say. "If my arm were just a bit more malleable—" The solution presents itself. I pull my arm back inside. "Bram, I think you have to have to break my humerus."

He recoils. "What? Absolutely not. I would never."

"We have no choice. I can almost reach the lever. If you wait until I'm in position, the break will give me a few more inches, and my arm should fall with enough pressure to lower the lever."

His face is a mask of horror. "We do have a choice. I'm not

going to use bone magic to hurt you."

I touch his elbow. "Hear me out. I used my magic in the first challenge to do a bone reading. Jacey has used hers twice to mix potions. Niklas carved the flute. Talon controlled the bird. But you haven't used your specific gifts yet."

He yanks away from me. "This is ridiculous. Neither has Tessa."

My gaze goes toward the bones on the table. The ones Tessa said were for healing.

Understanding dawns over Tessa's expression. "Saskia, no. I can fix the bone after it's broken, but I can't stop it from hurting in the first place. It would be excruciating."

"Yes, I know. I can handle it."

"Please don't ask me to do this," Bram says.

I give him a sad smile. "Too late. I already asked you."

He rakes his fingers through his hair as he paces across the length of the room. "This can't be how they intended us to escape."

I give a bitter laugh. "After that last room, I'm amazed you can say that with a straight face."

He stills. His lips part, but he doesn't speak.

"This has been a cruel challenge," I say. "I think this is exactly how they intended us to escape."

Niklas sighs and sinks into a chair. "I hate to say it, but I think she's right."

"Tessa?" The tightness in Bram's voice makes it sound more like a plea than a question.

Tessa closes her eyes and massages her forehead. "I wish I

could think of another solution, but I can't."

Bram spins back in my direction. His eyes flash with anger. "This is barbaric."

"I agree. But you said yourself that this place was built to train soldiers to withstand torture. So, let's withstand it." I shove my arm through the opening, wincing as I rotate my shoulder out of place. My fingers graze the top of the lever. "I'm ready."

Bram moves close to me. "I hate this," he whispers.

"I know. Me too."

"Saskia—"

"Just do it," I say. "Now, please."

Agony shoots through my arm as it snaps with a sickening crack. I scream. My limp hand slams into the lever.

And nothing happens.

I let out a choked sob. All that pain for nothing. But then a metallic screech pierces the air. The wall begins to move on both sides, splitting apart like a banana peel, and I quickly step to the side to avoid being dragged along. The additional motion is excruciating. It hurts so much more than I was expecting. I need to extricate my arm from the opening, but I can't move it. I try and fail to bite back a whimper.

Bram's hand finds the small of my back. "I've got you," he says, lifting my arm and gently guiding it through the opening. My eyes find his. "I'm so sorry." He looks like he's about to be sick.

"Don't be," I tell him. "It worked."

Tessa appears beside me. "I need a bit of your blood for

the healing spell." Her voice is all business, but her face is streaked with tears. She takes my uninjured hand in hers and pricks the pad of my finger with a sewing needle. A bright red drop wells at the surface and she squeezes it onto the bones. "Almost done."

A few moments later a wave of relief washes over me, and I'm not sure I've ever felt anything sweeter.

"Better?" Tessa asks.

"Yes," I say, giving her a weak smile. "Much better."

"It's going to be achy for a few days," Tessa says. "You should avoid moving it as much as possible."

Bram takes off his shirt and wraps it around my arm, creating a makeshift sling. He ties the ends around my neck. His breathing is ragged. He's close enough that I can feel the heat coming off his bare chest, and it makes my own breath go uneven.

"Is that comfortable?"

I can't trust myself to speak, so I just nod. Our eyes meet briefly and then Bram pulls his gaze away and puts his cloak back on.

"Should we get out of here?" Niklas asks.

The doors are fully open, and the fresh air, cold as it is, has never felt more welcoming.

I thought I'd seen the worst of Rasmus's temper when Bram and I snuck away, but I was mistaken. When he sees my arm in the sling, and finds out what happened, he screams at the Watcher who locked us in the Fortress until I'm stunned he has any voice left at all.

"How could you let this happen?" he shouts. "They are children, not soldiers." He punches a fist in the air. "It's grotesque, what you've done, and I promise you haven't heard the end of it."

Somehow his rage is a balm to my wounded soul. His words flow over me like a lullaby, making me feel treasured and protected.

"Look at her," the Watcher says, unfazed. "She's fine."

Rasmus's face goes bright red. "She's fine? *She's fine?* Her arm was just broken."

The Watcher shrugs. "Not for long. No permanent damage."

I think of Latham striding toward me with a knife in his hand. Of Jacey's panicked cries as she struggled inside the dark belly of a burlap death bag. Of Bram watching a fire consume someone he couldn't help.

And I wonder if the Watcher knows she's lying.

Just because no one can see it, doesn't mean there isn't any permanent damage.

Chapter Nineteen

he trip back to Ivory Hall feels completely different from the trip to Leiden. Less worried, but more somber. It's only been a few days since we were on the ship, but it feels like years. The impressions we had of one another when we left the capital have shattered, the broken pieces rearranging into a more complex, more broken picture.

But a more beautiful one too.

We sit on the deck of the ship, our shoulders hunched against the icy wind.

"Do you ever think it might not be worth it?" Niklas asks. "Bone magic, I mean."

Jacey pulls her cloak more tightly around her shoulders. "I

wonder that all the time. Especially lately."

"Maybe that's the point of the bone games," Tessa says thoughtfully. "To see who really wants it and who doesn't."

"So which are you?" Talon asks.

Tessa shrugs. "I'm not sure."

Talon indicates the space between me and Bram. "How about you two?"

The way he asks the question—like we'd both have the same answer—makes me realize we never corrected the impression among the group that we aren't a real couple. I wait for Bram to say something, but he doesn't.

I find a loose string on the hem of my cloak sleeve and wrap it tightly around my finger. "I don't think either of us knows what we want yet."

Bram turns toward me, his face limned by the setting sun, his eyes liquid. "Don't we?"

I search his expression for the answer to that question, but just like the illusions in the Fortress, I can no longer tell what's real and what's not.

Bram's heart is a puzzle box that I don't know how to open.

Jacey turns toward me, her hair gathered in her fist to keep it from blowing in her face. "So, will you tell us now?"

I raise my eyebrows in a question. Is she talking about me and Bram? Am I that transparent?

"Tell you what?"

"Why Latham wants you dead?"

The question makes something inside me recoil. I think of times I've trusted too easily and been betrayed. Like with

Declan. And on my other path, by Latham himself. But as I look around at their faces, I see my own fear and vulnerability reflected in their expressions. We are all raw and hurting. All of us had our secrets exposed in the Fortress. If I can't trust them, then I can't trust anyone.

So I take a deep breath and I tell them the truth.

The story spins out of me like a dropped ball of yarn. Some details unfurl quickly. Others tangle and jumble in the telling. By the end, my voice is as raw as my emotions.

My teammates sit quietly for a moment, digesting the details of my mother's death. Of Gran's.

"There's more," I say. "I think Latham is designing our challenges." The idea began to take shape in my mind after I saw Latham in the Fortress. And the more I've thought about it, the more I've become convinced. After the first trial, the other teams came back to Ivory Hall talking of mazes and obstacle courses, while our team got a challenge that seemed tailor-made to torment me with visions of a future spent on Fang Island. And after the horror of this last trial, I know I'm right. Latham must be using the bone games to torture me, to make my bones more powerful before I die.

"But that's impossible," Jacey says. "He couldn't design them unless—"

"Unless there's a traitor on the Grand Council who gave him control," I finish for her. "Yes, I know."

She sucks a sharp breath through her teeth. "Who?"

"I don't know," I say. "Maybe the Bone Charmer? He seemed to be watching me especially carefully during our first trial. Like he was enjoying my discomfort. But until we know, we need to be careful."

Tessa frowns. "We need to tell Norah. She can help protect you."

"Absolutely not," I say. "She reports to the Grand Council, and if she doesn't believe us, it could backfire."

"She'll believe us," Tessa says. "She cares about your safety. That's why she hired Rasmus. It's why . . ." She trails off, twirling a finger around a lock of her hair.

I sit up straighter. "You told Norah you'd spy on me." The moment the words leave my mouth, I know I'm right.

Tessa's hands drop to her lap. She turns to me, crestfallen. "No, it wasn't like that. Before you arrived, I agreed to look out for you. Make sure you were adjusting." Her gaze slides away. "And let Norah know how it was going."

Bitterness hits the back of my throat.

"Those are just pretty words for spying. It was exactly like that."

And then I think about how Bram waited outside the training room after my first session. About Norah whispering something to him before he joined our team. And suddenly it all clicks into place. I spin toward him and he flinches. The guilt is written all over his face.

"You too?" A swift waterfall of disappointment floods over me.

"Norah was trying to protect you," he says. "We all were."

I stare at him in stunned silence as he studies me with an expression full of questions. But I don't have any answers.

After everything I just confessed to them, I feel as if I've been kicked in the stomach, as if all the air has left my lungs.

Maybe it's my fate to be betrayed by everyone I care about.

"I was wrong," Tessa says. Her voice is small and soft. "I didn't know you then. I do now. And I won't tell Norah another thing without your permission, I promise."

"I promise too," Bram says.

I look back and forth between them. My heart feels made of lead. But I know what it is to have secrets. I have plenty of my own.

Talon lays a palm on my arm. "We won't let Latham hurt you." It's such an earnest statement that it makes my throat feel thick with tears.

"I'm not sure you can stop him."

Niklas leans forward, his elbows resting on his knees. "We can try."

"There are six of us and only one of him," Jacey adds.

Tessa puts an arm around my waist. "You don't have to do this by yourself."

I've felt alone for so long now that being surrounded by people who care about me is an unfamiliar sensation. But a welcome one.

"What do you need from us?" Jacey asks.

I wipe at my eyes. "I'm not sure yet."

The ship turns slightly. Jacey lets go of her hair, and the wind lifts it, blowing it behind her like a banner. "When you decide, let us know. We'll do whatever it takes to keep you safe."

I close my fist around the pendant Avalina gave me. "I don't know what to say."

Tessa nudges my knee with her own. "Just say 'thank you.'"

So I do.

Chapter Twenty

After surviving the Fortress, returning to my training at Ivory Hall feels false. Like I'm only pretending to practice bone magic.

Master Kyra leans against the table in the training room, watching as I tip a basin full of aviary bones—keel, rib, coracoid—onto the cloth in front of me and study them.

I started flame readings earlier this week. At least Master Kyra *thinks* I started them.

Master Kyra has given me a series of tasks—divining who would enter the room next, how many Mixer apprentices were crowded into the adjoining room, which bones the Masons were carving across the hall. I haven't made a mistake yet.

"You're making wonderful progress, Saskia," she says. "Your mastery tattoo should appear soon. Any sign of it yet?"

The question knocks me off-balance, as if an hourglass has been tipped over and it's only a matter of time before the sand stops flowing. How long until she actually checks for the tattoo and realizes I've broken the law? How long before I end up on Fang Island?

Or maybe Latham will get to me first. Either way, my fate seems bleak.

I put my hand into the pocket of my cloak and run my fingers over the parchment Avalina gave me. The address is the only lead I have for finding Latham. And finding him is a yawning need inside me. A hole that won't be filled until one of us is dead.

I look up to see Kyra studying me with a quizzical expression. She's still waiting for an answer about the mastery tattoo.

"No sign of it yet," I say.

She smiles. "Don't worry. It should be there any day now."

My gaze goes to the window and the rushing water of the Shard below. I feel like a tree branch caught in the current—bobbing along on the swells of fate, powerless to change direction. But maybe it doesn't have to be that way. I need to take control.

It's time to become the river.

"I'm going to find Latham," I tell my team later that night over the evening meal.

Talon pauses, a seasoned potato wedge halfway between his plate and his mouth. "Right now?"

"Not this very moment. In the morning. We have a few days before the next challenge, so the timing seems right."

Tessa wipes her fingers on a napkin. "What's your plan?"

I hesitate—what if she reports me to Norah? Tessa's mouth thins. She sets the napkin beside her plate. "I'm on your side, Saskia. I promised no more secrets, and I meant it."

I believe her, and yet my first instinct is to guard information carefully—pull it close to my chest and curl my entire body around it. But I fight the urge and answer her question. "I'll leave early enough that no one will be awake yet. Other than that, I'm not sure there's a plan to be made. All I have to go on is the address of a shop in the city. If I don't find anything there, it's a dead end."

"But what if you do find something?" she asks. "After seeing that vision of Latham in the Fortress . . ." She shivers. "Saskia, you can't go alone."

Bram tenses beside me. "I'll go with you."

"Yes," Tessa agrees. "Me too."

"Count me in," Niklas says.

My chest feels tight. "No, you guys, I can't put you all in danger."

"I don't mind a little danger," Talon says. "It makes me feel tougher than I am."

Jacey stabs a piece of roast beef with her fork. "It won't work. They lock the doors at night."

"How do you know?" Talon asks.

"My brother almost got expelled for trying to sneak out when he was here a few years ago. The doors were locked, and when he tried to leave, it set off some kind of silent alarm system."

My heart sinks. "Oh. Well, I guess I do need a plan then."

"They don't lock the upper-floor windows," Jacey says. She pops the meat into her mouth and chews slowly.

Bram shoots her an exasperated look. "Yes, because no one would be stupid enough to try to climb out a window that far from the ground."

Jacey swallows her food and grins at him. "If they had the right tools, they might be exactly that stupid." She uses her fork to point at Niklas. "Tell them what you've been working on."

Niklas pushes his hair out of his face. "Bone-carved climbing equipment. For hikers."

"Or for scaling walls," Jacey says, her expression triumphant.

Talon blanches, which makes his freckles stand out in even sharper relief against his pale skin. "When I said I didn't mind a little danger, I meant a *very* little. Doors are more my style than heights."

I ignore Talon and lean across the table toward Niklas. "Is that possible? Could you get the tools for us?"

He shifts uncomfortably in his seat. "I don't know, Saskia. It would require sneaking into one of the training rooms and stealing them. I could get in a lot of trouble."

His uneasy expression should be all the answer I need— Niklas isn't one to say no without a reason. But I need to find information—some clue about where Latham could have hidden my mother's bones. And then I need to make him suffer for what he's done.

"We'll put the tools back before anyone knows they're missing," I say.

"I'm not sure—"

"Please, Niklas. This is important."

A heavy silence settles over our table. Niklas fidgets with the ring on his index finger, spinning it around and around with the opposite hand.

Finally he looks up without quite meeting my gaze. "I'll see what I can do."

Niklas leaves the table and I feel as if I've swallowed a brick. It's more than I should ask of him. But I can't ask anything less. Tessa bites her lip. "I don't like this," she says.

"Do you think I'm making a mistake by trying to find Latham's shop?"

"No, of course not." Tessa massages her temples. "I just didn't think we'd have a plan quite this ... morally ambiguous."

I put an arm around Tessa's shoulders. "We don't all have to go, you know. I won't hold it against you if you don't come along."

She leans into me. "Of course I'm coming. I just wish we had a better option."

"So do I."

And it's true. I feel as if I've spent my whole life wishing for better options.

Three long days pass while Niklas tries to get his hands on the climbing equipment. The entire time, I'm so impatient that I want to crawl out of my skin. But finally he comes through with six sets of grips fashioned from the bones of black bears and shaped like claws.

We're gathered in the room Tessa and I share, staring at the window. The horizon is just visible in the predawn sky. We decided to leave in the wee hours of the morning. The instructors are more vigilant at night when they expect rebellious apprentices might attempt to sneak out. I doubt they'd anticipate an escape at dawn. And our presence in town is less likely to cause suspicion in daylight. If we can manage a clean getaway, it will give us a few hours before we're expected to be anywhere.

But now I'm second-guessing myself. The ground is alarmingly far away.

"These are called descenders," Niklas says, handing a set to each of us. "You'll want to make sure at least one stays in contact with the outside wall at all times. And don't look down."

"You're sure they work?" Talon asks. He shifts his weight from one foot to the other. "I'd really rather not die today."

"As sure as I can be, considering I've never tested them," Niklas says.

Talon's eyes bulge. He swallows. "A simple yes would have sufficed."

Niklas goes first, reaching through the window to anchor one of the descenders to the wall before climbing out. He starts to descend, sliding the claws down one at a time, moving faster than I would have thought possible for such a long distance. He drops to the ground below and he's so small, I can barely see his hand moving as he waves up at me.

My mouth goes dry. His quick descent made it look easy, but every time I glance out the window, I feel like I might be sick. But I have to go next. I can't ask my friends to put themselves in danger if I'm not willing to do the same. I close my eyes and take a deep breath. Then I try to imitate Niklas as precisely as I can, placing one of the tools on the wall before carefully lifting myself through the window.

But I make the mistake of looking down.

The ground spins beneath me and I gasp. My sweaty palm slips on one of the claws and I lose my grip. It stays attached to the wall while my body flings outward. I'm dangling by one hand. I'm going to plunge to my death. My vision goes blurry and I squeeze my eyes closed. My heart slams against my rib cage.

"Hang on," Bram says. "You're doing fine."

I pull in a deep breath, and with all the force I can muster, I swing my body back toward the window. My fingertips graze the tool stuck to the wall, but I can't quite reach it. I try again. This time I get closer and my fingers close around claw, but my torso slams against the wall with a thunk. It hurts, but still a wave of relief goes through me. I press my entire body against the bone facade, but I don't move. I don't dare. What if my hand slips again? My pulse pounds in my neck. I'm not close enough to the window to climb back in, but the ground is so distant that one wrong move would end me. So I cling to the side of the building, frozen.

"Saskia, look at me." Bram's voice is gentle but commanding.

I lift my eyes to his. "Good," he says. "Now slide your right hand down just a bit."

I bite the inside of my cheek and inch my hand down without ever taking my gaze from him.

"Yes. Now your other hand."

Soon I find a rhythm—one hand and then the other—until my toes touch the ground. I sink onto the grass and pull my knees to my chest, shaking as I watch the others scramble down the wall.

The sun has fully risen by the time everyone is on the ground. But before we set off, Niklas quietly collects the tools from each of us and carefully places them in his satchel. Guilt worms through my stomach. He's obviously worried about what we've done.

I touch his elbow lightly. "Thank you."

He nods. "I hope you find what you're looking for."

I pull out the parchment Avalina gave me and offer it to Talon. Watchers are notoriously good with directions. It's a must for controlling animals. "Will you lead the way?"

He snatches the page from my fingers. "Yes. I'll do anything you ask as long as my feet can stay on solid ground."

We hike down a path behind Ivory Hall in the opposite direction of the pier and I agonize about our half-baked plan the entire time. What if we don't find the shop Avalina told us about? What if I risked Niklas's future for nothing? And then we round a bend and the city comes into view. Awe snatches away my worry.

I've seen Kastelia City dozens of times in different readings, but I've never spent any time exploring on my own. My experience with the capital has been limited to the pier and the view from Ivory Hall.

A beautiful stone bridge arches gracefully over the Shard, and couples walk hand in hand on the cobbled streets that run alongside the river. Sunlight glints on the water. Farther ashore, the boulevard is lined with small shops and bundled shoppers. A flash of memory: warmer weather, full trees, flower boxes spilling colorful blooms perched in every window. I don't know if I'm remembering my own experiences on my other path or recalling a reading from someone else, but Kastelia City feels both familiar and foreign. Both exactly what I expected, and nothing like I thought.

Talon leads the group, and when he stops walking to study the parchment I gave him earlier, I'm forcefully pulled back to reality.

"I think it's just up this way," he calls over his shoulder.

"Relax," Jacey says, "before you break that in half."

I follow her gaze and, with a start, realize that my fist is closed around the pendant at my throat. My fingers went there without my permission, needing the comfort of knowing I'm safe from Latham's prying gaze. My stomach clenches and I drop my arm back to my side.

We pass storefronts painted in bold colors—cobalt, seafoam, coral—with their names brushed in swirling gold script. Outdoor stalls selling bouquets of flowers and fresh vegetables. Magic shops filled with shelves of bones already prepared for a variety of uses.

Finally Talon stops in front of a nondescript shop with peeling white paint and darkened windows. "It looks abandoned."

"I don't suppose anyone knows how to pick a lock?" I say, trying not to let despair creep into my voice.

But Bram is already hunched over, poking at the mechanism. I glance around to see if anyone is watching us. We can't just break in. What if someone catches us? What if we find Latham inside?

I grab Tessa and Jacey and the three of us move in front of Bram to hide him from view in case anyone strolls by. I try to look casual, but I'm certain I don't. "Maybe this was a bad idea."

Talon snorts. "It was most definitely a bad idea."

"Got it," Bram says as the door swings open.

"Where did you learn to do that?" I ask.

Bram shrugs. "I have many hidden talents."

"Impressive," Talon says, clapping Bram on the back.

"Someone should stay out here and keep watch just in case," Jacey says. "Anyone want to join me?" It's a good idea, but it's not going to help us if Latham is inside.

"I will," Niklas says. The two of them walk to a stone bench on the other side of the street, where they'll have a good view in every direction, while the rest of us enter the shop. My gaze sweeps over the space—empty shelving, glass cases covered in dust, cobwebs gathered in the corners. It doesn't look as if anyone has done business here in years. I run a finger over the wooden partition that separates the customers from the shopkeeper, leaving a trail through the dust. But then my gaze is pulled downward.

"We didn't leave footprints," I say.

Talon gives me an odd look. "What do you mean?"

"This whole room is covered in dust," I say. "Shouldn't the floor be filthy too?"

Understanding dawns over Bram's expression. "Someone is trying to cover their tracks. Literally."

My pulse speeds. "Let's split up and search."

"What are we looking for?" Tessa asks.

"Anything that looks out of place. Seams in the wall. Trapdoors beneath us."

We start exploring and it feels just as if we're back in the Fortress, only this time we're trying to get into a space instead of escape one.

"I think I found something," Bram calls. I join him at the back of the shop, where a row of bookshelves rests against the wall. "Notice anything unusual?"

I examine the area carefully. Most of the bookcases come all the way to the floor, but one ends just a fraction above it. "You think it's a door?"

"After what Avalina said? I think it's possible."

We run our hands along the frame, searching for anything that feels amiss, but it seems like just a normal bookcase. Bram and I trade places, and go even more slowly, trailing our fingers over every inch of the wood, looking for anything that might be a mechanism to trigger the door.

But there's nothing. Maybe the room Avalina was talking about doesn't exist anymore. And maybe this floor just doesn't collect dust.

Tessa comes up behind me and lays a hand on my shoulder. "We didn't find anything. Any luck over here?"

"No," I say. "We should go. Everyone in Ivory Hall will be awake soon, and someone will notice we're missing."

Bram searches my face. "Are you sure?"

"I don't know what other option we have."

Talon leans his back against the bookcase and lets out a heavy sigh. "I'm so sorry, Saskia."

I shrug. "We only had a slim chance of finding anything. I shouldn't be surprised."

Talon grins. "Maybe we should stop on the way back and get dessert? I bet a pastry would cheer you up."

"Yes, if my death is imminent, I should probably take every opportunity to enjoy my life."

"Excellent point. Let's go." Talon's voice is full of grim sarcasm. He pushes off the bookcase.

And the bookcase follows him.

My breath catches. It really was a door. Bram and I must not have put enough pressure on it to engage the unlocking mechanism.

Talon spins around. His eyes widen as he takes in the gap behind the shelf. "Did I do that?"

"Yes," Bram says, "I think you did."

"Surprise," he says, and then gives a little bow.

I attempt a faltering smile, and the playful expression slides from his face.

"Go ahead," he says. "We'll be right behind you."

I hesitate, my hand clutched around the edge of the

bookcase, bracing myself for the avalanche of disappointment that I'm certain will follow. Latham is like a ghost—appearing when his presence is unsettling but impossible to see when I'm trying to find him.

My knuckles have gone white. I gather my courage and push open the door.

A roar explodes in my head. My emotions careen from one to the next like a child's toy, spinning from shock, to disbelief, to horror. But then the whole world goes silent and still. My emotions distill into a sharp, hot point. Rage.

The room is overflowing with bones.

And they belong to my gran.

Chapter
Twenty-One

ran's bones are everywhere.

They're spread across the long wooden table in the center of the room, piled in boxes near the door. I spot her left humerus painted with her mastery tattoo—a series of interlocking lines that look a bit like a tree, with branches reaching upward and roots reaching down. Her right hip bone with the tattoo—a bright purple flower in bloom—that she claimed appeared the first time she danced with my grandfather. Grief chokes my throat. I grab a box and start to gather the bones. We have to get out of here before Latham comes back.

But then something draws my eye and I freeze.

In the corner of the room are a set of shelves lined with

dozens of glass jars, each housing a broken bone suspended in nutrient solution.

They look identical to the solution my mother and I used to heal Gran's broken bone. But why would Latham break these bones on purpose? Especially when he worked so hard to get them. Questions roll around my mind, but the answers keep spinning away.

"Saskia?" Bram says. "Are you all right?"

I had completely forgotten the others were here. They all look stunned. Shaken.

"No," I say, "I'm not."

He cups my elbow gently. "Explain this to me."

"I'm not sure I can." My voice collapses. My knees feel weak.

Bram guides me to a chair, and I sit. He crouches next to me. Speaks softly, as if I'm a scared animal who might bolt at any moment.

"These bones . . . they belong to your mother?"

My mother. A wave of nausea rolls over me. In my shock over seeing Gran's bones, I hadn't thought about my mother's. Where are they?

I shake my head. "Gran's."

Bram opens his mouth to ask another question, but Tessa speaks before he has a chance. "Saskia, how did Latham get this?" Her voice is quiet, but it has an edge that sends a chill down my spine.

I stand. "Get what?"

Tessa holds up a vial of blood. "It's marked with your name."

My palm flies to my throat. I think of kissing Declan. Of

pressing the numbing needle to his skin. The only reason Latham would need my blood is if he were reading my future. I press the back of my hand to my mouth. When did he get my blood? How? Whoever he's working with at Ivory Hall must have helped him. Could it be Master Kyra? I prick my fingers with needles in her presence all the time. Maybe she's found a way to collect my blood from the bones I used in readings. I shiver as I think of the challenge in the Fortress. The blood smeared on my neck after my vision of Latham. Did he gather my blood then?

"No," I say softly. "No, no, no." As if repeating the word will change reality. But it won't. It can't.

I thought I understood Latham's plan. He needed to kill and collect the bones from three generations of Bone Charmers. He has Gran's bones. He has my mother's. Now all he needs are mine, and he'll have unimaginable power.

So what is all this? What is he doing?

And why steal my blood instead of killing me? What is he waiting for?

"Is he doing *readings* on you?" Tessa asks.

I touch the pendant at my neck, grateful I've continued to wear it. "He must be."

Talon shuffles his feet. "What do you need us to do?"

But I can't form the words to answer him. My gaze keeps darting back to Gran's bones—dozens of them—broken and suspended in nutrient solution. I think of the horrified expression on my mother's face when just one of Gran's bones fractured, of her desperation to find a way to heal it before both of my paths disappeared. Is that what Latham is doing?

Trying to make people disappear? But who?

And why?

"Saskia?" Bram says. "What do you need?"

"I need some air." I push past him and hurry outside. I lean against the side of the building and slide to ground. The backs of my eyes burn, but I don't shed a single tear. I can't. The sight of that shop has burned through me and tears aren't nearly powerful enough for what I'm feeling. I'm just a dry, angry husk, ready for revenge.

Tessa comes outside and sits beside me. "You don't have to do this today."

I massage my temples. "Yes, I do. We're running out of time."

She rubs small circles on my back with the heel of her hand. "So let's go back to our room and figure out where to go from here."

She thinks I'm saying we need to get to Ivory Hall before all the other apprentices wake—and we do—but it's not what I meant.

"I have to face this now. Latham will catch up with me soon. He'll kill me."

Her face registers surprise and then anger. "No, he won't."

She's wrong, but I don't have time to tell her because Talon and Bram both come out of the shop. Jacey and Niklas see them, and jog over to join us.

"You've been gone a long time," Talon says. "We thought we'd better check on you."

"Everything all right?" Bram asks.

The question turns my spine to steel. "No," I say, "but it

will be. One way or another, Latham is going to pay for this."

I gather my courage and lift myself to my feet. I need to read those bones, see what paths they represent. Maybe then I'll know what Latham is planning.

The need to get back to Latham's shop is restless inside me—a hungry beast that will attack unless fed.

I take a deep breath. "I'm going back inside, but the rest of you should go back to Ivory Hall. I don't want you to risk getting in trouble."

"Not a chance," Jacey says. "We're staying."

I try to argue, but none of them are having it. Talon agrees to stay outside and keep watch, while Jacey and Niklas follow us into the shop.

Even though I'm prepared this time, nausea still swims up my throat when the bookcase swings open.

Behind me, Jacey sucks in a sharp breath. "It's like a workshop devoted to evil."

I steal a glance at Niklas. His face has gone pale and tight. His gaze is fixed on a table shoved against the wall. It's overflowing with Mason-made items—huge flutes, intricately carved boxes, weapons. My eyes settle on a sword and the blood freezes in my veins. I'd know that weapon anywhere. I've seen it a thousand times in my nightmares.

It's the sword that kills me.

My throat closes.

Bram touches my shoulder. "Tell us what you need."

I need Latham dead. I nearly say the words out loud, but I suppress the impulse.

"I'm going to try to read a few of the bones."

"Do you need blood?" Tessa holds out her hand. "You can use mine."

"No." A lump forms in my throat.

"But how will you—"

"These bones are intensifiers."

Tessa lifts her eyebrows. A silent question.

"Forbidden magic," I explain. "Because Latham killed my gran violently, they're especially powerful."

A shadow falls over her face. She doesn't ask how I know or if I've ever used such an abhorrent thing before, but I wonder if she's thinking it.

I pull one of the glass jars from the shelves and twist open the lid. Latham has placed the two halves of the fractured bone so far apart that they haven't begun to knit together yet. He must not want them to heal right away. The realization raises new questions that crowd my mind like cobwebs. But I have to sweep them away if I have any hope of focusing on the task ahead. Carefully, I remove both halves of the bone and lay them on a velvet cloth in front of me. A fist closes inside me as I notice that the edges are charred. Latham has already used these in a flame reading.

I cover the bone with my palm and close my eyes.

Color bursts behind my eyelids as if the bones have been waiting for me. I understand now why the intensifiers were a temptation on my other path. I underestimated the thrill of using them—the crisp clarity, the way the vision is vibrant and alive. It's unlike any reading I've ever done.

I hover—birdlike—over an array of paths fanned out in front of me like the branches of a giant tree. None of them are brighter than the others. It's as if this bone represents small choices instead of large ones. What was Latham looking for?

I choose a path at random and begin to explore.

Suddenly I'm watching Latham as a young boy of perhaps seven or eight. I'm not sure how I recognize that it's him, but the knowledge burrows inside me as certain as my own name. He perches on a windowsill, small hands pressed against the glass, waiting. His body vibrates with anticipation. When he sees his father coming up the path, uncomplicated joy leaps in his chest. He runs to the front door and throws it open, flinging himself into his father's arms.

"Papa!"

Latham's father chuckles and scoops his son off the floor. "How's my little mouse?"

"I'm not little," Latham says, attempting a pout, but unable to keep a smile from teasing at the corners of his mouth.

"Ah, then what shall we call you? 'Big mouse' doesn't sound quite right. Maybe 'my rat'?"

"Ew, no!"

Latham's father sets him back down and ruffles his hair. "Then I guess you're stuck with 'mouse,' little mouse."

Latham's father takes off his cloak and hangs it near the door. Latham follows him into the kitchen, where he plants a kiss on his wife's forehead. Latham covers his eyes, and both his parents laugh.

"So what did you do today, Papa?"

"Council work. Mostly making lots of important decisions."

"Like what?"

"Well, we voted on a new member of the Grand Council."

"Who did you vote for?"

"A Bone Mason named Jonas."

"Did he win?"

"Yes, he did. By just one vote."

Latham's father dips a spoon in the pot bubbling over the stove and brings it to his lips, blowing gently before taking a bite.

"When I grow up, I'm going to be on the Grand Council so I can make lots of important decisions."

"That's wonderful," his father says.

I can't tell if he's responding to the sauce, or to his son. And before I can find out, the path abruptly comes to an end.

I choose another path. It begins identically, with Latham at the window, eagerly awaiting his father's return. But here, his father comes home in a foul mood. He doesn't call his son "little mouse." He brushes off his boy's questions.

"Are you mad at me, Papa?"

Latham's father sighs. "No, of course not. Just a difficult day at Ivory Hall, that's all."

Latham perches on the back of a chair. "What made it hard?"

His father ruffles his hair. "A vote that didn't go my way."

Outside the vision, gooseflesh races over my arms. I explore another path, and then another. And they all end at the same moment: when Latham's father describes who got voted onto the Grand Council.

My hands are trembling as I pull them away from the bones. The implications slide down my spine like ice.

Latham is trying to replicate what happened with the bone I broke. When this bone heals, only one of the potential paths it represents will be real. But unlike before, these aren't future paths. These decisions happened long ago. Gran used to say that the past is a rigid and unchangeable thing. But in my head, I hear my mother arguing with Latham before she died. *Some things can't be altered.*

Remembering his response makes a slow beat of dread pulse through me. *With enough power,* anything *can be altered.* Latham isn't trying to control the future.

He's trying to change the past.

Chapter Twenty-Two

n the way back to Ivory Hall, I lag a bit behind the others, lost in thought. Every so often Tessa or Bram casts a concerned glance over their shoulder. I can tell they want to pummel me with questions but are fighting the urge. I'm grateful for the space.

Leaving Gran's bones behind made me physically ill, but I had no choice. If I had taken them, Latham would know I'd been to the shop and we'd lose our only lead on his whereabouts. I'd never find my mother's remains. Never be able to stop him.

I make a vow in my heart that I'll go back soon to bring Gran safely home. And I'll make Latham pay for this day along with all the other horrors he's brought into my life.

As we crest the hill, I hear Tessa's sharp intake of breath, and my gaze snaps up. A knot wedges beneath my breastbone.

Norah is standing at the front door, waiting for us. Her hands are on her hips, and her expression is enraged.

Niklas freezes. His arm reflexively tightens around the satchel slung over his shoulder, and I think of the bone-carved tools stashed inside. If he gets caught with them, he'll be expelled. I move in front of him, blocking him from Norah's view.

"All of you get inside," she says through clenched teeth. "Now!"

A dull roar fills my ears as we file past her. She slams the door behind us, then turns to the handful of apprentices milling around the grand foyer.

"Find somewhere else to be," she growls. They scurry away, and Norah begins to pace along the room, her boots clicking on the bone floors. Several tendrils of gray hair have escaped from her bun and flutter around her face as she walks. Finally she stops and fixes the full weight of her gaze on me.

"When you first arrived, was I unclear about my expectations?"

"No." My voice sounds as small as I feel.

"And yet you pull a stunt like this? I'm trying to protect you, Saskia." She presses a wrinkled hand to her brow, and it reminds me so much of Gran that a wave of remorse goes through me.

"I'm sorry," I say. "I didn't mean to worry you."

"Do you have a death wish?"

The question makes everything inside me go silent and still. I can't find the words to answer.

"I don't want to frighten you, Saskia, but your life is in danger"—she pulls in a deep breath—"and I can't protect you if I don't know where you are."

"We weren't far," Talon says. "We just went into the city."

She purses her lips and gives him a look that could slice through stone. And then her eyes travel over the rest of the group, lingering a bit longer on Tessa and Bram, who both squirm under her gaze. Neither of them utters a word.

"I'm so disappointed in you all," she says before turning back to me. "Saskia, I'm afraid I have no choice but to assign Rasmus to your security detail full-time. For the remainder of your time here, he goes everywhere you go. No exceptions."

Panic fists around my heart. How will I ever make it to Latham's shop again if I have a bodyguard following my every move? I can't just leave Gran's bones there for Latham to exploit.

"Please," I say, "that's really not necessary."

Norah holds up a hand. "I don't want to hear it. You can stay here and tolerate Rasmus, or you can quit your apprenticeship and leave without him. It's your choice."

But it's no choice at all. I've finally made progress in finding Latham. I can't leave now.

"Well?" Norah asks.

"I'll stay," I tell her. "Of course I'll stay."

"Finally a wise decision from you today. See that it's not the last one."

Just then Rasmus comes down the staircase and joins us in the grand foyer as if Norah has somehow managed to summon him with nothing but the power of her anger.

She gives him a curt nod. "I'll let you take it from here." She turns and walks away, but she only goes a few steps before she pauses and swivels around.

"One more thing. Some tools went missing from the Mason training room last night. I certainly hope they turn up before an investigation is launched." And with that she stalks out of the room.

Niklas goes rigid. Color drains from his face and his hands ball into fists at his sides. "I'll be expelled. My father will be furious."

"No," Bram says. "If she were going to expel you, she would have done it already."

But Niklas doesn't look convinced. I feel terrible for putting him in this position, but what choice did I have? If we hadn't gone into the city, I never would have found Gran's bones and never would have realized what Latham was intending to do.

Later that night the six of us are gathered in the library, huddled around a table in the corner. Rasmus leans against the wall on the other side of the room, his gaze glued to me. But at least he's far enough away that he can't overhear our conversation.

"I don't understand," Jacey says. My voice is raw from all the hours I've spent trying to explain what I saw in my reading at the shop and what it means. I've told them everything. Everything except my history with Bram. "Why do the different versions of the same event convince you that Latham is trying to change the past? Maybe he was just trying to understand what happened back then."

I lean forward and rest my elbows on the table. "Before Latham killed my mother, he complained about the Grand Council. He thought they exerted too much control over magic, hoarded too much power. And when we visited Avalina, she mentioned how angry Latham was with his father and the other members of the council for keeping the two of them apart. I don't think it's a coincidence. I think he's trying to choose a path that remakes the Grand Council in a way that benefits him."

Niklas worries his bottom lip with his teeth. "So why can't we just take all the bones from the shop? If we destroy them, he won't be able to change the past."

I sigh. "We can't destroy them. After Gran's bone broke at my kenning, my mother said that if it didn't heal, all of my potential futures would disappear."

"But that was a reading of your future," Tessa says. "This is a reading of Latham's past. Maybe if this bone doesn't heal, all of his paths will disappear. Wouldn't that be the perfect solution?"

"I don't think it's that simple," I say. "I haven't read all of the bones. We can't be sure he didn't use them to do readings of other people. In which case, they would disappear too."

"He had a vial of Saskia's blood," Bram says softly. "Destroying any of those bones is out of the question."

Tessa inhales sharply. Her hand flies to her mouth. "Saskia, no. What if that's his plan? To erase you?"

I squeeze her hand. "Don't worry. Latham doesn't want me to disappear. If I don't exist, he can't kill me."

"How comforting," Bram says dryly.

"When your gran's bone broke, did you choose which path would survive when it healed?" Jacey asks.

I shake my head. "I didn't even know what was on the other path—not until later."

Her brow wrinkles. "So what makes Latham different? The bones could heal in a way he doesn't expect and the past could stay exactly the same."

It's the same question that's been prickling at the back of my mind too. But I don't think he intends to allow the bones to mend without intervention. I think of how far apart the two halves were in the nutrient solution. As if he wanted to keep the bones viable but not allow them to begin merging until he can control the outcome.

It's no accident that he fractured Gran's bones and not my mother's. As a First Sight Charmer, Gran's would have more power to reveal the past. My mother's would be most useful to see how those changes to the past might affect the future.

Jacey is still watching me, head tilted to one side, waiting for an answer to her question.

"He'll be able to choose whichever path he wants after he kills me," I explain.

I have Second Sight—Latham will use me to determine how the bones heal in the present.

◆——————◆——————◆

I decide to use my next session with Master Kyra to try to see Latham.

We've moved on to harder tasks, and more powerful bones. But until now I've been holding back, worried about revealing myself as more skilled than I should be. And also worried about Kyra asking to see my upper arm, and discovering that my mastery tattoo has been there—all three corners of it— since before I arrived.

But I don't have the luxury of protecting myself anymore. If I have any chance of defeating Latham, I'll need to take more risks. No matter the consequences. And for all I know, she could be the traitor working with Latham.

So when Kyra drops a set of feline rib bones into a stone basin, I'm ready.

"The Mason apprentices started a new project today," she says. "I'd like you to tell me what they're working on. In as much detail as possible, please."

I chew on my lip, already trying to nudge my mind toward Latham, as Master Kyra lights the incense.

She pats me on the shoulder, misinterpreting my anxiety. "You can do this."

I set the bones alight. Extinguish the flames. Tip the basin onto the cloth in front of me. And then I close my eyes. First, I make quick work of spying on the Masons. They're working on crafting household items—goblets that continuously fill with water until the drinker's thirst is quenched, torches that stay illuminated without flame, bowls that keep food warm until it's ready to be eaten. Niklas sits at one of the tables, carving the small delicate hands of a bone clock. His dark hair flops across his forehead, and he keeps pushing it out of his eyes with his wrist, never setting down his knife. I linger on him a moment longer than the others. As soon as I'm confident I have a clear enough picture to answer any of Kyra's questions, I shift my attention to finding Latham. It will be infinitely harder without his blood, but if I can just focus well enough . . .

An image of him floats into my memory—angular face, dark hair shot through with silver, smile that can change from sincere to sneering in a single breath.

But even with a clear picture of him in my mind, I struggle to find him in the vision. I think of the necklace in my pocket. Defensive magic. I know from my other path that Latham was using it by the time I arrived at Ivory Hall. Maybe I need to go further back. He's probably impossible to see in the present.

I try to find familiar anchor points that connect the two of us—my house in Midwood, the ship where I saw him in a vision talking to Declan all those months ago—but the memories are full of so much pain, my mind flinches away.

I take a full breath and try to sink deeper into the reading. I need this to work. I need more information before I can figure out what he's trying to do with Gran's bones. An image of the shop flickers at the edge of my awareness.

The moment I focus on it, the shop transforms.

The peeling paint disappears, replaced with a crisp white exterior. Letters unfurl above the door in swirling gold script: *Perfectly Tuned.*

A young Latham—probably not much older than I am now—stands outside. His hair is much shorter than I've ever seen it, and a richer, deeper color too. His stomach churns with anxiety. He takes a deep breath before pulling open the door. A bell attached to the handle announces his arrival. The shop is captivating. Peacock-blue walls, wooden slat floors, a variety of musical instruments displayed on tables and shelves.

A woman bustles around the room, humming to herself as she works. She's tall and wiry—all angles, and no curves. She turns when Latham enters, her expression melting into a smile that softens her whole face.

"Latham. What a nice surprise."

"Hello, Mother."

"What brings you here in the middle of the day?"

I can't make sense of the flash of irritation that goes through Latham. At the way his muscles tense, making the cords on his neck stand out.

"I wanted to see if you'd had a chance to talk to Father," he says. His voice is all politeness and deference. Nothing like the storm of emotion that swirls in his chest.

His mother picks up a cloth and begins to dust one of the tables. She doesn't meet his gaze. "About?"

A gust of rage flies through him, so strong that I'm sure he's about to explode. But he pulls it back. Deliberately turns off his emotions, as if he's blowing out a candle.

"About Avalina? You promised to speak to him about allowing me to keep the match."

His mother waves a hand in front of her, swatting away the question as if it's an irritating housefly. "That girl isn't right for you."

"Isn't that for me to decide?" His voice is carefully neutral. She pats his arm. "Why don't we leave it up to fate? If you're meant to be with her, it will all work out."

He stares at her, incredulous. Because fate already decided. And still it wasn't good enough for his parents. They only care about fate when it agrees with them.

In the reading, time shifts, pulling me forward at breathless speed. Images flash by so quickly that my stomach spins. I think I might be sick. I try reaching for the edges of the vison, to get some purchase that will make it stop moving so fast, but I seem to have lost all control. If my eyes weren't already closed, I would squeeze them shut. Finally the vision slows. Comes to a halt.

And I'm still standing inside the shop.

The paint on the walls is a vivid orange now. The displays have changed.

Latham walks through the door again, but this time he's years older. He finds his mother and kisses her cheek. She chats with him for a while about mundane things—gives him an update on her vegetable garden, muses about the weather, shares a bit of gossip about one of his childhood friends. I nearly abandon the vision to try for something more meaningful when she clears her throat.

"So have you given any more thought to the Grand Council vacancy? Say the word and your father will make sure you're seated."

Latham gives a low chuckle that hides something much darker. His emotions are well concealed, even from himself. But I catch a few glimpses of old grudges and deep resentments as they dart through his mind. "I think I'll pass."

His mother's face falls. "I wish you'd reconsider. Your father always hoped you'd be on the council one day."

"I have every intention of taking my place on the council. But not now. I have a few projects I'd like to complete first. Though, if Father is interested, I do have a recommendation for a different Charmer."

"Oh? And who is that?"

"Della Holte. I trained with her at Ivory Hall. She'd be perfect."

His mother's eyes spark with interest. "Is she matched?"

Latham laughs. "Don't even think about it. She's already with someone. But I would love to connect with Della again. She would be . . . helpful . . . to my goals."

I yank my hands away from the bones and the training room slowly comes back into focus. I blink once. Twice.

Master Kyra is watching me expectantly.

My thoughts are spinning, and I've forgotten what I was supposed to be looking for. I stare blankly ahead.

"Any luck finding the Masons?"

The Masons. My brain lurches slowly into motion. It seems like she gave me the assignment days ago.

"Household items," I say. "They were making goblets. Torches. Clocks."

"Excellent work. And it took you a little longer than usual. I'm glad we seem to have found a task that challenges you."

But her words barely register. My mouth feels stuffed with cotton. Latham was trying to get my mother on the Grand Council long before I met him. Did he want us to move to Kastelia City so we'd be easier to spy on? Easier to kill?

Would it have made any difference if he'd succeeded? Would she have died sooner if we'd lived in the capital, or would events have unfolded entirely differently? Would she still be alive today?

Ever since I started studying Gran's healed bone, I can't stop comparing my two paths. Wondering at their differences, marveling at what stayed the same, torturing myself with all the things I might have done differently to save my mother. It's become a compulsion. And now every choice—every branch point on my path or anyone else's—seems fraught with uncertainty.

But one thing is clear: My visions of Latham seem to circle around the Grand Council like a vulture above a carcass. He's been trying to manipulate it for years, though I'm still not sure of his motives. Control? Power? But those are both things that three generations of Bone Charmers will give him in spades.

Unless . . . An idea starts to simmer in my mind. What if this is all about Avalina? What if he's not trying to remake the council to amass power, but to punish the people who kept him from being with the woman he loved? The two paths on the broken bone in Latham's shop were about which member was chosen to sit on the Grand Council. Could it be that Latham intends to change the past so that a different member is seated? One who wouldn't go along with his father's plans to keep the couple apart? Maybe he wants revenge instead of power.

Or maybe he wants both.

Chapter Twenty-Three

"*I* need to get back to Latham's shop."

The six of us are crammed into the room I share with Tessa. It's the only place I dare say the sentence aloud, the only place where a solid door separates me from Rasmus's watchful gaze.

"That's going to be a lot more difficult now," Bram says.

"I know." I rub my forehead. A headache is building behind my eyes. "But we'll get instructions for the third bone game any day. Who knows where we'll be sent? If I don't go now, I might lose my chance forever. But you're right. Rasmus is a problem."

Jacey slides to the floor, her back resting against my bed. "Is it just me, or is he getting more—"

"Annoying?" Niklas supplies. "It's not just you."

"He's trying to protect Saskia," Bram says. "He's just doing his job."

Talon raises one eyebrow. "And yet we seem to be discussing how to make him fail."

Bram's mouth twists into a frown. "Point taken."

Talon's statement makes guilt squirm in my stomach. I don't want to deceive Rasmus. I like him.

But he's also standing between me and finding a way to exact revenge on Latham.

Tessa sits on the bed and crosses her legs at the ankles. "So what are our options?"

"Distraction seems like the only thing that will work," Niklas says. He turns toward me. "Maybe we can find some way to occupy Rasmus while you slip away?"

Bram and I share a look.

"Not an option," I say.

Niklas's chin juts forward. "But how else—"

"I was hoping Jacey could help."

Jacey's eyes lift to mine. "What do you mean?"

I swallow. "We could make him fall asleep. Aren't there a number of potions that would do the trick?"

"I don't know, Saskia. That would be harder to pull off than it sounds. You don't think it would draw attention if he suddenly collapses where he stands?"

Bram shakes his head. "Even if we could figure out that part, poisoning him won't work. Breakers are trained never to accept food or drink while on duty. Rasmus won't ingest anything he hasn't seen prepared. And he'd be especially suspicious of anything we offer him."

Jacey chews her thumbnail. "If only I were matched to lotions instead of potions."

Talon laughs. "Lotions instead of potions?"

"Lotions, potions, and explo-shuns," Jacey says in a sing-songy voice. The terminology makes me smile. Mixers can be matched to one of three specialties—topicals, ingestibles, or explosives. Jacey works with ingestibles, so her magic is limited to things you can swallow.

"There's more than one way to administer a sleeping tonic," Jacey continues, "and in this case, a topical would be easier to use without Rasmus knowing what we were up to. But even so, that doesn't solve the problem of him collapsing on us."

Talon gives a low whistle. "Remind me never to cross a Mixer."

Jacey playfully punches his shoulder. "You're only just learning this now?"

"So is it possible that you could make a topical?" I ask. "Do you know how?"

A hush falls over the room. Jacey pulls her legs to her chest. When she speaks, her voice is low and nervous. "I probably could, but I don't know if I dare. After what happened with Jensen . . ."

"I would never ask if it weren't important."

Jacey's eyes drop to her lap. She traces patterns on her knees with her fingers. The silence in the room grows into a thing with claws.

"Never mind," I say. "Forget I said anything."

Her hands go still. She lifts her eyes to mine. "We learned

about something interesting in training last week."

I hold my breath and wait for her to keep talking.

"What was it?" Talon asks.

"Waking sedative potions," Jacey says. "They're often used when Mixers are working with Healers—given to patients to reduce anxiety."

"But how would that help us with Rasmus?" I ask.

"Because it also affects memory." She wraps her arms tightly around her legs and rests her cheek on her knees. "I think I could make a version that could be absorbed through the skin. And then we'd need to find some way to actually make him touch it."

"Jacey . . ." But I don't know how to finish the sentence. I hate that I've put her in this position, and yet I can't bring myself to reject her offer.

"It's not as if it would hurt him," she says.

Tessa shifts uncomfortably in her seat. "So how would it work?"

"We'd find a way to give him a dose before we ever leave Ivory Hall, and he shouldn't remember anything from when it kicks in until it wears off."

"But he won't be unconscious?"

"No, he'll function completely normally. He should be able to protect Saskia should the need arise. He just won't remember any of it."

"I don't know how I feel about this," Tessa says.

Jacey shrugs. "We volunteered to help. What else are we supposed to do? Politely ask Rasmus to back off so Saskia can go investigate the man who wants to kill her?"

Bram clears his throat. "Speaking of protecting Saskia . . . if we're going to go back to the shop, I think we need to take more precautions. We were reckless before."

"I've been thinking the same thing," Niklas says. "I could carve a bone flute for Talon if he can borrow a bird. That way at least we'd have some surveillance capabilities."

"That won't be a problem," Talon says. "I've already charmed half the birds in the training program and I'm sure I could convince one of them to follow me."

Tessa's fingers curl around my hand. "Obviously, I'll be ready to help too," she says, without offering a specific plan. We all know if we need Tessa's skills, something has gone terribly wrong.

"Good," Bram says. "From now on, I plan to have my breaking pouch with me every time we leave Ivory Hall."

Warmth floods my chest at their concern. Their loyalty. I think of how lonely I felt leaving Midwood. How utterly solitary in the world. But now I'm surrounded by people I care about. Somehow the bone games have taken the threads of our individual lives—our hopes and our fears alike—and woven them together so that they are one fabric. I wish there were a word for it, this intangible thing that's stronger than friendship. Even deeper than empathy.

It's how I felt about my mother. About Gran. And then I realize there is a word.

It's called family.

Niklas suddenly sits forward in his chair. "Sas, what's on your arm?"

I look down to find a thick gray band situated halfway between my wrist and my elbow. My gaze skips to my other arm. An identical marking. Tessa gasps. "I have them too."

We all do. Fresh new tattoos have etched onto our forearms. When we stand side by side, it's as if they form a chain that links us together.

The next day, I wake up to find my pendant tangled in my bedsheets. It must have fallen off during the night, which feels like a bad omen considering what we're planning. I take a deep breath before Tessa and I step out of our room, determined not to let anything unusual show on my face. Rasmus is leaning against the wall, his arms folded over his chest. He looks up as I open the door.

"Good morning," I say.

He dips his head in my direction. It's as friendly a greeting as he ever gives.

"We're going into the city today," I say. "Talon wants a new bone flute, and we heard about a shop that sells instruments."

He shrugs and pushes off the wall to follow us. "No need to ask my permission."

"Oh, I know. I just thought I'd keep you apprised of our plans. I mean . . . if you don't want to go, we could probably find another day."

He snorts. "It's fine."

"I figured as much," I say. "It just seems like you never

have any time to relax, and—"

Tessa shoots me a quelling look. I'm being too talkative. I press my lips together.

"You don't need to concern yourself with how I spend my time," Rasmus says.

I open my mouth to apologize, but then decide that perhaps I can't be trusted to speak. Tessa and I walk in silence as Rasmus trails us down the stairs. Bram, Talon, and Niklas are all waiting for us in the grand foyer, but Jacey is nowhere in sight. A spasm of panic goes through me. Our entire plan depends on Jacey. I asked her for details last night on how exactly she plans on dosing Rasmus without him knowing, but she brushed me off.

"I'm working on it," she said. "Don't worry."

"Good morning, Rasmus," Talon says brightly once we reach the bottom. "I'm in the market for a bone flute."

"So I've heard," Rasmus says dryly.

Time seems to shuffle along as we wait. We make small talk. We glance anxiously to the upper level.

"Should I go try to find her?" Talon asks.

"She'll be here," Niklas says. "Let's give her another minute."

Finally Jacey appears, bounding down the stairs like she's just heard good news.

She gives us all a big smile. Then she turns to Rasmus and wrinkles her nose. "You have something on your face."

His eyes widen in surprise. He rubs his cheek with his fist.

"Other side," Jacey says.

Rasmus wipes the opposite cheek.

"Ew. Now you've gone and smeared it everywhere."

He turns a deep red. He spits on his palm and scrubs furiously at his face.

"Oh, for bones' sake," Jacey says, rummaging through her satchel. "Here." She holds out a handkerchief, pinched between her thumb and forefinger like it's a rattlesnake.

I hold my breath. Rasmus will never fall for it.

But he doesn't even hesitate before snatching the cloth and attacking his skin like it's the bottom of a crusty pot.

"You got it," Jacey says after a moment. Either he doesn't hear or doesn't believe her, because he keeps moving the handkerchief over his cheeks. He's going to end up dosing himself with far too much of the potion. She touches his shoulder. "Rasmus, it's all gone."

"You sure?"

"Yes, I'm sure."

He holds the cloth out to her. "Here you go then."

Jacey looks at the handkerchief and then up at Rasmus. She cringes. "You keep it."

"Fine," he says, shoving it into his pocket.

I didn't think Rasmus had any weaknesses, but Jacey seemed to instinctively know how to find the chink in his armor. His pride. He doesn't want to be seen as a fool. Which makes me feel even worse about what we're doing.

But as we start down the path to Kastelia City, Rasmus seems to relax. All the tension leaves his shoulders. He catches my gaze. Gives me a wide smile. With a start, I realize I've never seen his teeth before.

We pass a bakery, and Rasmus stops, planting his nose against the glass. "My gramps was a baker. Did I ever tell you that?"

"No," I say, "you didn't."

"He made the best pie crust. Buttery. Flaky. Makes my mouth water just thinking about it." His expression gets dreamy and faraway. "I should eat more pie. Do you eat much pie, Saskia?"

Tessa turns to Jacey and widens her eyes. "You gave him too much."

Rasmus starts humming softly and Jacey laughs. "I gave him the perfect amount. And I think it's a huge improvement over his usual personality."

Rasmus is still gazing fondly at the pastries. I touch his upper arm. "Should we keep going?"

"Yes," he says, "you go and I'll follow." He lowers his voice to a conspiratorial whisper. "It's my job to make sure no one kills you."

Somehow the casual honesty of the statement lends it weight. I press my lips together.

Bram slaps Rasmus on the shoulder. "And you're doing great. Let's keep moving."

We get to the shop, and Rasmus watches with interest as Bram picks the lock. "Are you breaking in?"

"Kind of," Bram says.

"Norah isn't going to like this."

"I suspect you're right," Bram says.

Niklas rifles through his satchel and produces a small bone flute. "I'll wait out here with Talon. This place gives me the creeps."

Talon presses the bone flute to his lips as the rest of us file into the shop. When we open the door to the hidden room, Rasmus gives a low whistle. "What is all this?"

"Practice for the bone games," Jacey says without missing a beat. She's a better liar than the rest of us combined.

His brow furrows. "Norah didn't mention—"

"Just like at the Fortress?" Jacey gives a sympathetic shake of her head. "You're always the last to know, right?"

Rasmus opens his mouth, like he might mount an argument, but I can tell his heart's not in it. He shrugs and stands against the wall. He keeps his gaze on me, but it's different than usual. It's the way one might watch a group of children playing a game. Like he's not really expecting anything bad to happen, but intends to pay attention just in case.

As I look at the bones on the shelf—the vast array of paths that I need to study—I'm hit with a wave of exhaustion. But there's no other way. I'll need to read every single option if I hope to understand how to stop Latham.

I start toward the shelf, but something on a nearby table stops me in my tracks. I make a choked sound at the back of my throat. Behind me, Bram gasps.

Latham knows we've been here.

In the center of the table is the spell book he left in my room at Ivory Hall. The one made from my mother's skin.

He must have retrieved it from Bram's room and brought it here.

Bram's hand closes around my wrist. "We should go. This isn't safe."

"What's not safe?" Rasmus asks. "What do you need?" His

eyes roam around the room, but he doesn't seem particularly alarmed. Or especially capable of springing into action should the need arise.

Bram spins toward Jacey. "You've rendered him useless."

"He'll be fine. He's still wearing his bone armor."

"That protects him from Breakers. If he's too incapacitated to guard us, it hardly matters what he's wearing."

Her eyes narrow. "We wouldn't be here if not for me. I don't remember hearing *your* brilliant plan."

"My plan is to keep Saskia alive. Which means we need to leave. Now."

"Fine by me," Jacey says, her voice full of fire. "I was only trying to help."

I rake my fingers through my hair. "Stop. Both of you. We're not going anywhere."

"But—" Bram starts.

"That book is a message. Latham is trying to scare us away, and I refuse to give him the satisfaction."

"Saskia." Tessa's voice is full of warning. "You've seen yourself dying by a weapon in this room."

"And you've reminded me that it's only one potential path."

She falls silent. She can't very well argue with herself. Tension hangs in the room like a dense fog.

"I wish I had the luxury to run, but I don't. If we leave now, Latham wins. He changes the past."

I don't say the rest of what I'm thinking—that I would willingly trade my safety to assure that Latham pays for what he's done.

So I bury my fear deep inside myself, then settle into a

chair and pull the first broken bone from the nutrient solution. Gran's bones were originally prepared for my kenning, so each represents a set of different potential futures. I close my eyes and begin to explore.

I lose all sense of time or place as I wander down the different directions Latham's life could have taken. I see him as a baby, a child, a young man. I see him meet my mother. On another path, he never encounters her at all. But each has some branch point that involves the Grand Council—it must be why he chose to break these particular bones.

"The Grand Council is corrupt," he tells Avalina on one path. The two of them are walking through the streets of Kastelia City on a warm evening after a rainstorm. The cobbles are slick and shimmering in the lamplight.

Avalina threads her fingers through his. "What makes you say that?"

"They've been hoarding power for years." His thumb traces slow circles along her palm. "They want to limit it for everyone but themselves."

"What do you mean? Lots of people in Kastelia have magic. How could the Grand Council hoard it even if they wanted to?"

Latham gives her a gentle smile. "Did you know that there weren't always binding ceremonies?"

She tilts her head and looks up at him. "Really?"

He tucks a strand of hair behind her ear. "Really. People who had magic used to be able use it however they were able. But then the Grand Council decided too few people had too much power, and they started to assign new apprentices to specialize in one small area. And since unused magic withers and dies, it was an effective way to limit power."

Avalina's brow wrinkles. "But you said the council was *hoarding* power."

"Yes," Latham says, "because the rules don't apply to them. Council members are allowed to use any magic they wish. Bound or not."

"But the binding ceremony happens so young. Wouldn't their magic have been limited long before they were appointed to the council?"

"Exactly," Latham says, clearly pleased by the question. "Those members had to have been using unbound magic their entire careers. For well-connected, powerful families, the rules aren't enforced. While others face death for the same crimes."

Slow horror spreads over Avalina's expression. "That's horrible."

He squeezes her hand. "I'm going to change it. With you by my side, we can change the world."

Outside the vision, my breath catches. Before my mother died, we had a very similar conversation about the binding ceremony. Her words echo in my memory: *It used to be that magic was allowed to develop naturally, without so many boundaries. But now bones are bought and sold. Magic comes at a price. And we all suffer for the loss.*

My mother would have agreed with Latham that changes needed to be made. The realization knocks something loose inside me.

And it also gives new shape to Latham's actions. He was

already angry with the council. And then they nullified his match with the woman he loved.

I travel down paths where Latham has multiple conversations with his father, asking cleverly disguised questions to discover each member who agreed to keep him and Avalina apart. On some of the paths, he keeps a list of their names on his bedside table. He studies it obsessively.

And then I come across something that makes my blood run cold. A murdered council member. One who died in mysterious circumstances that bear a striking resemblance to the murders in Midwood a few months ago. The Bone Charmer who sat on the Grand Council was found dead in her home, throat slit. The killer was never discovered. She was the Charmer who performed Avalina's second kenning, the woman who matched her as a chef and claimed she had no suitable love match in the entire country.

I think back to the council vacancy Latham discussed with his mother. Latham created it. And he attempted to fill it with my mother. Earlier, I assumed he wanted her close so that she'd be easier to kill, but now confusion rages in my chest. Did he want her on the council because he wanted her dead or because she agreed with him? Did he think of her as an enemy or an ally?

I keep going. Path after path until my mind is muzzy, and I can't think clearly anymore.

I pull away from the bones and massage my temples.

"What's wrong?" Bram asks. "What did you see?"

"I know what Latham wants," I say, "but I can't figure out how to stop him."

"What does he want?" Tessa asks softly.

I stand up and pace the length of the room. "He wanted change before he became consumed with revenge. He's targeting the council members who kept him and Avalina apart. But he also wants power. He craves it. His father made every decision for him as a child. Controlled every aspect of his life."

Jacey sighs. "And then invalidated the result when fate stepped in."

"Yes," I say, "exactly. He's bitter. Angry. How he chooses to heal these bones will change the past, but I can't see how."

Niklas stands against the wall, the back of his hand over his mouth. His cheeks are sallow. "Let's just take the bones and get out of here."

"We can't. If we steal the bones, we can prevent them from mending, but that could destroy all of us." I think of what my mother told me after Gran's bone fractured. I wanted to do nothing. To simply allow both of my potential paths to exist simultaneously, but my mother made it clear that wasn't an option. *If the bone doesn't heal, all of your futures will disappear.*

I don't know what would happen if none of the bones healed, and I'm not sure how long we have. A month? Two? How long can fate stay suspended until it snaps? I dig my fingers into my hair. "I wish I could see what Latham was trying to accomplish in the future by changing the past."

"So he can see what will happen because he's a Third Sight Charmer?" Tessa asks. "Or will he need to use your mother's bones?"

Her question turns a page in my mind. I've been going

about this all wrong. I can't just focus on what options were available in the past. I need to see where they lead in the future. If I can see the outcomes, I can predict which Latham will choose. Then we can find a way to heal the bones in a way that preserves this reality exactly as it is before he heals them in a way that will change it.

"Tessa, you're brilliant. I need to do a Third Sight reading."

A curtain of confusion falls over her expression. "But can you do that?"

It's as if the ground beneath my feet has shifted, and I've lost my balance. I let my guard down. I said too much. I think of Tessa's expression when she claimed I didn't trust her. And with sharp clarity, I realize I don't. Not entirely.

And it's because of Jensen. The seed of mistrust that his trial planted hasn't thrived—not in light of the bone games and all we've been through together. But until this moment, I hadn't realized that it wasn't entirely dead, either. It sprouted roots that are hard to pull up.

If I tell her the truth, will she turn her back on me?

"Can you?" she asks again.

I bite my lip. "Yes. I can." Her eyes slide to the spell book and then back to me.

"Then what are you waiting for? Do it."

Reading the future is far more challenging than seeing the past. Before, I could simply access a reading that Latham had already done. It was relatively effortless, like perusing someone else's diary. But this—pushing past the point where the path dwindles away and forcing the vision to extend into the future—is more demanding than any reading I've ever done.

And it's not just that it taxes my magical abilities. It drains me emotionally. Every time I start down a path that shows a glimmer of happiness for Latham, my mind recoils. It was one thing to see Latham's past—as an innocent child or a love-struck new apprentice—but exploring his future when I know what choices he's already made, when I fully understand his potential for evil, demands a level of strength I'm not sure I can maintain for long. How can I watch him find happiness when I know he doesn't deserve it?

So I force myself to pretend he's a stranger. To watch his potential futures unfold as dispassionately as I can. Unlike the First Sight readings, this time certain pathways are more brightly lit than others, so I explore them first. On one path, it's clear Latham was able to be matched with Avalina, and the two of them fall more deeply in love. I see him move with her to Leiden. They walk along the beach at sunrise, watch the waves lap at the shore, sink their bare feet in the warm sand. The ocean calms him.

He becomes Leiden's Bone Charmer. It suits him—gently guiding the future of the townsfolk, knowing they trust him implicitly. Avalina brings out the best in him. She tempers his ambition—softens it just enough that it serves him well instead of turning him into a monster. They have a houseful of children—three sons and two daughters—who are treasured and adored.

Their home is filled with chaos and laughter and love. He and Avalina drift off to sleep each night with their hands intertwined as if they want to be connected even in their dreams.

But other paths are well lit too, and as I explore them, I find a very different Latham. In some, I watch him take his place on the Grand Council. Other paths keep him teaching at Ivory Hall. I watch as the council members responsible for keeping him from Avalina are punished—disgraced with scandal, put on trial for crimes they didn't commit, brutally murdered.

I notice a pattern. The paths always seem to branch in two opposite directions: choices that lead to vengeance and choices that lead to Avalina. The two never overlap. Seeking revenge leads Latham further and further from the woman he loves. But choosing her means the members of the council never get their comeuppance.

He can't have it both ways. He has to choose one or the other.

I have to take frequent breaks. I'm bleary with exhaustion.

"Maybe we should come back another time," Bram says. I've just come out of a vision, and I stretch my arms over my head, knead at a knot in my shoulder. I feel as if I've been awake for days.

"I have to keep going," I tell him. The spell book sits on the table like a warning. Now that Latham is on to me, I don't know how much time I have. And I shouldn't leave the bones out of the nutrient solution for too long—if the bone dries out, it will die off and lose its ability to heal. I pick up a sewing needle. "Maybe blood will make things easier." I prick my finger. Speckle Gran's bones in crimson. Try again.

I stand at the branch point between two paths. On one, Latham's father not only succeeds in having Avalina's parents imprisoned, but manages to secure the same fate for her as well. On the other path, Avalina goes back to Leiden after she's dismissed from Ivory Hall. I already know what happens on the second path, so I turn down the first.

And I'm suddenly back in Midwood, standing in my bedroom. I hover above the vision and turn in a slow circle. The blood must have connected me to my own future on this path and not Latham's. I'm just about to pull my fingers from the bone and try again when my mother walks by, her arms full of boxes.

"Saskia," she calls, "could you come in here and give me a hand?"

All the breath leaves my lungs. My mother. Alive in the future.

I sink deeper into the vision, until I feel as if I'm one with the Saskia who responds.

"Be right there."

I follow myself into the kitchen, where my mother is carefully placing dishes into boxes.

"I don't want to go," I tell her.

She leans across the table and strokes my cheek with the back of her hand. I can feel her fingers against my face, smell the sweet vanilla fragrance that she used to dab behind each ear. My chest fills with an exquisite blend of joy and grief, expanding so quickly, I feel like I might burst. I desperately want to control this future version of myself. To force her to lean in, to fit herself into the hollow at my mother's side and the safety I always felt there.

But I'm helpless to do anything except watch.

"I know you don't, bluebird, but it's not safe here anymore."

Outside the vision, I want to scream questions. Not safe *where*? Midwood? All of Kastelia?

"Maybe we won't have to leave," I watch myself say. "Maybe the vote won't go through."

My mother purses her lips. "It will. It's a sham vote designed to avoid an uprising. By this time next week, Kastelia will be a kingdom, and Latham will be sovereign."

The vision ends abruptly, and I pull away from the bones, gutted.

For months I've tortured myself with my mother's death. With what I might have done differently to save her. In moments where I was feeling gentle with myself, I reasoned that there was nothing I could have done to change the future.

But I was wrong. There were a series of events that would have saved her life. That would have saved us both.

Is it possible that Latham can change the past without killing me? And if I let him have his way—allow him all the power he could ever want—will I get my mother back?

I swipe at the tears running down my face.

Tessa's hand falls on my shoulder. "What's wrong?"

Could I heal this bone before Latham returns? Could I be the one who chooses the future?

I squeeze my eyes closed, and all I can see behind my lids are my mother's hands. Her hands cupped around my face as she told me she loved me. Her hands gesturing wildly in the air every time she discussed something that made her angry. Her hands cold against my skin after she died.

I've always thought I'd do anything to have her back.

But would I?

It's an impossible choice. Latham as king would be disastrous. It would be everything I've been fighting to prevent. But my mother would be alive. We'd leave Kastelia—she'd take me somewhere far away—and we would be safe. We'd be together.

"Saskia, you're scaring me," Tessa says. "What did you see?"

I turn toward her, ignoring her question in favor of one of my own.

"Do you think you could get me some books on Mending?"

Her expression clouds. "I can tell you anything you need to know."

"But can you get me a book?"

"Yes," she says, "I'm sure I could."

"Good. I'm going to need to learn as much as I can."

Chapter Twenty-Four

I'm silent on the walk back to Ivory Hall. Thoughts move through my mind like dancers in an overcrowded ballroom—worries rustling against one another like silk skirts—with no space to move freely. It's suffocating.

"Do you want to talk about whatever happened back there?" Tessa asks once we reach the top of the hill.

I struggle for a way to respond that won't hurt her feelings. But I can't find one. "Not now. I think I need to be alone for a while."

She hesitates, her lips pressed into a thin white line. "Saskia—"

Jacey squeezes Tessa's shoulder. "Let her be."

I give Jacey a small, grateful smile and peel off from the

others. I wander around the grounds for a while, trying to collect my thoughts. I ache with how much I miss my mother. I ache with what it would take to get her back.

Memories of her blow through my mind, lifting and spinning like leaves in the breeze. I think of her confronting Audra about using bone readings for selfish reasons. Of the way she used to encourage me to remember those who had less than I did. Of how she chose a path that ended her life to spare mine. She would be so angry if I sacrificed all of Kastelia just to save her. And yet the temptation is there just the same.

A noise behind me makes me startle, and I whirl around. But it's only Rasmus. I had forgotten about him, and I'm not sure if he's been following me the whole time, or if he just arrived.

He's unsteady on his feet, as if he's had too much to drink, but the only acknowledgment he gives me is his usual curt nod. The potion is beginning to wear off then.

I keep walking, and Rasmus keeps a greater distance than normal, as if he senses my need for space.

I find a parapet overlooking the city and sit on top of the cool stone.

I watch the sun move lower and lower in the sky until finally it dips beneath the horizon, streaking the sky in hues of rose and gold. Kastelia City spills at my feet, golden and glittering. I think about the people below, and wonder how many of them are gathered around kitchen tables sharing a meal. How many children are hearing bedtime stories near the glowing fire of a hearth? How many lives would I destroy by letting Latham rob them of their freedom?

A familiar memory nudges at the back of my mind, and it takes me a moment to identify it. But then it clicks into place. I sat in this very spot with Bram on my other path. His cloak and hair were a smudge against the dark sky. My throat was thick with all the things I wanted to say to him but didn't.

A throat clears behind me, and I turn.

Bram.

As if my thoughts summoned him.

I can't read his expression—worried? Hesitant?

"I know you said you wanted to be alone." He says it like an apology. Like a question.

I pat the wall beside me. "I don't mind."

He sits and we both stare out over the city. "Will you tell me what happened in the shop?" he asks, finally. "Something you saw obviously upset you."

I listen to the rush of the Shard. When I was young, we had a flood in Midwood after a season of unusually high rainfall. I remember asking my father why it had happened.

"The river can only hold so much, bluebird," he'd told me. *"And then it spills over just like a bucket that's too full."*

That's how my secrets feel inside me—they've been pouring down like rainfall for months and I don't have space to hold them all anymore.

"I saw my mother," I tell him. "Alive on one of the paths in the future."

Bram sucks in a sharp breath. "That must have been . . ." He trails off. Shakes his head. "Actually, I can't even imagine what that must have been like."

"Terrible. Wonderful. Confusing."

"Was it a good future?"

"Not for most people, no."

"I'm sorry."

"Yes," I say. "Me too."

"What are you going to do?"

"I don't know. If I could see her again . . . there are so many things I wish I could say to her."

"Yeah, I know exactly what you mean." Bram was so much younger when he lost his parents. He must have a lifetime of things saved up to tell them.

"Watching all of Latham's paths unfold is exhausting. Even though most of them never happened, once I've seen them, they feel as real as anything else, you know?"

"Does *your* other path feel real too?"

"More than you can imagine."

"That must be strange."

I sigh. "To put it lightly."

Bram shifts on the wall, turning his body toward me, and then away again like he's not sure where he wants to be. He scratches the back of his neck. "Do you want to tell me more about what happened there? Between us, I mean?"

"Why, so you can laugh at me?"

His eyebrows pull together. "I never laughed at you."

"You did. When I first told you we were matched on my other path, you laughed."

"Not *at* you. The idea seemed so far-fetched then."

Then?

I trace patterns in the cobblestones with the toe of my boot. "And now?"

The corner of his mouth twitches. "Do you want to tell me about it or not?"

"We were matched," I tell him, "and you hated it. You were so angry with me at first."

"I was angry?"

"Yes."

"Why?"

"I wasn't very kind to you in the beginning. You remember the prison boat from when we were children?"

He nods.

"We each saw that event very differently. It took a while for us to trust each other."

His expression goes tight, as if he's remembering that day and the thick wall of resentment that used to be between us. But Bram has been different on this path. It's as if he'd already let go of his bitterness the moment he came back to Midwood. Is it because he felt sorry that my mother died? Is it because I'm different in this reality? Or did our connection on my other path imprint on us both somehow? Maybe deep in his soul he knows I apologized long ago for how things were when we were children, even if he never heard me say it.

"Is that why you brought up the prison boat before our first task?"

I shrug. "I thought it would make things better between us if you knew how sorry I was. It did on my other path."

"And then what?" Bram's voice is husky.

I shoot him a questioning glance.

"You said I was angry *at first*, and then what?"

I almost don't answer him. But I'm so tired of being afraid.

"You fell in love with me. And I died in your arms."

I don't look at him as I speak. I don't want to see his face right now. But the words dislodge an old wound from my heart, like removing a stubborn splinter.

Bram shifts in his seat. His hands grip the edge of the wall. And I wonder if I've only transferred my discomfort to him.

"The tattoo on your wrist . . . ?"

"Not from Declan." But he already knew that from our visit to Avalina. I can tell he wants to press the point further, but he doesn't, and I'm glad I don't have to say it out loud. That I was in love with him once, in another life. That I'm in love with him in this life too. As much as I've tried to tell myself the feelings aren't real, I can't deny them any longer. Imagined feelings would have faded by now. My tattoo would have faded. Maybe love is love no matter how it begins.

I sneak a glance at him, and he's looking at me with the strangest expression. He lays a palm against my cheek, his thumb feathering against my skin, and I melt inside.

He leans toward me, so close that I can feel his breath against my face. And then something shifts in his expression and he sits back. His hand falls to his lap.

"Saskia, I need to tell you something." His voice sounds sad, resigned.

A roar grows in my ears.

"Is it going to break my heart?"

He flinches. "I'm afraid it might."

I feel my rib cage curl inward, as if preparing to protect my vital organs from a blast. "Then don't tell me."

"But—"

I stand and rest my hand briefly on the crown of his head. "Please. Just let it be. I don't think I can handle any more heartbreak tonight. Good night, Bram."

And with that, I turn and walk away.

I've been trying so hard to protect my heart, to convince myself that my feelings for Bram weren't real, but I didn't lie to myself as well as I thought. Somehow a bit of hope trickled in. And it's been gathering power. A cresting wave of optimism that just violently crashed.

I go straight to my room, but it's hours before I fall asleep. I vacillate between thinking about Bram, about what we had on my other path—what we don't have here—and imagining embracing my mother again. Hearing her laugh. Listening to her stories.

There's nothing I can do about Bram, but I could see my mother again. I could bring her back.

But she didn't raise me to be that selfish.

I wish I'd never seen that path. Having to make the choice to let her go is like losing her all over again. And I've lost far too much. A surge of anger swells in my chest. Latham stole my mother from me twice, and I'm not sure any amount of vengeance I inflict would be enough to satisfy me.

But I'm going to try.

Getting my hands on a set of Bone Mending books turns out to be more difficult than Tessa and I thought. Rasmus is watching us all the time, and ever since the librarian found me in an unauthorized area, she's especially vigilant whenever any of us step foot among the stacks.

"We'll have to get someone else to loan you the books," Tessa says, "but I still don't understand why you need to learn. Why can't I just heal the bone for you?"

"Just trust me," I say.

I don't tell her the truth. Latham is closing in on me. I can feel it like a hot breath against my neck. When he catches me, I don't want my friends to be anywhere close. Besides, I've seen myself dying in a dozen visions, and Tessa wasn't there in any of them. She won't be able to help me in the end. This is something I need to do alone. If I'm going to stop Latham, I need to learn how to mend bones.

Tessa worries her bottom lip with her teeth. "Give me some time and I'll find a way."

And she does.

I'm leaving the workshop the next day when someone taps me on the shoulder. I spin around to find a Healer. He's short and slight with a pair of thick-rimmed spectacles that have slid halfway down the bridge of his nose. It makes him look years younger than the rest of the apprentices—he looks seven instead of seventeen.

"Saskia, right?"

"Yes," I say, "and you are?"

"Tessa asked me to find you. She said you might want some

help from me?" He struggles to keep pace beside me as I climb the stairs.

"Oh, you must be a Mending Healer."

He nods. "So what kind of help were you looking for exactly? Tessa didn't really say."

"I want to learn everything there is to know about mending bones."

His eyes go wide and he shifts the large stack of books he's carrying from one arm to the other. "Like, you want a tutor?"

"No, no, nothing like that. I was hoping you might have some reading material I could borrow. Tessa says you have quite a large collection."

"But aren't you a Bone Charmer?" He shoves his spectacles back into place. The hint of suspicion in his voice is exactly why we didn't get the books from the library ourselves.

We reach the top of the stairs and enter the grand foyer.

"I am, yes. But I'm working on a reading for a Healer. A Mender like you. And it would really help if I understood his craft a bit. My accuracy improves if I'm more informed."

His face relaxes. He shifts his books to the other arm. "Oh, that makes more sense. For a moment I thought . . ." His cheeks flush.

"It's an odd request, I know. But Charmers have to learn a bit about everything. And Tessa says you're the best."

At that his cheeks go from slightly pink to scarlet. "Oh. Well, Tessa," he stammers, "she's . . ." He swallows. Collects himself. "That's very kind of her."

"It's very kind of *you*," I say.

He gives me a sheepish grin. "I could get the books for you right now, if you want to wait?"

"Thank you," I say. "I can't tell you how much I appreciate it."

The Healer hurries up the stairs toward the men's dormitory. I throw a glance over my shoulder at Rasmus, who is watching me with something like a smirk. He was too far away to hear the conversation, so I'm sure it looked like I was flirting.

I miss the days when I could humiliate myself without an audience.

A few minutes later the Healer returns with a different stack of books that he presses into my arms. "That should be a good start," he says, "but let me know if you have questions. And tell Tessa . . . tell her I said hello."

I rush to my bedroom to study the healing book—it's something to think about besides the looming third bone game and the possibility of a traitor at Ivory Hall—and then spend every free moment over the next few days scrutinizing each page. I read all about blood clots and calluses and using magic to repair fractures. In truth, I'm not sure I can heal the broken bones on my own, even if I am willing to break the law.

When I first discovered the bones, I thought I'd be content to prevent Latham from changing the past. But the Grand Council seems no closer to apprehending him than they were when I first arrived at Ivory Hall. And if he has someone on the inside—maybe even someone on the council—it seems unlikely they will. As I've thought about everything I've seen in Latham's past and in his future, the shape of his plan has begun to emerge in my mind. Once he has my bones, he can heal each of Gran's individually, carefully choosing the paths that will shape his life any way he pleases. And understanding his plan has made my own crystallize.

I'm not content with preserving the past anymore. If the Grand Council can't find Latham to punish him, then I'll do it with the bones he broke. I'll change his past to give him the worst possible outcomes.

I'll gift him with the future he deserves.

I just need to figure out how to do that without the benefit of my own bones to complete the spell. And for that I'll need Bram's help.

But something inside me recoils at the thought of approaching him for help. We haven't been alone since the other night when I all but confessed I was still in love with him. And he didn't return the sentiment.

I've been avoiding him.

My heart is too bruised to risk it again. And yet I can't stop picturing Bram's lips inches from mine. That unexpected swell of hope that crashed into bitter disappointment. I take a deep breath. I need to pull myself together. There's too much at stake to let my wounded pride stand in the way of doing whatever I can to stop Latham and find my mother's bones.

Before I can change my mind, I hurry to the men's dormitory and tap softly on Bram's door. He probably didn't hear. I should try again, but I hesitate, my fist suspended in midair, willing myself to knock. This was a terrible idea.

I turn to leave, but just then the door swings open.

"Saskia?"

Bram's hair is mussed, as if I've woken him from a nap. His feet are bare. My stomach flutters.

I give him an apologetic smile. "Can I come in?"

His gaze darts to Rasmus, and then back to me. He opens the door wider and gestures for me to come inside.

"I'm sorry," I say after the door clicks shut behind me. "Having a bodyguard makes things awkward."

"Sure," Bram says lightly, "that's what makes it awkward."

What little confidence I had vanishes. "Should I not have given you details? About the other path, I mean?"

He rakes his hands through his hair. Paces around the tiny space. "Yes. No. I don't know."

If hearing more about our relationship on my other path makes him this uncomfortable, he isn't going to like what I'm about to ask him.

"Maybe I should come back another time," I say, reaching for the doorknob.

His hand darts out and circles my wrist. "No, Saskia, wait." He gently spins me around. "Don't go. What is it?"

His eyes are soft. His face is too close to mine. I swallow. "I need your help. If you're willing."

"I'm listening."

"I was wondering if you could teach me . . ." I bite my lip. It's the wrong way to start. I try again. "I heard once that you can pull magic from the bones of someone living."

His face goes ashen. "Where did you hear that?"

"Esmee told me."

A crease appears between his brows. "You know Esmee?"

"No. But I did on my other path. You introduced us."

His expression is guarded. Wary. I can tell he's weighing whether to believe me or not.

"She loved you," I say.

"Loved? I assume she still loves me unless I've done something to offend her."

A bright spark of surprise goes through me. Esmee is alive in our reality. It hadn't occurred to me until this moment. I've seen the fire that killed her so often in my readings of Gran's healed bone that I've thought of her as gone. But she's not.

I smile. "I think she wishes she saw you more often, but yes, I'm certain she still adores you."

"I don't understand. Why would I introduce you to Esmee? And why would she tell you that?"

"Is it true? Can you pull magic from the bones of the living?"

His gaze holds mine. "Yes."

"Can you teach me?"

He gives me an uneasy look. "Why?"

"Latham needs my bones to choose which paths survive. It would be nice if I could heal them before he does and save him the trouble of killing me."

"You want to figure out how to pull magic from your own bones?"

"Well, it's that or the rest of you are going to have to kill me and then use my remains to stop Latham yourselves."

"That's not funny."

I lift one shoulder. "It wasn't meant to be. So, is it possible?"

He scrubs a hand over his face. "Maybe? I'm willing to try."

I let go of a long breath. "Thank you."

"When would you like to start?"

"How about now?"

He laces his fingers behind his neck and touches his elbows together. "I don't know. It's not a quick skill to learn."

"Maybe I catch on faster than your other apprentices." I'm teasing him, but a spasm of pain flashes across his expression. He drops his arms to his sides and shifts his weight from one foot to the other.

I'm not sure what I did wrong, but I clearly made him uncomfortable. "Never mind." I open the door. "We can do this another time."

"No." His voice is soft, but forceful. "Now is fine."

I hesitate, my hand on the doorknob again. "Are you sure?"

"I'm sure. Let's get started."

The task makes us forget our discomfort with each other.

Bram tries to explain the sensation of drawing magic from bones that haven't been prepared—bones that are still inside a living body.

"In some ways it's exactly the same," he says. "When I was young, I didn't even realize I was doing it at first. But now that I think about it, the technique is slightly different—push instead of pull. Does that make any sense?"

"Not really."

"When the bones aren't prepared, it takes more focus. More control."

"More control how?"

He cocks his head to one side and stares at the wall. "It's

hard to articulate. Maybe you should just attempt it, and I'll try to guide you."

So I sit across from Bram, trying to focus all my attention on my own bones. I cradle my elbows in my palms and feel the pointy contours of my olecranon. I try to envision it just as I would if it were lying on a velvet cloth in front of me. I can sense the magic, but it's distant—like a scent on the breeze that vanishes as quickly as it arrived.

"It doesn't feel right," I say. "I don't think it's working."

"How do you usually feel bone magic?"

The question takes me by surprise. It never occurred to me that it wouldn't feel the same for everyone. "It's usually like a pull in my belly."

"Like the magic drawing you in?"

"Yes," I say, "exactly."

"I have an idea." He offers his hand and pulls me to my feet. Then he moves so he's standing behind me. "May I touch you?"

My breath stills. I nod.

He lays a palm on my stomach, and every thought flies out of my head. If he imagined this would help me focus, he was mistaken.

"You're trying to feel the magic here, right? Like a tug that pulls you forward into a vision?"

I have to force the answer from my lips. "Yes."

"So I need you to try the opposite. Imagine you're trying to pull my palm toward your spine. Draw power out of the bones and reel it in. Instead of falling forward into magic, you're gathering it in your center."

His breath ripples against the nape of my neck. My heart bumps against my ribs.

"Close your eyes and try again."

I obey. My stomach feels hot beneath his hand. I can't think with him touching me. I wish . . .

What, Saskia? What do you wish? Bram's voice floats to me on a memory. The two of us standing on the deck of a ship. Stars glittering overhead. My two paths melt together in my mind, become undistinguishable.

A knock on the door makes my eyes fly open. I spin around, and Bram's hand falls away. He studies me with a careful expression. With eyes that belong to the Bram from *this* reality, not the Bram from the other one.

Not the Bram who was in love with me.

I try to swallow my disappointment. I feel like a fool.

Bram takes in my stricken expression and his face changes. "Saskia . . ."

"Aren't you going to answer that?"

His gaze flicks between me and the door.

"It could be important," I say.

Finally he sighs and pulls it open.

Niklas stands on the other side. "Oh good, you're both here. Norah wants us in the workshop."

"Why?" Bram asks.

Niklas shrugs. "Everyone is speculating it's about the next bone game."

"We should go," I say, pushing past Bram and joining Niklas in the corridor. "We don't want to be late."

"Saskia, wait."

I pause and lift my eyes to his.

Niklas moves away to give us privacy.

"I care about you," Bram says, "but I'm not the same person I was on your other path."

"I know that," I say softly. My memories of Bram feel like the treasures I used to carry around in my pockets when I was a little girl—broken rocks with shimmery bits inside, old coins whose faces had been rubbed bare with time, the colorful feather of a small bird. But now I feel as if I've opened my fist, excited to share my precious things, only to realize the truth as they lay on my palm: They are worthless to anyone but me.

I give him a tight smile. "Thank you for your help. I'll try practicing on my own."

"Saskia, I'm trying—" He blows out a frustrated breath and rakes his fingers through his hair. "I don't know what you want from me."

My gaze falls to his bare wrist.

"I want something you can't give," I tell him. "I want you to remember."

"Remembering isn't the problem." His voice is soft. Careful. He opens his mouth to say more, but something about my expression makes him abruptly stop talking. I feel as if he's punctured my heart with a pin, and I can feel it shriveling in my chest.

He catches my fingers in his. "Please, let me explain."

But I'm already backing away. I don't want to hear him say he's not in love with me. I hurry into the corridor, where Niklas is waiting.

Niklas wrinkles his forehead in concern. "What's wrong? What did he want to tell you?"

"Nothing I don't already know." But for just a moment, I wonder if I'm wrong. Maybe Bram was trying to tell me something else. But then I push the thought away. I can't keep stoking the fires of false hope. We're not meant to be.

Not in this reality.

Chapter
Twenty-Five

he workshop is louder than usual. I assumed Norah had summoned only our team, but it appears every apprentice at Ivory Hall is here. And they're all talking at once. The air hums with anxious conversation—worry and speculation and excitement blend together to create a low roar that makes my head ache.

Norah steps onto the amphitheater stage. "Take your seats, please." She speaks into a bone-carved trumpet that amplifies her voice across the workshop. The chatter dulls as we all file into our color-coded sections.

A sorrowful feeling steals over me as I sit on one of the red-painted benches reserved for Bone Charmers. I've grown accustomed to being with my team, and I feel their loss sharply. Regret knots inside me. I should have never let myself grow so attached. My connection to them has made me more vulnerable. It's so much easier to lose something you never expected you'd care about than to lose it after hope has taken root.

My eyes slide to Bram.

Norah claps her hands and the room falls silent.

"Congratulations, apprentices. You've nearly made it to the end of the term, and now the final bone game is upon us. This one will be a bit different from the others."

Norah paces from one end of the stage to the other as she speaks. Every pair of eyes in the room is glued to her. "Up until now, each of the challenges has been custom-designed to test your team's strengths and reveal your weaknesses. But in real-life situations, this won't be the case. Difficulties will arrive without respect to your readiness or your skill. So, for your final bone game, we have replicated real-life scenarios that actual town councils have faced. Each group will receive the name of someone who has broken the law, and your task will be to find the clues you need to locate and apprehend the criminal." She smiles. "We will use actors, of course, but the details of each case will unfold precisely as they did then—with each team acting as an independent town council."

It sounds similar to our first bone challenge, except this time instead of convicting a criminal, we have to catch one. But for the other teams, who only had to contend with obstacle courses and puzzles, it will be much harder.

"But this time," Norah continues, "the stakes are higher.

The first team who solves their challenge will have their choice of assignments at the completion of their apprenticeship."

A murmur ripples across the room. Graduating apprentices don't typically get a say in where they're sent. Most end up back in their own towns, or the towns of their mate if they are romantically attached.

"And unfortunately, any team that doesn't apprehend the criminal in time will fail the challenge. Best of luck to all of you."

As soon as Norah leaves the stage, the apprentices peel apart like petals on a blooming flower. One moment we're organized into distinct sections by cloak color, and the next the room is a kaleidoscope of jumbled hues.

Tessa reaches me first. "What do you think? At least all the challenges are roughly the same. It doesn't sound like we'll be tortured this time."

Jacey comes up behind us. "That's a low standard."

I laugh. "True, but I'm still relieved."

One by one, the others join us. I carefully avoid Bram's gaze.

"This game actually sounds kind of fun," Talon says.

"Don't be fooled," Niklas counters. "Knowing Norah, she selected this challenge because the solution is something arcane, like locking ourselves in a wooden box and going without food and water for days."

A throat clears behind us, and Niklas spins around to find Norah, lips pursed, one hand on her hip. "I don't design the games myself, you know," she says. "Nor are they difficult just for the sake of tormenting you."

Color rushes to his cheeks. "I'm . . . I didn't mean . . ." he stammers. "I was only joking."

Norah's eyes flash. She makes a dismissive, throaty sound, and then turns her attention to me. "Saskia, may I have a word?"

My pulse spikes. "I . . . Yes, of course."

She gives me a curt nod. "Follow me."

Norah's boots click on the bone floors as we climb the stairs and make our way through the grand foyer to her office on the other side of Ivory Hall. Unease snakes through me. Maybe she has an update on Latham. The thought is surprisingly disappointing—I've grown attached to my own plan for revenge. Then again, maybe I'm being punished. I've broken so many rules that I'm not even sure what I should be most worried about.

Norah unlocks her office door and steps aside so I can enter. The room is softer than I would have expected considering her temperament. Two cream-colored plush chairs are situated opposite a large desk. Thick pale blue drapes frame tall windows. A vase of bright pink peonies sits on a low table. On the other side of the room, a cheerful fire glows in a small stone hearth.

Norah settles behind her desk, then waves me toward one of the chairs.

"Please," she says, "make yourself comfortable."

I sit, but I'm far from comfortable. "Is something wrong?"

"Rasmus has been removed from your security detail."

A bright spark of surprise goes through me. "What? But why?" I look behind me to try to gauge his reaction, but he's not there.

Norah sighs. "I'm afraid we've had some negative reports about his job performance."

"From who?"

"It doesn't matter. What matters is that they were credible, and we had no choice but to take action."

"I don't understand. What did the reports say about him?"

"He's been accused of unseemly behavior." Her eyes slide away from mine.

My mouth goes dry. "What kind of behavior?"

"Abandoning his post. Sleeping on the job. Drunkenness." She presses her lips together and shakes her head. "I'm sorry, Saskia. We owe you better than that."

A slow pulse of dread goes through me. "No, Rasmus would never. . . . He's done a good job."

She arches her eyebrows. "And yet you didn't notice his absence until just now."

I can't let Rasmus be punished for something he didn't do. But how can I refute her without exposing myself and my team? If I confess, she won't let me out of her sight. Latham will change the past. All of Kastelia will be in danger.

"Please," I say, "you can't do this. He's been a good body-guard."

"I admire your loyalty, Saskia. Really, I do. But his actions are unacceptable. He put your life at risk. You'll be assigned someone new, but the replacement won't arrive for a day or two. So I need you to be particularly cautious until then. No going off by yourself. No leaving Ivory Hall. Understood?"

My fingers twist together in my lap. I can't let this happen to Rasmus. It's wrong. Unjust. But I don't know what else to do.

I nod. "Understood."

Norah taps the desktop lightly. "Good. Now let's go. I'll walk you to the training wing and hand you off to Master Kyra."

Hand me off. I cringe. She makes me sound like I'm a baton in a footrace. Just an object to be safeguarded instead of a person with feelings.

But the thought brings a swift pang of guilt that hits me hard in the chest. I treated Rasmus as even less than that—like he was just an obstacle to get around instead of someone with a reputation. A reputation I've just ruined.

My private training is an exercise in futility. I can't focus. My thoughts are slow and sticky.

"You're distracted," Master Kyra says, not unkindly. "Worried about the next bone game?"

"Yes," I say. But it's a lie. The games haven't even crossed my mind since I left the workshop.

I'm thinking of Rasmus. Of Bram. Of how my entire team is in danger because of me. I've been so selfish, so focused on defeating Latham, I haven't appreciated how devastating the consequences would be if my friends were caught helping me. What would Jacey's punishment be for dosing Rasmus with a walking sedative? Or Talon's penalty for using training birds to spy for me?

They've taken such good care of me and I haven't returned the favor. I sink my teeth into my lower lip.

"It's late," Master Kyra says. "Should we call it quits for

today? Perhaps try again when you're not so preoccupied?"

The question makes my throat feel thick. Because I'm quite certain there will never be a time when I'm not weighed down by worry. And with the third bone game approaching next week, I don't have time to waste. I need to find my mother's bones. To stop Latham.

"No," I say, "let's keep going."

I barely listen to her instructions. I have no intention of trying to see anything except Latham.

Master Kyra drops a handful of bones into the stone basin in front of me, and I set them alight. Extinguish the flames. Tip the bones onto the cloth in front of me. The magic leaps in my belly and I'm sucked into a vision.

It takes me a moment to get my bearings, but then the familiar bone-white walls of Ivory Hall come into focus. The dripping chandeliers. The curving dual staircases.

Norah hurries through the foyer, a bundle of packages tucked under her arm. I can't tell if I'm in the past, present, or future. The capital is quiet. No apprentices bustling between classes, no clanging of dishes in the dining hall, no one lounging on benches or studying spells. Maybe everyone is in training sessions. Or maybe the term is over, and everyone has already gone home.

I follow Norah up the stairs, down the corridor, toward the men's dormitory. She stops at one door, and sorts through her stack until she finds a parchment marked *Notice of Exam Failure*. She presses her lips together and shakes her head as she folds the paper and slides it under the door. Then she makes her way down the corridor, delivering letters from home, invoices for damaged library books, instructions to attend extra training sessions. She finishes in the men's dormitory and heads toward the women's. When she stops at my door, my heart clenches. Maybe we're in the future and I've failed the bone games. But Norah doesn't pull a paper from her stack. Instead she reaches for the doorknob. It turns easily at her touch.

She enters the room. A neatly folded stack of linens sits on the end of each bed as if no one lives here yet. So I'm not in the present. Does that mean I'm in the past? In the future?

Norah props a package on one of the pillows. It's wrapped in brown paper stamped with delicate red designs. A tag is attached to the front, and Norah flips it over to reveal a single word written in elegant script: *Saskia*.

The air freezes in my lungs, making it impossible to draw breath. Latham didn't leave the spell book in my room.

Norah did.

But she couldn't have known what she was delivering. Could she?

I shift my attention to her face, hoping if I just study her carefully enough, I might be able to read her intentions. Outside the vision, my stomach rolls over and I think I might be sick. The vision dims and I nearly pull my hands from the bones, but then a shaft of moonlight falls across Norah's face. I've moved forward in time, but Norah is in the exact same place again. She stands in the middle of my room. But now I lie in bed, my hair unbraided and fanned across my pillow. My face is relaxed, as if for once my dreams are untroubled.

Norah pulls a cloth from her pocket and holds it over my nose and mouth. A heavy stone of dread drops into my stomach. Am I in the future now? Is she trying to suffocate me?

In the vision, I swat my hand over my face, as if trying to scratch an itch, but then I go suddenly limp. My hand falls heavily back to the mattress. Norah pulls a bone needle from her pocket and plunges it into a vein at my elbow. Outside the vision, my pulse thunders in my ears. It's exactly like the needle I used on Declan to steal his blood—made from the wing of a vampire bat, infused with the animal's numbing saliva so it pierces without pain. The chamber inside the needle fills with my blood as I lie motionless, drugged by whatever potion Norah soaked into the cloth.

I think of Tessa's horrified expression as she lifted the vial of my blood in the shop. *Saskia, how did Latham get this? Is he doing readings on you?*

Suddenly the pieces fall into place. Norah discouraging me from going after Latham. The way each bone game has seemed specifically designed to torture me. Norah firing Rasmus as an excuse to leave me exposed. The realization is like a knife to the gut.

I was right that Latham had someone working for him on the inside. But the traitor isn't someone on the Grand Council.

The traitor is Norah.

Chapter
Twenty-Six

I stumble from the training room with my hand pressed to my mouth. Bile coats the back of my throat.

Bram is waiting in the corridor and his eyes go wide. "What's wrong?"

Master Kyra is quick at my heels. "Oh good," she says when she sees Bram. "Saskia needs a Healer. Can you walk with her? Tell Master Dina that she overextended herself during a reading and needs something for nausea." But she's wrong. There isn't a medication in the world that can ease my rolling stomach.

Bram takes my elbow. "Yes, of course."

I think of Norah saying she'd hand me off to Master Kyra. Did I just get handed off to Bram? I pull my arm away and his hand falls to his side. I ignore his wounded expression and hurry down the corridor.

He races to catch up with me. "What happened?"

But I don't answer right away. Betrayal, as it turns out, feels a lot like grief. It comes in waves, nearly suffocating me, before receding into something manageable only to gather strength and pummel me all over me again. Norah sat in my home in Midwood. Her eyes welled with tears when I told her what had happened to my mother. She held my hand as she promised to help find Latham and get justice for my family. And yet she was working with him all along.

Just like Declan.

I wait until we're far from the training wing before I dare speak. Then I spin to face Bram.

"Are you still spying for her?" I ask the question through clenched teeth.

"For who? For Norah? Of course not."

"Then why were you waiting for me back there?"

"Because we left things in a weird place before. I wanted to talk to you." He rubs a palm against his cheek. "Saskia, what's going on? What happened back there?"

I lay a palm flat against my stomach. I feel like fate is mocking me. Using my life like a child's toy—a quick turn of a kaleidoscope that keeps rearranging everything I think I know. All I can do is wait for a new image to appear.

"Latham didn't leave the spell book in my room. Norah did."

He goes very still, and then rage flashes across his expression so suddenly, I take a step back. His hands curl into fists at his sides. The air around him seems to crackle.

"I had nothing to do with this," he says.

"I trusted her," I say softly, as much to myself as to Bram.

"I did too. If I'd had any idea—" He takes a deep breath and pinches the bridge of his nose. "What do you want to do now?"

Thoughts whirl around my mind, spinning feverishly until they grow too weary to keep moving. Slowly, like exhausted puppies, they settle and grow still.

And with the quiet in my head comes clarity. "I want to confront her."

Bram's expression is tight, his eyes dark. "I'm coming with you."

My calm doesn't last. As we hurry down the corridor, my pain catches fire and builds into a seething fury. Norah will pay for this right along with Latham. We're nearing the staircase when Talon comes running toward us waving a parchment in front of his face. Jacey, Tessa, and Niklas are close behind him. "We've been searching everywhere for you." His face is flushed. He rests his hand on the banister and sucks in a big gulp of air. "We just got the details for our final bone game, and—" His voice dies as he takes in our expressions. "What's wrong?"

"Norah is working with Latham," Bram says.

There's a slow beat of silence and then they all start talking at once. Questions. Shock. Outrage. But it blends into a dull roar that makes my stomach turn. I can't just stand here talking. I have to do something before the anger inside burns me alive. I might not be able to get to Latham right now, but I can get to Norah.

I spin on my heel and race down the staircase. The others follow, their steps thundering behind me.

When I get to Norah's office, I don't knock before throwing open the door. She sits on a plush chair in front of the hearth, her face lit by crackling flames. She's sipping a cup of tea and a plate of pastries rests on a small table beside her.

"Saskia," she says, "what a nice surprise. Is there something I can do for you?" Her tone is light. Friendly. As if she doesn't have a care in the world.

It enrages me.

"You're a liar." I practically spit the words.

Norah's eyes narrow. She glances at the rest of my team standing behind me. "Excuse me?"

"You promised to help find Latham, and instead you've been helping him this entire time."

A spasm of something flits across her face—surprise? Regret? Guilt? But she quickly regains her composure and her expression smooths into tranquility. She brings the cup to her lips and blows delicately.

"I'm afraid I don't know what you're talking about."

Bram takes a step toward her. "We'll report you to the Grand Council. Maybe a little truth serum will improve your memory."

She gives a brittle laugh. "Are you *threatening* me?"

Bram fixes her with a cold stare. "Yes."

Norah sips her tea. "That would be unwise."

She's so unruffled that it unsettles me, blankets me with a cold that seeps into my veins.

"You won't get away with this," I tell her.

Behind me, Tessa lays a palm against my shoulder blade. "She's right, you won't."

Norah sets the teacup on the table beside her. "What is it you want, Saskia?" Her gaze is glued to me. She doesn't even look at the others, as if she knows this is between the two of us.

"Here's what's going to happen," I say. "You're going to confess to the Grand Council that you've been working with Latham. That you've been allowing him to manipulate the bone games. And then you're going to give them whatever information they need to find him."

Her eyebrows arch, and her mouth twists into an amused smile. "That's a lovely story, dear. Now let me tell one of my own." She presses her hands together in front of her like an excited child playing a game. "We'll all go to the Grand Council together. You'll tell them your suspicions, and then one of them will ask how you came to believe such a preposterous claim. You'll stammer a bit, before finally admitting that you saw it in a bone reading. Of the *past*."

She stands up and begins to pace in front of the hearth. She looks exactly as she does when she's lecturing in the workshop, like she's savoring every moment. Drawing out the suspense for maximum effect. A heavy cloak of dread falls across my shoulders. I feel myself slumping under its weight.

"You might protest that it was just that once—an accident, a mistake—but then I'll point out a similar question that was recently put to rest by this very team. I'll ask the Grand Council to demand you show your mastery tattoo."

I feel a shock wave go through my team, and Norah laughs. "You've been keeping secrets, I see. Would you like to show them now?" Reflexively, I fold my arms across my chest and press my palms over my upper arms. She turns to the others. "Saskia's mastery tattoo is quite lovely. Very intricate. And it has three corners. Poor Jensen is on Fang Island at this very moment being punished for something Saskia is guilty of too. Ah, the irony. Imagine what the Grand Council would think of that."

A twinge of sadness flashes across Jacey's expression, but it quickly hardens into defiance. "It doesn't matter," she says. "The rest of us can testify that we know what you've done."

"I wasn't finished with my story," Norah says. "See, when I fired Rasmus, I found something strange in his pocket. A cloth that had been soaked in a waking sedative potion. He claims he got it from you, but that can't be, because you're matched to ingestibles. Unless . . ." Her eyes go deliberately wide. "Did Saskia encourage you to use unbound magic?"

Norah taps her bottom lip with her index finger. "The stolen climbing equipment will be a problem for Niklas. I have it on good authority that Talon borrowed a bird from the menagerie. And, Tessa and Bram, you haven't been helping Saskia learn even *more* magic she isn't bound to, have you? Because that would be unforgivable in the eyes of the council."

It's as if the air has been sucked from the room. We're all robbed of speech. She's right. Every single one of us has committed offenses that would result in our expulsion if the Grand Council knew. Or worse.

"So *here's* what's going to happen," Norah says, echoing my earlier statement. Her voice has taken on the sharp edge of broken glass. "The six of you are going to keep your mouths shut, keep your heads down, and complete your final bone game. If you're successful, you'll finish your apprenticeships in a few weeks, leave Ivory Hall, and get on with your lives. But if you decide to start spreading rumors, please understand, I will *destroy* you. Are we clear?"

Our stunned silence is all the answer she needs.

"Good. Now kindly leave. My tea is getting cold."

I turn to the others. "Go. I'll be right there." Reluctantly, they shuffle out, but I hang back. Norah's betrayal stings like acid in a fresh wound. I want answers.

"Why?" I ask softly. "Why would you help him?"

Norah's expression gentles, but I can't tell if it's false or genuine. "I'm no fan of Latham, but in this case, our interests happen to align. I'm in a unique position to see how Kastelia hamstrings some of our best and brightest talents by limiting their potential. I've tried for years to get the binding lifted, but the Grand Council won't listen to reason."

"But Latham is evil. You're really willing to sacrifice my life so he can get his way?"

She gives me an apologetic frown. "Even evil people are right sometimes. And leadership is all about difficult choices."

Master Kyra said something similar not too long ago, but I don't think this is what she had in mind.

"Is our final challenge even real? Or is it just another way for Latham to torture me?"

"Can't it be both?" she asks. Our eyes lock for a beat, and then she sighs. "Of course it's real. And maybe if you succeed, we can both get what we want."

I don't have the courage to ask if *both* means me and Norah or Norah and Latham. But even if I did, I'm not sure she'd tell me the truth. Either way, Latham's trap is well laid.

And if I want to find him, I have no choice but to walk into it.

The night air is frigid. Fog rolls across the hilly terrain. I shove my hands into the pockets of my cloak, and my fingers close around Gran's healed bone like it's a lifeline. I think of watching myself sail away from Midwood on my other path. How I gazed up at the sky dotted with stars and thought they looked like bones scattered on velvet. I felt as if I could divine the whole world's fate if I only knew how to read them.

But tonight the clouds are so thick, I can't see a single star. The fate of Kastelia is a mystery.

The six of us hike down the now-familiar path into the city. We could have waited until morning to leave Ivory Hall, but our meeting with Norah left us all raw and restless. None of us would have felt safe enough to close our eyes within those walls tonight. And so we gathered enough supplies to make it through the next few days and then we left. The city streets are deserted. Lamplight puddles on the cobbles.

We find a bench and sit, huddled together against the cold.

"I'm sorry," I say, finally. "I've ruined this for everyone."

"Latham ruined it," Bram mutters. "Norah did."

"Why didn't you tell us about your mastery tattoo?" Tessa asks. Her voice is soft. Careful. But I don't miss how it's shot through with an undercurrent of pain.

"You knew I could use Third Sight. You saw me do it in Latham's shop."

"Yes," she says gently, "so why not tell us about the tattoo?"

"I don't know. After Jensen—"

"Latham did it on purpose," Bram says. "He gave us a trial that would make Saskia feel like she couldn't trust us. It was designed to be a wedge."

He's right. Of course, he's right. Latham has been controlling the bone games to torture me as much as possible this whole time. But the way Bram says it—as if he's come to some realization that's left him troubled—gives me the nagging sense that I'm missing something.

"Well, it didn't work," Jacey says. "We're not going to abandon you."

I sigh. "Maybe you should."

Talon snorts. "That's ridiculous. We would never." His hand is still clutched around the details for our next challenge, which has grown limp with sweat.

Niklas drops his gaze to the folded parchment. "We should probably see which criminal we're supposed to find."

"I guess we should," Talon says. His hands shake as he opens the document and spreads it over his lap.

My heart takes off at a gallop. I'm fully expecting to see Latham's name staring up at us—it would be fitting for him to design a final bone game that forcibly lead us to him. So when I see the name Rayna Roe printed in neat block letters, a long breath sags out of me. I'm not sure if it's relief or disappointment. On one hand, I'm itching for a confrontation. The rage that burns in my chest needs a target before it destroys me from within. Then again, I don't feel ready to face Latham just yet. I'm not sure I ever will.

Jacey taps the page with her fingertip. "She's a Bone Handler."

I gaze down the list of crimes and my stomach curdles. Preparing illegally obtained bones. Selling stolen goods. Facilitating murder. I'm reminded again of Declan—the sharp sting of betrayal when I found him selling my father's bones in the shadow market, the horror at realizing he'd helped arrange the murders of two members of Midwood's town council. Perhaps that's the point—Latham wants me to remember the wounds of the past. To be tortured anew. The more I suffer, the more powerful my bones will be when he finally kills me. But I won't give him the satisfaction. I'll treat this challenge like the game it is. I push aside my feelings and clear my throat.

"It looks like she worked here in the city before she went missing. Maybe we should start at the bone house."

"I agree," Jacey says. "It seems like that's where the council would have started when they were searching for her."

Talon yawns. "Do you think we could close our eyes first? Just for a little while?"

"The bone house won't be open at this hour anyway," Bram says. "Rest. I'll keep the first watch."

I've never been more exhausted, yet more certain I won't be able to sleep. Even so, maybe I'll close my eyes for just a moment—it's better than nothing. I must drift off, because the next thing I know, sunlight is filtering through the clouds.

But my future still looks as dim as ever.

Chapter
Twenty-Seven

he bone house in Kastelia City is nothing like the
one in Midwood. It's huge—a stone structure that looks more
like a castle than a cottage. And when we step inside, instead
of one Master Bone Handler and an apprentice, we find
more than a dozen of each. Apprentices sit at large circular
tables, hunched over bones in various states of preparation.
Some of the Handlers work on cleaning the bones—scooping
out marrow with small wooden spoons, dunking bones in
bleaching solutions, or clearing off dust with small brushes.
Other Handlers sit at tables painting on replicas of tattoos. Still
others poke holes in the bones with small metal pinners and
submerge them in various solutions.

The sight deflates me. There are so many Bone Handlers here. It will take hours to question them all, and we don't even know where to start. But then I remember that Rayna Roe has probably been rotting on Fang Island for years already. This is a reenactment of a case. I glance around for anyone who looks like they don't belong. Who looks like they might be an actor instead of a real Bone Handler.

An apprentice approaches us, tall and gangly, a thin coat of white dust covering his green apron. "Can I help you?"

"We have a few questions," Tessa says. "We're looking for someone who might have trained here. Or maybe trained others?" She bites her lip as she glances down at the parchment. "There's no age listed."

The apprentice cocks his head to one side. "Does this person have a name?"

Tessa blushes. "Oh. Yes, of course. Her name is Rayna Roe."

A dark cloud passes over the apprentice's face, and his Adam's apple bobs in his throat as he swallows. He glances over both shoulders as if he's worried someone overheard the question.

"Sorry. I don't know anyone by that name."

"I think you're lying," Bram says.

The apprentice shoots a furtive look at the pouch hanging from Bram's belt. He licks his lips. "I don't want any trouble."

Ice slides down my spine. He doesn't seem like he's acting. He seems genuinely afraid.

"Let us be clear," I say. "We're not trying to break any rules. And we're not asking *you* to break any rules. We're just wondering if you've ever heard of Rayna Roe. Please? It's important."

"We could always try asking someone else," Talon says, standing on his tiptoes and glancing around the room.

The apprentice puts a hand on Talon's forearm. "Don't bother. No one will tell you anything."

Bram gives him a pointed glare, and the apprentice seems to wither under his gaze. "I don't know much," he says. "Only that there were rumors a while back—"

"Sven," one of the Masters barks from across the room. "What's going on over there?"

"Just answering some questions." His voice wavers a bit, and even from here I can see the Master's eyes narrow in suspicion.

"What kind of rumors?" I ask, my voice low and urgent. The Master starts to head in our direction.

The apprentice shifts his weight. "Some said that Master Rayna was doing work in a shadow market near the Mandible District."

"Thank you," I say, just as the Master reaches us.

"Is there something I can help you with?"

"We were just asking a few questions about Rayna Roe," Niklas says.

The Master's face goes ashen. "What kind of trouble have you gotten yourselves into?"

Suddenly I'm certain that Rayna Roe is not a captured criminal. No one can act this convincingly. Latham and Norah sent us after a Bone Handler who hasn't been apprehended yet.

Another apprentice hurries over and tugs on the Master's sleeve. "Have you seen the neutralizing powder? We just had an acid spill and it's eating through the floor."

The Master groans. Then he points a bony finger at us. "I'll be back in just a moment. Wait right here."

But we don't. The moment he looks away, we run.

The Mandible District is on the outskirts of Kastelia City in the opposite direction of the bone house. We walk all day, chasing the sun as it moves lower and lower in the sky before it finally sinks below the horizon. The gas lamps that line the street grow farther and farther apart until they disappear altogether. Gradually, the broad streets transform into narrow, crooked alleys. Stray dogs rummage through trash heaps, their ribs clearly visible under patchy fur. And then a dog walks by with no fur at all. No skin. No eyes. Just an animated skeleton that is clearly the result of dark magic. I resist the urge to gag.

We pass a gambling den where patrons toss dice made of bone. Dice that have the power to reward or punish bets on the spot—winners receive the prize of pleasure; losers pay with pain. Through the window we can see a woman sitting with a crowd at a round table, a pair of dice sitting near her clenched fist. Her head is thrown back, her mouth open in a silent scream. I'm not sure if she won or lost.

A man stumbles out of a building, clutching a drink in his hand that sloshes over his shoes.

A well-dressed woman walks by with a tiny whistle dangling from her bright red lips like a cigar.

Another storefront with darkened windows has a Breaker guarding the door. I make eye contact and he tosses a set of cervical vertebrae in the air, catches them, and rolls them over his knuckles like he's performing a magic trick instead of issuing a threat.

"I hate this," Tessa whispers.

"Just keep your head down and keep moving," Bram says.

As we travel through the Mandible District, I can't help but wonder what horrors the shadow market is concealing. The thought sends gooseflesh racing over my arms.

I've only been to a shadow market once in my life, and it was one time too many. In Midwood, the market was housed on a merchant ship that docked somewhere different each night to escape the notice of the town council. But as this shadow market finally comes into view, I realize they have no such worries about the Grand Council. The market isn't hidden; it's on display like a jewel in a glass case.

A huge complex made of clear glass stretches as far as the eye can see. Even though it's after dark, inside it's as well lit as if it were broad daylight.

And the patrons are dressed in finery worthy of a ball. Silk cloaks with intricate patterns embroidered in threads of gold, gowns with rows of tiny bone-crafted buttons, oversized jewels that glitter on every throat and finger. It's both a celebration of the Mandible District's debauchery and a mockery of its poverty. It's grotesque.

But I can't let it show on my face. We have to convince the Breakers standing at the entrance to let us in. I stop and turn to the others.

"I should go in alone." I incline my head toward the guards. "They'll never let all six of us through."

Talon scratches the back of his neck. "No. That's a terrible idea."

"I agree," Niklas says. "We'd have no way to know if you're in trouble."

I turn toward Tessa and Jacey, but both of them have identical expressions of worry on their faces.

"I don't know," Tessa says. "It seems too dangerous."

I sigh. "I'm the one Latham wants. I should be the one to take the risk."

"I'll go with you," Bram says.

I turn toward him. "You don't have to—"

"Of all of us, I'm the one best equipped to protect you if something goes wrong."

"It makes sense," Jacey says. "I'd feel better if Bram went too. I think we all would."

"Fine. Let's go." But before I can move, something scurries across the top of my foot. I let out a yelp and jump back. A huge rat disappears into the gutter.

I press my hand to my chest. "Did anyone see that?"

Talon's eyes dart from the ground to something in the distance. "That was no ordinary rat."

"I know." My heart is still beating at twice the normal speed. "It was huge."

"Not just that," Talon says. "It was Watcher-controlled." He nods to a woman across the street, and jolt of recognition goes through me.

"I saw her a few minutes ago," I tell him. "I thought she had a whistle, but it must have been a tiny bone flute."

"*Spy* rats?" Bram says, his voice disbelieving.

"I'm afraid so," Talon says. He looks at me. "I don't like this."

"Neither do I, but what choice do we have? If we bail now, we fail the challenge. You'll all be stripped of your magic and go home with nothing. And if I don't find Latham, I won't ever get my mother's bones back."

I don't add that my thirst for revenge is propelling me forward more than it ever has before. That I would do anything to watch Latham suffer.

Tessa grabs my hand and squeezes my fingers. "Be careful."

I turn and pull her into an embrace. "I'm just going in to ask questions. Rayna Roe probably isn't even here. I'll be fine."

"I'll come find you if you're not back soon."

"Sounds like a plan." But we both know she's unlikely to get past the guards. If I don't come back, there's very little she can do about it.

I try to keep my breathing even as Bram and I approach the entrance to the shadow market. I have the advantage of seeing Audra do this once before. It's important that I project confidence. Act like I belong.

But when we get to the door, the guard doesn't hesitate. "Not a chance," he says without looking at us. "Move along."

"We're here to see Master Rayna."

He snorts. *"Master* Rayna?"

My neck goes hot as I realize my mistake—the show of deference seems out of place here. I make my expression go steely.

"If you knew her, I think you'd find she prefers the title. Now, can you let us pass?"

He turns a withering gaze on me. "You have a lot of nerve attempting to command me."

Panic closes my throat. But I force myself to stay calm. "And you have a lot of nerve to deny me entrance."

We stand there a moment, eyes locked in a battle of wills.

"I'm not leaving until I get what I came for," I say finally.

He laughs. "And what exactly did you come for?"

"Revenge."

Something like grudging admiration washes over his expression, as if I've finally convinced him I belong in a place like this. He chuckles. Then he steps aside and motions me forward with a gallant sweep of his arm. "Far be it from me to stand between a lady and her vengeance."

"I've never seen anything like this," Bram says as we wander through the shadow market. His voice is a mixture of horror and awe. It's exactly how I feel.

In one booth, a Healer works on a man's face—changing the shape of his nose, the height of his forehead, the fullness of his lips. At first, I assume it's for vanity's sake, but then it occurs to me that the man is probably a criminal changing his appearance to evade punishment.

In another booth, Mixers offer patrons small goblets of potions in electric colors—bright greens and blues and oranges. Other patrons sniff finely milled bone powders from glass trays.

We pass tables of stolen goods, clothes studded with bone fragments, weapons in all shapes and sizes.

I spot a tannery displaying a selection of leather products— some of them tattooed—and revulsion swells inside me. Is this where Latham had the spell book made?

All around us things are happening that would shock us if we saw them in isolation. But gathered in one place, it's a tsunami of illegal activity that leaves me craving a shower.

Finally I spot a woman working with a set of tools I recognize—small brushes, tiny spoons, flat blades. I think of Ami back in Midwood using an identical set in her duties as a Bone Handler.

"Maybe that's her," I whisper to Bram.

He touches my shoulder lightly. "I'm right behind you."

The woman is tall and slender with raven hair that falls past her shoulders. Rubies shaped like teardrops dangle from her earlobes and she wears at least a dozen thin gold bracelets around each wrist. But as we approach, she pushes back from her chair and saunters away.

Bram and I exchange a look. Did she spot us coming?

We keep our distance as we follow her. We weave through the shadow market, trying our best to both catch up with the

Bone Handler and to stay out of her line of sight. My breath stills when she glances over her shoulder. But she must not suspect us, because her pace stays the same. Slow. Measured. Like she's not running from anyone. Finally she stops at a set of booths tucked into a corner. They appear to be workrooms instead of display areas. Thick curtains block their contents from view. The woman pulls back one of the panels and horror pushes up my throat.

The sight is nothing like either the bone house in Midwood or the one in Kastelia City.

Floating inside glass urns filled with liquid are severed body parts. Feet. Hands. Individual fingers and toes. All with bloated flesh that is starting to separate from the bone.

I gag.

Bram makes a choked noise. His face is ashen.

I don't even want to think about how these body parts were taken. It horrifies me that there's a market for this—people willing to buy the stolen bones of the living.

"It must be some kind of acid," I say, looking over the containers. "She's trying to accelerate decomposition."

"I guess the Forest of the Dead is too slow when you're trying to turn a profit." Bram sounds as repulsed as I feel.

An image flashes through my mind of Latham running from my house in Midwood with my dead mother cradled in his arms. A wave of nausea rolls through me. He wants me to know what he did to her. I stuff my knuckles into my mouth.

Grim determination settles inside me.

"Let's get out of here," I say, my voice catching on the words.

I don't care about completing the bone games. I'm going to go back to Latham's shop and heal the bones to get the future I choose. I'm going make his every nightmare come to life.

I grab Bram's hand and hurry back the way we came. And then we round the corner and freeze.

Latham stands near a booth filled with weapons. He's squarely between us and the exit. He's grown a beard since I saw him last. It's dark and trimmed close to his face.

"Hello, Saskia."

Bram's hand tightens around mine. But I feel strangely calm, as if Latham and I are just keeping an appointment we made long ago.

Latham lifts an eyebrow. He sweeps his hand around the booth. "Were you looking to purchase something? Anything I can help you find?"

"No," I say, "I'm all set."

He tips his head to one side. "So, which way did you decide to go?"

"I'm sorry?"

"I saw two distinct paths for you. I'm wondering which you chose?"

A cold trickle slides down my spine as I think of the vial of my own blood on the shelf in his shop. The vision of Norah plunging a needle into my arm.

"You've been doing readings on me." It's not a question.

He laughs. "Would you have expected anything less?"

No. I wouldn't have. I touch the pendant in the hollow of my throat and think of all the times I've had to remove it for training. All the times I've woken in the morning to find it lying on the floor or tangled in my blankets.

My mouth goes dry.

It's as if I've walked off the edge of a cliff. I'm falling. Flailing. Bracing for impact.

I take a step back. "Please. Just let us go."

He frowns. "You know I can't do that."

"Get away from us!" I scream. We're in the middle of a busy market made of glass—visible to throngs of people both inside and out—and a crowd of curious onlookers have started to gather. Someone will intervene. Someone will stop him.

But no one does.

I'm like a bird in a cage. People might pause and stare, but none of them are going to unlatch the door.

I take another step back. "So what now?" I'm stalling for time. "What did the bones tell you about how this ends?"

My eyes flick to where a bone-carved sword rests on a high shelf, and a ping of alarm goes through me—it looks familiar. Latham follows my gaze. Takes a step toward the weapon. Runs a slender finger over the bone-carved hilt.

"Come here, Saskia."

I try to remember the details of my nightmare—the quality of the light in the room. Bright colors, and weapons made of bone. Where I'm always standing when the sword falls. The details are hauntingly similar.

I swallow. "I think I'll stay where I am."

His hand drops back to his side. He leaves the sword where it is.

"Aren't you tired, Saskia?" He asks the question softly, almost tenderly. And it nearly breaks me. Because I am. I'm so, so tired. Is that it then? I'm so exhausted that I simply give up? No. I refuse to choose that path.

"I'm not too tired for justice," I say.

He gives me an evaluating look. "Justice? I think you mean revenge."

"In this case, they're the same."

"Are they? You'd choose vengeance over seeing your mother again? When it would be so easy to bring her back? I must confess, I'm astonished. I had no idea you were so cold."

Even though I know he's trying to manipulate my emotions, I'm still stunned by how effective he is. The thought of abandoning my mother forever when there is any other option—it feels like vinegar poured over an open wound. I make an involuntary sound, and I can see that it pleases him.

"You never found your mother's bones." His tone is light. Conversational. "It was important to you."

It was more than important to me. It was vital. And the reminder of my failure is a vice around my heart.

"Perhaps you didn't know where to look." His fingers trail lazily across the weapons on the shelf—bone knives, arrows, throwing stars.

Beside me, Bram reaches into the pouch at his side. I hear the snap of a small bone, but nothing happens.

"Would you like to know what I did with them?"

My voice sticks in my throat.

It's a game, a trick. I think of Latham's question months

ago. *Would you like to embrace your mother one final time?*

And my answer. A tight whisper. *Yes.*

But the moment she reached me, he stabbed her in the back. So now I clamp my lips shut even though I want to answer, long to beg him to tell me.

"No?" he says. "Not even a little curious?"

The sound of his voice ties my stomach into knots. I wish he'd stop talking. I can't think with his voice in my head. Can't plan. Latham's gaze flicks to Bram and understanding drops into my mind like a stone in a lake. He wants me to let go of Bram's hand. To separate us so I'll be more exposed. But I won't do it.

"I've heard Bram's teaching skills are being put to good use once again," Latham says, continuing his one-sided conversation.

"Don't you dare, you worm." Bram's voice is infused with heat. My stomach clenches like I'm bracing for a blow.

Latham expression is smug as he turns to me. "Have you gotten the hang of it yet?"

"Stop it!" Bram shoves his entire fist into the pouch at his waist, and a dozen bone snap at once.

But Latham just laughs. "Tell her."

Bram tugs on my hand. "Let's go."

I don't move. "Tell me what?"

Bram stares at me. His mouth opens, and then he snaps it shut.

"Tell me what?"

"It took me a while to catch on too," Latham says, "but once I did, it was such a *useful* skill. It made breaking the lock on your father's bone box a breeze. Bram is a good teacher. You're lucky to have him."

My heart slows, seems to shudder to a stop. My vision fractures.

I let go of Bram's hand and take a step back. "You helped him?" My voice comes out high and shrill. "You helped him steal my father's bones?"

Bram's expression is haunted. "Saskia, no."

"So he's lying?"

"It wasn't like that. I didn't know who he was then. What he was capable of."

I didn't think that Latham could hurt me any more than he already has, but I was wrong. I think of Bram showing up in Midwood after my mother died. I asked him how he found out what had happened. How he knew to come.

Master Latham let me know. . . . He's kind of taken me under his wing this year.

Declan sold my father's bones in the shadow market. But Bram helped Latham steal them in the first place.

I take another step away from him, but then I freeze. I've just moved closer to Latham, who laughs darkly.

"What if I told you that on one of your paths—maybe even *this* one—you come to me willingly?"

"I wouldn't believe you," I say.

He smiles. It's the smile of someone who knows something I don't.

He picks up a large bone flute from among the cache of weapons and artifacts. He turns it over in his hands, and a flash of color catches my eye. A yellow-orange sunburst.

Time seems to slow. Still. Turn backward.

I am a little girl, no more than seven. The wind whips through my hair as my mother pushes me on the swing hanging from the tree in our backyard.

"You should try it, Mama," I say, tipping my head back so that my long hair brushes the blades of grass at the bottom of the swing's arc. "It feels like flying."

And she does. She climbs onto the swing and I put my hands on her knees and give her a push. Her laugh mingles with the birds chirping in the branches. She swings back toward me and I push her again. The fabric of her skirt bunches around her knees. A flash of yellow-orange. A tattoo on her thigh.

"What's that?" I ask as she flies away from me.

"I always thought it looked a bit like a sunburst." She smooths her skirt over her legs. Swings back in my direction.

"How did you get it?"

"It appeared when your papa surprised me with this house. Our first home together." Her toes drag in the grass and she comes to a stop. "It was a burst of pure joy," she says, touching her fingertip to my nose. "Kind of like right now."

The memory fades. But I still remember the glow in my chest. The way warmth spread through me.

And now Latham is holding a bone flute with the same sunburst tattoo.

Bone flutes are used to control animals, and they're made from the bones of the same type of creature they are meant to command. But what if a bone flute were made from a *human* bone? What if that bone belonged to my mother?

Latham watches as the realization floods over me. As it turns my blood to ice.

He smiles. He puts the flute to his lips and begins to play. My mind goes blank. And then, distantly, I hear a familiar lullaby—one both my mother and Gran used to sing to me.

> *Come with me to the dreaming place*
> *Where the owls call and the children race*
> *Come with me to the dreaming place*
> *And stay by my side for-ev-er*

"Come, Saskia," my mother says. I see her in front of me, arms outstretched. Joy leaps in my chest.

"Mama?" I stand and take a step toward her.

"I missed you," she says.

A sob chokes my throat. "I missed you too."

"Saskia!" A shout pierces the air and the music stops. My mother wavers. Starts to disintegrate.

I look around, confused.

"Saskia!"

Bram's face swims in front of me. His hand closes around my arm. "Come with me."

The music starts again. *Come with me to the dreaming place.* . . .

My mother grows more solid. She opens her arms.

I'm yanked violently to the side. Bram's face. *Come with me.* My mother's. *Come with me.*

The music stops abruptly. A cacophony of noise erupts around me. Voices shouting over one another. Things being knocked to the ground. I feel as if I'm waking up from a dream—the images of my mother slowly breaking apart, ethereal and impossible to hang on to. Followed by the sinking disappointment she was never here at all.

And then I look up and my nightmare comes to life. Latham stands in front of me, a sword in his hand. His eyes are bright and eager.

A small, round table sits between us. I can use it as a shield. If he can't reach me, he can't kill me.

I put a hand on the silky wood to keep him from moving it out of place. He gives me that shrewd smile again, as if he's still playing the bone flute and I'm still dancing to his tune. What does he know that I don't?

A raven flies into the room, frantic and shrieking. It dives for Latham. Aims for his eyes.

Relief cascades over me. Talon must be close.

The bird's sharp beak draws blood. Latham grunts and slashes the sword in the air. He misses. Tries again.

And then a desperate, injured squawk. An explosion of black feathers and innards. My stomach pitches. I taste bile at the back of my throat.

Latham advances on me, but I keep one hand on the table between us. I won't let him get close enough.

He raises the sword.

"Saskia, watch out!" Bram's voice cuts through the air. But I don't take my eyes off Latham. Dimly, I wonder why Bram doesn't break Latham's bones—snap his humerus so the weapons slips from his hand. Sever his femur to topple him. A faint memory flits at the edge of my awareness. Did Bram already try and fail? Maybe that's the knowledge that keeps twisting Latham's lips into a smirk.

The sword swings downward. I see it like I'm traveling along a path in a vision. Disconnected from myself. Moving slowly, as if time is a bit of molasses dangling from a spoon, stretching and stretching but never landing.

The sword falls, but it isn't headed for my throat or my heart or my lungs.

The blade slices through the slender red tattoo at my wrist. Pain seizes me, white-hot and blinding. I scream. My hand detaches from the rest of my arm. Blood spatters my cheeks and pools on the table. There's so much of it.

I feel suddenly cold.

Black spots rush into my vision and the world goes dark.

Chapter Twenty-Eight

*V*oices float toward me from a distance. I try to open my eyes, but the effort is too much.

"What if she never wakes up?" That must be Jacey. Her words are soft and shot through with worry.

"She will." Tessa's voice. "She has to."

My wrist throbs.

The surface beneath me shifts, and my head lolls to one side. An arm under my neck. Someone is cradling me. I force my eyes open. Bram's face hovers above mine. I blink, confused. My dreams sometimes start this way, but I'm never this disoriented. Never in this much pain.

I try to stretch. To open and flex my hands, but something feels off.

My hand.

Everything comes rushing back and I let out a whimper.

"Don't worry," Bram says. His face is tight. His mouth thin. "You're safe now."

We're outside, in some kind of alley. It's dark out—the only light comes from a barrel fire burning nearby. Bram must have carried me out of the shadow market. When I realize my head is resting in the crook of his elbow, my broken heart aches. He helped Latham. Taught him the magic he needed to steal my father's bones.

"Put me down." Pain flashes through Bram's eyes, but he complies, gently setting me on the ground.

At the sound of my voice, the others hurry to my side. They're all here, their faces illuminated by firelight—Tessa, her face tear-streaked and swollen; Talon, who looks like he hasn't slept in at least a week; Jacey and Niklas, who are leaning against each other as if they might fall over otherwise.

I gather my courage and look down. My arm is wrapped in blood-soaked bandages. My hand is missing.

"No," I say softly. "No, no, no."

Tessa lets out a choked sob. "I'm sorry, Saskia. We tried . . . We tried so hard to stop him, but we couldn't do it. He was wearing some kind of armor, so Bram couldn't break his bones. Talon tried with the raven, but . . ." I think of Latham's blade arcing through the air. The burst of black feathers. "He was too strong."

All of my time spent worrying and I never once considered that Latham didn't actually need to kill me to finish what he started. He didn't need *every* bone in my body, just a few.

We must not have moved very far from the shadow market, because I can still hear the din of corruption in the background—customers bartering for a better deal on stolen bones, Breakers calling out bets on who will die in their next snapping battle, the barking of Mixers advertising drugs for sale.

I lift my head, and Bram helps me sit. The sky spins, and I squeeze my eyes closed. A wave of nausea rolls through my stomach. A distant ache pulses at the wound, and I can tell whatever pain spell Tessa administered is beginning to wear off.

"I can make you a new hand," Niklas says. His voice is tentative. "I've studied how to do it in training. The bones wouldn't be yours, of course; we'd need a donor. But it would function."

I don't want a new hand. I want *my* hand. But the earnest expression on his face unravels me and I nod. "Thank you."

They all look so bleak that guilt twists in my stomach. I never should have let them come with me to the Mandible District. Not when I knew it was a trap.

"I'm sorry," I say softly. "I'm so very sorry."

Niklas touches my knee. "No, *I'm* sorry. Saskia, I saw that bone flute the first time we were in Latham's shop. I wasn't sure it was human, but I suspected, and it sickened me. I should have mentioned it. If I'd had any idea . . ."

I think of how studiously Niklas avoided entering the shop after that first time. His haunted expression as his gaze swept across the room. But how was he to know? The shelves were full of horrors—broken bones suspended in nutrient solutions, strange weapons. He couldn't have suspected the flute was carved to control me.

And the truth is, once I saw Gran's broken bones, I didn't explore the rest of the shop either. If I had, would things have turned out differently?

"You couldn't have known," I tell him. But he still looks unnerved. And I know how he feels. I will be haunted forever by the ghosts of paths not taken.

I climb to my feet and the world tilts to one side. I nearly topple over, but Bram catches me. Puts a steadying hand around my elbow.

"Don't touch me," I say. "Please."

"Saskia." Bram's voice is raw, pleading. "Let's talk about this."

The others are looking back and forth between us, confused. But I don't explain.

I pull in a deep breath and then I take a few shaky steps forward.

"What are you doing?" Talon asks.

"I have to go after Latham."

Tessa's eyes widen. I can see the reflection of flames in her pupils. "Saskia, no. You're still weak. You've lost too much blood."

"I don't have a choice. He's going to use the bones in my hand to change the past. I have to stop him."

"You're in no condition to go running after anyone." She presses a palm to my brow. "We need to get you to a Disease Healer. I did what I could for pain control, but you're warmer than you should be. I'm worried about infection."

I shake her off. "None of that matters if Latham heals one of Gran's bones."

"We'll go to the Grand Council," Tessa says. "Tell them what we know. They'll be better equipped to handle this than we are. And they'll have more resources, too."

"It would be pointless. One of them might be working with Latham and Norah. The only people in the world I can trust are right here."

"But what makes you assume we'd have any better luck?" Jacey asks gently. "We're not even sure where he went, and even if we could stop him—"

"He'll go back to his shop. He has everything he needs to change the past now, and he won't waste any time."

Tessa folds her arms across her chest and cradles her elbows in her palms. "Let's try the Grand Council first. And then if they don't—"

Frustration builds inside me. A pressure behind my eyes. A weight in my chest. "I'm going now," I say. "With or without the rest of you."

They all go silent. A held breath.

And then Bram clears his throat. "I'll go with you."

"I will too," Talon says.

Tessa digs her fingers into her hair. "Of course I'll come along." She looks at Jacey and Niklas, who both nod. "We all will. But not until I change those bandages and give you another pain spell."

But she can't heal what really matters. She can't crack open my chest to find my heart—bruised in shades of black and blue, yellow and green, tattered with grief and betrayal—and make it whole again.

Some things can't be mended.

Before we leave the Mandible District, we go back inside the shadow market and gather supplies. Knives and daggers, cords made of bone fragments that clamp down with struggle.

We walk through the night to make it back to Latham's shop. I'm weak from blood loss, and the others take turns letting me lean on them for support. All except Bram, who stays at the back of the group.

I've lost track of time, but I know we haven't eaten or slept in far too long. And we don't have time to do either right now.

As we travel, I bite my cheek against the throbbing in my hand, before I realize that my hand is no longer there. A phantom pain that hurts just as much as if it were real. Like my other path on Gran's healed bone. The ache of expecting something that isn't there. The agony of absence.

And so I focus on my anger instead. I let it fester and ooze. My father once said that anger was like paint on a wall—it might be the first thing you notice, but it's always just covering up something else. You can't actually build anything from it.

But I think he's wrong.

I think if the anger is big enough, maybe it could build a whole world. A different future.

As we draw closer to Latham's shop, a thin strip of pale pink light hovers above the horizon. Bram draws up beside me and touches my shoulder lightly. "Can we talk?"

I start to pull away, but he catches my fingers in his. "Saskia, please. Just let me say this."

I stop and spin to face him. "What? What could you possibly have to say to me?"

The others exchange nervous glances and back off a little to give us space.

Bram swallows. "I didn't know who Latham was when he asked me to help him. If I'd had any idea he would use that knowledge to hurt you. To hurt *anyone* . . ." He rakes a hand through his hair. "I never should have trusted him. But I was flattered that one of the Masters thought I was gifted. Once I realized what he'd done, I was horrified. I've been tortured about this for months. I tried to tell you, but you asked me not to. I should have told you anyway."

Confusion washes over me. He never tried to tell me about this—but then I remember. That day on the grounds outside Ivory Hall when I thought, for just a moment, he might kiss me.

Saskia, I need to tell you something.

Is it going to break my heart?

I'm afraid it might.

"I thought you were going to tell me you still found the idea of being with me amusing."

He shakes his head. "I stopped finding it amusing a long time ago. And I can't let you go into Latham's shop without telling you how I feel."

334

My pulse speeds. "So tell me. How do you feel?" My heart feels like an open wound—raw and vulnerable to more damage.

"I don't want to lose you. Not ever again."

But he could be lying. Declan lied too. He pretended to love me at Latham's instruction. And then, in the end, he led me right into a trap.

My eyes fall to Bram's wrist. It's still bare.

"You don't have a tattoo."

He groans. Tunnels his fingers through his hair. "You can be so infuriating sometimes. I've done nothing but try to help you take down Latham. I've been by your side. I've kept your secrets. So if I'd done all those same things with a red line around my wrist, that would have made me more trustworthy?"

"You helped Latham destroy my family."

"Before I knew what he was doing!" Bram's eyes blaze, and I look away, stung.

He puts a single index finger under my chin and gently lifts my face. His gaze finds mine and I feel like I'm drowning.

"Please forgive me. I made the wrong choice and trusted the wrong person. I won't do it again."

I feel as if he's swept my feet out from under me. Turned the world on its head. I've spent months wishing he'd say what he just said. Wishing he'd look at me the way he's looking at me now—like nothing else matters if things aren't right between us. But now that he has, I don't know if I can trust him.

And I don't get the chance to sort out my feelings before Talon steps forward and clears his throat. "I don't mean to rush"—he waggles his fingers between us—"whatever is going on here, but we should probably make a plan."

I tear my gaze away from Bram. Shake my head to clear my thoughts. "Yes, you're right."

"What do you need from us?" Jacey asks.

"Latham will be wearing protective magic," I say. "If we can work together to remove it, he'll be vulnerable to attack. The five of you can try to kill him, while I work on healing the bones."

An awkward silence envelops us. They all avoid meeting my gaze. They're not murderers.

"If you don't want to kill him, then incapacitate him instead. Tessa, do you think you can control my pain while I work?"

"I'll do my best," she says.

Niklas twists the ring on his finger. "Maybe I can help. I fuse bone pieces together sometimes when I'm creating objects. It's probably a similar magic to mending."

I turn and give him a small smile. "I'm sure you could attach the individual pieces, but I don't think it would work to change the past. I think the bone needs to be healed as if it were inside a body."

"Why not let Tessa heal the bone?" Jacey asks. "Wouldn't that work better?"

I squeeze Tessa's fingers. "I don't think she can. I think it has to be me. My bones have to be used to complete the spell."

Jacey's mouth twists. "How are you going to manage that?"

I glance at Bram. "I'm going to try to draw the magic from my own bones to heal Gran's. Bram and Tessa, I might need both of you to help coach me if I get stuck."

Talon throws his hands up in the air. "So I'm the only useless one here?"

Jacey nudges his shoulder with her own. "Did you bring
your flute? You could provide some background music."

He glares at her in a way that belies his affection, and my
heart pushes against its borders. My mind is flooded with
memories of our last few months together, and I have the
sudden urge to refuse to heal anything so I can protect this
version of reality—one where their friendship is a certainty. I
don't want to lose any of them. But I have to take the risk. If I
truly care about my friends, I can't leave them in a world where
Latham could be sovereign. Even if I have to lose them trying
to give them a better one.

I turn and take in each of their faces. Tessa's fiercely loyal
expression. Jacey, whose chin is trembling just a little despite
how hard she's trying to hide her worry. Niklas and his quiet
strength. Talon, who—even now, when things are dire—looks
only a moment away from laughter.

And Bram.

Even with everything that has happened, I'd give anything
not to lose him again.

"If this works, everything might be different between us," I
tell them, letting my gaze fall on them one by one. "We might
not remember this path. We might not remember one another
at all."

Talon grins. "I'm like one of those ivy plants. Easy to find,
but hard to get rid of once it's taken root. I'll be around whether

you guys remember me or not."

Bram puts a reassuring hand on my shoulder. "If the worst happens, we'll find one another again. We've done it before."

I take a deep breath. "We should each take a weapon."

Talon holds open the satchel from the shadow market. I choose a small dagger—the most I can manage with one hand—even if it is my dominant one.

"We're ready when you are," Jacey says.

As quietly as we can, we move closer to the door. I pull a pin from my hair and hand it to Bram, who quietly works the lock. We step over the threshold. The outer room is silent and still. What if we're too late? What if Latham has already changed the past?

A single crimson drop splashes on the ground beneath my feet. My wound has started seeping again and the bandage is soaked in fresh blood. If Latham had already healed one of the bones, my hand wouldn't still be missing.

"Stay behind me," I whisper to the others as we creep to the hidden bookcase and ease open the door.

The room looks different in the dim light. A collection of shadows and oddly shaped objects. Candles flicker throughout the space, bathing the room in a soft glow. Shadows climb the walls and spill across the floor.

Latham is seated at the long wooden table in the center of the room, hunched over a set of Gran's bones. He's so focused on his task that he doesn't hear us enter. Next to him is a jar filled with clear liquid. My hand floats inside, a bright red tattoo visible at the wrist.

I clamp my lips together and fight the wave of nausea that rolls through me. A mix of relief and rage bubbles in my chest. He hasn't completed the spell. He hasn't changed the past, at least not yet.

But the sight of my own bloated fingers bobbing in acid makes the loss of my hand feel even more real than my bandaged arm does.

From the corner of my eye, I see a sudden movement on the other side of the room.

"Latham, watch out!"

The Bone Handler from the Mandible District moves out of the shadows. Latham spins around. His hand closes around the hilt of a blade as his gaze lands on me.

"Rayna, get back."

But the warning is too late. Bram has already dipped his fingers into the bone pouch at his waist. Rayna lets out a bloodcurdling scream and her leg gives out beneath her. She crumples to the floor, her face a mask of agony.

"Get away from my gran's bones," I say.

Latham doesn't move. His eyes fall to my arm. "Haven't you suffered enough?"

Bram reaches into his pouch again and snaps one of the small bones clean in half, but it doesn't have any effect. Latham's fingers go to the claw-shaped clasp at his throat. Protective magic. But if it blocks Bram's abilities, it must be far more powerful than the pendant Avalina gave me.

"My suffering will be minuscule compared to what I'm going to do to you." The dagger in my hand trembles. It's slick with sweat and slippery against my palm. I feel faint.

"This will all be over soon," Latham says. His voice has lost its usual edge. He says it almost tenderly. "Let me finish and your pain will vanish. You'll be safe."

Talon inches closer to the table. In a flash, I understand what he's doing. I have to keep Latham's attention focused on me long enough for Talon to grab the jar that holds my hand. Latham can't finish the spell without my bones.

"I'll be safe? You've been trying to kill me for months. You don't care about my safety."

I push my hair off my forehead with my wrist. Talon takes another step.

Latham cocks his head to one side. "What do you think will happen to you when the Grand Council finds out about your mastery tattoo? The fate I have planned for you is far more merciful than a lifetime spent on Fang Island."

"You don't get to plan my fate."

He smiles as if I've told a clever joke. "I do now."

Talon's hands close around the jar, and at the same moment, the rest of us rush forward. We try to pry the claw from Latham's throat, but it holds fast. I let out a cry of frustration, but then a raven flies into the room at full speed and rams into Latham's collarbone, tugging at the clasp with its beak. Finally it comes loose and clatters to the floor. At the same moment, Bram breaks one of the bones in his pouch and Latham's femur snaps in half. His eyes go wide. He tumbles from the chair.

His scream is music to my ears.

"Tie him up over there," I say.

Niklas fishes the bone cord from the satchel and pulls Latham's arms behind his back. He wraps the cord around his wrists several times. Latham struggles and the cord digs even deeper into his flesh. Rayna is still whimpering in the corner, and Niklas drags Latham across the floor and deposits him next to her.

I gather supplies and bring them to the table—a bone knife, a needle, a velvet cloth. Then I carefully take all of the jars from the shelves and bring them to the table.

Gran's bones line up in front of me—broken, yet full of possibilities. They could be combined in endless different ways to change the past.

A sense of calm settles over me.

I don't know if what I'm attempting is even possible. But if I fail, at least I will fail trying to avenge my mother and Gran.

I remove the first bone from the nutrient solution and place it on the cloth. I touch one half and then the other—my fingertips resting on each just long enough to remind me of what I saw when I last read them. Latham at seventeen. One side of the bone, Latham's father splits his coin between a kenning and matchmaking reading for his son. On the other half, he devotes the full amount to the kenning—more valuable bones, more expensively prepared.

But I don't want either option.

I sift through my memory of a small, slender path I saw on one of the other bones. A path where Latham's father lost a great deal of coin on a bad investment.

It was an unlikely outcome in any reality, but I'm going to make it happen.

"You don't know what you're doing," Latham says. His voice rattles from his throat, strained and full of pain.

"Yes," I tell him, "I do."

I open the jars one by one and touch each bone half until I find the one I'm looking for. I think back on one of the volumes on Bone Mending I've been studying. I practically memorized the section on bone grafts. Healers sometimes use donor bone fragments in their work—bits of bone belonging to another person that can be used to repair the bones of their patient.

If I can use the same principle, I should be able to create one bone from many, allowing me to carefully select the exact paths that will bring Latham the most misery. But first, I'll need to slice a small piece from this bone—just the corner, where I read the possibility of Latham's father going broke.

He can't provide his son a deluxe kenning if he has no coin.

I'm so focused on the task, I startle when a strangled noise pulls my gaze upward.

The world goes silent and slow.

Tessa stands in the doorway. A man I recognize is positioned behind her. It's Latham's Breaker, Lars, the same man who killed Declan in Midwood. Who protected Latham so he could kill my mother. He must have just arrived, and now he has one arm pressed across Tessa's shoulders pinning her back to his chest.

"I'm sorry, Saskia," Tessa says. "I lost focus for just a moment. And I—" Her voice cuts off as he squeezes her windpipe with his free hand.

I turn to Latham.

"Tell him to let her go."

"Tell your friend to give me the jar."

I hesitate, my gaze skipping between Tessa and Latham. My mind scrambles for a way out of this. For a way to protect Tessa without giving up my hand. But I can't think of one.

"Give it to him," I tell Talon.

"Saskia—"

"He'll kill her," I say. "Give it to him."

"Are you sure?"

"Give it to him." My voice is flat.

Talon steps forward and places the jar on the floor halfway between me and Latham. Latham grimaces as he inches forward and snatches it up. He cradles it in the crook of his elbow.

"Now tell your Breaker to let Tessa go," I say. Latham gives a small nod to Lars. I turn and wait for him to release her.

But he doesn't.

He snaps her neck.

Chapter Twenty-Nine

essa's eyes go wide. Startled.

And then they go blank.

Lars lets go, and Tessa slumps to the ground. I run to her. Her head is bent at an odd angle. I press a palm against her cheek and try to turn her face toward me. I lift my other arm, but then I drop it back to my side; I don't have another hand to help her.

Behind me, commotion erupts. Bones snapping, furniture toppling, the crash of broken glass. But I don't take my eyes from Tessa.

"Don't die." I say it over and over, like a prayer. *Don't die. Don't die. Don't die.* My father's face flashes in my memory.

My mother's.

Gran's.

I've lost too many people. I can't lose Tessa, too. But her eyes are vacant.

Jacey kneels beside me. Her breathing is ragged. She presses two fingers to Tessa's neck. "She gone."

I shake my head. Wipe my nose with my sleeve. "No."

Don't die. Don't die. Don't die.

"Saskia, there's nothing you can do."

But there must be.

A yawning chasm of despair opens inside me. This is all my fault. Tessa didn't want to come. She practically begged me to go to the Grand Council instead of handling this on our own, but I wouldn't listen. And now she's dead.

What have I done?

I look up, tears blurring my vision as I take in the scene of destruction. Shards of glass glitter at my feet. Gran's broken bones are strewn across the floor.

Suddenly I'm hit from behind. It knocks the wind out of me.

Lars.

He grabs me roughly around the waist and drags me forward. I try to struggle free, but he's too strong, and I can't land a blow. What is he doing? He doesn't need to get close to me to end me. He could kill me from afar, snap my neck like he snapped Tessa's.

And then I see it. His bone pouch has come loose and is lying across the room. Bram's pouch rests alongside it, and a handful of small bones are strewn across the floor between them.

Lars is using me as a shield.

"Put her down!" Bram shouts. But Lars doesn't even acknowledge him. He handles me like I weigh no more than a rag doll. My head bounces up and down with each step.

And then abruptly, he drops me. My hip hits the floor and I cry out. Lars sweeps both bone pouches into his fist, and races toward Bram. I try to crawl to my feet, but my leg throbs.

A sickening crack splits the air. My throat closes.

No. Bram. No.

My gaze flies to him, my breath trapped at the base of my throat, terrified of what I'll find.

Bram stands over Lars, who lies in the corner in a heap. Dead. Bram's face is a mask of rage. His eyes are bleak.

"You did this?" I ask him.

"I couldn't let him kill you." His voice his haunted.

A sob rips from my throat. "Tessa is dead."

He scrubs a palm over his face. "I couldn't let him kill you too."

I think of Declan standing in my house in Midwood, helping Latham until the end.

Bram isn't Declan. Latham used him, but he never meant to hurt me. I stand and press my hand against his cheek.

"What are you doing?" Talon's voice echoes off the walls like a blast. My gaze snaps to Latham, and my stomach plummets. His restraints are gone. They must have broken in one of the spells Lars and Bram were exchanging. And now Latham has crawled to the center of the room and gathered Gran's bones in front of him. The bones from the jar—from my hand— are clutched in fingers, still wet. Skin still clinging to them.

He's trying to heal Gran's bones to change the past. And

my bones will give him the power to do it.

I throw myself toward him, and try to wrestle the bones from his grip, but the spell has already started. The moment I make contact, a tug low in my belly yanks me into a vision with him. The paths feel like his paths always do. His familiar yearning for vengeance flares inside me—white-hot, insistent, all-consuming.

But with a start I realize it's not Latham's path I'm seeing. It's my own.

I watch myself convincing Niklas to steal climbing equipment from the Mason training room, pressuring Jacey to use unbound magic to make a potion to drug Rasmus, and then doing nothing when his reputation is destroyed. All because making Latham suffer was more important than anything else.

A sharp moment of clarity steals the breath from my lungs.

I've been making the same mistakes as Latham. His whole life was consumed by a burning desire for revenge. He had something lovely with Avalina, but he let his bitterness become more important than anything else. He was willing to let happiness slip through his fingers in pursuit of making those who had wronged him suffer.

And I just sacrificed Tessa chasing my own retribution.

I struggle to break free from the bones and push Latham out of the way, but his magic is too strong. He's going to win. He's going to change the past into something horrific.

Unless . . . an idea circles at the edges of my mind. It could work, but it means giving up the only thing I've wanted since the moment my mother died.

Once, when I was a little girl, I told my parents a rumor I'd heard about a boy who had bitten another child, and then when his tutor reprimanded him, he bit her too. My father asked the boy's name, and when I told him, his eyes went soft with sympathy.

"No one gives grief like the grieving," he said. Later I asked my mother what it meant.

"It means sometimes when people are sad, they do things that make other people sad too."

"Maybe they want someone to be sad with them so they won't be so lonesome," I said. I still remember how her face changed, as if I'd said something profound.

"Yes," my mother said, "that's exactly right."

I can choose which bone heals, but I'll need Latham's cooperation to do it. I won't be able give him a life that makes him miserable. I'll have to give him a past that makes him happy. A past I can tempt him to choose.

The thought makes my throat raw. The wrongness of it—to reward him after my mother and Gran's death, to allow him joy after what he did to Tessa—sets my teeth on edge. But I'm out of other options.

I wish I had more time. More time to research mending. More time to learn how to pull magic from my own bones. More time to tell Bram I accept his apology. What if I succeed in changing the past, but he disappears from my life forever? What if we don't find each other in a different future?

But time is a luxury I don't have.

Instead of fighting Latham, I join my magic with his. I wander down the paths of Latham's childhood. Find branch points that could shape him—a moment when his mother has the choice to offer a compliment instead of a criticism. A time when a friend could choose to betray a confidence, or exercise loyalty.

I repeat the process again and again, giving Latham devoted friends, gentle correction, experiences that boost his confidence and enlarge his empathy. When I get to Avalina showing up in Kastelia City, I'm especially careful. The paths where his parents are accepting of the match are dimly lit and challenging to isolate.

But they exist. In some version of reality, Latham's parents cared about his happiness more than his prestige, and those are the paths I choose.

Now I need to knit them together so they heal. I need the power from my own body. I focus on feeling the bones inside me—the curve of my ribs, the jutting knobs of my knuckles, the flat surface of my shoulder blades. I pull the power from deep within and push it toward the bone beneath my fingers.

Latham resists. And he's not just drawing on the magic in my severed hand. He uses what he learned from Bram to access the power in my body too. I feel it draining from me as he yanks me toward a different path. Toward the future.

A sharp stab of grief goes through me as I see my mother. Latham is choosing the path where she lives. She walks through an orchard, plucking ripe blush-red apples from the trees and placing them in the basket tucked beneath her arm. She hums softly as she works. Her face is serene.

She turns to someone and smiles. My breath catches when I see myself smiling back.

"Would I be an irresponsible mother if I made pie for dinner?" I laugh. "I won't tell if you won't."

A weight presses against my chest. An ache so fierce, I can hardly breathe. I could bring my mother back. All the small things I've missed about her could be mine again: the comforting weight of her hands on my head as she brushes my hair, the cadence of her voice as she lectures me about the future, the way her laugh sounds like music. I sink into the vision. Luxuriate in all the ordinary things I used to take for granted.

It would be easy. Effortless. And I wouldn't be an orphan anymore.

I give in to Latham. I feel the bone starting to mend beneath my fingers.

But then my mother's face rises in my memory. Her head tilted to one side, her lips pressed together in a disappointed frown. She wouldn't want to be alive in a world ruled by Latham.

As tempting as it is, I can't choose my own happiness over hers. I won't abandon my friends to a version of the future where they aren't free. I push Latham's magic away and take it back for myself. Then I use every last bit of my strength to yank him down a path of my choosing. I force him to explore all his potential in the past—paths where he laughs and cries, and no heartache is bigger than the love at home waiting to soothe it.

I feel him sinking into the past like I sank into the future. The images I show him wear down his resistance. They soften him.

Outside the vision, his hand brushes against mine. Magic pulses between us where my skin touches his, and I can feel the exchange of energy like we're playing a game of catch—tossing a stick back and forth between us so quickly that it blurs as it sails through the air and I can't tell anymore if he threw it last or if I did.

Power gathers inside me—bright and glimmering, but also dangerous. The way fire is both life-giving and deadly.

Bram's voice is gentle near my ear. *Don't fall forward. Draw power out of your bones. Reel it in. Gather the magic in your center.* I don't know if he's speaking now, or if I'm remembering what he said earlier. Past or present? Either way, I concentrate on the contours of my bones, and feel tendrils of power lifting inside me, reaching out for something to hold on to.

Bone charming magic tugs me forward again, and I push back, afraid that if I'm swept into a reading, I'll lose focus and Latham will retake control. That the wrong bones will heal. But the pull is overwhelming. Irresistible. I can feel the bones mending beneath my palm, joining together in one giant mis-shapen mass connected in odd places. Images rush past.

Latham as a dimple-cheeked baby. As a toddler, serious and slow to smile. As a young boy, anxious to please. I see his mother raise her hand to strike him. Watch his brow crease in fear. Power flows from my fingertips and the vision hiccups. Time flows backward. Latham's mother lowers her hand. Lifts it again and brushes the hair from her son's forehead instead. Latham's brow smooths, like a tranquil crystal-clear lake the moment before a tossed stone breaks the surface. But the stone never comes. Not anymore. Latham's life speeds by me. I try to see into his future—to give him the power he needs to change the Grand Council without the past that made him into a monster. But I don't know if it's possible. I see him argue his ideas to his colleagues, hear the passion in his voice as he tries to convince them he's right. I try to lead him toward a path where he chooses persuasion instead of force. But the magic is slipping. I'm losing control.

I lose track of Latham. Other images fly past. My father bouncing me on his lap. Gran humming to herself as she prunes a rosebush. Bram biting into a ripe peach, laughing as the juices dribble down his chin. Talon. Niklas. Tessa. Jacey. I try to keep them all with me. Preserve a future where they're still part of my life.

The vision spins faster and faster. People blur together then break apart, disintegrating before my eyes. My stomach lurches. Something is wrong. I try to pull back, but the magic has too strong a grip on me. And yet I feel weightless. Detached from my body, as if I only exist in a memory.

I wiggle my fingers, searching for Latham, but I can't find him. It's like he vanished. Maybe we both have.

Behind my closed eyelids, I see a sudden flash of light so intense that it cracks through my skull—blinding and painful. And then utter darkness.

I'm not sure if we remade the past, or if we destroyed it.

Chapter Thirty

ust motes dance lazily in the air above my head.
I blink once. Twice.

My memories come back sluggish and confused, turning slow circles in my mind as if they're lost children. I sit up, and my head screams in protest. A tight fist of fear clenches in my stomach. Where am I? Sunlight pours through narrow windows, illuminating shelves of boxes. Nearby, someone groans.

Tessa. Her dark curls are tangled around her face. She rubs her forehead.

"Saskia? What happened?"

Competing memories war in my mind like two people arguing—I can hear them both shouting over each other but I can't make out the details of either one. Tessa and I were just in the library studying a bone map for an upcoming exam.

And yet . . .

I was also just on the floor of Latham's workshop, attempting to heal Gran's broken bones. In a fight with Latham for who would control the past. And Tessa was lying at my feet, dead.

It's like waking up from a particularly vivid dream—daylight washing away an invented life in favor of the real one.

Except I'm not sure which memories belong to the dream and which don't.

"Tessa? Is it really you?"

Her brows pinch together. And then I watch her face transform. "A Breaker grabbed me," she says. "I almost . . ."

I jump to my feet and throw my arms around her. "You're alive," I say. "Oh, thank the bones. You're alive."

A bright glimmer of hope lights inside me. Could my mother and Gran be alive too? But there are no competing memories of them. The pain of their deaths is still a raw wound inside me. Did I only change one thing, then? Did I manage to bring Tessa back, but nothing else? And what does that mean for Latham?

A throat clears behind me, and I turn. "Did it work?" Talon. "Did you change the past or did Latham?" His ginger hair sticks up in all directions and his pale cheeks are colored with splotches of bright red.

"I'm not sure," I say, distracted.

My gaze sweeps over the rest of the room. Jacey is lifting herself from the floor, and behind her, Niklas brushes the dust from his pants.

"Where's Bram?" I can't help the panic that seeps into my voice.

Talon's brows pull together. "Who?"

I make a strangled sound. My heart seizes in my chest, and then shatters into sharp, jagged pieces.

Talon takes in my expression and his face goes instantly repentant. "Saskia, I'm only teasing." He dips his head to the side. "He's fine."

I have to crane my neck to see Bram, but finally my eyes find his, and I choke back a sob. I run to him and fling myself into his arms. My whole body trembles. A tear trails down my cheek, and he wipes it away with his thumb. He holds me close and his breath is a soft sigh against my neck.

"I'm here," he says, stroking my hair. "I'm right here."

The words radiate through me, melting into my relief and setting something else ablaze. Bram traces the long line of my clavicle from one shoulder to the other. His thumb rests in the hollow of my throat. Our lips are only inches apart. And then his mouth is on mine, gentle and sweet at first and then urgent and demanding.

I feel my pulse everywhere. In my neck. My stomach. The tips of my fingers.

Talon groans. "Give it a rest, you two."

I pull away from Bram and spin toward Talon. I jab a finger in his chest. "You don't get to say anything. If I weren't so relieved, I'd kill you."

He gives me a sheepish grin. "I'm sorry?"

"Is that a question?"

"No?"

His expression—all wide-eyed innocence, while the little quirk of his mouth hints at mischief—is both infuriating and endearing. Memories of three different paths jostle in my mind—Talon lying in the grass underneath a tree, his head cradled in his palms, quizzing me on the uses of amphibian bones; Talon trying to cheer me up after a long day by pulling silly faces from all the way across the workshop; Talon pretending to sing off-key to make us all laugh, even though his voice is pitch-perfect. And before I know it, I'm laughing and crying at the same time. I'm hollowed out, exhausted, and limp with relief. I'm not sure if we succeeded, but at least we're all here.

"I should wring your neck," I say, lifting my arms to mime the action, "but I won't."

His eyes go wide. "Saskia, your hand."

My hand. Conflicting memories nudge against one another, and the pieces click into place. I look down. I have two hands again, but one is streaked with five black tattoos that run from each fingertip to the red line around my wrist, as if tracing the bones beneath my skin. Echoes from another path.

It's enough to finally convince me.

"It worked," I say, in awe. "We changed the past."

◆——◆——◆

We woke in some kind of storage area. Shelves laden with boxes fill the center of the room. High, narrow windows on one end overlook a door on the other. We search the entire room for the bones I healed, but we can't find them. They seem to have vanished along with the past we left behind. And Gran's bone has disappeared from my pocket too. I feel the loss like a hole in my heart. My access to my other paths—both of them—now lives only in my memory.

Bram threads his fingers through mine. "It's probably a good sign that we can't find them, right? Maybe it means Latham never stole the bones at all."

But I have no idea what it means.

"I think this is Latham's shop." Jacey is spinning in a slow circle, her eyes scanning the shelves.

At first I think she's wrong. The spaces couldn't feel more different. But on closer examination, I realize she's right. The bookcase has been replaced with an actual door, and the windows are different—they're bigger, and let in more light—but the room is the right size and shape.

"So what do we do now?" Niklas asks.

"We should probably go back to Ivory Hall," I say. But the thought makes me feel as if I've swallowed a stone. I have no idea what will be waiting for us there. Will we be safe? Are we even apprentices in this reality? Yet the moment I have the thought, I'm flooded with new images of the six of us competing in bone races, eating together in the dining hall, studying for exams. And we all still have the gray bands tattooed around our arms that connect us. We belong together on this path too. I'm sure of it.

"Do you think we've been gone a long time?" Tessa asks. "Have we missed the last bone game?" Her expression falters, and I can see her struggling to reconcile the same kind of fuzzy new memories I've been grappling with—events that didn't really happen in the reality we just left, yet the ghost of them lurks in both of our minds because they happened to us *here.* Tessa frowns.

"Hopefully there's still time to find the hikers," Niklas says. He fidgets with an emerald ring on his index finger. Wasn't his ring silver before? And what is he talking about?

Tessa must have the same question because confusion washes over her face. "What hikers?"

My heart sinks. Something is wrong with Niklas.

"The third bone game," Jacey says, "the hikers trapped in the Droimian Mountains? We're supposed to be figuring out how to rescue them?" She shakes her head. "I swear, I'm the only one who listens in workshop."

And then it hits me. We have different memories of the past. Not of the one where we confronted Latham, but of the new past I created.

"There were no hikers for us," I tell her. "Our third bone game involved designing a new town hall."

Talon's mouth falls open. "I remember the town hall too."

I tried so hard to bring each of them along with me when I healed the bones, but I lost track of them at the end. I succeeded in getting us all together in the present, but we must have arrived here on slightly different paths.

"So . . . what's real?" Tessa asks.

My eyes automatically find Bram. It's the same question I've been asking myself for months. "It's all real," I tell her.

"We just remember it differently."

She bites her lower lip. "I'm not clear how this works."

I take her hand and squeeze her fingers. "I'm not entirely sure either. But there's only one way to find out. Let's get out of here and go back to Ivory Hall."

I open the door. We step into the adjoining room. And run headlong into an older woman.

She screams and drops the box in her arms, spilling a cascade of bone-carved harmonicas across the floor. I suck in a sharp, startled breath. I should have been more careful. It hadn't occurred to me that the shop might be occupied. But it is. It's a brightly lit music store, just as it was when Latham was a child.

The woman presses a hand to her chest. "Where in bones' name did you come from? You frightened me nearly to death."

I grab Talon's arm and shove him toward her. "My friend wants to buy a new flute. He's been looking for weeks."

"Of course," the woman says, threading her arm through his, our trespassing immediately forgotten. "We have a wide selection of very fine bone flutes. We'll find you something perfect."

As she leads him away, Talon looks over his shoulder and glares at me, but I just smile sweetly back.

After the scare he gave me, I owed him a little payback.

Ivory Hall looks just as it always has—gleaming bone floors, elegantly curved staircases, chandeliers dripping with crystal—

reassuringly predictable when so much else has changed. But I think how different *I've* been every time I've walked through these doors. First as an apprentice. Then as a fraud. And now, if someone could peer into the recesses of my heart, I think they'd find it looked very much like the bone I healed. Oddly shaped by dozens of different paths. Scarred over. Healing from the many times it's been broken.

Norah strides into the foyer and gives us a reproachful look. "Where have the six of you been?"

Seeing her sends a jolt of anger through me. I want to shake her until she goes as limp as a rag doll, to scream at her, to demand to know why she betrayed me. It takes me a moment to rein in my anger. To remind myself that she didn't. Not on this path. Still, knowing what she's capable of will change the way I see her forever.

It's both the blessing and the curse of being a Bone Charmer. Seeing people for who they really are and for who they could have been in a different life. Knowing the potential for good and evil in all of us.

"Well," Norah says. "Care to explain yourselves?"

Bram rests a palm in the curve of my lower back. "We lost track of time."

Behind me, Talon snorts softly. "That's an understatement."

Norah presses her lips into a disapproving line. "You're late. All of you get to your tutoring sessions. Now."

We scurry up the stairs to the training wing, but when we get there, we hesitate before separating. The others look as restless and agitated as I feel.

Finally it's Jacey who gives voice to what we're all thinking. "I'm worried that all of you might disappear if I let you out of my sight."

"I feel the same," Tessa says, and then to me, "Is that possible?"

"Of course not." Though even I can hear the doubt that creeps into my voice. The truth is, I don't know if the past is stable or if the future is secure. I won't know until I find out what became of Latham in this reality. But Gran used to say that she'd never met a problem that couldn't be made worse by worry. "Everything will be all right."

"But if something *does* change," Talon says, "it will probably be that I grow even more handsome."

Jacey slugs him on the shoulder. "Unlikely."

"True. It's hard to improve on perfection."

Niklas cocks his head to one side and taps his finger against his cheek. "Saskia, is there some bone we can heal that will make him less insufferable?"

Bram's hand shoots in the air. "I volunteer to do the breaking."

I laugh. "Doubtful. But I kind of like Talon just the way he is."

Talon narrows his eyes. "Are you saying nice things just to make me feel guilty for teasing you earlier?"

"Depends. Is it working?"

"Yes."

I grin. "Then yes."

We hear footsteps on the stairway and turn to see Norah glaring at us with fire in her eyes. "Did I not make myself clear?"

We mumble apologies and reluctantly go our separate ways. I find Master Kyra sitting alone in the training room, strumming her fingers on the table.

I slide into the chair across from her. "I'm sorry I'm late."

Her eyebrows rise just a fraction. "It's not like you. I assume you had a good reason?"

I swallow. "Yes. A very good one."

She studies me for a moment, but she doesn't press for details. "All right then. Why don't we begin by having a look at your mastery tattoo?"

I go numb with panic. I should have known that it was too good to be true. My troubles are about to follow me from path to path, relentless.

"Is there a problem?"

"No," I say softly. Ami warned me that my instructor might ask to see my tattoo as a way to gauge my progress. Whether I show her or refuse, she'll know something is amiss.

I should have held Bram for longer. I should have kissed him one more time. I should have told him that I love him—on this path and every other. But now it's too late. The moment Master Kyra sees my tattoo, my fate will be sealed. I won't get to say goodbye.

Woodenly, I shrug off my Bone Charmer cloak. Pull up my sleeve.

Master Kyra stands. Her warm fingers are gentle but firm as she traces the tattoo. Healing the bones didn't change it. She makes a disbelieving sound, but she doesn't speak.

My breath feels trapped in my lungs. Like I'm desperate for air, but a heavy weight rests on my chest and makes it impossible to breathe.

"Remarkable," Master Kyra says, letting my sleeve fall.

"What?" My voice comes out little more than a squeak.

"Your tattoo is looking excellent, Saskia. Much more balanced now. All three corners are equally developed in both size and color." She pats me on the shoulder. "I'm so proud of you."

My thoughts move so fast, I can't catch them. Master Kyra knows I have all three Sights. And she's not angry about it.

Something changed in the past that altered the rules. Latham got what he wanted—a world where everyone is free to reach their fullest magical potential. It must mean that he has true power here. It's a chilling notion. Or a hopeful one. I don't know yet.

I think of Norah's statement before we left for the third bone game. *And maybe if you succeed, we can both get what we want.* Is this what she meant? Fewer restrictions on magic *without* Latham becoming king?

Then I think of Jensen and my heart swells. He'll be safe on this path. Home with Boe and Fredrik. I search my memory of the bone games in this reality, and images of a different trial float to the surface of my mind—a woman who used healing magic as a torture device—to cause agony instead of alleviating it. This time, my guilty vote wasn't fraught with inner turmoil.

If only I could have brought my mother back too. I wonder if her absence will always feel like this. Like a wound that never really heals. I wonder what she would think of my choices.

"Everything all right?" Master Kyra asks.

"Yes. I'm just glad you're pleased with my progress. I've been . . . worried."

"Well, you shouldn't have been."

She scatters a handful of bones in the bottom of the stone basin that rests between us. "I thought we'd do a little First Sight memory work today."

"Memory work?"

"Occasionally you'll work with Healers to help their patients access long-forgotten memories. Or memories that haven't been recalled for many years and need to be accessed for emotional healing. But in order to help others retrieve their memories, it helps if you can learn to find your own."

A thrill goes through me and I can't tell if it's anticipation or fear.

"So what is the task?"

"I'd like you to do a First Sight reading on yourself," she says. "Find a memory that has been lost to the sands of time and experience it again. See it in as much detail as possible."

I sprinkle the bones with my blood and set them alight. Then I extinguish the flame with a heavy iron lid and tip the bones onto the cloth in front of me.

The magic leaps from my fingers and pulls me into the vision the instant I make contact with the bones. I'm swept away before I'm fully ready.

I'm so accustomed to reading possibilities that the view of my past startles me. It isn't a network of ever-branching paths, but one long, glimmering ribbon, as if this one life was always inevitable. I walk down it in reverse, starting with opening my eyes in Latham's shop and moving through the memories of my training at Ivory Hall. Backward even further, to my kenning, where my mother matches me as a Bone Charmer—no First, Second, or Third Sight designation necessary. And she pairs me with Bram. I'm unhappy, but I don't reach for the bone. Don't break it.

I keep wandering backward, luxuriating in the familiar sights and smells of Midwood—the subtle fragrance of the pale pink blossoms on the trees, the gentle burble of the river in the distance. I sit with Ami on the banks of the Shard, our feet dangling in the cool water. I find my father and delight in hearing his voice again. At smelling the remnants of paint wafting from his skin. At feeling the scratch of his whiskers on my cheek when he kissed me good night.

I stand in the kitchen with Gran, shelling peas while she tells me stories. I lie in the cool grass under the stars and listen to the soft hoot of an owl.

And then I go to my mother. I find a moment when I am very young. I've just had a nightmare, and she pads into my room, barefoot, hair loose and hanging nearly to her waist. Her face is limned in moonlight. Her expression is gentle.

"I had a bad dream," I tell her.

She sits on the edge of my bed, pushes my hair off my forehead. "Yes, I heard."

"Will you stay with me for a while?"

"Of course I will." She pulls the covers up and tucks them under my chin. "Do you want to hear a story?"

"Yes, please."

"It's a true story," she says. "And it happened just the other day."

In the vision, I give a disappointed sigh. "True stories aren't as good as made-up ones."

She laughs. "That's usually true. But I think you'll like this story. It's about you."

That gets my attention and I perk up just a little.

"I was doing a bone reading, and I saw you. In the future."

I yawn. My mother seeing my future is nothing new. This story isn't starting out exciting at all.

"You were sitting in a training room studying bone charming, and do you know what you saw in your vision?"

"What?" I say, bleary with exhaustion, my eyes already sliding closed again.

"You saw this very moment. You saw yourself having a nightmare and me coming in here to talk to you. I saw a future where you saw the past. Isn't that amazing?"

"I don't know," I say sleepily. "What does it mean?"

"It means you'll never lose me." Her voice is husky with emotion. "It means we're connected forever. Across space and time."

"Why would I lose you?"

She's quiet for a moment. "In the vision, you missed me very much," she says.

"Homesick?" I ask softly, tucking my palms beneath my cheek.

"Something like that."

In the vision, I roll over. My breath grows deep and even. But my mother keeps talking.

"I saw a future where you wondered what I would think of your choices. So I want to tell you: I saw a woman who is brave and strong and capable. A woman who tries to do the right thing even when it comes at great personal risk. A woman I'm so proud to have raised."

She's not talking to me in the past. She's talking to me right now. I'm breathless with the magic of it. With this golden, glimmering gift of fate.

"I love you, Saskia," she continues, "with every fiber of my being. I will love you always."

In the vision, she leans over and presses a kiss to my forehead. I feel her lips on my temple. Smell the vanilla scent of her skin.

"I love you too," I say in the present—outside the vision. I say it even though I know she won't be able to hear me. The only Saskia she can hear is right beside her, fast asleep.

And yet . . .

My mother smiles softly. "I know you do, bluebird."

The vision fades. I open my eyes and wipe the tears from my cheeks.

Master Kyra is studying me with a thoughtful expression. "Memories can be so healing, don't you agree?"

Chapter
Thirty-One

Bram and I walk hand in hand through Kastelia City. Moonlight glimmers on the water. Musicians stand at each corner, strumming instruments and singing love ballads. I feather my thumb along the slender red tattoo on Bram's wrist. It appeared after we changed the past—bright and fully formed, as if it had been there all long.

When I first saw it, my eyes met his. "Is that . . . ?" I looked away, suddenly shy. "Is it from me?"

He shrugged. "Could be from anyone. I'm not familiar with this path."

I stared at him, unamused. A teasing smile tugged at the corner of his mouth. I tried to punch his shoulder, but he caught my fist in his hand and pressed it tightly against his chest. I opened my palm. Felt his heart go erratic.

"I think there's only one explanation for that tattoo," he said.

"Tell me."

"I don't think it matters at all." He smiles as I raise my eyebrows. "Whether I have a love tattoo or I don't is irrelevant. My path could split a thousand times, and I'd find you and love you on all of them."

"Even if I can be infuriating sometimes?"

"Even then."

I tipped my face up to his, and he kissed me until I felt like I was made of bubbles. Until I was so giddy, I couldn't think straight.

And now, as we walk, I'm filled with wonder that finally we are in the same place at the same time with the same memories.

A gift of fate. Or finally, a series of good choices. Either way, I'm grateful.

We start across a bridge. On the far end, a couple stands, looking out over the water. They huddle close together, their fingers intertwined. The man says something that makes his partner throw her head back in laughter. He laughs too and then pulls her closer. She rests her cheek against his shoulder.

"Maybe that will be us twenty years from now," Bram says. "Still in love enough to hold hands and take moonlit walks."

The thought makes me feel as if I'm sipping a hot drink on a cold day. Warmth spreads through my center. As we get closer, the couple shifts, revealing a man standing on the other side of them. I stop walking.

"What's wrong?" Bram asks.

But words fail me. I'm frozen in place.

Bram squints into the distance. "Is that . . . ?"

"Yes," I whisper.

It's Latham.

Tears spring to my eyes, unbidden, and I try furiously to blink them away. Bram's hand tightens around mine.

"We'll go another way," he says. But it's too late. Latham has spotted me.

He nods politely to the couple as he maneuvers around them. They laugh as he exchanges some pleasantry I can't hear. And then he comes toward us, smiling in a way that is entirely unfamiliar. It makes me feel unsettled and off-balance.

"Hello there. It's Saskia, right?"

I don't say anything. I spot the gold knot on the shoulder of his cloak that designates him as a member of the Grand Council. My tongue feels glued to the roof of my mouth.

"I'm Master Latham," he says, holding out his hand. "We met briefly when I lectured at Ivory Hall earlier this year." I wonder if the other paths left any imprint on him. If he has vague recollections of me he can't quite place.

I search my memory, but I can't find this version of him there. Maybe all the other iterations are too powerful to be overwritten. My arm lifts without my permission, as if good manners are more instinctual than common sense. His hand folds around mine and I resist the urge to yank it away.

I've tried so hard not to think about Latham over these past few weeks. I've tried to stem the tide of hatred that spills over my heart like poison. I've thrown myself into doing well on our last bone game, tried to distract myself with perfecting my charming skills. But in quiet moments—when I have too much time to think—my heart still feels dark with hate. I wanted this man dead, and yet he stands before me with so much of what he wanted. A seat on the Grand Council. The power he always craved. He radiates contentment.

And a storm rages in my chest. Bram's palm rests on the small of my back. He doesn't say anything, but the reminder that he's there—that if I bolt, he's ready to go with me—is a comfort.

"I was so sorry to hear of your mother's passing. She was a good friend."

A good friend. To Latham. I swallow.

My mother didn't come back to me when I remade the past. Neither did Gran. I can only assume it's because their bones were used in the magic that changed everything, which made them lost forever. I know from Ami's letters that everyone in Midwood remembers Gran dying of old age, and my mother dying of illness.

"Thank you," I manage.

And then my gaze falls to his wrist. It's bare. A spark of panic zips up my spine. What if I erased Avalina when I remade the past?

"What is it?" Latham asks. "Are you all right?"

I take an unsteady breath. "I just—I thought my mother once mentioned you being matched. But I must be thinking of someone else."

His expression grows wistful. "Avalina." He says her

name tenderly. "You're not mistaken. She trained at Ivory Hall with me and your mother, and we *were* matched back then. But I had all sorts of ambitious plans, and Avalina wanted a quiet life. We decided we were happier apart." He leans a little closer, as if sharing a secret. "I adored her, but she's better off. I'm not the easiest man to live with."

Relief washes over me. Avalina is safe. Her parents are safe. Latham still had to choose between love and a path toward power—he wasn't emotionally healthy enough to have both—but at least in this life he didn't leave a trail of destruction in his wake.

He stares off in the distance for a beat as if lost in a memory. And then he sighs deeply and seems to come back to himself.

"If you need anything—anything at all—please don't hesitate to ask. Your mother was extraordinary. Everyone who knew Della cared deeply for her."

I've heard Latham lie many times. In many realities. I've experienced some of his lies again and again as I explored the path on Gran's healed bone. I know the exact timbre of his voice when he's being deceitful, the precise look on his face. And that's how I'm sure he's telling the truth. He's sincere in his admiration for my mother. His sadness is real.

A sudden realization pierces my heart—a pinprick that lets enough light in to chase away the darkness. I *did* succeed in killing Latham. The man who murdered my mother was unmade. Swept from existence. And I didn't let a quest for vengeance destroy my life.

I didn't get revenge, but I got something better.

I became the woman my mother raised me to be.

Midwood is in full bloom.

Cherry blossoms dust the cobbles in the town square like sugar on a pastry. The leaves in the Forest of the Dead are thick and green again after a long winter.

I stand at our family tree and marvel at how much has changed.

At how much hasn't.

I trace my mother's name—carved in Oskar's hand now instead of Bram's. Changing the past didn't bring her back from the dead, but it did return her bones to me. I found them safe and sound at the bone house in Midwood. And Gran's too. If I ever have a child, their kenning will be rich with the wisdom of the women who came before.

I sit at the base of the tree and rest my back against the trunk. Tip my head toward the sky. Run my fingers through the blades of cool grass.

"I miss you," I say aloud.

Ever since Master Kyra assigned me to do a reading of my own past, I can't help but wonder if my mother saw me in the future more than once. If, perhaps, she saw me over and over again. The possibility—however remote—has opened a wellspring of hope inside me that makes me feel as if she's been returned to me in some small way. As if we've been returned to each other.

And so, I talk.

I tell her everything. How I've mastered all three Sights.

How our team won the last bone game, so we all chose assignments in towns close to one another.

How she was right about Bram all along.

"He's perfect for me, Mama. I can't believe I didn't see it before."

"I can't either," Bram says, cresting the hill and sinking into the grass beside me. "How could you be so clueless?"

"It's impolite to eavesdrop." My voice is stern, though I have a hard time keeping a straight face when he's smiling at me like he can't decide whether to tease me or kiss me.

"I wasn't eavesdropping. I made as much noise as possible on my approach."

"Oh, was that you clomping through the forest? I thought it was a moose."

He laughs. "So you'd share your secrets with a moose but not with me?"

"Only a moose I trust implicitly." I brush a lock of hair from his forehead. "And I don't have any secrets from you."

He leans back on his elbows. "None?"

"Do you have secrets from me?"

"No." He tilts his head thoughtfully. "Well, maybe one."

"Are you going to tell me?"

"We're matched on this path," he says. "It's almost time to declare if we accept or not."

"And your secret is that you plan to break my heart?"

"Of course not. But sometimes I worry . . ." He plucks a blade of grass and spins it between his fingers. "Would you still have chosen me if we weren't fated to be together?"

The vulnerability in his voice tugs at my heart.

I thread my fingers through his. "Do you know why they call it the joining ceremony?"

"Well, I always assumed it was because two lives were being joined together. But I'm guessing this is either a trick question or you're trying to boost my confidence with the easiest exam ever."

"My mother once told me the ceremony is the moment fate and freedom join hands. Being matched is about discovering the person who's right for you. The joining ceremony is when you choose to love them."

I lean over him, my hair cascading around his face like a curtain that cocoons us in our own private world. "I choose to love you, Bram Wilberg. Today and always. In this reality and every other."

"Can we just stay on this path from now on?" he asks, his fingers tracing my jawline. "I've grown quite attached to it."

"I'd love nothing more."

His lips meet mine and the whole world falls away.

I feel at once like I'm drowning, and like I'm breathing for the first time.

Like fate and freedom just joined hands.

Acknowledgments

This book has been so much fun to write, and I have so many people to thank for helping bring it into the world.

First, to my amazingly talented editor, Ashley Hearn: Thank you for pushing me to be better, dig deeper, and do more. This book is so much stronger with you than it ever would have been otherwise.

I'm so grateful to Kathleen Rushall, who is supportive, wise, and kind—everything an agent should be. Thank you for everything!

My sincere appreciation to the entire team at Page Street: Will Kiester, Lizzy Mason, Lauren Cepero, Lauren Wohl, Tamara Grasty, Trisha Tobias, Chelsea Hensley, Meg Palmer, Hayley Gundlach, Marissa Giambelluca, Kylie Alexander,

Mina Price, and the fabulous sales team at Macmillan. And special thanks to Kaitlin Severini for copyediting.

To my mom, Sharon Berrett: Thank you for foisting my books on coworkers, strangers, and airline pilots. You're the best! And to the many other family members who have gone above and beyond to come to events, rally friends, and generally be supportive: Edna Berrett, Dalena Berrett, Davonna Wachtler, Randy Wachtler, Tebin Berrett, Ted Berrett, Melissa Berrett, Don Shields, Ginny Shields, Christy Shields, Steve Shields, Jill Shields, Britnee Landerman, David Landerman, Cameron Berrett, Nicole Berrett, and Derek Berrett.

I'm so blessed to have writer friends on this journey who get both the ups and the downs: Katie Nelson, Kate Watson, Emily R. King, Rosalyn Eves, and Tricia Levenseller. Thanks for always being there!

To my nieces and nephews: Keaton, Kaiser, Danica, Jaden, Kennedy, London, Maverick, Cassidy, Paul, Tom, and Jimmy. Look, kiddos! Your name is in a book!

To my children, Ben, Jacob, and Isabella, who continue to fill my life with more happiness than I ever thought possible. I love you guys!

And always and forever to Justin. What would I do without you?

About the Author

Breeana Shields is an author of fantasy novels for teens, including *The Bone Charmer*, *Poison's Kiss*, and *Poison's Cage*. She graduated from Brigham Young University with a BA in English. When she's not writing, Breeana loves reading, traveling, and playing board games with her extremely competitive family. She lives in the Washington, D.C., area with her husband, her three children, and two adorable, but spoiled dogs. Follow her on Twitter @BreeanaShields, or find her on her website at breeanashields.com.